BY

SUSAN CAROL McCARTHY

A Place We Knew Well

True Fires

Lay That Trumpet in Our Hands

A PLACE
WE KNEW
WELL

A PLACE WE KNEW WELL

A Novel

SUSAN CAROL MCCARTHY

BANTAM BOOKS

NEW YORK

Copyright © 2015 by Susan Carol McCarthy

All rights reserved.

Published in the United States by Bantam Books,
an imprint of Random House, a division
a Penguin Random House LLC, New York.

BANTAM BOOKS and the HOUSE colophon are
registered trademarks of Penguin Random House LLC.

LIBRARY OF CONGRESS CATALOGING-IN-PUBLICATION DATA
McCarthy, Susan Carol.
A place we knew well: a novel / Susan McCarthy.
pages; cm
ISBN 978-0-8041-7654-5 (acid-free paper)
eBook ISBN 978-0-8041-7655-2
1. Families—United States—History—20th century—Fiction. 2. Cuban Missile Crisis,
1962—Fiction. 3. Life change events—Fiction. 4. Domestic fiction. I. Title.
PS3613.C35P58 2015
813'.6—dc23
2014049123

Printed in the United States of America on acid-free paper

www.bantamdell.com

2 4 6 8 9 7 5 3 1

FIRST EDITION

Book design by Barbara M. Bachman

FOR TRAVIS

A PLACE
WE KNEW
WELL

*A*s I WHEEL RIGHT INTO DAD'S DRIVEWAY, A SIX-FOOT CHAIN-link fence jumps up out of nowhere. I stomp on the brakes. My car heaves to a stop within inches of the padlocked gate.

My hands, shoving the gearshift into park, switching off the ignition, are shaking. I rest my head against the wheel, my heart still skidding inside my chest. *Stupid, stupid!* I think, only now remembering Clem's phone call two weeks ago. "DEP recommends it, Charlotte," Dad's attorney told me, asking my okay for the expense of the fence. "Plus, it'll secure the property against vandals. Or vintage collectors looking for a five-finger discount."

But the sight of Dad's station turned ENTRY RESTRICTED fortress, flanked by the tall fence lined with green sight-blocking screens, is still a shock.

My entire life the busy corner of Princeton and the Trail was always wide open and welcoming, usually with Dad waving me in and striding out to hug me hello. Now, leaning over to retrieve the FedEx packet launched to the floor by my abrupt stop, I realize I've never felt so completely *un*welcome here, or alone.

After fishing out the keys—one marked GATE, the other marked STATION—I take a last look at Clement T. Grimes, Esquire's extensive Property Inventory, then sidestep my way to the padlocked gate.

"We already have inquiries from CVS and Walgreens," Clem's cover letter said, "and the Broker's Open isn't till Thursday." This is the new Florida, I think, resentfully eyeing the Rite Aid across the street. Instead of a gas station, every busy intersection needs at least two competing drugstores.

The shiny new Master Lock opens easily enough, but shoving the gate against a stubborn patch of weeds on the other side, I have just enough room to squeeze through.

Oh, Dad, I sigh, dismayed by the view: the once gleaming white canopy and station front are desolate and dirt-streaked. The pumps and all the windows are dingy. I'm glad you're not here to see how swiftly a lifetime of careful stewardship gives way to a few scant months of inattention.

Left of the pumps, there's an odd scattering of small dirt mounds. Suspecting gophers, I see instead they're the geologist's drill holes for the state's mandated assessments of soil and groundwater, another in the seemingly endless number of hoops yet to be jumped.

Moving quickly to the office door, I unlock it and stand still, relishing the lingering smells of petroleum, cigarettes, and strong coffee that, as long as I can remember, meant "Dad's work." The sight of his desk, the old cash register he refused to replace, and the small porcelain-on-tin sign on its back facing every customer who ever walked through the door tightens my throat. The desk and the register are empty, of course. Cal and Steve saw to that. Both service bays cleaned out as well.

"The back room is a treasure chest," Clem's letter said. "Three different antiques dealers are salivating over the chance to sell whatever you don't want of your father's collection. You're lucky he had the good sense to hang on to this stuff."

Flipping on the back room's light, I have to laugh at the tin signs that line every available square foot of the walls and ceiling, most bearing the classic red-and-green Texaco star. I asked Dad once why he chose Texaco over the more popular Shell or Gulf Oil brands. "It was the star, Charlotte: same five-pointed star as on my air force uniform. To me, that star meant freedom . . . not just to fly and fight the enemy, but to come home, marry your mom, and build our American dream. Besides, I just couldn't see myself running around with a sea-shell or an orange ball on my chest."

Me neither, Dad. I lift the latch on his locker and pull open its nar-row, green metal door. Inside, a spare green uniform, cleaned and pressed, hangs next to his work jacket. I pull out the jacket and bury my face in it, rewarded by the fragrant mix of oil and Old Spice. Oh, Dad, for a while anyway, your American dream went exactly as planned. But then, when it didn't, you made the best of things better than any of us. I slip on the jacket and trace the red embroidery on front that says simply WES.

I poke around in search of the item listed on the Inventory as "1 floor safe, locked, contents unknown." After a few minutes, I spot the disk-shaped dust cover in the floor. Dropping to my knees, I lift the protective cover easily enough, but the combination dial atop the sunken cylindrical safe looks rusty and corroded. "We never used it," Cal told me. Over the phone, Steve added, "Not for years, but even then it was always your dad's private place."

I stare at it a moment, remembering the start of seventh grade, coming home completely baffled by the shiny new black-and-silver lock that was supposed to secure my gym locker. "All combination locks work essentially the same way, Kitten," Dad explained, patient as ever. "It's a simple three-step process; the only hard part is coming up with a combination of three numbers you won't forget."

Silently invoking Dad's okay, I take a deep breath and reach in and force the dial left, slowly and with some difficulty, to "0." Hoping my hunch is right, I twist the dial left again, three times around, and stop at "8." With no idea whether I've guessed correctly, I turn the dial right, one full rotation, then stop at "3." Almost there, I twist the dial right again and return directly to "3." Beneath my fingers, I feel the lock disengage but, after several pulls, the safe door remains barely cracked.

I sit back on my heels. The concrete floor is cold and hard, and my knees aren't what they used to be. Who but Dad would stick with the same lucky number for sixty-plus years? Eight-three-three was Mom's factory ID number during the war. "Without it, without your mother," he'd insisted, "I'd have probably gone back to farming, spent my life trailing the north end of a southbound mule." I doubted that. But Dad never did.

Determined to find out what, if anything, Dad left behind in his "private place," I lean in, grasp the edge of the door, and yank it *hard* to open it. I put my hand into the hole and grasp the only thing there—a small brown leather pouch, zippered closed on top, and embossed on the front with the vaguely familiar logo of The State Bank of College Park, gobbled up by SunBank when I banked there in the 1970s, and morphed sometime later into today's SunTrust.

Has this been in there since the '60s? Or did Dad just hold on to it the way he held on to so many other things?

The pouch feels empty, but, steeling myself against disappointment, I open it anyway to be sure. Inside, the small white paper napkin with the black Steak 'n Shake logo (*"In sight, it must be right!"*) makes me smile. How many nights over how many years did my high school friends and I cruise the scene at "The Steak"? Way too many to count. But removing it from the pouch, I spot the handwritten note on the back—*IOU for 4 Cokes 4 me & the twirls. XO, C!*—and am jolted backward in time. It was my senior year, late October 1962, when after cruising The Steak I drove my friends here to the station, ostensibly to raid Dad's Coke cooler, but specifically to show off Emilio to them. I shake my head against a sudden flood of memories. Not going there. Not today anyway.

Three things remain in the pouch. A white palm-sized rectangle turns out to be a business card from Bayshore Realty in Tampa. KATHARINE AYRES, LICENSED AGENT. Oh, Lord. No wonder he buried this here instead of at home, or in their safe-deposit box at the bank, where Mom might have found it. On the back, in loopy feminine handwriting, I read, *Call me at the Cherry Plaza,* with the phone number of what was once Orlando's ritziest hotel. "Oh, Dad,"

I sigh. For the first time, I feel that invading his "private place" is a mistake.

The final two items in the pouch are a complete surprise. A small, suede drawstring sack, like a boy's marble bag, with an old, oddly broken screw inside. What's that about? I have no idea. And . . . Dad's dog tags? I wonder, fishing out the metal ball chain looped with two modest metal tags. Like others of his generation, Dad was mum on his World War II experiences. All he would say was, "The real heroes are the ones who didn't make it home." Moving the tags out of my shadow into the light, however, I'm stunned to see not Dad's name, but *mine*. And not only my name, but my birth date, my blood type, and our old address and phone number on Bryn Mawr. Obviously, a specially ordered item, but one I've never laid eyes on until now. Why was that?

My brain swims with questions. And my heart hurts with the thought that these things—the napkin, the business card, the marble bag, and the dog tags—are related somehow. Remnants of the same time, the same week even—that singular week, my senior year in high school, when each of us, and all of it, fell apart. What was I thinking, coming here, doing this, *now?* An unsettling sense of trespass and regret overwhelms me. Are there places in a person's heart, in the private remnants of his life, where no one, no matter how loved, should presume to go?

Gently, I put everything back into Dad's leather pouch and return it to the safe. Slowly, I close the lid, spin the lock, and secure the outer door in the floor. Struggling stiffly to my feet, I eye Dad's stars on the ceiling as I switch off the light and leave. At the front door, I turn for one last look around, then, impulsively, step back to the register and pry off the tin sign that was always there, always Dad's favorite. Tears blur the words. Though, of course, I know them by heart. "Good-bye, Dad," I whisper as I lock the station door for the last time.

Outside, the sky is darkened by clouds heavy with rain. I run to the gate, hugging Dad's jacket against the chill wind. Outside the fence, I padlock the gate and make it to my car just as the first stinging splats of rain begin to fall. I set Dad's small sign—YOU CAN TRUST YOUR CAR TO THE MAN WHO WEARS THE STAR!—on the seat beside me, a comfort and a consolation against the long, wet ride home.

1.

WES AVERY STOOD AT THE BACK OF THE PLYMOUTH WAGON holstering the nozzle on the silver Sky Chief pump. He noted the amount, spun the gas cap closed, then turned to scan the traffic in the busy intersection where Princeton crossed the Trail. Still no sign of the parts truck from Holler Chevrolet or the special-order camshaft he'd been promised "by noon, Wes . . . one at the latest." He pictured dragster Jimmy Cope's hopeful face, convinced the new Crower cam would drop his quarter-mile ET from the low 13s to the high 12s in tonight's "Run What Ya Brung" race at the Big O Speedway. Hope springs eternal, Avery was thinking, but . . . no part, no start.

Just then a sharp, shrill scream sent him quick-stepping to the wagon's rider-side window.

The baby had startled awake with the kind of heart-piercing shriek that scares the bejeezus out of new parents and jerks even experienced ones alert with a worried "Now what?"

Behind the wheel Marjorie Cook lunged sideways, hands outstretched, spilling the contents of her open purse everywhere.

Pelted by a pair of shiny lipsticks and the pointy end of a rat-tail comb, the baby yelped even louder and bucked herself perilously close to the edge of the bench seat. Seeing what was bound to happen next, Avery ducked his head and thrust in his arm. Just as the child fell, face-first, toward the floorboard, he grasped a wad of pink shirttail and hauled her back up to safety. She was really squalling now. Her little arms and legs flailed every which way, as he handed her gently over to her mother.

Marjorie's face, pale and frozen a moment ago, flushed blotchy red with relief. "Oh, Mr. A!" she said, eyes wide with what-if.

In the backseat, three-year-old Tommy squinched up his face, stuck his fingers in his ears, and cried, "Mommmmy, make her stop!"

Beside him J.J., his barely older brother, snapped, "Shaddup, wouldya," and launched a swift kick at Tommy's sneakered foot.

As little Tommy dissolved into howling outrage, J.J. retreated to his corner and met his mother's over-the-shoulder glare—"You *boys!*"—with an innocent shrug. "I didn't do nuthin'," he insisted.

The bald-faced lie launched his brother onto him with fists flying.

"Tommy, *stop* that . . . *now*," Marjorie hissed.

Avery shifted his gaze, backseat to front, wondering, What the heck happened? Only minutes ago, the baby girl was sound asleep, the boys drowsing in the back. A sleeping cherub, he'd thought, cleaning the windshield: same blond curls and pink cheeks as her mother, same fairy dust of freckles as both her big brothers. But now the pink cherub was flaming red, tiny lips calibrating a frightened cry into a furious screech.

"It's okay, Lissie, you're okay . . . ," Marjorie was saying when, abruptly, they both heard what the baby's sensitive ears must have picked up ahead of them: the high, keening squeal and thunderous rumble of massive turbojet intake roaring into view.

Avery raised his head to watch the two B-52 bombers, monstrous eight-engine Stratoforts from Orlando's SAC base, climb into standard three-ship cell formation. Their companion, a huge KC-135 Stratotanker, lumbered behind, refueling boom at the rear retracted like a scorpion's stinger at rest.

Odd time for takeoff, he thought, as the air, the very ground beneath his feet, trembled under the combined jet power passing overhead. And poor Marjorie, as the engines' roar set off another round of pained howls inside the car.

Avery slid a practiced eye, courtesy of the United States Army Air

Forces, over the second bomber's sleek silver fuselage to the manned quad-fifty turret at its tail. Catching the shadowy shape of the tail-gunner there, he raised a commiserating hand. Normally, the big birds of the Strategic Air Command left mid-evening, carrying their heavy bombs in long figure-eight patterns east over the Atlantic, past Gibraltar to a tight turnaround just short of the Soviet border then back, with the help of in-flight refueling, around sunset the following day. Leaving now meant a long, late-night flight home over black water—which always upped the ante on a potential SNAFU.

"Ohhhhhh ...," Marjorie bristled, "I'd like to throttle the guy schedules a gol-durn exercise during naptime!" She'd wrestled the baby to her shoulder. "There, there, Lissie," she murmured, patting the plump cloth-diapered behind. She blew a damp strand of hair out of her face and looked over the scattered mess of her purse. "My wallet," she said, frowning, "it's here somewhere."

Avery nodded sympathy. "Look ..." He chucked his chin toward the groceries in the back. "Your ice cream's melting, and so's that little cupcake. I'll make a note. You drop by later, anytime tomorrow; we'll settle up then."

Marjorie resisted, at first—"Oh no, I'll just ..."—but he waited while she worked out the logic: If she left right now and put the kids straight to bed, she'd have time to take in the groceries, repack her purse, maybe put in a load of laundry before they were up again clamoring for *Adventures with Uncle Walt*.

He shot a wink at the two boys in the backseat, sullen and sulking in their respective corners. Some other day he'd tell them that smiling, mustachioed Walt Sickles—WDBO-TV's popular Uncle Walt—lived just up the road in Lockhart and was a regular customer, same as them.

Resolved, Marjorie fired the ignition. "Thank you," she called over the baby's blubbering. "You're a peach!"

Avery acknowledged the compliment with a modest show of both palms. He stepped back to wave her off, but his hand dropped midair at the shimmy in her left rear tire. He'd have to check that when she returned.

"Ready?"

Steve stood in the office doorway holding up their lunch pails. Avery nodded and, with another quick glance at the traffic, strode inside. On a small pad, he wrote Marjorie's name and $5.58 gas debt— Marjorie Cook she was now, he reminded himself, not Franklin as she'd been in high school. He added *Ck. Rr. Shimmy,* then punched open the cash drawer and slipped the note into the twenties slot.

Steve put their pails on the desk beside the chessboard he'd retrieved from the bottom drawer. As Avery took the swivel chair, long legs stretched out to the side, Steve sat down opposite on the station stool.

Squat, ropy-armed, with a steel-gray buzz cut and a petty officer's swagger, Steve had a two-pack-a-day habit (Camels unfiltered) and, according to Avery's daughter, Charlotte, "the face of a sad, old hound dog." His real name was Ira Stephens, but shipmates called him Steve during the war and that's what he had embroidered on the white name patch of his Texaco-green uniform. While Avery flew in B-29s over Japan, Steve had been a gunner's mate at Iwo Jima and Okinawa. Their widely differing views on warfare showed up in their chess play: Steve's strategy was naval, full speed ahead to capture the center and continually attack, while Avery was more circumspect, deflecting from the outside then diving into a defensive weakness. "Backward into battle," he called it, the tail-gunner's mantra.

Steve watched Avery pop the top on his RC Cola and study the game in progress without comment. Although they were both the same age, forty-two, Avery was a head taller, still airman-slim and, in Steve's mind, solid as the day was long. Lately, however, he'd seen the tiredness puffing Avery's eyes, the worry tugging at his lips, and couldn't help but wonder . . .

"What?" Avery asked, catching his stare.

"Sleep much?"

Avery shrugged him off.

Steve bit into his bologna and cheese, took a swig of his cola, then pressed, "Everything okay on the home front?"

Avery dropped his gaze to the board. It wasn't his nature to complain. Besides, even though he considered Steve his best friend, he felt it would be disloyal to Sarah to say, *My beautiful wife doesn't sleep, hardly eats; she seems tied up in knots, constantly on edge, yet she can't or won't say why. . . .*

Instead, Avery short-castled his king and said quietly, "Fine, everything's fine."

Steve heard the hesitation, though it lasted only a fraction of a second. He was considering his next move when, suddenly, another thunderous three-ship flyover rattled the front windows and clanked the empties stacked next to the Coke cooler.

"Laggin' today!" he said, scowling.

As quiet gradually returned, Avery chewed the inside of his cheek. Summer out at the base had been nuts with "large joint military exercises in the Caribbean," the *Orlando Sentinel* reported. "Gettin' ready to kick out Castro," locals added cheerfully. But for the past two months, things had settled back down to normal with the usual flurry of evening takeoffs and just-past-sunset returns.

A short while later, as Steve bent to light his after-lunch cigarette, a third flyover obliterated the flip and click of his navy Zippo.

Avery checked his watch. They were spacing the takeoffs twelve minutes apart. He uncrossed his legs, leaned forward, elbows on his knees, and rolled his shoulders against the ball of tightness at the base of his neck.

Thirteen minutes later, he did the math: Four flyovers meant eight long-range bombers plus four tankers were in the air—over half the 4047th Strategic Wing based out at McCoy.

Normally, no more than a *third* of the wing was gone. *Half* the wing gone meant something was up. Something *big*.

Avery shut his lunch pail and stood to stretch his legs. Had Khrushchev made good on his threat against Berlin? Recalling the Krazy Komrade's latest rant—"Berlin is the testicles of the West. Every time I want the West to scream, I squeeze on Berlin."—he switched on the station radio for the top-of-the-hour news.

At two o'clock, WABR reported that President Kennedy had left Washington for Chicago on "a three-day, seven-state campaign trip in support of upcoming midterm elections." If this was an international crisis, Avery reasoned, surely the President would have stayed at the White House. Steve shelved the still-unfinished game and returned to the tune-up in his service bay.

Avery walked out to ask the Holler Chevy delivery guy, "Since when did 'one at the latest' mean two oh eight?" He carried the stock boxes into his bay, popped the hood on Jimmy Cope's '61 Roman Red Impala SS (feared and revered locally as "Brutus"), and began the careful process of removing the old camshaft and installing the new one, plus lifters and triple valve springs.

By three o'clock, four more flyovers meant the *entire* wing was in the air. In seventeen years here, *that* had never happened.

"This is no exercise," he told Steve. "More like a complete evacuation."

"Why? What now?" they wondered.

A battered brown Ford coupe pulled through the pumps and parked beside the office. The driver, a young man in a white short-sleeved shirt, skinny black tie, and coffee-stained suit pants, wandered into the service bays.

"Joe Riley," he said, addressing both mechanics, "*Orlando Sentinel,* looking for Mr. Wes Avery?"

"You found me," Avery said, wiping his hands on a red work rag to offer the guy a shake.

"Oh!" Riley blinked pale eyes as if he couldn't believe his luck. His face spread into a delighted grin.

The guy's youth, his red-peppered freckles and rust-colored hair, made Avery think, Jimmy Olsen, cub reporter, in the flesh. Resisting the urge to ask, *Where's Clark Kent?* he said instead, "What can I do you for?"

"Well, I was just at your house, interviewing Mrs. Avery about the big show on Sunday. You know, Civil Defense?"

"Yup." Preparations by the Civil Defense Committee of the Orlando Women's Club had consumed Sarah's every waking hour for weeks.

"Got a peek inside your bomb shelter. Pretty nifty."

Avery shrugged. "Came with the new house. Fellow we bought from built it."

"Yeah, your wife said that. She also said . . ." Riley pulled a flip-top notebook out of his back pocket and thumbed through the pages. "Here it is. . . ." His hushed tone oozed reverence. "You helped drop The Bomb on Japan?"

"Not *The* Bomb . . . ," Avery said firmly. (No doubt, if asked about his service, Sarah had said, "My husband helped bomb Japan," but that's not what the reporter, or most folks, wanted to hear.) "'Bout every other kind of bomb you can think of, though. Thirty-seven missions, seven tons apiece—that's pert' near eighteen hundred tons of bombs-away from our crew alone. And there were hundreds more crews just like us."

"Oh . . ." Poor Riley flushed disappointment.

Steve dropped the hood on the Dodge Polara in his service bay and tossed in, "This guy's forgotten more about bombs than most experts know."

Avery shot him a *back off* look. It was a simple truth: Most people didn't care about the *real* air war on Japan. You ever wonder, he might've asked, why it was Hiroshima got The Bomb? Ever think that, after that spring and summer of near-nightly firebombing by over a thousand Superforts, Hiroshima was one of the last cities still standing? Ever imagine the war was as good as won without The Bomb? No? I didn't think so.

"So . . ."The kid was obviously scrambling. His hoped-for scoop— EXCLUSIVE: INSIDE THE SHELTER OF THE MAN WHO DROPPED THE BOMB—was blown. Now what? "So . . . uhm . . . you thinkin' that shelter of yours could withstand The Bomb?"

"Which one?"

"What do you mean?"

"Well, the A-bomb dropped on Hiroshima . . . maybe. But the

H-bomb, like that fifty-megaton monster the Soviets set off last spring? That's four thousand times the yield of Hiroshima. Not a shelter on the planet could survive a direct hit from that one."

"That's interesting." Riley pulled a pen out of his shirt pocket and scratched a note. "So . . . what's the point of having a shelter then? Or Civil Defense even?"

"Beats me," Avery said and instantly regretted it. Irritation with the kid's questions, and the subject of Civil Defense in general, had cracked his habitual reserve.

"Can I quote you on that?"

"Nope," Avery said. The young reporter's face fell. "But look here," Avery added, "you need a quote, I'd go with the one from General Omar Bradley: 'Only real defense against a nuclear war is to make sure it never starts.'"

Riley scribbled furiously, then stopped. "Omar?" he asked, knitting red brows. "Was he one of ours?"

Steve rolled his eyes and stalked off into the office to file his paperwork.

Avery pretended patience. "You still have a reporter down there name of Tom Dunkin?"

The kid nodded. "Yes, sir."

The gas bell rang; both turned to watch the shiny black Riviera brake beside the pumps. "You go ask Dunk if Omar Bradley was one of ours, okay? Now if you'll excuse me . . . ," he said curtly and strode out to work.

Around four, Steve was squaring away his service bay when Emilio Alvarado, the lanky Cuban teenager who would help Avery till closing, arrived.

Emilio waved off his ride with a quick thanks and sprinted into the office. "Hey, Mr. A, how's it goin'?" he asked, tossing his school books beneath the register. A sharp-looking kid who hustled around the station with an athlete's ease, he made a beeline for Steve. "You hear the Twins released Naragon today?"

Steve shrugged. "His age—guy's better off coaching than catching. They'll be fine without him."

Avery held up a flat palm to silence them. The radio was declaring a breaking update: "*. . . large tropical storm off the Bahamas . . . upgraded to hurricane status.*" Hurricane Ella was *"gathering strength and headed northwest toward central Florida."*

Avery swept a hand through his hair, then walked out of his bay, past the pumps, out from under the canopy to the curb.

The air had turned heavy with humidity and storm smell. A stiffening wind was bullwhipping the fronds atop the station's only palm tree. At the corner, he turned his back on the afternoon sun, shaded his eyes against the glare off the front windows, and stared east out Princeton Street, past the big packinghouse of DR. P. PHILLIPS, WORLD'S LARGEST CITRUS GROWER.

A massive steel-gray anvil of clouds dwarfed the southeastern horizon—"rain-heads," the old farmers called them—replete with hammering thunder, like distant cannonade, and the white metallic strikes of lightning.

Obviously, the SAC base had advance warning of the storm, he decided. So they were diverting their new eleven-million-dollar-apiece aircraft, not to mention their powerful thermonuclear cargo, out of harm's way, right?

He gnawed his lower lip. Two years ago, they'd survived a glancing blow from Deadly Donna, the most damaging hurricane on record. But Sarah had been a nervous wreck. When the howling winds tore a giant limb off the old oak beside the house and dropped it within inches of Charlotte's bedroom, Sarah had come unglued. It was a waking nightmare Avery would never forget: the crash of ripping wood, shattering glass, and his daughter's screams; the shock of opening her door, seeing twigs and leaves plus razor-sharp glass shards all over her bed, glittering in her hair. Worse yet was Sarah's volcanic fury—at the storm and "life in this godforsaken place! Isn't it enough," she'd raged, "we have to battle the blasted bugs, the infernal snakes, the alligators around here, but *hurricanes* . . . hurricanes, *too*?"

"But, Mama, I'm *okay*," Charlotte had reassured her in a small, pinched voice.

"Yes, baby, and thank God for that!" Sarah cried, then collapsed beside the bed, a heap of raw, inconsolable sobbing.

"Careful, Mama," Charlotte had whispered, cutting anxious eyes toward Avery. "There's glass."

Sarah's meltdown had left him and Charlotte tenderfooting around her for weeks. He'd been shaken to the point of mentioning it to Mike Martell, the family doctor, after Rotary in the parking lot of Tony's Italian.

"Only a couple weeks since her surgery, right? Unfortunately," Martell told him, "there's a reason why *hysterectomy* and *hysterical* have the same Latin root. It's a hard thing on a woman, losing her female parts, getting tossed into the change of life way sooner than expected. I'll adjust her medication. But you," he'd said with a finger tap on Avery's chest, "you've got to give her a wide berth. And time. These things take time."

Within that wide berth, Sarah had insisted on moving out of the old neighborhood—where "every third person on the sidewalk is pushing a baby carriage," she'd complained—to the fancy new split-level on the lake. She'd packed the place with all-new Danish modern furniture that looked, to him, like something out of *The Jetsons;* and they had a walk-in closet now—her two-thirds crammed with a wardrobe that would rival Jackie Kennedy's—plus a stocked-to-the-gills, built-into-the-house bomb shelter. For a while, it had all seemed to make Sarah happy; though lately . . . And what would she do if another hurricane struck?

Avery exhaled a small worried whistle. The ball of tightness at the back of his neck had grown heavy and hard. He hunched his shoulders against its weight. Wearily, he turned back toward the station when a sliver of light (bright metal sparked by the sinking sun) caught his eye in the middle distance. There it was again, just above Dr. Phillips's rail-side water tower. He stepped to the curb to get a clearer view and cocked his ear toward the inbound rumble.

Staring hard, he counted the number (three, six, *twelve*), the distinctive shape (needle nose, swept-back wings), and the descending

trail formation of the fully loaded supersonic fighter squadron screaming into view. The concussion of sound—a dozen F-105 Thunderchiefs swooping down to pre-landing level—stopped thought
altogether. Behind them in the distance came a dozen *more.*

Car traffic on both sides of the busy intersection came to a screech-
ing stop. Drivers opened their doors, craned their necks to follow the
bright orange glow of the afterburners southwest toward McCoy's
twin runways. "Fighters in Orlando?" "Fighting what?" "Who?"

Still at the curb, Avery folded his arms across his chest, tucked his
hands into his now damp armpits. He looked up to study the fishnet
of old and new contrails from the departing heavy bombers and arriving jets. When a sudden gust of wet, roaring wind struck his left
cheek, he wheeled abruptly to consider the bigger-than-before mass
of hurricane clouds advancing from the coast. Foreboding wrenched
his chest. Beneath the heel of his right palm, he felt the pump of his
heart awash with heat.

SARAH AVERY STEPPED THROUGH the dining room's swinging door
into the kitchen. "Hello, Avery residence, Mrs. Avery speaking."

"Sarah? Edith Murray."

Sarah sagged against the Frigidaire. She closed her eyes and pictured the caller's sharply chiseled face.

"Sorry I couldn't make the interview with Jean Yothers. How'd it
go?"

"Miss Yothers couldn't make it, either," Sarah answered. "They
sent a nice young man named Joe Riley."

"But I specifically requested Jean Yothers! Who's this Riley fellow? I've never heard of him."

"He's new, apparently."

"Good Lord, they sent us a *nobody?*"

Sarah heard the annoyance in Edith's inhale and imagined her
long, blue-veined fingers holding her cigarette to thin, red lips, the
hard sparkle of multiple diamonds, the twin funnels of smoke stream-

ing out her nostrils. Sarah had joined the Women's Club at the urging of her next-door neighbor Elsie Stout and, when presented with a list of committees, blindly signed up for Civil Defense. With their new shelter and all, it seemed a natural fit. "Oh, my dear," Elsie said when she heard, "if only you'd asked me, I could've warned you off the Dragon Lady."

"Well," Edith was saying, "tell me he got a photo of your Granny's Pantry thing."

"Grand*ma's* Pantry, Edith. Yes, he did." It had been Sarah's suggestion to make "Grandma's Pantry"—the federal government's list "for proper family preparedness" of canned foods, medical supplies, and key items such as soap, blankets, buckets, flashlights, and a portable radio—part of the committee's presentation at this Sunday's first-ever Family Survival and Fallout Shelter Show.

"Well, good. I'm sure I mentioned I play bridge with the publisher's wife. I'll call Martin Anderson myself and insist on front-page placement."

Two more days, Sarah thought. *Two . . . more . . . days.*

Oh, Edith had seemed nice enough at first, promising that theirs was "important, potentially lifesaving work," bragging about her support among the area's "movers and shakers," even hinting at a potential invitation for the Averys to join the prestigious Orlando Country Club. Ironically, she'd reminded Sarah of her mother. Her voice had the same cultured, precise tone as Mama's: polite, Old South aristocratic. But where Mama—who insisted manners were the true measure of one's class—was always a firm hand in a velvet glove, Edith was nothing but a slave driver in a pillbox hat! And I'm the one with the word SAP blinking across my forehead in neon lights.

Typical. How many times over how many years had she found herself in exactly this position? High-stepping in, holding up hope and good intentions like the flags of a color guard, only—inevitably, it seemed—to trip and fall and find herself facedown in a ditch spitting dirt while the rest of the world marched blithely by.

"Now, let's see . . ." Edith was no doubt scanning her endless to-do list. ". . . have you confirmed the Mininsons? What time are they due in Orlando?"

Inviting Melvin and Maria Mininson—the Miami couple featured in *LIFE* magazine for spending their two-week honeymoon in a bomb shelter—was Edith's Big Idea. She considered them "the stars of our show!"

"Haven't talked to her since Tuesday, but I know they're planning to drive up tomorrow morning."

"Plans change, my dear. You should confirm the final details today, and also their room at the Langford Hotel."

"All right, Edith."

"Has the printer delivered your brochures yet?"

"Not yet."

"Okay. I'll make that call and the one to the *Sentinel.* You'll confirm the Mininsons and the Langford?"

"Yes, Edith."

"Good," the old crow cawed and was gone.

Sarah hung the receiver on its hook and went in search of Maria Mininson's phone number. She'd stored it carefully, but where? Not in the stacks of file folders cluttering the dining room table; nowhere in the living room, of course. Had she carried it with her when she showed the shelter to the reporter? She crossed the hall and let herself into the middle bedroom, which—with its heavy metal door, twelve-inch reinforced-concrete walls, twin stacks of fold-up metal cots, and floor-to-ceiling shelves of supplies—was the family's in-house safe room. She flipped on the overhead light and saw the folder where she'd set it atop the five-gallon jugs of drinking water.

After he'd photographed every part of the shelter—from the kitchen area with its sink, racks of dishes, pots, pans, and Sterno cans for cooking; to the medicine cabinet's bandages and first-aid supplies; to the flushable toilet in the corner stall between baskets of toilet paper and Renuzit air freshener—the reporter had asked her to stand in front of the food shelves filled with the bulk of items on the government's "Grandma's Pantry" list.

"Not that you look like any grandma I've ever seen," he'd said. Shyness flushed his freckled face.

Flattered—somehow, despite everything, she'd managed to hang on to her looks—she'd set down her file and stepped into the picture, hoping his popping flashbulbs wouldn't reveal the extra layers of concealer she'd slathered on the dark circles under her eyes. She'd been up all night, cleaning, stacking, and restacking the shelves in preparation for today's visit by Jean Yothers, the *Sentinel*'s popular "On the Town" columnist, and Edith Murray. When both women canceled, she'd considered telling Joe Riley to forget the whole thing.

"I've never actually spoken with The Press before," she'd admitted.

"Well . . ." Riley had grinned, looking like Andy Griffith's Opie all grown up. "You're my first official interview so, between us, we should be fine."

Groggy from no sleep, she'd done the best she could, but now . . . what was it she'd come in here for? The file in her hand reminded her.

Back in the kitchen, she dialed the Miami number. "Hello, Mrs. Mininson. It's Sarah Avery from Orlando, hoping to confirm your arrival time tomorrow."

"Oh, well, I'm not really sure. . . ."

"You mean . . ."

"With the hurricane and all, I don't know if Mel . . ."

"Hurricane?"

"Haven't you heard? Hurricane Ella, they're calling it . . . headed right toward you."

"Why, no, I . . ." Sarah turned to look out the kitchen windows. The view of her hibiscus bushes shaking as if throttled by a giant unseen hand, the queen palms bent low toward the lake, the lake itself quaking with small whitecaps, raised the hairs on the back of her neck. A hurricane? *Now*, when the season was supposedly over?

October, she thought. Ever since she was six years old, October— with its grinning jack-o'-lanterns and Mama's tears, and her own broken heart over losing little Robbie to the scarlet fever; Robbie, who loved Tom Mix, Pick Up Sticks, blueberry pancakes, and both his big sisters, Kiki and Sare-Bear. "The meek don't inherit the earth," Mama complained bitterly at the cemetery, the fall-leaf funeral wreaths too bright beside the small pale blue casket. "It swallows them whole." And later, hollowly, as they arrived home: "Just imagine if Robbie had been my only child."—October, Sarah thought, was really the cruelest month of the year.

In Sarah's ear, Maria Mininson was saying something about ". . . till Mel gets home from work . . . morning might be better." Then, as if from very far away, Sarah heard her front doorbell.

"I understand." A confounded *hurricane*! "You'll call me soon as you decide, then? Thanks so much, Maria. . . ."

In her hands, she felt the thrust of the wind against the door. In the sudden whoosh off the front stoop, the potbellied man held his cap on his head and a clipboard against his chest. "Got yer brochures right here, ma'am." Behind him, storm clouds loomed black across the sky, darkening the afternoon like a curtained room.

"Thank you," Sarah said and stepped aside to let him in.

He placed the clipboard facedown on the uppermost of three boxes stacked atop a metal dolly and, still holding his cap, rocked the dolly to an angle and wheeled it across the threshold. "Where you want 'em?"

She caught the whiff of tobacco plus some chemical she assumed was ink. "Next to the dining room table, if you don't mind."

"Sure thing."

Something bright—a yellow leaf from the Gilberts' sycamore across the street—was attached to his shoe and came off in front of her. She stooped to pick it up and toss it back outside. She frowned as, closing the door, she saw the scatter of other leaves just like it littering her front lawn, shifting across the driveway. Sarah had only evergreens in her yard, because falling leaves reminded her of poor Robbie, and all the other bad luck and lost babies that followed. Was it any wonder she hated this time of year?

"If you'll just sign here . . ." The printer had unloaded the boxes, had a pen from his pocket clicked to ready, and handed her the clipboard. She signed. "And here's yer sample," he said, removing the sheet from beneath the receipt.

"But it's not folded."

"Yeah," he said, suddenly sheepish. "As I told the other lady, our folder's broke. Got a new part comin' in from Jacksonville on Monday."

"But the show's on Sunday!"

"I know. Sorry. But the other lady, Mrs. Murray, said to go ahead and deliver 'em and the committee would fold 'em."

"Three *thousand* of them?"

"Sorry," he said again, halfheartedly, and wheeled his dolly out the door.

Sarah returned to the living room dazed. Of the original committee, two women had privately fumed over Edith's heavy-handedness and then, claiming other obligations, politely quit. The other two were as overwhelmed by Edith's endless demands as she was. There'd be no help there. She glanced aimlessly around the room, stopping for no good reason at the mantel clock. Ten past four. She could hear its insistent *tick-tick-tack* in the empty room; and outside, high overhead, the drone of an airplane, then another; and out back, the worried twitter of the family parakeets in their cages on the screened porch.

She shivered against the idea of another hurricane and the sudden thought that in the room's growing shadows lay remnants of her old anxiety, the depressive darkness that sometimes trailed her with the glint of hungry eyes, a blur of feral fur at the edge of her peripheral vision. Abruptly, she switched on the lamps at each end of the sofa and beside Wes's chair and forced herself to take stock. Charlotte was at majorette practice, with plans to work on the senior float in the school Ag Barn, then attend a slumber party at her friend Brenda's tonight. Wes would be at the station till closing at nine. She had five hours to fill, plus three thousand brochures to fold for a Civil Defense show that might not even happen because a hurricane was headed their way.

She moved to the stereo, stacked the turntable with some sooth-ing Verdi, a Bizet, and the new Leontyne Price, then drifted into the kitchen. She needed a glass of sherry—or something stronger—to calm her nerves. Or maybe a couple of her little yellow Nembutals?

Perhaps, she decided, both.

2.

"WHEW!" SARAH AVERY EXCLAIMED, OPENING THE SIDE DOOR. "Wet enough for you?"

"Ya think?" Jimmy Simms said with a laugh. Water dripped off the end of his bulbous nose and ran off the hem of the red slicker covering his white T. G. Lee Dairy uniform.

Behind him, gale-force winds blew the heavy downpour sideways. Rain pummeled the back of his milk truck and battered the front of the house.

Behind her, Wes Avery called from the breakfast nook, "Come on in, Jimmy; have a cup of coffee."

Simms held his wire crate of foil-topped, one-quart milk bottles and shifted his gaze to Mrs. Avery. It was company policy, not to mention plain old horse sense, that no employee set foot in a domicile without the express permission of the lady of the house. *This lady especially*, Simms thought. He'd always appreciated that, while most of her neighbors were still shuffling around in their pink hair curlers and pajama robes, Mrs. Avery was up early and nicely dressed—crisp white blouse atop black slacks today, dark hair swirled in a stylish French twist. She was always pleasant, too, thanking him with that low, husky voice of hers. Deep for a woman's, like—what's-her-name, married Bogie? Lauren Bacall, that was it.

She took the crate and elbowed the door open for him. "Cream and sugar, right?"

"Yes, ma'am." Simms stopped to shrug out of his slicker. He hung it on the coat hook beside the door, wiped his feet on the mat, then ambled across the kitchen to where Avery sat at the white Formica dinette.

"The ol' Crackers had a sayin' . . ." Simms gingerly lowered his bulk onto the chrome chair. ". . . July—stand by; August—look out you must; September—remember; October—all over." He scowled at the water-streaked view of the lake writhing under Ella's outer bands. "Exception to every rule, I s'pose."

"Yup," Avery agreed, shifting a discarded section of the newspaper out of Simms's way.

"Radio says she might be turning north," Simms added. "Any luck, we'll catch a break later today or tomorrow."

"Oughta make the cows happy," Avery said.

"I hope you're right," Mrs. Avery said with an obvious shudder. Her hand, placing the steaming mug in front of him, pointing out the cream and sugar, had a visible shake. "If I never see another hurricane, it'll be too soon for me," she added, topping off Avery's mug and carrying her own empty to the sink.

"Cows don't mind the rain, y'know," Simms said amiably, pouring cream, spooning in sugar. "It's the planes make 'em nervous."

It was no secret to anyone that T. G. Lee Dairy's pastures lay in the southeastern flight path of McCoy Air Force Base.

"Ones arrived yesterday?" Avery said. "Thunderchiefs. Louder than all get-out."

"Them, yeah." Simms sipped coffee. "But it's the black ones really spook 'em. Comin' and goin' during early milkin'. Big black suckers, like a flock of giant turkey buzzards. Take off funny, too, almost straight up"—he traced the ascent with his hand—"like a rocket."

Avery set down his mug. "Black, you say?"

"Black as tar." Simms leaned in, relishing his role as insider, and dropped his tone. "Guy at the plant says they're some kinda spy planes, like the one got shot down by the Russkies couple years back."

Avery stiffened, like a hunting dog on point. "A *U-2*? They've got a U-2 out there?"

"That's it, but not just one. They's a whole flock of 'em flew in this week, parked off to theirselves outside the old parachute hangar. Know where I mean?"

"Of course. We went to the open house same as everybody else."

Four years ago, thirty thousand people had jammed the tarmac for the bittersweet celebration of the air base's name change from Pinecastle to McCoy AFB. The event memorialized popular base commander Colonel Mike McCoy, who, rather than eject out of his malfunctioning B-47 and risk crashing the local neighborhood, flew it fatally into a nearby field.

"What a zoo that was!" Simms chuckled. "Half of Orlando and most of 'em thinkin' that drinkin' our milk entitled 'em to park in our pastures."

Avery's eyes were wide with excitement. "A U-2! Might be worth a drive over after church to see one of *those*. Heh, Sarah?" he asked.

Mrs. Avery stood at the open Frigidaire transferring the milk bottles from Simms's crate to the top shelf. Her tone, when she answered, was distracted. "You go ahead if you want to. Lord knows where I'll be."

Simms followed Avery's gaze and, frankly, enjoyed the view. Mrs. Avery was beautiful in a way he thought particular to the South—all that dark chestnut hair and pale porcelain skin, tall and slim yet delicate somehow, like the thoroughbreds at the Ocala stables, where his brother-in-law worked. He wondered, not for the first time, how they'd met. He'd heard Avery's story: Georgia farm boy turned crop duster turned airman who'd done some training in Orlando then came back after the war. But Mrs. Avery was less forthcoming and, therefore, more intriguing. Wartime romance, Simms imagined, wishing he knew more. She was a beaut all right—*fine china married to a tin cup.*

"Well," Simms said, suddenly uncomfortable in the extended silence. "I best get goin'." He hoisted himself up off his chair and carried his mug to the counter. "Mighty fine coffee, ma'am," he murmured. "Thank you."

"You're most welcome," she said as he picked up the crate of empty returns.

At the door, he pulled on his slicker then, ducking his head against the wind and rain, called brightly over his shoulder, "Be seein' ya!"

AVERY WAVED SIMMS OFF, elated. He'd had a hunch the milkman might know something about the unusual activity out at the air base, but Simms's news—*A real live U-2!*—was extraordinary. Two years ago, Ike had denied the super-secret spy plane even existed—until Khrushchev produced not only the plane but US pilot Francis Gary Powers, shot down over Sverdlovsk. Now, if Simms could be believed, there was a whole squadron of U-2s here in Orlando?

While Avery sat planning when, and how, he could get out to the base to see for himself, Sarah set his ready-to-go lunch pail on the counter, then moved to open the cabinet left of the sink. He saw her take out the blue Bromo-Seltzer bottle and matching glass, plus the smaller amber vial of her Nembutals. She shook two capfuls of crystals into the glass, added tap water up to the fill line, then swirled and drank down the fizzing water in a series of grimacing swallows.

Feeling his gaze, she shrugged and said, "Just trying to clear my head and"—she popped a couple of her yellow pills—"calm my nerves."

He knew she'd been up and down all night, a shaky silhouette moving from window to window, wincing at the rifle-like cracks of lightning, worrying over the whistling winds and heavy rain, agonizing over Charlotte's safety at her slumber party, and whether Sunday's Civil Defense show would be on or off.

But even after her six a.m. phone call confirmed Charlotte was fine, she'd remained a bundle of nerves.

Avery hoped the Bromo and her pills would help. In the meantime, he was due at the station. He rose from the table, thanked her for his lunch, then asked, "Anything I can do before I go?"

She stood at the sink staring out at the storm-chopped lake, arms crossed as if she was cold. "Stop the rain?" she said quietly. "The clock? The world—and let me off?"

Avery took a long breath. Sarah's blue moods always gave him the feeling of a dark intruder between them, one that, try as he might, only she could repel. He squeezed her shoulder gently. "Darlin'," he said, his exhale a soft sigh, "you know I would if I could."

SATURDAYS, THE STATION OPERATED on staggered shifts: Steve opened at eight and worked till four. Avery arrived at ten and stayed until six. And Emilio came in at one and closed at nine.

While Steve attended to engine work in his service bay, Avery spent a miserable morning out at the pumps. The station's canopy offered scant protection against the rain gusting sideways in Hurricane Ella's advance winds.

In the office, they kept the radio on for storm updates. Just after noon, they heard the cautiously optimistic news that, despite coastal winds of 115 miles per hour, Hurricane Ella seemed to be weakening. Better still, she was veering slowly north toward coastal Georgia.

Just before one, Emilio dashed in and ducked into the back room to change into his uniform. Father Thomas O'Meara, the burly Catholic priest who usually dropped the teenager off, parked his Chevy at the curb and lumbered in without an umbrella.

"Afternoon, Mr. Avery. Might I have a word?"

Avery had never met a Catholic priest, much less talked to one, until this one walked into his station last month, broad red face atop a tight-fitting white collar, bushy brows, and a flop of white hair combed like an ocean wave.

At that first meeting, Avery had found the man's Irish accent hard to understand, except for the part about "Twenty-five Cuban boys, Mr. Avery. *Twenty-five!*"

It had taken almost half an hour for the priest to explain and for Avery to understand that Bishop Moore, Orlando's Catholic high school, had taken in twenty-five teenage Cuban exiles; that the diocese was housing them in the local Catholic retreat camp; and that the boys needed jobs "to earn money for extras." It was all part of some hush-hush church charity program—Operation Pedro Pan, O'Meara called it, Spanish for "Peter Pan"—to help Cuban Catholics get their children out of the clutches of "that infidel Fidel."

"Fourteen *thousand* children airlifted out so far, Mr. Avery. Can you imagine?"

No, Avery couldn't. "Where you putting them all?"

"Catholic parishes all over Florida and twenty-nine other states," the priest answered proudly.

Was a parish the same thing as a congregation? Avery wondered. And what the heck was a *di-oh-sees*?

In the end, Avery had agreed to one job for one boy. It was good timing, he told the priest, since his previous help, Billy Jameson, had just gone off to college in Gainesville. No special skills required, he said, so long as the boy was reliable and spoke English.

Steve had expected some kind of teenage Ricky Ricardo, small and dark, so Emilio's height, his sandy-blond hair, and his aqua-blue eyes surprised him. But Avery, who'd spent two months in over-water flight training at Batista Field outside Havana, shook his head. "You'd be surprised how many blue-eyed, blond Cubans there are."

Turned out, Emilio's English was impeccable and his customer sense outstanding. Almost immediately the boy intuited that although the tourist trade was important at the pumps, it was the locals who kept the service bays busy. Like Avery, he checked each car's license plate first thing and paid special attention to those whose Florida plate began with No. 7, the state's designation for Orange County. Lady customers were charmed by the teenager's good looks and proper, Continental manners. Asked to do anything extra, he'd grin and say, "It would be my pleasure." And by all appearances, it was. Back in the service bays, Emilio amused the mechanics with tales from his obviously privileged childhood in Cuba, which he pronounced *COO-ba* with quiet pride and affection. His stories—about Antonio their chauffeur's passion for Havana showgirls; Marcellina the cook's hapless attempts to catch a husband; and trips to his grand-

father's coffee plantation on a mountainside honeycombed with pirate caves—were full of intrigue and laughter, but often ended with a
frown passing like a cloud across his sunny features. "Of course, that
was all *before* . . . ," he'd say darkly, turning to spit in the nearest trash
can, ". . . *Fidel!*"

Now, for some reason, the priest was back, brushing rain off his
freckled forehead and the shoulders of his black suit.

"Please, uh . . . *sir,* have a seat," Avery said. In his mind, the term
Father was reserved for prayers to the Almighty.

The priest nodded, sat, and began. "It's been a month, Mr. Avery.
I'm making the rounds, checking how our boys are doing."

Overhead the gas bell, triggered by the arrival of a powder-blue
Ford Fairlane, rang its rapid *ding-ding.* Both men turned to watch
Emilio snap the sides of his clear plastic rain poncho, straighten his
cap, hustle out to greet the driver, then sprint around the car to the
red Fire Chief pump.

"Great kid," Avery said. "Gets along with everybody . . . even old
Steve in there, the station grump."

"Heard that," Steve called from under the big Merc in his service bay.

"I know it," Avery called back. "Turns out they're both nuts about
baseball. Same team, too," he told the priest. "What is it, Steve? The
Senators?"

"The *Twins!*"

"Yeah, that's it. I can't keep up. Anyway, the boy's a walking ency-
clopedia on Cuban ballplayers. Played catch as a kid with one of the
rookies. What's his name?"

"Tony Oliva!"

"Ah, yes." The priest nodded. "They're from the same town in
western Cuba. Pinar del Rio. Pines by the River."

"Well, you should've heard those two howling over the World Series last weekend."

"Damn Yankees!" Steve complained, then remembered himself.
"Sorry, Padre."

The priest winked a sky-blue eye at Avery. "I understand, my son.
Red Sox man myself."

"So you in mourning, too? Over the end of the season and all?"

The priest chuckled. "Not a fan, Mr. Avery?"

"More of a basketball man myself."

"Ahhh . . . Russell or Chamberlain?"

"Russell. No contest."

"Indeed!" The priest beamed. "Boston is twice blessed by her sporting teams." Then, raising his voice to carry, the priest called to Steve in a comforting tone, "Four months, my friend. Pitchers and catchers report for practice in a mere one hundred fourteen days."

Avery jerked his head toward Steve's feet, the only part of him that was visible. "He and Leo already made plans for opening day at Tinker Field." The Twins' spring training park was in south Orlando.

The priest's forehead furrowed. "Leo?"

"Sorry. That's Steve's nickname for Emilio. He doesn't seem to mind."

"The boy enjoys it here, Mr. Avery. And we sincerely thank you for your support, but, um . . ." The priest turned briefly to eye Emilio, now cleaning the Fairlane's dipstick. "Come spring . . . there's no telling where he'll be by then."

"What do you mean?" In the service bay, Avery heard the wheels of Steve's work trolley roll out from under the car.

The priest pursed his lips. "There's word from the monsignor in Miami—credible word—that very soon the marines will finish what the Bay of Pigs failed to start, if you know what I mean. Once Castro's gone and Cuba's free again, the boys will return to their families, just as soon as it's safely possible."

Steve, now standing in the doorway, locked eyes with Avery in a solemn stare.

One question rose higher than all the others crowding Avery's mind: *If we squeeze Castro out of Cuba, won't Khrushchev cut off Berlin?*

DESPITE THE IMPROVED FORECAST, pounding rain and gusting winds continued throughout the afternoon.

Avery was in the left service bay replacing the fan belt on DeeDee Martin's Corvair.

Nearby, Steve had spent the better part of the past half hour explaining to Emilio what a thing of beauty the 413 cross-ram Max Wedge engine was in attorney Clem Grimes's Chrysler 300F. The only flaw, unfortunately, was the difficulty in reaching and replacing the spark plugs. Attempting to do so had set Steve off on a grumbling, foulmouthed tirade.

Avery shot Emilio an amused wink. Both turned to scan the pumps to make sure no customers were in earshot.

"That the Reverend Steve I hear, warming up for tomorrow's sermon?" a familiar voice called from the office: Charlotte Avery, dark ponytail damp and curling with rain.

"Hey, kiddo, what's up?" Avery called, delighted, dropping the Corvair's trunk lid with a resounding *thunk,* wiping his hands.

Though Charlotte grinned at Steve and Emilio, she didn't stop to chat. Instead, his daughter headed straight toward him. Avery noted her graceful toes-out gait (the product of six years' ballet at Mrs. Pounds' Dance Studio). But her eyes, always a window on her feelings, were clouded.

"What?" he asked, worried.

Charlotte stepped close, her back to the other bay, and said softly, "Mr. Beauchamp came by the Ag Barn while we were working on the floats. They counted the votes. He wasn't supposed to tell, they're not announcing it till Monday, but . . ." Tears welled in her eyes. "I'm in the Homecoming Court."

"But that's great!" he said, confused. "Isn't it?"

"Noooo," she said, widening her eyes, willing him to understand. "Now I *have* to go to the dance. I mean, I was, but with the twirls. We were going as a group. Now . . ." She gave a ragged sigh. "Well, all the boys in the court have girlfriends. They'll be pairing up at the dance. And I'll be all dressed up"—her lower lip quivered with misery—"with nobody to dance with."

Avery slung a comforting arm around her, pulled her to his chest, and felt the flicker of outrage over the stupidity of the boys in her class.

At age thirteen, his daughter had shot up to five-nine, the tallest girl in eighth grade. It had taken a couple of years for the boys to catch up and pass her. In the interim, her braces had come off and her frame had changed from lean, like both her parents, to downright curvaceous. Charlotte was, to him, a dark-eyed, dark-haired knock-out, but the sting and shyness of being over-tall remained. And now this . . .

He squeezed her close. "Poor Kitten," he murmured. With a girl like Charlotte, the average guy would probably figure he hadn't a chance. Why risk the embarrassment of asking, or the potential humiliation of being told no? Easier by far to do nothing and accept that you were—same as *I* was, back then—a tongue-tied, ham-handed oaf.

"Leo could take her," Steve suggested softly.

Avery took a slow inhale. Over Charlotte's head, his eyes sought Emilio. The boy's ears flushed red, but he nodded earnestly. He could.

"What?" Charlotte asked, turning around to peer at Steve. "What did you say?"

"Leo can take you," Steve repeated confidently, problem solved. "And I'll bet you a ten spot he's a better dancer than any of the local clodhoppers."

Emilio stepped forward. "When my sister was in Cotillion, I was her practice partner. Enrique Jorrín, the man who invented the cha-cha, was our teacher," he told Avery proudly. Then, respectfully dipping his head toward Charlotte, he said, "It would be my great honor to take you."

Nicely done, Avery thought. I'd never have had the nerve.

Charlotte stilled head-to-toe, but her face flashed delight, then indecision, then, in the glare of their communal stare, froze with embarrassment. She glanced at the floor and raised a flat hand to blot the tears clotting her lashes.

Emilio politely averted his eyes. Steve took a sudden, keen interest in the rain pelting the station canopy like gravel. But Avery's attention remained on his daughter. Watching her sly appraisal of Emilio's profile—his height, probably, and handsome good looks—he tried to guess her thoughts.

From the beginning the two teenagers had been shyly friendly. The first week Emilio started work and school, Avery had heard them comparing class schedules. Emilio had admitted his hardest was trigonometry, which Charlotte had aced last year. "The formulas are tough at first," she'd told him, "but once you get to factorization, it's kind of fun."

Her least favorite was speech. "I get so nervous in front of the whole class," she'd confessed.

Emilio's face had softened with understanding. "Back in Cuba, our teacher told us to forget about the crowd, pick out one or two friendly faces, and speak directly to them. It helps," he'd said.

Just last week, she'd thanked him for the tip. "It does help," she'd told him. And because her college applications were top-of-mind, she'd asked him his plans after graduation.

"I'd always hoped to study law like my father but . . ." He'd trailed off, at an obvious loss.

In response, Charlotte had blushed almost as bright red as her Edgewater Eagles sweatshirt. "Oh, Dad," she'd told Avery later, "I was just so certain that, as a teenager with no parents, he was having all kinds of fun, and freedom. But it never occurred to me—until then—that, coming here, Emilio not only left his parents and his past behind, he lost the future he'd always planned. I felt like such a dimwit!"

"What about you?" Emilio had asked quickly, his eyes curious, his lips curving in an *it's okay* smile.

"Aeronautical engineering," she'd told him; though that wasn't something she normally admitted outside the family, for fear, she'd said, of being labeled a brainiac.

"Like a lady astronaut?"

"More like a rocket mechanic."

They'd shared a laugh over that one, but this going to the dance together, Avery thought, was something else entirely.

Now, apparently resolved, Charlotte lifted her chin. "Thank you, Emilio," she said. "I'd like that very much."

"Great!" Steve crowed and turned on his heel back to the Chrysler.

Emilio's delighted grin matched Charlotte's, but before he could say more the *ding-ding* of the gas bell drew him out to the pumps.

"But of course," Charlotte said quietly, favoring Avery with the *Daddy's girl* look that never failed to sway him, "*you'll* have to square it with Mom." Pointing out a slight letup in the rain, she added, "This be a good time to run me home?"

"Sure, honey," he said. The sooner Sarah was in the loop on this thing, the better. He grabbed his keys. "Hey, Steve, she's all yours for a few."

"Roger Wilco, Cap," Steve called back from under the Chrysler's hood.

With waves to Emilio, Avery and Charlotte dashed through the splattering rain to the green pickup, which Charlotte had nicknamed Otto for the words—ORANGE TOWN TEXACO, PRINCETON AT THE TRAIL, COLLEGE PARK—painted on both doors beneath the red-and-white Texaco star.

College Park was a burgeoning Orlando neighborhood that could boast neither a college nor a park. It was originally conceived as Orange Town, because it was bordered on the east by Orange Avenue, the main drag into downtown, and on the west by busy State Route 441, known locally as the Orange Blossom Trail. It was renamed College Park, however, when the developer's wife suggested "classing up" the titles of its red-brick streets to Harvard, Yale, Dartmouth, and the like.

Thus far, the community had two dubious claims to fame: First, it was the neighborhood that Colonel Mike McCoy had crashed himself to save. Second, it was the place where poor old Mrs. Kerouac's son Jack, having barely survived a trip to Mexico, arrived on her doorstep flat broke, spent the summer of '57 on her back porch, mostly drunk, writing stories about his bum friends in San Francisco, and, that fall, received word that *The New York Times* thought him "the Voice of the Beat Generation." Whatever that was.

Avery wheeled east over the Southern Seaboard Railroad tracks, past the cottage on Princeton that had been their first home and was now one of three rentals he owned. At the light, he turned left on Northumberland, crossed Smith, Vassar, and the inadvertently misspelled Radclyffe, then headed right on Bryn Mawr into the low-slung split-level on pocket Lake Silver.

He pulled in under the cover of the carport and parked beside Sarah's Buick. Entering the kitchen, they heard the low rumble of her voice.

"I *told* them the storm's turning, Edith . . . ," she was saying and, seeing them, rolled her eyes at the woman on the other end of the phone line. ". . . the husband's refusing to make the drive." She compressed frustrated lips. "I said that, too. . . ."

"Hey, reinforcements!" Elsie Stout called from the propped-open doorway to the dining room, waving a handful of folded brochures.

"Would *you* like to call him?" Sarah was asking. "I have the number right here."

"I've got to get back," Avery told Elsie, "but maybe Charlotte . . ."

The half smile Charlotte had worn all the way home spread wide at the sight of their next-door neighbor. "Reinforcements for what?" she asked brightly, obviously relieved that, with Elsie there, any discussion of her date with Emilio was delayed till later.

"Right this way," Elsie said, ushering her out of the room.

"I really don't think . . ." With the fingers of her free hand, Sarah pressed and circled the spot between her brows where she tended to get headaches. Avery gave her shoulder an encouraging squeeze, then returned, driving back through the renewed downpour, to work.

At the station, Emilio was out front, replacing the wiper blades on Dick Johnson's Rambler. In the office, Steve was packed up, ready to go, and smoking a cigarette. He gave Avery a wary look. "Sarah okay with this?"

"She was tied up on the phone, couldn't talk, so I came back."

"Think she'll be okay?"

"We'll work it out," Avery said.

I hope so, Steve's look said.

Fifteen years running and his wife and his best friend still seemed unable to fathom each other. Although Steve thought Sarah classy and attractive, he misjudged her natural reserve as stiffness, her wry sense of humor as arrogance. And while Sarah admired Steve's work ethic, she often mistook his habitual gruffness for deliberate rudeness when, in fact, the guy was all bark, no bite. It was ironic, Avery thought—or was the word *sardonic?*—that the two people who knew him best so often misunderstood each other.

"I was thinkin'"—Steve flicked ash into the desktop tray—"they usually put the girls in a convertible for the parade. Charlotte can ride in The Admiral, if she'd like. And I figure Leo can borrow it for the dance."

Avery hiked his eyebrows and rocked back on his heels in mock shock. The Admiral was Steve's pride and joy. A jet-black, cherried-out '59 T-Bird with custom red leather bucket seats; a special-order, 430-cubic-inch, four-hundred-horsepower Super Marauder engine; plus three two-barrel Holley carburetors. It was the envy of every hot-rodder in town.

Steve shrugged. "Just a thought."

Avery smiled. For all his bluster, Steve could surprise you. "That'd be great. Thanks."

Steve peered out at the renewed rain and ground out his smoke.

"You heading out now?" Avery asked.

"Good a time as any, I s'pose."

"My regards to Miss Lillian," Avery called in lieu of good-bye.

Although he'd never laid eyes on Steve's lady friend, Avery knew she was a nurse who lived on the coast in New Smyrna Beach. They'd met at one of Steve's "Don't Drink" meetings and shared a passion for surf fishing, baseball, and races at the new Daytona Speedway. That summer, in fact, she'd somehow arranged for Steve to be in the pit for local hero Fireball Roberts's back-to-back wins at the Daytona 500 and the Firecracker 250. Steve had come back flush with speed- and power-boosting secrets from Roberts's mechanic, Smokey Yunick, plus a bunch of track trivia: Like the fact that Fireball's nickname sprang from his blistering fastball as a star pitcher at Apopka High.

And that Roberts didn't mind the fans applying it to his fearless racing style, but his friends called him Glenn, and the other drivers
called him simply, respectfully, Balls.

Avery had relished the inside scoop, but worried that Steve was
planning to make a move. At summer's end, he'd asked Steve directly,
"You considering the coast full-time?"

"Nah," Steve said. "If it ain't broke, why fix it?"

Watching his friend drive off, Avery wondered, had two divorces
soured Steve on marriage forever? Whatever happened to "third
time's the charm"?

JUST AFTER SIX, AVERY surrendered the station to Emilio—"She's all
yours, son"—and drove home through the pouring rain. As usual, he
made a beeline for the master bathroom to shower, shave, and change
for supper. In the kitchen, he saw the dinette was set for two.

"Where's our girl?" he asked Sarah.

"Oh, a few of the twirls came over to help fold brochures, and
after they got word that tonight's game was canceled, they all went
off to see that new Pat Boone movie—*State Fair*, I think. Going to
the Steak 'n Shake after." She set a plate of steaming tuna noodle casserole with a side of green beans in front of him.

Avery, suddenly starving, spread his napkin in his lap and waited
for her to do the same. She'd brushed her hair, he noticed, left it loose
the way he liked it. She'd put on fresh lipstick, too, but her eyes were
red-rimmed with fatigue, her face drawn and tired.

"Tough day?"

"Just awful. Edith was a raving maniac over the Mininsons not
coming—even though it wasn't till five o'clock that the general decided tomorrow's show is still a go." Sarah sighed. "At least we got the
brochures done. I just have to pack up the Grandma's Pantry stuff and
get it down there and on display by nine a.m." She picked up her fork.
"How about you?"

"Rain slowed things down a bit." He took a bite and winked his
appreciation. The combination of creamy tuna, sweet peas, and the

extra-sharp cheddar she got from a shop in Winter Park was one of his favorites. After a moment, he asked, "She tell you the big news?"

"What news?"

Inwardly, Avery winced. Charlotte hadn't talked to her mother about the dance or done anything to make this any easier for him.

For some time, she'd reminded him of a young filly pawing the rails of the paddock. No longer content to trail alongside her mother, as she had for years, she was testing boundaries, bucking conventions she considered too conservative, and regularly tossing her head at Sarah's concerns. For the most part, he tried to sidestep their occasional dustups.

But now, with Charlotte gone and Sarah watching him expectantly, eager for "the big news," he needed to tread carefully.

"Apparently, Mr. Beauchamp stopped by the Ag Barn hinting that Charlotte was elected to Homecoming Court." He leaned heavily on the word *hint*.

"He did?" she asked, eyes brightening. Then a flush of hurt blossomed at the base of her graceful neck and spread up to her cheeks. "Nobody said a word about it . . . to *me*."

"Well, it's not for sure *yet*," he added hastily. "Maybe she didn't want to get your hopes up," he lied, rushing on. "In any event, she stopped by the station fretting about not having a date for the big dance. And Emilio, polite as you please, offered to take her."

"Emilio?" Sarah said quietly. "You can't be serious."

"Well, actually, darlin', our girl said yes. Mind of her own—like her mama, I s'pose," he said, as smoothly as he could manage.

Her angry flash at the words *like her mama* warned him away from that particular tack.

"Just like *that*? He asked and she said *yes*?"

"Pretty much," he said, deliberately not mentioning it was Steve's idea.

"But the boy doesn't even go to her school."

"Could be an advantage, I'd say. The locals had their chance, and lost it."

"But he's your employee, Wes. Not to mention Catholic and a

Cuban"—she searched for the word—"*exile*! Why, he doesn't have a
penny to his name except what you give him. What would he wear?
How in the world could he even get there?"

"Turns out . . . Steve's offered to lend him The Admiral."

"Oh, great," she said coolly. "Popeye plays matchmaker."

"But he's a *good* boy, Sarah, from a very good family. His father's a
judge, remember? And his mother lectures at the local art museum."

"Or *so* we've been told." She'd drawn herself up, shoulders high
and square. And she was holding her face in that way that reminded
him of her mother, locking her real thoughts and feelings in, locking
him out.

"But, Sarah, the priest—"

"—was interested in getting the boy a *job*, Wes. Of course he
painted the rosiest picture possible. Just like you are now." She looked
down into her lap, jaw thrust out to keep it from trembling, then
slowly refolded her napkin and placed it on the table beside her untouched plate. "And I suppose Charlotte put you up to this . . ."

"Oh, honey . . ."

"Don't 'oh, honey' me, Wes." She rose to set her plate in the sink.
"That girl is too headstrong by half. And you . . ." She shook her head
wearily. "I suppose it's a gift you have . . . favoring everyone, friend
and foe alike, with a wink and a smile; getting us all fixed up just the
way you like." She had the habit, when upset, of placing one hand on
her hip, the other on her belly, fingers splayed as if taking the measure
of the long vertical scar on the skin beneath her clothes.

"I wish I had your gift, Wes. I really do. But mark my words," she
said slowly, as if she was only going to say this once and it behooved
him to listen, "this thing has disaster written all over it. Now if you'll
excuse me, I have work to do," she finished and was gone.

For a long moment, Avery watched the swinging door resettle itself. He heard her move through the living room and into the middle
room to pack up the supplies for tomorrow's show.

He turned to eyeball the window onto the lake, but there was
nothing to see except his own watery reflection. The darkness outside
was lashed with blue rain. Some fine messenger you are, he thought

miserably. Tried to reconstruct what just happened—and why?—but he couldn't get it straight, couldn't pinpoint the place where he might have kept things on track. All he could remember was the way her smile fell off her face and hurt bloomed on her neck.

Somehow he'd bungled it and was left to sort through the after-mess alone. Did Sarah really have a problem with Emilio? Or was it Charlotte's not-telling that set her off? Or was this just fallout from her nerves over today's storm and tomorrow's Civil Defense show? But why walk out like that? Why not sit and talk this through, the way most people do, the way they used to?

He covered her plate and put it in the fridge, then made his way reluctantly to the open door of the shelter. He leaned against the oversized doorjamb, hoping to reopen their conversation, but her look over the half-filled cardboard box warned him off.

Not now, Wes, it said. *Leave me be.*

"Can I help you pack, at least?"

She shook her head. "I have a system. It'll be easier to unpack to-morrow if I do it myself."

So he left her alone and retreated to the sunken living room and the Saturday-night lineup of their favorite TV shows.

INSIDE THE SHELTER, SARAH sat back on the fold-up metal chair and swallowed hard against a rising tide of upset. When was it, in the good cop–bad cop roles of parenting, I became the permanent bad cop, the spoilsport and chief disciplinarian—while Wes got to slide by on a wink and a smile? Is that why Charlotte went to him with her big news? Didn't she think I'd be as excited as the next person? Or did she go to the station in the hope of having Emilio ask her to dance? Where in the world did that come from? And then she was here all afternoon and never said a word!

Just like Kitty.

The chilling effect of those three little words, echoing inside her head in her mother's voice, made her shiver.

Oh, Lord, that's it, isn't it? When Wes looks at Charlotte, all he sees is Daddy's little girl all grown up. But more and more, I see Kitty—that scary tendency to leap without looking: go to a college fair and make up your mind after talking to a single recruiter, accept a date with a boy you hardly know because he's the first to ask—and all I can think of is what happened . . .

Oh, I'm sure Wes and Charlotte think I'm unfair, too strict, too much of a worrywart. But neither of them was *there*. They've never seen, as I did, how quickly a girl's life, her reputation, her entire family can fall apart over a single night's stupidity.

Sarah stopped short of letting her mind wander down that particularly painful path.

Life was so much easier and safer when Charlotte was little! What I wouldn't give to go back to the days of tea parties, ballet lessons, and hopscotch chalk marks all down the drive. Now the older and more independent Charlotte gets, the more potential disasters I see wherever I look.

What's happened to me? Why can't I be the person I used to be? Why? Because the velocity of *everything* has changed, sped *up*. And I can't escape the feeling that I'm two steps behind with no hope of ever . . .

Stop this! A part of her brain knew she was overreacting and wondered gently if the fog of her Nembutal wouldn't be preferable to dwelling on the ever-expanding list of her concerns. No, she told herself adamantly. There's simply too much to do. She needed to buck up, focus on the here and now, and leave worrying for later. She opened a new box, drew her mouth into a tight, determined line, and started stacking the canned applesauce atop the canned corn; though her hands trembled with the memory of packing up the big house in Tuscaloosa all alone after Mama died, with no big sister and no little brother to help. "You'll get through," Mama said on one of her last days in the hospital. "You always did; you always do."

I hope you're right, Mama. If I can just forget about the damn hurricane, get through this stupid show tomorrow, get Charlotte safely through homecoming next week . . . then the prom in the spring and graduation in June, and ... and into Stetson instead of FSU ...

"Mind of her own," Wes had said, "just like her mother."

Sarah shuddered. Oh, Mama, for the first time in my entire life, I haven't a clue how I'll get through.

AN HOUR OR SO later, Avery turned up the volume so she could hear the opening orchestral strains, the pop of the champagne cork of Lawrence Welk and His Champagne Music Makers.

When he heard the packing sounds in the shelter stop, he hoped for a moment that she'd join him, as usual, on the sofa. But instead, she strode past him and out the sliding glass door onto the screened porch. He saw the quick, familiar movements of her covering the birdcages for the night, then watched her let herself back in, walk past him, and return to her work in the center bedroom. He switched over to *Have Gun—Will Travel*. From there, he rolled into *Gunsmoke* and the comforting world of Marshal Matt Dillon and his faithful sidekick, Chester B. Goode.

At eleven, he punched off the TV and approached her once again.

"Coming to bed?" he asked.

"Not yet," she said, intent on checking items off her list.

Reluctantly, he left her and padded down the hall to the master bedroom at its end.

Later, he heard Charlotte return home; heard Sarah and her talking urgently back and forth. Heard Charlotte take her final stand—"I'm *going* with him, Mama. Let's just leave it at *that*."—and firmly shut, without slamming, her bedroom door. He heard Sarah call quietly, tiredly, from the hall, "Tomorrow, Charlotte. We'll talk this all out tomorrow."

Still later, he heard her moving around inside the shelter, late into the rain-soaked night.

3.

*T*HOUGH THICK CLOUDS SCUDDED OVERHEAD, THE RAIN THIS MORN-
ing had tapered off to a lackluster spit.

Avery woke at six to the sound of Sarah already in the shower. He
lay there trying to recall what time she'd come to bed. Had she been
up all night again? After a while, she emerged from the bathroom in
an elegant knit suit, pale blue with silver buttons, slim skirt, and
matching pumps.

"You look great," he said, sitting up.

"Thanks. Think you can help me load up the car?"

"Sure. Right now?"

"Well, they open the gates at nine so I want to get there by seven
to set everything up."

Avery threw back the covers. "Need me to go with you and help
unload?" He toed his feet into his slippers.

"No," she said from her vanity, fastening her wristwatch. "General
Betts promised Edith an entire unit of army reservists on hand to
help."

"Edith with an army of Weekend Warriors to order about?
Hooah!"

Sarah was retrieving a pair of white gloves from the vanity drawer.
She chuckled. "Poor lads have no idea what they're in for."

She strode out of the bedroom to "get some coffee going" while Avery, still in his pajamas, loaded her trunk with six large boxes of supplies from the shelter—each one coded in Sarah's careful hand. He put the three boxes of folded brochures in the backseat, and returned to the kitchen.

Sarah handed him a steaming mug, then turned to the counter, where her gloves lay beside her purse and car keys.

"Listen, Wes. It occurred to me," she said, pulling on a glove, "that when they announce the names at school tomorrow, Charlotte may have other offers for the dance. I mean . . ." She was pressing the fingertips of one gloved hand between the joints of the other. "It's not that Emilio doesn't have a certain, well . . . charm, but . . ." She reversed the process to the opposite hand. "Everyone knows he works for you, Wes. It looks more like a setup, a pity date arranged by her parents, than the real thing."

Something about her tone, and the way she raised her eyebrows seeking his agreement, reminded him of the way his mother-in-law, the very complicated Dolores Ayres, used to nudge people to do her bidding.

"A girl's got to keep her options open," she was saying, "not just jump at the first thing that comes along."

Avery leaned against the opposite counter and sipped his coffee. "That what you did with me?" he asked quietly.

"Oh, Wes," she replied with a long, hollow look. "I was hardly the prize Charlotte is."

"Not the prize?" Avery's mind raced with objections. He felt again his endless, aching eagerness—on the interminable troop transport flight to Sioux Falls and the sixty-hour train ride south to Tuscaloosa— to meet and marry his future wife. How many times had he read and re-read her answer to his airmailed proposal? Traced the letters *Y-E-S!* outlined and triple-underlined in red ink? They'd met by mail, on a nickel bet with fellow crewman Mac McNair over who might answer his thank-you letter to Inspector 833 at the Tuscaloosa B. F. Goodrich plant "for the rubber raft that saved my life."

"If you hear back at all, it'll be from some gray-haired granny," Mac predicted. "Nah," Avery shot back, "with my luck, it'll be some flat-footed 4-F-er."

Her first shy letter—"You're most welcome"—was, in retrospect, the turning point between all the tough breaks that plagued him before and all his good fortune since. In the V-mails that followed, love had opened like a flower between them, one petal-thin page at a time. Then *finally*, after all those anxious hours on the train, he spotted the red roof of the Tuscaloosa station, exactly as she'd described it, and there she *was*, waiting on the platform—a tall, slim beauty in a navy-blue suit with a white gardenia pinned to her lapel. He was stunned. Here was the girl whose shy revelations, wise observations, and witty, self-effacing "Tales from the Tuscaloosa Homefront" had captured his heart. But *in person*! He'd seen pictures, of course, but was unprepared for Sarah's refinement, elegant bearing, and, later, that amazing voice of hers, like velvet smoke. He'd panicked—what in the world would *she* see in *me?*—and braced himself for the inevitable crash and burn. But then she'd spotted him through the open train window. And he'd seen, like a miracle, her heart leaping into her eyes.

In the kitchen, he set down his mug and stepped forward to take her white-gloved hands.

"You were the blue-ribboned brass ring, the solid twenty-four-karat-gold jackpot . . . to me," he told her.

Her fingers returned his squeeze. Her face softened. "You were always a sucker for a pretty phrase." It was their old joke—along with *love at first write*—about their unconventional courtship and engagement.

He felt happy she'd recalled it.

"So . . ." She sighed, letting him go. "We'll talk to her when I get home tonight?"

The spell of the moment was broken. She was back on Charlotte. "What mean 'we,' Kemo Sabe?"

"You saying I'm the Lone Ranger on this thing?"

"Well . . ."

"Or that *you* should talk to her?"

"Me?"

"Maybe you should, Wes," Sarah said, warming to the idea. "She only half listens to me anyhow." She picked up her purse and keys. "I have to go. You'll come by after church? There are food booths. If I can break away for a few minutes, we could have lunch together."

"All right, darlin'." Seeing the relief in her eyes, he realized he'd just agreed to both lunch and to speaking with Charlotte about Emilio. Hi-yo, Silver, he thought.

WITH HURRICANE ELLA OFFICIALLY headed elsewhere, members of the congregation hailed Avery, on meet-and-greet duty inside the church vestibule, with thanks for the heaven-sent relief.

Handing out the day's bulletin, helping the old ladies to their seats, Avery kept an eye on Charlotte in the section off the right aisle favored by church young people. Her dark head bobbed as she whispered and grinned at the girls beside her. He'd let her sleep in, so they'd had to rush to get here on time.

At head deacon Ted Buck's signal, he closed the sanctuary's rear doors and took his seat in the back with the other deacons scheduled to pass the collection plates.

To Avery's ear, the choir's Call to Worship sounded thin without Sarah's rich contralto. Pastor Billy Wigginthal, in a new suit and recent haircut, steered the service along predictable lines, except for one thing: During the collection, a far-off rumble drew in close overhead and drowned out the bulk of the offertory hymn. A number among the congregation—veterans mostly—gazed upward at the sound. Thunderchiefs, Avery thought. The original squadrons from Friday? Or a new wave of arrivals now that the weather's cleared?

Avery tapped impatient fingers on the end of the pew, eager to head over to the base and see for himself.

At the end of the service, Pastor Billy extended the invitation—while the choir sang softly "Just as I Am, Without One Plea"—but nobody responded. Privately, Avery suspected the minister had set his sights on a bigger congregation: the big, new brick First Baptist downtown, maybe? The guy seemed skittish and rangy, like a horse in changing weather. Or a man looking to make a move.

Afterward, Avery waited at the base of the church steps till Charlotte joined him, calling to her friends, "Later, 'gators!"

Mabel Jenkins, a thin, hawk-eyed widow, turned and put a blue-veined claw beneath Charlotte's chin. "What a beauty you've become!" she exclaimed. "Just look at that face, that *figure!*" Her gaze switched bird-like between Charlotte and Avery. "Where on earth did those curves come from?"

Charlotte blanched and crossed her arms defensively in front of her chest. Over the summer a number of the coarser boys had taken to calling her "stacked." And now this old biddy was doing the same thing—on the church steps, no less!

Avery felt her embarrassment as well as the not-so-subtle swipe at Sarah. "My side of the family, I guess," he lied. "Good day, Mabel," he added curtly and, with a firm hand on the small of Charlotte's back, steered her away from the old bat to the truck.

THE PARKING LOT OF J. M. Fields looked like the circus was in town.

There was a series of brightly striped tents, flags flying, young men in orange vests directing cars where to park. But instead of WELCOME TO RINGLING BROS. AND BARNUM & BAILEY'S GREATEST SHOW ON EARTH, the entrance banner boasted CENTRAL FLORIDA'S FIRST EVER SHOWCASE OF FAMILY FALLOUT SHELTERS sponsored by the Office of Civil and Defense Mobilization.

Instead of Gargantua, Jo-Jo the Dog-Faced Boy, and the little house that caught fire, there were full-sized displays of walk-through fallout shelters: from the prefab Peace O' Mind steel-and-concrete vault (*with patented fluted design to resist shock waves*) to a fire-resistant California redwood Safety Shed (*A shelter for the family and workshop for Dad in one!*) to the small, dark Bee Safe Quonset hut (*with fireproof exterior surface of Gunite!*). Most of them were no bigger than one of his station's bathrooms. Avery peered in but refused to enter.

Truth be told, he hated dark, enclosed spaces and avoided them whenever he could.

He walked about, following Charlotte in and out of the tents in search of Sarah's "Grandma's Pantry" display. He listened to the barkers hawking the lifesaving advantages of their wares. He nodded, in acknowledgment but not necessarily agreement, at the government man's explanation that, although an underground basement was most easily adapted to family shelter use, Florida's high water table, its universal lack of basements, presented challenges that were "easily overcome so long as you followed government standards to achieve ninety-nine percent reduction in gamma ray exposure."

Avery heard the hype. He examined the shoddy workmanship of what one local contractor called his "guaranteed watertight, airtight, radiation-tight Florida Igloo in aqua blue." (The guy's primary business was building swimming pools.) He shook his head at the men walking around like clowns in transparent plastic bags advertised as "Civilian Fallout Suits, only $19.99."

Unfortunately for the hucksters, Avery was no rube on the subject. On V-J Day, he'd been a part of the massive American "Show of Strength" flyover above Tokyo Bay and the defeated emperor's Surrender Ceremonies on the deck of the USS *Missouri*. Heading back to base on Tinian Island, the crew had lobbied their pilot, amiable Cap'n Tex Ritter, to swing west for a bird's-eye view of what was left of Hiroshima and Nagasaki.

Avery, facing east in the tail turret, was the last to see the green islands dotting the blue Hiroshima Bay then, opening like a miles-wide mouth of hell, the decimated delta city recognizable only by its distinctive river channels, four fingers and a thumb, flowing into the bay. Worse yet was the sulfurous stench of fiery death that filled their plane at five thousand feet and lingered for days as a black taste on Avery's tongue. Circling back, Cap'n Tex said quietly over the intercom, "Seen enough, boys?" and headed home without further comment. In the tail, Avery got the last, long look at the devastation. How was it possible? he wondered, sickened that a single bomb dropped by a solo plane could do so much damage.

Photos published later in *The New Yorker* for the rest of America to see fell far short of conveying the actual horror that still haunted his dreams. John Hersey's chilling account of the bombing came closer, but did little or nothing to stop further nuclear testing by the Americans at Enewetak and Bikini, the British in Australia, the French in the Sahara, and the Soviets in Kazakhstan.

Avery knew, quite rightly, that no man-made structure could survive a direct hit from today's more powerful hydrogen bombs. And even if the hit was indirect, the chances that he and Sarah and Charlotte would be in the same place at that time were slim. For that reason, he agreed with Ike, who'd said, "If I were in a very fine shelter and [my wife and children] were not there, I would just walk out. I would not want to face that kind of world."

A barker strode by calling "Any Catholics in the crowd?" and thrust a yellow flyer into Avery's hand. It was a mimeographed copy of a magazine article by a Father L. C. McHugh proclaiming, *Nowhere in traditional Catholic morality does one read that Christ, in counseling nonresistance to evil, rescinded the right of self-defense which is granted by nature and recognized in the legal systems of all nations. To love one's neighbor as thyself,* the priest wrote, *is, undoubtedly, an heroic Christian virtue, but it is not a Christian duty.* Indeed, this Father McHugh implied, it would be misguided charity *not* to shoot a neighbor trying to invade one's jam-packed shelter!

Avery had had enough. He crumpled the flyer, tossed it into the waste barrel of a vendor hawking Double Decker Moon Pies, and called to his daughter's back. "Charlotte . . . Charlotte!"

She turned, eyes bright. "I think I see her . . . in *there.*" She pointed to the entrance of a nearby red-and-white striped tent. Beside it, one large poster proclaimed, MEET THE ATOMIC HONEYMOONERS! with a picture of the smiling Mininsons and diagonal red letters: CANCELED DUE TO HURRICANE. A second poster asked, GRANDMA'S PANTRY WAS READY: IS YOUR "PANTRY" READY IN THE EVENT OF AN EMERGENCY? and announced, CIVIL DEFENSE FOR HOMEMAKERS, PRESENTATIONS ON THE HOUR, EVERY HOUR.

Inside the tent, rows of empty folding chairs faced a stage whose metal shelves were filled with the supplies from their shelter. Near the wooden podium, Sarah stood talking earnestly to an imposing woman in a fire-engine-red suit, white pearls, and a royal-blue pillbox hat. The infamous Edith, Avery guessed.

"Hey, Mom!" Charlotte called.

The two women turned. As he and Charlotte came down the center aisle, Edith cast a withering glance in Avery's direction.

"Edith, this is my daughter, Charlotte . . . ," Sarah was saying.

"And your husband, Judas Iscariot, I take it. With friends like you, Mr. Avery, who needs enemies?" Abruptly, the older woman stomped off the stage and out the side exit.

"What the Sam Hill?" Avery asked, dumbfounded.

Sarah took a labored breath. "Oh, Wes, didn't you see the paper?"

"What paper?"

"This morning's *Sentinel*?" She walked to the podium, picked up and handed down the day's Society Section. It was his custom to separate the morning paper into his and hers portions: News, Financial, and Sports for him; Society, usually sheathed in weekend sales circulars, for her. So, of course, he hadn't seen the section's cover photo of Sarah, taken inside their shelter.

"Nice picture," he said.

"Read the last paragraph, Wes."

He scanned the column, under the byline of reporter Joseph A. Riley, to its end:

When asked to comment on local Civil Defense efforts, Mrs. Avery's husband, an incendiary expert who participated in the bombing of Japan, shrugged. "The only real defense against nuclear warfare is to make certain it never starts," Avery said.

"You *shrugged*?" Sarah asked in a tired voice.

"Let me see." Charlotte was peering at the paper.

"That's not at all what I—"

"'*Incendiary* expert,' Dad?"

Behind them, three women strolled into the tent chatting and took their seats midway up the aisle.

Still on stage, Sarah smiled and called, "Welcome! We'll be starting in"—she checked her watch—"another six minutes."

She bent down to tell Avery and Charlotte, "Lunch is out, I guess. I'm stuck with back-to-back presentations for the rest of the afternoon." When her eyes slid from Charlotte to Avery, she gave him a searching, lifted-eyebrow look, clearly asking, *You talk to her yet?*

His quick head shake told her, *No, not yet.*

Walking out with Charlotte, he was seething at the reporter's failure to credit Omar Bradley with his own quote, and at that battle-ax Edith for accusing him of some sort of betrayal.

Betrayal! Wasn't the real betrayal the whole idea behind this event? That the local Civil Defense plan—eleven designated buildings, mostly downtown, at a considerable distance from the suburbs where everybody lived—could save more than a handful of city bureaucrats? That the President's campaign suggesting people build their own private shelter was anything more than political eyewash, part of the Democrats' run-up to midterm elections?

Avery looked around, bewildered by the size of the crowd and the number of families trailing small children. Why were they here? Was it plain old curiosity or did they actually intend to buy this crap? He'd seen the options available, the obvious hucksters, the bloated price tags attached to the ridiculous shelters. *Shelter!* The very word was a joke. Do-it-yourself *tomb* was more like it.

"Can we eat?" Charlotte asked, tugging on his sleeve. "I'm starving!"

He stood in line for a couple of hot dogs while she found an open bench just inside the exit. They sat and ate their dogs in silence, basking in a patch of sunlight breaking through the clouds. Then Charlotte jumped up, intent on buying an "atomic mint chocolate" ice cream cone at a nearby stand.

"Want one?" she asked, joining the line.

"No, thanks."

Ignorance is bliss, right? he thought, surveying the crowd. But what about Sarah? She wasn't ignorant, not by a long shot. So what in the world was *she* doing here? Seventeen years and there were still parts of his wife that mystified him. Her moods, for instance. One day, she could be the queen of optimism and organization, blithely moving from household task to community project to school committee meeting. All poise and polish. The next, she could be laid low, composure fractured by the less than perfect, the unpredictable, or some other thing that was completely outside her control.

Charlotte had reached the counter and was giving him a thumbs-up. Avery thumbed her back, wondering what it was Sarah expected him to say to Charlotte. Was last night's upset, all her talk about "options" this morning, really about Emilio? Or was it that Charlotte had made up her mind without consulting her mother? Or anyone else, for that matter? And what was wrong with that? Truth was, he loved Charlotte's decisiveness, her desire to go her own way, to dream her own dreams. It showed character, didn't it? And reflected well on her parents: Without those same qualities, Sarah might never have left Tuscaloosa. And I'd still be a dirt farmer, fighting bad weather and boll weevils!

Charlotte plopped back down beside him. "Yummm," she said, licking her cone.

"It's turning your tongue green," he teased her.

"Maybe I'm radioactive!" she shot back, crossing her eyes and flicking her tongue like a lizard.

They walked out through the still-incoming crowd. In the parking lot, Charlotte tapped the truck's front fender and said, "Wake up, Otto! Time to make like an atom and split."

Firing the ignition, Avery said, "I thought it was, 'Make like a tree and leave'?"

"Well, yeah, if you're *twelve*."

"Oh, got it. So let's, uhm . . . make like an engine and run? Make like a gasket and blow? Or how 'bout, make like a pedal and put it to the metal?"

"Save it for the station, Dad."

Wheeling left on East Colonial Drive, Avery announced, "Scenic route!" A few miles later, he turned right on Route 436, through T. G. Lee Dairy's cow-spotted pastures to Bearhead Road, the northern perimeter of McCoy Air Force Base.

THE BARRICADE SURPRISED HIM.

A makeshift collection of sawhorses, guard shack, military jeeps, and uniformed air police blocked the normally public road 250 yards ahead of the main gate. Avery pulled the truck off onto the grassy shoulder, behind a gaggle of others who had done the same thing. Up ahead, a hundred yards from the barricade, a cluster of men, civilians, were gathered around a white Dodge pickup. He decided to walk up and ask what was going on.

"Want to come?" he asked Charlotte.

"Sure!" she said, already half out the door.

The circle of onlookers stood listening to a large man in denim overalls and mud-caked farm boots. His milk-colored truck sported the red T. G. Lee Dairy logo and held an assortment of field tools in the back. He wore a red T. G. Lee cap and the dark tan of a man who spent the bulk of his time outdoors. He'd pulled a stalk of sweetgrass from a nearby patch and held it between his lips. The trio of lime-green leaves at its tip quaked as he talked.

When Avery and Charlotte approached, the dairyman eyed Avery's starched white shirt, his Sunday suit pants, and shiny wingtips, and called, "Afternoon, Reverend. How was church?"

Avery held up innocent hands. "I'm a mechanic, not a minister. Just out for a drive on my day off."

"Come to see your hard-earned tax dollars at work?"

The dairyman reached into his truck's open window, pulled out a pair of black binoculars.

"Take a good look. Everyone else has."

The solemn faces surrounding him nodded. A few men toed the dirt like cattle wary of a shifting wind.

Avery put the binocs to his eyes, peering south beyond the huge ordnance depot, a beehive of busy front loaders, toward the row of hangars and plane docks off the flight line, far right.

What he saw shocked him. The US Air Force organized its air-craft into wings of three squadrons with twenty-four planes apiece. Before him, like a giant flock of silver seabirds blown off course, were at least two wings of F-105 Thunderchief fighters, another two wings of F-84 Thunderjets, and a third of F-100 Super Sabres—five wings, 72 birds each, equaled 360 fighters all told! Next to the fighters sat a dozen or so shiny silver Connies (Super Constellations) with their distinctive triple tails. Some were outfitted with radar hoods for re-connaissance; others, obviously paratroop carriers.

Avery lowered the binocs to make sure they weren't playing some kind of trick on him. But the packed view was the same with plain sight, only smaller and less detailed. He raised them back up, looked again at the magnified fighters, each armed to the gills with cluster, free-fall, and Sidewinder bombs, and felt his gut clench in genuine alarm.

In the uncomfortable group silence—Avery was stunned for a moment beyond words—he remembered Charlotte. Determined not to overreact, he took her arm and said, as casually as he could manage, "We were sort of hoping to see a U-2."

The dairyman's eyes flared with surprise as if to ask, *How'd you know about them?* After a moment, he said softly, "One came in 'bout fifteen minutes ago." He chucked the largest of his several chins. "Walk up another fifty, sixty yards and look left."

Avery led Charlotte in that direction, his senses assaulted by the sharp reek of jet fuel and the sucking roar of jet engines.

"Awful lot of planes out there," she said, betraying the same mix-ture of curiosity and dread that was gripping him. "Pretty scary, don't you think, Dad?"

Avery threw a protective arm around her. Hoping to distract her from the effect of all that firepower, he said, "Let me tell you about the U-2, Kitten."

He told her what little he knew about America's super-secret spy plane: How it supposedly flew twice as high as most other aircraft, up to seventy thousand feet, "where blue sky meets black space." How it had a single pilot, a single jet engine, and flew unarmed over enemy territory with a bellyful of special long-range cameras. How, for years, it was thought untouchable by enemy radar or ground fire until 1960, when a Soviet missile shot down U-2 pilot Frank Powers over Russia.

When they'd reached the point roughly midway between the dairyman and the guard shack, Avery stopped. He pointed out the hangar in the distance, now visible beyond the ordnance depot. The sight of the U-2s out front—five all-black plus another three in silver with the single air force star—took his breath away. Was this a joint CIA and air force operation? Was that possible?

The binocs provided further details. Milkman Jimmy Simms had compared the U-2's shape to a big, black buzzard. But to Avery, the aircraft's long, lean fuselage and significantly wider wings looked more like a cluster of fantastic dragonflies. The flurried actions of the ground crew drew his attention to one U-2 in particular.

"Hey, Dad?"

"Just a sec, hon."

A group was gathered at the all-black nose dock, canopy up, help-ing the pilot, moving stiffly in a silver pressure suit, out of the cockpit. Another bunch was busy mid-plane under the wide-open camera bay. And a third was loading a Metro Van with two heavy steel boxes. The film, Avery reasoned. Judging from the care with which the men han-dled the boxes, the sense of urgency in their movements, the boxes had to contain the spy plane's film!

"Dad ..."

Spellbound, Avery watched the Metro Van wheel toward a silver T-39 transport already on the flight line, hoses dropped, twin engines at fractional power, ready to go. In mere seconds they had the boxes and an armed escort officer aboard, and the T-39 was taxiing for take-off. Somewhere, Avery thought, there were men in high command waiting for whatever secrets that film might ...

"Sorry, sir." A brusque baritone demanded his attention.

Avery lowered the binoculars and felt a shiver at the nearness of the muscle-bound air police confronting them. He'd been so intent watching the runway that he'd ignored Charlotte's warnings and completely missed the staff sergeant's approach.

"Sir, observation of base ops is strictly limited to *approved* personnel. Please return to your vehicle immediately." The man's gaze was direct, his tone no-nonsense.

"Of course, Sergeant," Avery said, and watched the E-5's eyes glide toward Charlotte in an appreciative once-over.

"Let's go, Kitten." He took her arm, stepped back onto the asphalt, and headed toward the dairyman and his uneasy herd of onlookers.

"So what do you think, Dad?"

"About what?"

Charlotte gave him her *don't baby me* look. "All this . . ." She opened her palm toward the jam-packed runway.

Avery exhaled guilt. It was a mistake to bring her here; he should have insisted she wait in the truck. "Hard to say, honey."

"But . . ."

They'd reached the dairyman, who, after accepting the binocs and Avery's thanks, observed, "Looks like Gen-rill-leesimo Castro's 'bout to get his clock cleaned, don't ya think?"

Avery shrugged.

Charlotte waited until they were out of earshot to ask, "He's right, Dad, isn't he? About Castro?"

"Maybe, maybe not, honey. The U-2s mean they're investigating something. But with their range, it could just as easily be the Panama Canal or somewhere in South America."

They drove home in silence, Avery's thoughts darkened by dread. How in the world have we come to this? Why *now*? And why *here*, on Florida's front porch? Wasn't my war the one that was supposed to end all others?

Avery was watching TV with Charlotte when Sarah limped in around eight-thirty. She was in stockinged feet, purse in one hand, both pumps in the other.

He rose to greet her. "You're a sight for sore eyes."

"Sore *feet*," she said, holding up her shoes. "*Very* sore feet." She sounded hoarse, and looked exhausted, spent.

"Get you something?" he asked.

"If you don't mind, I'm going to bed."

"'Night, Mom." Charlotte waved, eyes intent on comedian Rip Taylor and *The Ed Sullivan Show*.

Hobbling toward the hall, Sarah stopped and turned back. "Anyone remember to feed the birds today?"

"I did," Charlotte replied. "Cleaned the cages, too, while Dad mowed the lawn."

"Well . . . thanks," Sarah said.

Avery nodded acknowledgment. After the unsettling discoveries out at the base, he'd attempted, for Charlotte's sake, to make the rest of the day as normal as possible.

The routine had calmed them both. But then the evening news announced that President Kennedy had unexpectedly cut his campaign trip short and returned to Washington. He'd caught a cold, a spokesman said.

A cold, my butt! Avery thought. *More like a cold war turning hot.*

"'Night, darlin', sleep tight," he called to Sarah, relieved she was too tired to ask about their trip to the air base or his true thoughts on Civil Defense.

4.

DRAGGING WITH EXHAUSTION FROM VERY LITTLE SLEEP, AVERY dressed quietly so as not to disturb Sarah, and padded to the still-dark kitchen to make his own coffee. He took a fragrant mug out onto the screened porch that spanned the back of the house.

Already Sarah's parakeets were up and chattering to have their cages uncovered. There were only three left of the four birds she'd brought home last summer. Originally, she'd named them Dianne, Peggy, Kathy, and Janet after the singing Lennon Sisters on *The Lawrence Welk Show*—until the morning she found Janet pecked to death on the floor of their communal cage.

When the vet decided that the brightly colored sisters were, in fact, brothers and should be housed separately, Avery suggested they rename the aggressive trio Moe, Larry, and Curly; or simpler still, so that even he could keep them straight, "How about Green Guy, Blue Boy, and Yella Fella?"

Both his suggestions were flatly rejected as "all wet" by Sarah and "pretty dorky, Dad!" by his daughter. Instead, they'd settled on Adam, Hoss, and Little Joe. And Avery had been hard-pressed to explain, to either his wife's or his daughter's satisfaction, the predatory nature of males, even among parakeets.

Annoyed by the birds' insistent chatter, Avery stepped outside and made his way across the dark, dew-slick lawn to the family dock. He walked out to the wooden bench at its end and sat to watch the dawn. While Sarah had been attracted to the neighborhood's quiet maturity and the split-level's modern kitchen, it was Lake Silver's watery expanse, waves lapping gently against the dock's pylons, and the occasional jump of fish and splash of birds that sealed the deal for him. Born on a hardscrabble farm in Macon County, raised during the worst drought on record, he'd had a childhood framed by ankle-deep cracks in dried red clay and the constant choke of rusty dust. If heaven has a lake, Avery thought the first time he saw it, it looks like this.

Today, however, watching the dawn finger-paint the lake and tattered clouds pink then peach then, inexplicably, bright red, he remembered his grandfather saying, "Red sky at morning, sailors take warning." This quiet lake felt like a surreal juxtaposition of all those war birds parked wingtip-to-wingtip on McCoy's tarmac, and the anxiety—images of an entire world in Hiroshima-like ruins—that had kept him awake most of the night.

In the sandy shallows, green-black wings fluttered. He turned to see the black-tuxedoed night heron give way, with a harsh squawk like the bark of a small dog, to a stocky green heron. The new day bird fastened Avery with a sun-bright eye and cried a sudden, loud *kyou* followed by a series of more subdued *kuk-kuk-kuk*s.

Changing of the guard, Avery thought, and wondered: What other changes are afoot today? If the President is planning to wage war on Castro, won't he need to announce it first? And to explain why, after backing off at the Bay of Pigs eighteen months ago, he's charging ahead *now*? What could be worth the risk of ticking off the Soviets? And whatever Kennedy's reason, when the announcement comes, how will the American people and our local customers respond? He made a mental note to check the levels on his underground fuel tanks first thing and call the depot in Tampa for a top-off.

Behind him, human sounds drifted down from the house. He turned to see Sarah moving past the now lit kitchen windows.

Charlotte was at the dinette finishing up her Frosted Flakes while Sarah stood silently at the stove scrambling eggs. When a car horn out front announced her ride to school, Charlotte rose in a sudden flurry, grabbed her books, slid her cereal bowl into the sink, and, rushing past him, grinned. "See ya, Daddy-O, gotta make like lightning and bolt!"

Sarah brought him his breakfast without comment. She'd coiled her hair in a simple bun at the back of her neck this morning and applied makeup to the deepening circles under her eyes. He'd heard her tossing and turning throughout the night.

"Catch up on your rest?" he asked.

"Hardly," she replied wearily, then added, "I gather you didn't talk to her?"

"Not yet."

She froze her face against it, but he sensed her frustration. "The principal will announce the names this morning. I figure I'll take her shopping this afternoon—there's no time to make her a dress and she's going to need two: one for the parade and one for the dance. Guess I'll try talking to her then."

Avery felt her disappointment wash over him. Rightly so. He'd agreed to speak with Charlotte, but his discoveries out at McCoy had crowded everything else out of his mind.

He got up from the table, and laid his hands gently on her forearms. "I'm sorry. I meant to, but . . ." Could he explain that, to him, Charlotte's choice showed character that reflected well on both her parents? Should he share what they'd seen, out at the airbase?

Sarah stepped back, freeing herself. "Nobody has better intentions than you do, Wes. But this . . . this was important. . . ." She smoothed the sleeves of her blouse where he'd touched her. The words *to me* hung unspoken between them.

He watched her tread slowly out onto the screened porch, uncover the protesting birds, and speak softly to each one. She was the only woman he'd ever truly loved, the one to whom he'd eagerly "pledged his troth"—that fine old-fashioned vow he'd always interpreted to mean "to keep safe and happy." And yet, in the events of this weekend, he'd failed on both counts. Her expression in profile was sadly bereft and, in his mind, he sent her the message, *I am sorry.*

She turned, almost as if she'd heard him, and, for a long second, met his gaze steadily, as if each were seeing a regret that ran deeper than either intended to reveal.

AT THE STATION, AVERY worked alone—Monday was Steve's day off—sticking the tank levels, calling in his fuel order, counting up Saturday night's receipts, preparing the credit slips for today's bank deposit.

In one of the cash register's coin drawers, he found a note from Charlotte written on a small, black-and-white Steak 'n Shake napkin. *IOU for 4 Cokes 4 me & the twirls. XO, C!* Avery could only guess that sometime Saturday night, Charlotte dropped by the station, perhaps to introduce Emilio to her friends. Did her determined face-off with Sarah, later that same night—"I'm *going* with him, Mom. Let's just leave it at *that.*"—mean the boy had passed muster with the girls?

Also, in the twenties slot, he found his own note about Marjorie Cook, the young mother who'd promised to come back and settle up her gas debt on Saturday. He was surprised but not worried. In addition to being his customer, Marjorie was his tenant in the little house on Princeton that had been his, Sarah, and Charlotte's first home. Marjorie was a good egg, Avery thought, just overwhelmed by three kids and a husband who, as a long-distance truck driver, was rarely at home. Worst case, he'd remind her when she dropped off her rent check next week.

Traffic was unusually brisk for a Monday, and the morning and early afternoon went fast. Normally, he enjoyed the rhythm of solo work out at the pumps—taking the order, setting the nozzle, checking the oil, water, and fluid levels, washing the windows, plus a quick look at the tread and inflation of all four tires. But today, even his regular customers seemed a bit off-kilter.

When Maggie Hayes, the postmaster's wife, came by in hair curlers and no makeup, he knew the car but hardly recognized her. "Don't bother with the windows," she told him despite their obvious need for a wash.

"Pete says the oil is fine," Ginny Howard insisted, though they both knew her husband, a county commissioner, couldn't tell a dipstick from a Popsicle stick.

It wasn't until his neighbor Valerie Gilbert, whose husband, Bud, was an administrator at the county schools, drove in to ask, "Top 'er off, Wes?" that the pattern occurred to him.

"Weren't you just here on Saturday?" he asked.

"Yes," she replied, "but Bud called from work. He wants it full."

Avery heard the flutter like a trapped moth in her voice. "Really?" he said, inviting further comment.

Valerie shot him a wild-eyed look and waved her list. "He wants the water jugs, the gas tank, and the pantry full, all full by the time he gets home. I'm headed to Winn-Dixie next."

When the pump clicked off, Avery holstered the nozzle and walked around to collect forty-seven cents for a gallon and a half. Valerie handed him two quarters and drove off without change or saying good-bye.

Hands on his hips, he watched her go, picturing the faces of all the other women who'd driven in today with knit brows and strained smiles asking him to "just make sure the tank is full." He noted the jobs held by their husbands: Postmaster Hayes, County Commissioner Howard, School Administrator Bud Gilbert; plus the wives of the school superintendent, a guy from the mayor's office, and a couple of city councilmen—all government employees. What do they know that the rest of us don't? he wondered.

At two o'clock, he turned up his transistor radio for the news:

"Presidential press secretary Pierre Salinger has announced that President Kennedy will speak on television tonight at seven p.m. Eastern Standard Time. Salinger said the topic will be 'of the greatest national urgency.'"

Avery pressed grim lips, adjusted his belt buckle atop his now churning gut. Here we go.

SARAH PARKED IN THE SCHOOL'S side driveway, checked her watch, and made her way to the open door of the band room. It was fifth period, band director Charles Beauchamp's planning period, so the large room—smelling of valve oil, Brasso, and musty sheet music—was uncharacteristically quiet and empty. She veered left at the small forest of chunky black music stands awaiting sixth-period band practice and knocked on the open jamb of Beauchamp's office.

Beauchamp looked up and smiled. "Why, Mrs. Avery, how very nice to see you!" He rose to walk around his desk and shake her hand. "I suppose you've heard our happy news?"

"Charlotte? Yes."

"And Barbara, too. For once, the cheerleader stranglehold on Homecoming Court is loosed—by not one but *two* majorettes!" The band director was beaming with pride.

"It does seem quite a coup."

"A coup? Yes, exactly! And of course," he said with a broad conspiratorial wink, "I'm hoping for a major-ette upset!"

Sarah chuckled. While some of the Band Parents—the dads, mostly—found Beauchamp a bit over the top, she thought him charming and his enthusiasm infectious.

"And that's why I'm here. Charlotte needs a new gown—well, two actually—and I was hoping to snag her early for a bit of shopping. If you wouldn't mind, that is."

"Not a-tall. In fact, since neither she nor Barbara will be marching this week, I've already excused them from sixth period. They're working on the floats down at the Ag Barn."

"Oh, okay," Sarah said blankly. She glanced down, wishing she'd worn different shoes.

Beauchamp followed her gaze. He put a flat hand to his chest. "Please, permit me to send a runner." He picked up his phone, and dialed someone, Sarah wasn't sure who, to request that Charlotte Avery return to the band room as soon as possible.

"Thank you."

"No problem whatsoever. And, as long as you're here, let me give you a copy of the week's schedule for the bonfire, the parade, the big game, and so forth, if"—he returned to the other side of his desk, frowning at the mess—"I can remember where I put it. Please, have a seat."

Sarah sat in the empty guest chair while Beauchamp riffled through the stacks of memos, sheet music, marching diagrams, competition applications, and grade books. As his search widened to one desk drawer, then another, then to the top of the credenza behind him, he began to hum quietly to himself. It was a slow, rather mournful tune that took Sarah by complete surprise.

"'Erbarme dich'?" It came out a shocked whisper.

He turned to face her, his own eyes wide with surprise. "I was listening to it this morning and got it stuck in my head. But . . . there aren't many people around here who would recognize it."

"I . . . sang it, once," she explained, slowly, "in a talent contest."

"You? Sang 'Erbarme dich'? But that song requires"—he was suddenly attentive, keen with curiosity—"a three-octave range."

"Yes." In the silence that followed, the air in the little room, which had felt close with oil and dust, seemed to open and expand.

He sat down. "And did you win? The contest, I mean. Some sort of prize?"

"Yes," she said, masking a deep breath, considering how much more she might say. It was a nice story, which would have been nicer still if . . . "The prize was voice lessons in New York with Frank La Forge."

"Frank La Forge?" He drew his hands together in a single appreciative clap. "How wonderful!"

"It might have been, if I'd gone."

"You didn't?"

"Just didn't work out." Sarah swallowed hard against the tremble in her throat. Spilt milk, she reminded herself firmly.

Beauchamp looked away. "I. Understand. Actually." He straightened a piece of paper, aligning it with the edge of his desk. "I was accepted to Juilliard. But the war and my local draft board got in the way."

A fragment of a poem, memorized decades ago, floated into Sarah's mind. Softly, she repeated it: *"From far, from eve and morning, and yon twelve-winded sky, The stuff of life to knit me, Blew hither: here am I."*

Beauchamp nodded, his eyes crinkling in a slow, sad smile. "A. E. Housman, the sad Shropshire lad of senior English. I don't think they teach him anymore."

"But they should."

"I completely agree, Mrs.—"

"Please, call me Sarah."

"If you will call me Charles," he said, reaching out to offer her his hand.

Sarah took it and shook it gratefully. She'd grown accustomed, over the last many years, to being *looked at* as Wes's wife, Charlotte's mother, and, more recently, Edith's underling. But it had been a long time, a very long time, since she'd felt *seen* as Sarah, a woman who could recognize a hummed aria when she heard it, quote an appropriate snatch of poetry, and, at one time, sing with a three-octave range.

"Heigh-ho," Beauchamp said, looking past her to the open door. "Here's our Charlotte!"

AT FOUR, WHEN FATHER O'MEARA dropped off Emilio for his afternoon shift, Avery was eager to get to the bank and assess the mood downtown. As soon as the teenager emerged from the back room in his green uniform, Avery told him, "She's all yours, son," and was on his way.

The lobby of the State Bank was packed with a long, snaking line of locals withdrawing cash. Avery noticed the rise in the communal pulse, the rapid shifting of eyes and feet, the nervous jingling of pocket change, and the odd tendency to grab the cash envelope without comment and stalk directly out the door.

Teller Bea Dittman accepted his deposit with the comment, "Nice to see something *coming in* for a change."

Outside, Avery's insurance agent, burly Ralph Kayhill, hailed him from the curb and waved him into his office next door.

"Guess you've heard." Kayhill heaved himself into his chair.

"Heard what?" Avery asked, playing dumb for news.

"Near as I can tell all hell's about to break loose over Cuba."

Avery bit back frustration. Kayhill was trolling for information. Same as he was.

"You know"—Kayhill leaned forward, chair creaking protest—"they've stepped up the Civil Defense drills at the schools, got the kids doing duck-and-cover twice a week now."

"Didn't know that," Avery said, wishing Charlotte had mentioned it, resenting a policy that promised schoolchildren ducking under their desk and covering their heads with their arms would keep them safe in case of an actual attack.

Kayhill opened his desk drawer, thumbed through a stack of envelopes. "Lot of schools, not ours, have been issuing the kids dog tags in case, well, you know, something happened while they were out in the open, marching on the field, say, or walking home from school."

Avery stiffened. Where was Kayhill going with this?

"So, you know, parents could identify the bodies and all," Kayhill continued, selecting a single envelope and holding it with both hands. "I know it's a grim prospect, Wes. But that's what insurance agents are for, to consider worst-case scenarios. I talked to the local principals, even went 'round the district office, but"—he furrowed his brow in aggravation—"no dice. So I decided, well, I hope you'll agree, that at the very least I want my clients to have the peace of mind that, under any circumstance, their children could be identified."

At this, he opened the envelope and handed Avery a metal dog tag on an aluminum linked chain.

The sight of Charlotte's name stamped in tin, above her birth date and address and blood type, made Avery want to retch.

"And, of course," Kayhill was continuing, "we have very reasonable rates on juvenile policies, especially . . ."

Clutching the tag in one hand, Avery shot his other hand out flat in front of Kayhill's face. *Stop right there*, it said. *Not another word.*

Kayhill stopped.

Incensed—not just at Kayhill, but at all of this . . . *insanity!*—

Avery got up, punched the fist holding Charlotte's dog tag into his pant pocket, and walked out.

Striding to the truck, still fuming over Kayhill's gall—"juvenile policies" be damned!—he railed against it being a Monday.

Any other day, Steve would be at the station and they could hash this out together. Steve could be caustic, his language colorful. But he prided himself on, and Avery counted on, his ability to "maintain an even keel." What's Steve thinking about all this? Avery wondered, checking his watch. Is he still in New Smyrna with Lillian, or on his way home?

For a brief moment, Avery considered dropping by the VFW. It might be good, he thought, to belly up to the bar with other veterans and talk over the day's ominous developments. Maybe someone had been out to the base PX and had a real update. Then again, the VFW was often overrun by negative blowhards who argued, in almost every case, that we should "just go ahead and nuke the bastards" and be done with it.

As perhaps the only local who'd actually laid eyes on Hiroshima, Avery had no patience with Bomb-worshippers. Unlike them, he carried his own involvement with the deaths of all those Japanese civilians like a deadweight, a guilt-laden drag on an otherwise upright life. He had, suddenly, no taste for drinking with potential warmongers.

Instead, he drove home. The empty carport, no sign of Sarah's Buick, surprised him. But then he remembered Sarah's plan to take Charlotte shopping. He sat in the truck a moment, and rejected his initial idea to toss Kayhill's dog tags into the trash. Not about to risk either Sarah or Charlotte finding them, he stashed the tags in his leather bank pouch, locked it in the glove compartment, then, for good measure, locked the truck.

In the kitchen, prominently placed in the middle of the fridge, he saw the container of leftover tuna casserole, plus Sarah's note: *350 degrees for 20 minutes.*

He put it in the oven, took his shower, then returned to the kitchen and ate his meal standing at the sink, watching the bland cloud-choked sunset.

As he was rinsing his plate, the phone on the wall next to the fridge rang. A young man's voice, a nervous cracking tenor, asked, "Is Charlotte home?"

"Not right now. Take a message?"

"Well, sure. Thanks. Could you tell her Todd Jenkins called? I'll call again later?"

"No problem," Avery said and hung up.

Jenkins was the son of Mabel from church, who'd admired Charlotte's looks after the service yesterday. He was also a short, pimply-faced drag racer who chain-smoked Marlboros in an effort to look tough. Hot Toddy, Steve called him, having replaced the clutch in the boy's '50 Ford Crestliner twice in the past six months.

"No way, Ho-zay," Avery announced to the empty kitchen.

Immediately the phone rang again. Now what?

"Hey, Cap." It was Steve. "Heard the news?"

"President's announcement, y'mean? In"—Avery eyed the kitchen clock—"forty-two and a half minutes?"

"Yeah, well, I'm back. Just talked to Leo. Poor kid's pretty bent outta shape over what's goin' on. Thought I'd swing by the station, watch the speech with him."

"Oh, Lord. Leo! Good idea." Imagine being *here* while your family was stuck *there* in the crosshairs of all that firepower out at McCoy? And God knows how many other American bases, too. Avery shook off a small icy shiver.

"Talk atcha tomorrow," Steve said, signing off.

At quarter till, Avery was in the living room, television on, listening to Chet Huntley and David Brinkley's run-up for President Kennedy's speech. Huntley in New York was his usual cool cucumber, but Brinkley, outside the White House in Washington, scowled concern. Though, Avery thought, it doesn't appear he knows any more than the rest of us.

At two till, Avery saw the Buick wheel past the front window into the carport, heard two car doors slamming and Sarah calling from the kitchen, "Has he started yet?"

"Not yet."

Sarah and Charlotte burst into the room, arms full of shopping bags.

"It was all the talk at Colonial Plaza," Sarah explained in a rush. "Stores up and down the mall setting up televisions in their windows. Baer TV had five color consoles in theirs!"

"Mom, shhhhh!" Charlotte dropped down on the sofa beside him. "Here he is."

The first thing that struck Avery was the President's face. Normally handsome, debonair, smiling, John Kennedy's face was grim; his jaw hard, his eyes steely grave.

He began simply, *"Good evening, my fellow citizens,"* and pulled no punches: *"This Government, as promised, has maintained the closest surveillance of the Soviet military build-up on the island of Cuba. Within the past week, unmistakable evidence has established the fact that a series of offensive missile sites is now in preparation on that imprisoned island. The purpose of these bases can be none other than to provide a nuclear strike capability against the Western Hemisphere. . . ."*

Avery's churning stomach suddenly stilled. He heard Charlotte's sharp intake of breath and felt Sarah's trembling fingertips press his shoulder. In his mind's eye, he saw the solemn transfer of the black film boxes on the flight line at McCoy, imagined the chain of custody from the photo developers and interpreters to the Joint Chiefs to the President's own hands. No doubt, *that* was why he'd returned to Washington.

Unmistakable evidence, Kennedy was saying, of the Soviets' urgent transformation of Cuba into a strategic Soviet base with large, long-range, and clearly offensive weapons of sudden mass destruction.

The words *"sudden mass destruction"* flooded him with an acute, seething anger. And Kennedy's listing of potential targets: *"Washington, DC, the Panama Canal, Cape Canaveral, Mexico City,"* felt like a body blow.

Clearly, Kennedy was angry, too—especially over Soviet foreign minister Gromyko's repeated assurances just last Thursday that there was no need for offensive weapons in Cuba and that the Soviet Union would never become involved in such a thing.

"False," Kennedy practically spat, *"a deliberate deception!"*

The U-2s' cameras must have caught them red-handed. But what in the world do we do about it? Avery sat frozen, staring at the screen.

"We will not prematurely or unnecessarily risk the costs of world-wide nuclear war in which even the fruits of victory would be ashes in our mouth—but neither will we shrink from that risk at any time."

Ashes in our mouth, Avery thought. And remembered well that same taste on his tongue.

The President outlined his immediate course of action to effect the withdrawal and elimination of the missiles: a strict quarantine on all offensive military equipment under shipment to Cuba, continued and increased close surveillance, plus orders to the US armed forces to *"prepare for any eventualities."*

Kennedy warned the Soviets that any nuclear missile launched from Cuba against any nation in the Western Hemisphere would provoke *"a full retaliatory response upon the Soviet Union."* Finally, he called upon Khrushchev personally to *"halt and eliminate this clandestine, reckless and provocative threat to world peace"* and to *"move the world back from the abyss of destruction."*

Sandwiched between his wife and daughter, Avery felt chilled to the marrow. On his left, Sarah trembled, twitchy with nerves. On his right, Charlotte had shrunk into stillness, like a field mouse sensing the dark overhead flight of a night owl.

The President's sign-off, *"Thank you and good night,"* left Avery wondering. Who in the country, or in the world, could possibly have a good night when the two superpowers were locked in a dangerous face-off, potentially on the brink of what scientists called MAD— Mutually Assured Destruction?

It was madness all right. He'd seen ample proof of it at Hiroshima seventeen years ago. But that bomb—Little Boy, they called it—was a mere fledgling compared with the hundred-times-more-powerful thermonuclear bombs perched atop missiles on both sides today. Bombs that, like hell's chickens, had come home to roost just ninety miles south of Florida's Key West. Less than five hundred miles— eight to ten minutes in missile time—from his living room.

5.

*T*HE *HONK-HONK* OF A CAR HORN IN THE DRIVEWAY TELE-graphed its message: *Hurry up!* Avery opened his eyes, groggy and confused. His first thought—he was at the station and someone wanted gas on the double—didn't square with the fact that he was still in bed. He rolled over to squint against the view through the bedroom window: azure sky, clear and unclouded; the lake winking gently back at the sun. It was bizarre. How could the morning appear so normal after last night's dreadful announcement that the nation, the very notion of life as we knew it, had been manhandled to the brink of—what did Kennedy call it?—"the abyss of destruction."

He sat up and rubbed his eyes and bristly cheeks with both hands. The President's speech had given frightful form and detail to his nightmares. What little sleep he'd gotten was fractured with awful images: Russian mechanics adjusting wires and winches to attach their nuclear horror atop long, red missiles and hoist them vertically against a range of green mountains. A cloud full of fireworks rising up into a foreboding mushroom shape across the lake, dwarfing the pale peaks of Edgewater High's gymnasium. Smoldering human forms bearing dog tags.

He'd tossed and turned until sometime after midnight, then been awakened just after two a.m. by the long, mournful whistle of a freight train approaching the crossing at Silver Star Road.

It wasn't the whistle that startled him. It was the sound, the low growling grasp of wheel on track, of a fully and heavily loaded *southbound* train.

Normally, trains headed south through central Florida were empty, or nearly so, their wheels clattering lightly on the rails, bound for a turnaround at the loading docks of Miami, the muck farms and sugarcane refineries on the shores of Lake Okeechobee, the giant phosphate mines due south in Polk and Hardee counties, or the big citrus packinghouses in Lake Wales and Orlando. For Avery, whose station was sandwiched between the Trail and the Southern Seaboard Railroad tracks, the difference in sound between an empty and a fully loaded freight train was as clearly distinguishable as a tenor and a bass.

And the two a.m. train wasn't only fully loaded, it was *long*! Half an hour long, at least. How many boxcars and flatbeds and engines did it take to make a train thirty minutes long?

When a second train whistled and rumbled by at three twenty-two, equally loaded but longer—forty-two minutes long!—Avery remembered the President's order to the armed forces to "prepare for any eventualities." His brain churned with lists and images of the vehicles, ordnance, and armaments that were most likely rolling past them in the dark of this night.

At four forty-five, exhausted, a different image came to mind: his grandfather's face leaning in across the farmhouse table, giving Avery his eagle eye; his grandfather's knuckles reaching out across the bleached oak tabletop.

"That's enough, son," he heard his grandfather say, heard his knuckles' quick rap, only twice, on the planked oak. "That's enough."

After the terrible, too early death of his father, Avery's grandfather had come down off his West Virginia mountaintop to "serve as ballast for you and your mother, till she makes up her mind which way she wants to go."

The fifth son of a coal miner, Old Pa had gone down to the Norfolk docks in 1885, lied about his age, and joined the Merchant Marines. He'd worked colliers mostly, transporting black tons of American coal to US ships and bases all over the world. He'd helped fuel Admiral Dewey's victory in Manila Bay and transported horses for Teddy Roosevelt's Rough Riders at San Juan Hill; though, a man of few words, he rarely spoke of it.

His quiet presence, however, had been the rudder of Avery's adolescence and provided the encouragement he'd needed to leave the farm and join the air force. Although Old Pa died in late '44, while Avery was en route to Tinian Island, the old man remained, in memory, a steadying force, helping Avery to finally fall off for a couple hours of fitful sleep.

Now reaching for his robe, he heard Charlotte—"Later, Mom. Tell Dad I said bye!"—and the bang of the front door as she flew out to catch her horn-honking ride to school.

He regretted sleeping in and not seeing her. More than that, he felt grieved. She should have come home smiling, happy to show off and even model her new dresses. He would like to have seen her twirling around in them, preening like a princess.

But instead she'd huddled beside him, pale and drawn, fists pressed against her lips, eyes blank with disbelief. Her one comment, an attempt at humor—"There goes homecoming!"—fell flat in the face of both her parents' barely suppressed horror.

Later, after Sarah insisted he unload her trunk (still full of the boxes she'd brought home from the shelter show) then disappeared into unpacking mode, he'd returned to the living room to check on Charlotte. She wasn't there or anywhere else inside the house. He'd finally found her outside in the backyard, staring up at the cloud-smudged dark. "I heard planes," she told him. "Wanted to make sure they were ours." He'd done his best to comfort her. But she'd seen too much out at the air base, and knew too much from the President's speech, to blindly accept his lame reassurances. He hoped she'd slept, which was more than he could say for Sarah. She, as far as he knew, had been up restocking the shelter most of the night.

When he entered the kitchen, Sarah was on the phone frowning, clearly annoyed by what she was hearing. She wore a faded house-dress, and with no makeup, her hair pinned haphazardly out of her eyes, she seemed to have aged years overnight.

She acknowledged him with a distracted wave toward the dinette, where his breakfast was waiting: pancakes and link sausage tented with tinfoil.

"I understand, Edith, but I couldn't possibly ... Well ..." She sighed, her shoulders slumped with resignation. "If you insist, I'll take the Langford and First Baptist today; and the Cherry Plaza tomorrow. But after that ..."

Avery studied her, wondering what Edith wanted now. Sarah looked and sounded exhausted. Her hand, making a note on the wall pad beside the phone, trembled. "Good-bye, Edith," she said and stopped just short of slamming the receiver onto its hook.

"Now what?" he asked.

"General Betts"—Orange County's director of Civil Defense—"was so impressed with our committee's work at Sunday's show, he's asked us to inspect the public shelters, make sure they're organized properly."

"Wants the Women's Club Seal of Approval, does he?" Avery asked, thinking, Now, *that's* a propaganda move if I ever saw one. "Complete with *Sentinel* photographers to reassure the general public the government's got their back?"

"Something like that, I s'pose." She turned to open the cabinet door, popped the top off the brown vial, shook out two small yellow pills, and tossed them down without water.

He'd eaten a few bites but realized he had no appetite. Besides, he was running late. He thanked her for her efforts and rose to open the fridge and remove his lunch pail from the shelf where she always left it for him.

"Sorry I have to run, darlin'." He leaned in to kiss her pale cheek. Her hair had an odd, musty smell. Like the shelter, he realized distractedly. "My best to the Dragon Lady."

Good luck, he might have added, but didn't. Clearly, the good general and Edith were sending her on a fool's errand, a PR stunt to keep the locals from panicking. But aren't we all fools today? Going through the motions of normal life—as if everything and everyone doesn't hang in the balance? As if the unspeakable—the unthinkable— isn't staring us in the face just across the Florida Straits?

NORMALLY ON TUESDAYS AND Thursdays, Avery opened, Steve closed, and Emilio was off. But yesterday, to accommodate Friday and Saturday's homecoming events, he'd switched to a three-shift schedule to give Emilio the weekend off. Avery was glad he'd made the change. If today was anything like yesterday—and after the President's speech, how could it not be?—he'd need the extra help.

He barely had time to get the doors open and turn the lights on before the deluge began. The gas bell was ringing off the wall for fill-ups, top-offs, and a few random men in pickups looking to load up their fifty-five-gallon drums. Avery refused them, on account of they weren't regular customers and he wasn't inclined to support hoarding.

Rumors were rampant; everyone claimed an inside track.

Connie Diggs, who worked the Rexall counter across the street, told Avery with a nervous, sideways glance down the Trail, "You hear they're evacuating Miami? Everybody's s'posed to be packin' up and headin' north. 'Cept for the Cubans in Little Havana. They're refusin' to go."

Avery doubted that one was true.

"Our boy's Spanish teacher?" whispered housewife Billie Watts, pink nose and lips twitching like a scared rabbit. "Been workin' nights out at McCoy, teaching the paratroopers basic phrases, for after their drop into Cuba."

Avery considered that one credible.

Herb Benson, who ran the family fruit stand around the corner, stopped in to say, "My neighbor's an engineer out at Martin-Marrietta. They got the biggest building under roof in the state, y'know. And with what they're doing out there? Says they might as well paint a giant red bull's-eye on top."

Probably right, Avery thought grimly. Any Sputnik spy satellite worth its circuitry would pick up the Beeline Expressway running stick-straight from the giant defense contractor's back door, less than ten miles south, to Cape Canaveral's coastal launch pads. Though, in Avery's mind, Orlando's SAC base at McCoy was the more likely target, and it was closer still.

Either way, Avery knew, a fifteen-megaton bomb like the one the US tested on Bikini would drop a lethal blanket of radioactivity over central Florida 40 miles wide and, depending on the wind, 220 miles long. Just last year, Khrushchev boasted the Soviets now had thirty- to fifty-megaton monsters in their arsenal—a bomb that big would sink the entire state.

At nine-thirteen, another southbound train rumbled by behind the station, the other side of Dr. Phillips's packinghouse. Avery heard it, clocked its length at twenty-two minutes, but was unable to leave the pumps to walk to the corner and watch it go by.

Steve arrived at ten, providing Avery with his first chance to call the depot in Tampa and ask about the fill-up of his own underground tanks.

"I don't know, Wes," the dispatcher warned him. "Phone's ringing off the hook here. We got all our tankers out on deliveries, but you're—let's see now—number twenty-seven on the list. Tomorrow afternoon, maybe? I'll have to get back to you."

Just after noon, Marjorie Cook wheeled into the parking space beside the office and got out, wallet in one hand, baby girl on her hip in the other. Both boys trailed behind her.

Avery was on his way out the door to return a customer's Texaco card and get the credit slip signed. "Be right with you," he told her.

Back in the office, he noticed her eyes were red-rimmed. "I've come to settle up," she said, handing off the baby to J.J., the bigger of the two boys, "and also to serve notice."

"What do you mean?" Avery had opened the cash register and was retrieving her gas bill.

Marjorie pushed back damp curls off her forehead with the palm of her hand. She was dressed sloppily for her, in a man's plaid shirt and rolled-up jeans.

"Jimmy's on a long haul to Nebraska. Called home long-distance Friday night. Said there's all kinds of scary talk on his CB radio."

The baby whimpered and waved her arms, wanting her mother. Marjorie handed over her keys instead, then, laying her wallet on the counter, fished a balled-up handkerchief out of her pocket and blew her nose. After that, the words boiled out in a rush.

"Said he wanted me to go to the U-Haul shop, rent a trailer, pack up the kids, and meet him at his daddy's house in High Point, North Carolina. Wanted me on the road by Sunday night but, with the kids, I just couldn't get everything done till today." She stopped to collect a ragged breath and slipped the crushed handkerchief back into her pocket. "Said to tell you sorry for the short notice and all. But since we already paid first and last, you'll be covered. And maybe"—her face flushed pink with the effort of asking—"if you get somebody before the end of next month, you'll send us a refund?"

"You're leaving for good?"

"With everything going on around here, Jimmy's convinced we'll be safer up there."

"Sorry to hear that," Avery told her gently. His eyes fell on the note in his hand, the words *Ck. Rr. Shimmy* he'd written on Friday. It now seemed like centuries ago. "U-Haul, you said?"

"Just a small one. Kids' stuff mostly." The cottage on Princeton was rented furnished.

Avery frowned. He needed this today like he needed a hole in his head. "Well, look here ... The other day when you left, I saw a shimmy in your car's rear end. See, I made a note." He held it out. "Before you go hooking up a trailer, I better put it up on the rack and take a look."

"On the rack?" Her voice wobbled, her eyes rounded in dismay. "I promised Jimmy we'd be on the road by noon."

"Won't take but a sec," he assured her, concerned she might bolt. "You'll be climbing mountains to get to High Point. A woman with three kids and a trailer doesn't need car trouble on top of everything else. How 'bout some nice cold Cokes while you wait?"

Marjorie bit her lip. Then she sighed and nodded.

"Here, Lissie." She took the child from J.J., handed over the keys to Avery, then sank slumped into the chair, the baby on her lap. "You boys sit here," she ordered, pointing to the floor.

Avery got them Cokes out of the cooler. He gave the boys a small container of metal washers and suggested a game of tiddlywinks. Then he drove the wagon into the service bay and raised the rack, hoping for something simple, like rear tires out of alignment. But the alignment was fine.

The problem, he discovered, was worn rubber bushings in the rear suspension links that attached the axle to the frame. Steve manned the pumps while Avery wrenched off the pivot bolts, drove out the old bushings with an air chisel, then beat in the new ones with a ball-peen hammer. Mercifully, he was done in under an hour.

Marjorie looked up from the child fast asleep in her arms. "First time I've sat down in three days," she whispered.

"Better here than alongside a mountain road," Avery told her, mentally sidestepping the thought of what might have happened if he'd let her go. He added the cost of her prior gas bill and the parts, then announced, to wipe the worry off her face, "Labor's on me."

Marjorie rose, shifting the sleeping child from her lap to her shoulder. He was reminded of Charlotte at that age, a soft snuggling bundle fragrant with shampoo and Johnson's baby powder.

"Thanks, Mr. A." Marjorie opened her free arm, offering and inviting a hug. Avery was surprised by the strength of her grasp, the moist warmth as she drew him in and murmured, "You've always been just . . . swell."

She held him tightly, then released him hastily, and it startled him to think he didn't know when, or even *if* he'd see her again.

"God bless you," she said, tearing up.

"You take care," he told her lamely.

Outside, waving good-bye, he could still feel the imprint of mother and child against his chest, within his arms; and the scent of apples in

Marjorie's hair. How long had it been since he'd held Sarah and Charlotte in a single embrace like that? Years. How long with just Sarah alone?

From the beginning, Sarah had been subject to the occasional dark mood, the near-monthly headache. For years, she dismissed it as simply her hormones talking. Charlotte was two when they'd begun trying in earnest for another child. She was five when Sarah had her first miscarriage. Three more miscarriages after that (or was it four?—a couple happened so early on, it was hard to keep track) before the final disaster two years ago this month: the tubal pregnancy—of *twins,* though he and the doctor had kept that detail to themselves—that ended in her emergency hysterectomy. "I've been fixed? Just like a dog?" she'd raged at them and at the zipper-like scar, navel to pubis. *Barren,* she called herself now, a harsh, unforgiving term that reminded him of the worst of the windblown drought of his youth.

He'd waited patiently for her recovery, gently given her a wide berth and plenty of time. Her Nembutal helped get things back to normal, though she complained the pills made her feel stupid and foggy. Then last Tuesday night, something had gone amiss. He'd reached for her in the night and she'd refused him with a dejected "Oh, Wes, what's the point?" What had he done to deserve that? He had no clue.

And now there were missiles in Cuba and God knows what else. And Sarah was off on a propaganda goose chase for Civil Defense. Had too much Nembutal addled her brain? They'd been warned it was habit-forming and she might need to switch. He considered giving Doc Mike a call, asking him to drop by. But the thought depressed him. And the gas bell continued to ring like the Salvation Army at Christmastime. And then the first of the convoys darkened the Trail out front, headed south to Miami and beyond.

STEVE HAD BROUGHT IN A SMALL, portable television to watch the President's speech with Emilio last night. He'd left it on the desk, and at lunch they opted for checking breaking news over their usual game of chess. Customers, seeing the TV, got out of their cars and crowded the office to watch:

In New York, delegates to the Organization of American States voted their unanimous support for the navy's quarantine (to cut off all Soviet military shipments to Cuba). Adlai Stevenson, America's ambassador to the United Nations, delivered a fiery speech about the Russians' premeditated deception, their flagrant violation of the UN Charter, *"clearly a threat to this hemisphere and to . . . the whole world!"* And in Havana, Castro was calling the quarantine *"a total blockade"* that he considered *"an act of war and a violation of the Cuban people's sovereign rights!"*

Secretary of Defense Robert McNamara was pale and baggy-eyed when he announced that, per the President's order, the US Navy's quarantine of Cuban ports would commence at ten a.m. tomorrow. American ships would draw a line on the sea eight hundred miles off Cuba's shore; no ship carrying military cargo would be allowed to pass.

Meanwhile, all afternoon, beneath a sky stunningly blue and clear, the long green convoys continued to roll past.

Avery and Steve and customers in their cars turned to watch the seemingly endless war parade with numbing dread. Were all those trucks—jeeps, eight-, ten-, and twelve-ton trucks, buses, transporters with semi-trailers—different groups converging on the Trail or one long, organized procession? Who knew?

Were the GIs—all *so* young, some smiling and waving back, others dismally downcast or fast asleep—bound for the big bases at Miami, Homestead, or Key West? Would they wind up on the beaches of Cuba or the backstreets of Berlin? Either way—Avery and Steve exchanged knowing looks—war would be a far worse experience than any of those boys could possibly imagine.

The sight of so many soldiers, vehicles, trailers hauling long cylindrical shapes barely camouflaged with green canvas—not to mention the trains rumbling behind the station on parallel tracks—was both shocking and sobering. Clearly, something potentially life and history changing was about to occur off Florida's south tip.

Midafternoon, there was a break in the action at the pumps—most likely the result of the twenty-six-minute train crossing Princeton behind them and the convoy of green semis in front of them on the Trail. Emilio was late for work.

Steve grabbed two RC Colas and joined Avery at the curb. "Wanna bet he's sittin' in traffic other side of the tracks?"

"Probably so," Avery replied, taking an icy swig. His eyes followed the passing tank strapped to a rolling flatbed, the boxcars filled with napalm cylinders piled, like cordwood, roof-high. "How'd he handle the speech last night?"

Steve scowled. "Not as surprised as I was."

"He wasn't?"

"Turns out a couple of the boys had heard stories from family still stuck on the island. Big trucks in the middle of the night. Corner fences run down by trailers too long to make tight turns."

"So they knew something was up?"

Steve nodded. "I'd say he was more steamed than anything else."

"Steamed?"

"'Just when you think things are as bad as they can get,' he said, 'Castro goes and makes 'em worse.'"

"Oh, man." Poor kid.

"Really worried about his parents and grandparents."

"And his sister, the dancer?" Avery recalled. "Is she still there? Or did they send her here, too?" He found himself wondering, not for the first time, what it would take—how bad would things have to be?—for him and Sarah to send Charlotte away, alone to another country, dependent on the kindness of strangers. He couldn't conceive of it.

"Didn't mention her." Steve turned to appraise the progress behind them on the Trail. "Can't imagine all this hardware's gonna help him feel any better."

Avery cleared his throat. "Think we should talk to the priest about it?"

Steve shrugged, drew a bead on his soda bottle. "Can if you want to, Deacon." As a rule, Steve steered clear of men of the cloth.

WITHIN MINUTES OF THE train's passing, the priest's Chevy pulled up and Emilio leaped out, worry creasing the space between his brows.

"It's all right, son," Avery called to him. "Got caught, right?"

Emilio nodded, cast a startled glance at the line of canvas-covered trucks on the Trail, then ran inside to change. Avery strode out, signaling the priest to stop.

"Sorry for the delay, Mr. Avery," the priest called out the open window. "We were quite trapped—"

Avery waved off further explanation, leaned in. "Not a problem. But, look, uh . . ." As usual, he was at a loss for what to call the guy.

The priest chuckled. "*Father* is a Catholic term, Mr. Avery; doesn't trip easily off the Protestant tongue. No need to dance an Irish jig around it. Please, if you prefer, call me Thomas." He stuck out his hand.

Avery returned his grip. "Wes," he said.

"How can I help you, Wes?"

Guy must be good at what he does, Avery thought. Somehow, in the brief pause between their handshake and his question, he'd sensed Avery's intent. One moment those bright blue eyes were smiling, crinkling at the corners, the next they were soberly attentive, inviting whatever was to come.

"It's not me, Thomas," Avery said. "It's Emilio. Steve says the speech last night really riled him."

"All the boys, I'm afraid. It's a double bind, you see? On one hand, they want the island liberated so they can go home. On the other, they're terribly afraid for the family members still there."

"I was wondering what we might do for him."

"Indeed, Wes, you already have. The dance date with your daughter? It's a bright spot, a bit of normal to look forward to. Thank you, and please thank your wife for your, uh, support. And Mr. Steve's offer to buy him a new suit?" His eyes crinkled again. "Over-generous but also much appreciated."

EMILIO WAS OUT AT THE PUMPS when Steve stopped for a smoke break. Avery watched his friend's familiar ritual: the left-handed pat, slide, and shake out of the pack; his right-handed extraction, tap, and tip of a single cigarette onto his lip; the arc, flare, and click of his Zippo expertly tossed back into his shirt pocket; the hungry pull giving way to a satisfied stare.

"New suit, huh?"

"Well"—Steve rasped a gruff cough—"he needs one, don't he? Figured you're on the hook for a fancy dress or two."

"Where you gonna take him?"

Steve squinted, blew a jet of smoke, and watched it fade. "Figured we'd go see Dahling."

Avery grinned. "Well, that ought to cheer him up."

Dahling was a popular local saleswoman in Belk-Lindsey's men's department. Nobody remembered her real name. But thanks to her curves, her Zsa Zsa Gabor–like accent, the way she called every man "Dahling," her nickname was born. She could tell a man's suit size on sight, and pick out the perfect tie "to match your eyes, Dahling!" In addition, she dyed her hair a different color every month to match the season. "Boring I'm not, Dahling!" This being October, it could as easily be pumpkin orange as ghostly white or pitch black, "depending on my mood when I sit in the chair."

"When were you planning to go?"

Steve turned to eyeball the single customer in a dusty Studebaker wagon paying his bill. "What d'ya think?"

"Well, it's Tuesday. Couple days for tailoring, if he needs it. You should probably go now."

"Prob'ly should," Steve agreed, grinding out the stub in the desk ashtray.

Avery smiled. A bit of normal, Thomas had said. Without even talking to the guy, Steve was giving Emilio exactly what the priest recommended.

Emilio, normally playful, came in subdued. He placed the cash in the register without comment, then stepped aside, staring blankly at the green trucks passing by out front.

Avery noted the dark circles under his eyes. "Tough night?" he asked.

The teenager turned, eyes drooped, shoulders stooped like a much older man. "Guys out at the camp . . . ," he began in a quiet voice. "How can I explain?" He drew a breath. "When we were kids, Cuba"—he pronounced it, as always, *COO-ba*—"Cuba was the queen of the Caribbean. The largest island and the most successful, with the most modern cities, the most talented artists, the most beautiful hotels . . ."

"And women," Steve added. "The most beautiful women."

"Yes, of course," Emilio agreed, with the flicker of a smile. "But then *Fidel*—" He turned to look for a place to spit. "Fidel rode out of the mountains with a white dove on his shoulder, calling himself a man of peace. *Peace!*" His pale eyes snapped angrily. "Overnight, our American friends were driven out and the Russians arrived to protect us from Yankee Imperialism! The thing is"—he looked out the window, remembering—"we all considered the Russians—with their World War Two airplanes and fifteen-year-old trucks—a *joke*. Those trucks were always breaking down. We'd see them parked by the side of the road for weeks, waiting for a part from Moscow. And now," he said bitterly, "Fidel's let them turn Cuba into their launching pad, the queen of the Caribbean nothing but *dirt* beneath their *boots*." He scowled. "We were up half the night arguing."

"'Bout what?" Steve asked.

"About whether we should all go down and join the army."

"The *army?*" Steve recoiled, ripe with a navy man's disgust.

"Or navy," Emilio said hastily. "Or air force even," he added with a nod toward Avery.

"What'd you decide?" Avery asked it quietly.

"Me?" Emilio shook his head. "I told them I didn't dare. My mother went through hell to get me out of there. She'd *kill* me if I came back!"

Avery blew out a pent-up breath.

Steve jingled his keys with relief. "We're thinking this'd be a good time to go see a lady about a suit."

Avery reached over, punched the cash drawer open, pulled out the fiver that Emilio had just put in. "And bring back some Mister Donuts, would ya?"

Emilio flashed a grin, a glimmer of his usually sunny self. Although nothing in this country came close to Cuba's pineapple *pastelitos*, the teenager insisted, Mister Donuts toasted-coconut-with-banana-cream-filling were the next best thing.

WHEN THEY RETURNED, Avery was outside under the canopy, collecting for a tankful of premium he'd just pumped into Charlie Novak's brand-new cherry-red Corvette convertible.

Novak, generally a jokester, was complaining about "all this hand wringin' and foot draggin' over Castro! Ike shoulda taken him out years ago, day after he announced he was Red. Been a piece a cake then. Now, with these damn missiles stuck up our butt, it's a helluva mess, ain't it?"

Avery waved Novak away, his eyes on Emilio, who was cautiously easing The Admiral into Steve's parking spot beside the truck. Steve got out of the passenger's side, popped the trunk, and removed the black Belk-Lindsey suit bag.

"A perfect forty tall, Dahling," Steve said with a wink. "No tailorin' required."

"What color was her hair?" Avery asked.

Steve's gaze sobered. "Blond. French twist. Said she'd planned on ghoulish green, but things were scary enough without it."

Avery nodded. Even Dahling was feeling the heat.

Emilio trailed them both into the office, handed Steve his keys, and offered Avery the box of Mister Donuts.

"No, thanks," Avery said. "Eat what you'd like, then take the rest back to the camp, okay?"

"Thanks, Mr. A, Mr. Steve." The teenager's sea-colored eyes swam with a sudden wave of emotion. His first attempt to say what he obviously felt he needed to tell them failed. He took a shaky breath and tried again. "Somehow . . . someday . . . I'll find a way to pay you both back."

"It's okay, son," Avery said.

"Just wish we could do more," Steve added gruffly.

Before leaving, Avery called the depot one last time, but the line was still busy. He'd stuck the levels in his underground tanks and was alarmed by the results. The two 8,000-gallon regular and premium-grade tanks were just under the 1,825 mark, roughly 23 percent full, and the 4,000-gallon mid-grade tank showed 1,095, or 27 percent. At current fill-up rates, they'd be out of gas in seventy-two hours.

"Hate to say it," he told Steve, "but until that tanker arrives, I think we'd better limit sales to ten-gallon allotments."

"Customers won't be happy 'bout that. . . ." Squinting out at the pumps, where activity appeared to have tapered off, Steve asked, "Start first thing in the mornin'?"

Avery thought about it and agreed. Steve would be opening, and neither of them felt right subjecting Emilio, who'd be closing alone tonight, to the first wave of upset customers.

Now ready to leave, Avery was surprised to see his wife's LeSabre glide into view with Charlotte alone at the wheel.

"Hey, kiddo!"

"Dad . . ." She seemed out of breath. "Mom sent me to Publix. The twirls are coming tonight . . . to see my dresses and to show me theirs. We're planning pizza, plus root beer floats, so Mom sent me for vanilla ice cream. I drove over there. But, Dad"—her eyes were enormous—"there wasn't any. No ice cream, no milk, no eggs. Whole shelves *empty*. People have gone *ape*! I saw two ladies in the parking lot fighting over a box of Tide. It's like Nowheresville over there!"

She bored into him with her *tell me the truth* look. "Has the war started already? Is this . . ." Her voice broke. ". . . the beginning of the end?"

"Oh, Kitten."

From the first moment he'd held her as a screaming, squirming infant until now, all he'd ever wanted to do was protect her. From harm, from unhappiness, from worry over dangers she was still too young to comprehend. But now? He hated the awful truth that the Russians had brought front and center—that the future was no longer a given, that our enemies were not to be trusted, that as long as those missiles remained in Cuba no one was safe. The news flew in the face of everything he'd brought her up to believe. And it broke his heart to see its effect on her. He reached in, gently lifted the lock of dark hair crowding her cheek, and tucked it behind her ear.

"Nobody—not even that crackpot Khrushchev—wants a war. You have to believe that, Charlotte. The President's going to work this out. In the meantime, people get spooked and do crazy things. Who in their right mind picks a fight over a box of laundry soap?"

He could see in her eyes the struggle between her need and her reluctance to believe him. In kindergarten, she'd nicknamed him Happy Pappy, discerning, even at age five, his determined optimism. Her childhood drawings of him were always smiling. But clearly, the problems they were facing today were so much larger, and scarier, than he had the power to resolve. That realization—her recognition that all the positive thinking in the world couldn't mask the fact that he was as powerless as she was—pained him no end.

"I bet," he said, grasping for something, anything, he could do for her, "if you go across the street and sweet-talk Mr. Hammond, he'll give you enough ice cream for your party. In fact, c'mon, I'll go with you."

Avery opened the car door, took her elbow lightly, and escorted her across the intersection to the Rexall Drugs & Soda Fountain on the opposite side of the Trail.

On the surface, he was willing himself calm. But his mind was racing, conjuring up old, odd, unsettling images: a silent Gary Cooper escorting Grace Kelly down a deserted street; clock faces ticking toward a terrible confrontation; and somewhere out there, Soviet ships plowing east across the Atlantic toward the US Navy's line of interdiction in the waters off Cuba's coast.

The quarantine was set to start at ten o'clock tomorrow. *"High noon on the high seas,"* one newsman called it. In the movie, Gary Cooper's six-guns triumphed over the evil gang of four. In real life, would America's broadsides be enough to face down the Soviets?

Bo Hammond greeted them from behind his old-fashioned brass cash register. In his white pharmacist's coat, pale pallor, and silver hair helmet, he never failed to remind Avery of a deep-water fish. "Ten floats, you say? What do you think, Connie?" he called to Connie Diggs behind the counter. "A quart? Half gallon?"

Connie nodded. Hammond turned tired eyes back to Avery. "Ice cream I've got. But first-aid kits, bandages, flashlights, transistor radios? All out. I don't think I have a single battery left."

Charlotte had wandered off to the magazine rack. She picked the one with a picture of Ozzie and Harriet Nelson's handsome son Ricky on the cover beside the headline: LONELY TEEN IDOL, ARE YOU THE GIRL HE'S LOOKING FOR?

Hammond lowered his voice. "Wish I carried shotgun shells. Coulda sold a *ton* of those."

Avery shook his head. A loaded shotgun was the poor man's version of Civil Defense—perceived comfort, but no real protection against thermonuclear disaster.

"Here ya go!" Connie called, holding up the hand-packed container. "Put the ice cream in first," she advised Charlotte, "it's less of a mess."

Back across the street, Charlotte asked Avery, "You heading straight home?"

"I was."

"Great," she said, handing off the ice cream with a smile. "I'd like to say hi to Emilio . . . long as I'm here." Her eyes shifted toward the office; big smile for the guy behind the register with half a doughnut in his hand.

"I'll tell your mother you're right behind me."

"Oh, and Dad . . ." He'd turned to leave, but the warning in her tone drew him back. "You should know . . . Mom's really upset with me."

"With *you*?"

"Two other boys asked me to homecoming. Todd Jenkins"—she made a face—"and Greg Lund."

Avery arched a questioning brow. Lund was popular, the good-looking son of a local banker, and Edgewater High's all-star running back. He was somebody Sarah, and even he, would deem a catch.

Had Sarah succeeded in getting Charlotte to change her mind? Avery glanced back at Emilio, now carefully wiping his hands and face with a napkin and moving toward the office doorway.

"Mom 'bout had a cow," Charlotte was saying, "because . . . well . . . you know Greg. And the football team votes on the winner and all. But, Dad . . ." Avery braced himself for bad news. "Dad, *you're* not mad, are you? I told them both I already had a date."

He'd been holding his breath, pulling, in this case, for the filly to outmaneuver the mare. And she *had*. He covered his guilt-ridden pleasure, and relief, with an amused chuckle. "Good for you, kiddo," he assured her as Emilio approached.

Avery shifted the container of ice cream to one hand, and fished for his keys with the other. "She's all yours, son," he told Emilio. It was his standard exit line.

"Roger Wilco, Cap." Emilio mimicked Steve's usual reply.

Between them, Charlotte blushed bright red, suddenly shy.

Avery saw her and frowned, mock stern, at Emilio. "The station, not the girl. Ten-four?"

Emilio straightened. "Ten-four, sir," he echoed, snapping off a recruit's salute with a sideways smile.

Backing out, Avery watched them through his windshield, chatting eagerly, laughing easily with each other, so young, and for the moment—he felt the wrench in his heart—so normal.

"This thing's got disaster written all over it," Sarah had said. He wished she were here now to see them. *Those kids aren't the disaster,* he would've told her. *We are; every one of us who saw this thing coming and didn't do everything in our power to stop it.*

SARAH MET HIM AT THE DOOR. "Oh, finally, you're *here!*" She seemed flustered and genuinely relieved to see him, until she noticed the ice cream in his hands.

"Where's Charlotte?"

"Right behind me," he said, striding to the freezer, attempting nonchalance. "Be here in a few."

He turned to find her backed up against the counter, arms folded. "Well, of *course* she went running straight to *you.*"

"It wasn't like that, darlin'," he said, softening his tone. "Publix was cleaned out—no ice cream, milk, eggs, anything. People in the parking lot were acting nuts. It spooked her. But fortunately, Bo and Connie at the Rexall had half a gallon to spare."

Sarah pressed stiff fingertips to the center of her brow. "I was really hoping you'd be on my side this time."

"Always," he said pleasantly.

"No, Wes." She dropped her hand, gave him a pained look. "*Not* always, not lately."

"I don't know what you mean."

"Well, there's my side. What I'd call the side of reason, which says Greg Lund's an ideal date for homecoming. Then there's yours and hers, the side of—what, exactly? Pity? Charity? Romance?—that says, 'Stick with the Cuban boy in the borrowed car and rented suit.'"

Avery bit back his thought—*Emilio has a suit, and he'll be driving one of the hottest cars in town, thanks to Steve.*

"Fact is I've never understood what he's doing here. Him and his twenty-four *amigos.* If they'd stayed with their own kind in Cuba, where they *belong,* fought against Castro and the Communists, maybe those missiles wouldn't be there. And the rest of us wouldn't be sucked into their mess."

"He's only seventeen, Sarah."

"Yes, Wes. And how many seventeen-year-old American boys did you know lied about their ages to jump into the fight against Hitler and the Japs?"

"It's just a dance," he said calmly. "One and done."

Sarah stiffened. "Homecoming is *just* a dance? And Civil Defense is *just* a bunch of government PR? And what would you call those missiles in Cuba, Wes? *Just* peashooters? And, and the Russian warships? *Just* t-target practice?"

All the color had drained from her face. She was bone white and shaking. Avery heard an odd sound that could only be her teeth chattering.

"Hey." He stepped forward to touch her. "You okay?"

"Okay?" she echoed.

"You look a little . . . tired, darlin'. Why don't you lie down for a few minutes, get some rest. I'll pay the pizza boy. And Charlotte will be here shortly to set things up."

"Oh, Wes, pizzas!" she cried, her eyes bright with terror. "You have to run to Tony's and pick up the pizzas!"

"Pick them up? Tony delivers."

"I don't know. For some reason, he can't. Please, go!"

"Okay . . . ," he said carefully, as she moved to the cabinet where she kept her pills. Tomorrow, he resolved. He would definitely call Doc Mike tomorrow morning.

Tony's was a popular Italian restaurant conveniently located between College Park's two high schools, public Edgewater High and Catholic Bishop Moore. Owned and run by the Virellis, Tony and his wife, Gina, it had two dining rooms: one for fine dining on pink tablecloths, and a second, brightly lit, with long wooden picnic tables for pizza. The family lived in a tidy concrete block home on the wooded lot behind the restaurant.

Avery entered the small lobby and was welcomed by the tantalizing smells of garlic and tomatoes and by Tony Virelli's gleaming smile; white teeth tented by a trim Don Ameche mustache. As ever-present host, Tony's role was to usher patrons irresistibly left or right through the appropriate padded red leather door. Behind him, a third door led to the kitchen, where Gina and their three daughters presided over both dining rooms' food and table service. Normally, their son, Tony Junior, drove deliveries.

Virelli greeted Avery warmly with a two-handed shake. They knew each other from the monthly Rotary lunches held in Tony's fine dining room.

"Tony Junior sick?" Avery asked.

The smile dimmed. "No, he's here. Working in the back."

"Not enough deliveries to keep him busy?"

"No, and it's not the car, or the gas, either," he confessed glumly. "It's Gina. She's scared to death that when the bombs fall the family won't be together. Until this blockade business is settled, she wants all of us under the same roof. She didn't even want to let the kids go to school today. Thank God Bishop Moore is just up the street."

One of the daughters, pretty dark eyes with a cloud of dark hair not unlike Charlotte's, elbowed her way out the kitchen door carrying three pizza boxes.

"For Avery?" Virelli asked, with a rich rolling of the *r*.

"Yes, Papa."

"Gratzia, Nina," he told her. He took the boxes and handed them over. "For your trouble, ten percent discount."

"Tony, that's not necessary."

Virelli frowned, made a gesture as if tossing a ball from one hand to the other. *"Da cosa nasce cosa,"* he said. "One thing leads to another."

Avery thanked him, paid, and walked out, surprised by how swiftly the pale twilight had dropped off into dusk. Up the street, the lights were on inside the sanctuary of St. Charles, the ultramodern Catholic church adjacent to Bishop Moore High. A large illuminated sign invited passersby to PRAY FOR THE PRESIDENT, OUR NATION & THE WORLD.

Through the open doors and etched-glass windows, Avery caught the flicker of candles, the shapes of shoulders and bowed heads, the movements of a burly, white-robed priest. He was certain it was Thomas O'Meara. Ordinarily, the man conducted evening Mass, then picked up Emilio and several of the other Cuban boys to take them home to the retreat center where they lived.

Somehow, Avery was relieved that Catholics all over the country, maybe the world, felt profoundly connected to President Kennedy and were praying for him, for everyone, that night. But as he passed his own darkened church and those of the Methodists and the Episcopalians, also dark, relief turned to letdown. Where was everybody else? Why weren't the Protestants out in droves as well—praying that God, or *somebody*, would turn those Soviet ships around, swerve them off tomorrow's showdown with the navy?

Entering his own neighborhood, Avery slowed to pass the tow-headed Moyer kids darting across the street in a wild game of Kick the Can. He saw the teenage Tobin boy sneaking a smoke behind his mother's hibiscus hedge; and his neighbor Bud Gilbert out with a hose, filling the dirt wells around his roses. On any other evening, these events would have brought him comfort, *a bit of normal* affirming his sense of community and surprising good fortune. But not tonight.

Tonight, for more reasons than he could comprehend, Avery felt cut off from normal. And terribly, inexplicably, alone.

It reminded him of when his father died. Five years younger than Avery was now, his father had been crushed by a failed hydraulic tractor jack. A careless mistake—he'd trusted the jack and neglected to set protective blocks—that cost him his life. Avery, only ten at the time, came home from school to a farmhouse crowded with neighbors from their rural community. As word of the tragedy spread over the next few days, the number of mourners doubled, then tripled, spilling out of the house onto the lawn, the barnyard, into the barn itself, its dirt floor still darkened with his father's blood. Avery had wandered among them feeling lost, forgotten, and desperately alone.

Only his grandfather had been able to reach him. Overhearing a local churchman tell Avery "this was God's will," Old Pa had pulled him aside, among the jar-filled shelves of his mother's pantry, and told him firmly, eyes blazing, "God had *nothing* to do with this!"

Turning into his driveway, Avery saw, with an audible groan, that all ten of the twirls were already there, their cars parked chocka-block in his way. He parked on the street and walked in with the pizzas. The girls greeted him at the door in a floral-scented female rush.

"Hey, Mr. A!"

"Mmmm, pizza!"

"Great! I'm starving!"

Most were in lovely long dresses, a few with elbow-length gloves. They fluttered and squawked and hopped around him, calling to mind the flock of long-legged white pullets his mother used to raise.

But instead of his mother's cheerful chiding, it was Sarah kneeling on the floor, strawberry-shaped pincushion on her wrist, hemming stick against the bottom of Charlotte's red dress, who called rather sharply, "Hush now. Settle down! Nobody eats till we're done."

The twirls fell silent, their bright faces dimmed with discomfort. Charlotte's eyes flew to Avery's. He shot Sarah a look that he hoped counseled patience. Maybe even an apology?

Sarah sat back on her heels, eyes watering and a bit wild. Her mouth opened and then closed, empty. She seemed, at that moment, undone, and as surprised as Avery was by her rudeness. As a rule, Sarah was never consciously rude to anyone.

After a long, painful pause, she pulled herself slowly to her feet with an over-bright smile all around. "Okay, everyone," she said, slipping into a deliberately honeyed purr. "We're almost done here. Wouldn't want to get red pizza sauce all over your pretty dresses," she said, oozing patience. "Please change and then we'll eat." She added with a courteous nod to him, "If you're hungry, Wes, please help yourself."

He wasn't, and didn't.

Instead, he retreated to the master bath to shower and scrub any residue of the day's dirt and oil off his body. It was a farmer's ritual, established early by his mother, who claimed the mark of a considerate man was scrupulously clean hands, nails, ears, and hair. He'd hoped to wash away the darkness of his mood as well.

But there it was, staring back at him in the mirror, with a constriction in his chest muscles like curved staves around an empty barrel.

Inside, he felt hollow, helpless against the slow, steady drip of rising dread.

AFTER THE HUBBUB OF the pizza party, the kitchen seemed over-quiet. Sarah needed a Nembutal and a bit of sherry badly, but more than that she needed to speak with Charlotte.

"Charlotte?"

Sarah saw her halt mid-step, in the exact same way she'd done as a child playing freeze-tag with the neighbor kids in their old back-yard. Only her eyes moved, wary as a chained dog.

"Please. Just hear me out."

Charlotte's eyes stopped just short of rolling; her look turned in-stantly sullen. She was tired and wanted to go to bed. One hand sought the doorjamb, the other slid to her hip.

Sarah draped the dish towel over the lip of the sink and turned to face her. "Growing up, I had a sister," she said quietly.

"Kitty, right?" Charlotte saw her mother's face blank with surprise.

"How in the world would you know that?"

"Grandma Do told me."

"Mama?" The very same woman who'd warned her and Wes never to mention Kitty to Charlotte? "Don't go soiling that child's mind with your sister's dirty laundry," she'd scolded.

"When?"

"I don't know. Years ago. Grandma Do took me to downtown Tus-caloosa to pick up a hat she'd ordered. The lady at the shop said something about Kitty, about me being the spittin' image of her. So I asked Grandma who she was. She said Kitty was the pretty one, but you got all the talent. She also said not to mention that . . . to you."

Sarah compressed peeved lips—the old family judgment still ran-kled. She'd have to stew on that, and on her mother's deception, later. "When Kitty was your age," she continued, "she was up for Home-coming Queen, too."

"Really? Did she win?"

"Yes. But that's not the point." Sarah sighed, willing herself on.

"Kitty had her pick of dates. But she chose a boy she hardly knew, a college guy she'd met at a hamburger joint near U of A. He was handsome. She liked his car, she said, and his New York accent."

Sarah looked down vacantly at her hands. When had they turned into her mother's—same elegant length, same narrow, ridged nails, same web of wrinkles and emerging liver spots? She squeezed them into fists to make the wrinkles go away, then opened them flat again to see Mama's hands return.

"Homecoming night," Sarah said, old, still-painful images flashing through her mind, "he showed up with a bottle and, like most boys, only one thing on his mind. He got her drunk at the dance and, on the way home, took advantage. It was a major catastrophe, Charlotte, and a huge scandal. It changed everything for all of us."

"Is . . . is that when she died?"

"No," Sarah said truthfully. "But it was the beginning of her downhill slide."

Charlotte glanced toward the door, then returned her mother's pained look.

"Couple of things, Mom," she said. "First, do you really think it's possible for me to walk around high school with these"—she spread her open palms beneath her ample breasts—"and not be aware what 'most boys' have on their mind? Second, two of the girls here tonight—don't ask me who—are saying that if we're all going to hell in a handbasket, they're not leaving without losing their virginity." Shock flattened her mother's face. "I'm not one of them, Mom. And Emilio's not like that. Besides . . . he'd never do anything that might disappoint Dad or Steve." She turned on her heel and left.

"I hope you're right," Sarah said to Charlotte's retreating back. "I really do," she said, now addressing the empty kitchen. She poured herself a large glass of sherry, tossed down a couple of pills, and went out onto the back porch to nurse the insult and irony that, of all people, Steve's opinion mattered more than hers.

Par for the course, she thought desolately.

Outside, the lake was dark under a barely there, final-quarter moon. Down to its last dime, her daddy would have said. Small, pale wisps of mist rose off the water like smoke from a circle of country cabins. Or a gathering of old ghosts, Sarah thought, sipping sherry. She paused briefly to cover the birdcages for the night, then fighting off exhaustion—*Stay busy or go crazy, right?* Mama's motto ran through her head—she trudged back to the dining room to hand-stitch the pinned hem of Charlotte's homecoming dress.

6.

WEDNESDAY MORNING,
OCTOBER 24

THE KITCHEN WAS ODDLY HUSHED. OVERNIGHT, A THICK FLEECE of fog had formed on the lake, crept up the dock, captured the back lawn, and laid siege to the house. Beads of moisture striped by watery rivulets cloaked the rear windows. Beyond them, there was nothing but diffuse gray silence.

Avery hated fog like this: too thick, too quiet, too close for comfort. Fog like this took him to a place he never wanted to go again: the living hell of January 27 and 28, 1945, the worst thirty-seven hours of his life, when after flying eight hours from Tinian to Tokyo, dropping their load on the Mitsubishi aircraft plant, and circling back, Cap'n Ritter announced, eight hours in, that they were still two hours from base. The race between strong headwinds and dwindling fuel would be "close." Ninety-two nerve-racking minutes later, Ritter announced, "Close but no cigar, boys," and rang the bail-out bell. Isolated in the tail turret, Avery opened his escape window and, seeing other crew members already in the air, stood, snapped on his chest parachute, lifted the life raft pack that served as his seat cushion, attached it to his chute harness, and dove out into . . . nothing but clouds rushing and roaring in his ears and, after the *pop* of his chute, a sea fog so inpenetrable he never saw the water surface coming. Stunned by the impact, he had no memory of inflating his Mae West, ditching his chute harness, or pulling the inflation straps on his raft. Alone, unable to see his feet, he was certain he'd landed in hell—not the fire-and-brimstone kind favored by preachers in his youth, but a cold, wet wasteland inhabited by unseen monster waves that came at him, one after another, in a nauseating, unending roller coaster, while every bump beneath the thin rubber membrane of his raft was, in his increasingly addled state, the nose of a shark, the fin of a killer whale, or the lines of a surfacing Japanese sub. More likely, he decided as the hours rocked by, he'd suffer death by vomiting and its attendant dehydration surrounded by an undrinkable sea. It was, in the end, thirty-seven hours of shivering hell before he heard the muffled *chug-chug-chug* of an engine and saw the megaphone-shaped sweep of a searchlight atop a ship he could only hope was American. It was, in fact, a Merchant Marine cargo ship (a final parting gift from his grandfather, who had passed on six weeks before?), its crewmen angels with grizzled faces whose strong tattooed arms, not unlike Old Pa's, lifted him up and out of hell and set him down in the heaven of a steaming shower. (It was later, when he was reunited with his surviving crewmen—they'd lost four out of eleven that night—for one week's R&R at a camp on Waikiki Beach, that he hit upon the idea of sending a thank-you to Inspector 833 for the rubber raft that saved his life. Eight-three-three was a number he'd easily recalled and taken as an omen, he explained in his note, since it was also his mother's birthday: August 3, 1903.)

Weather like this, palpable as cotton, set Avery's nerves on edge. Earlier, he'd paced around the kitchen, an uneasy captive, while Charlotte downed her cereal and milk. He'd followed her out the door, calling to her friends in the car, "Take it *slow!*" He'd returned to the kitchen to refill his mug, then moved, antsy, into the dining room.

Sarah, up late sewing, was apparently sleeping in. Her handiwork—Charlotte's multilayered red dress, each layer neatly hemmed—hung off the top ledge of the china cabinet. A second dress, the sparkly white one for the parade, hung beside it, bristling with silver pins.

Ground clouds had flanked both sides of the house and were reassembling near the sidewalk and in the street. Avery checked his watch and stepped out on the front stoop to wait.

He heard the distinctive squeal of the Divco brakes first. Then he saw the twin lights, the white snub-nose, and the square top of Jimmy Simms's milk truck roll into view. He moved quickly onto the walk, intent on asking the big man for an update on activity out at the air base. But something in Simms's manner stopped him.

Normally a smiler, a greeter, a glad-handed gossip, Simms lumbered up the drive in silence, solemn as a pallbearer. He held out the crate of glass bottles like a condolence offering. Once the transfer was made, his eyes made a darting circuit of the door, the drive, the fog-filled street, then returned to Avery, narrowed with warning.

"DefCon Two," he confided in a low voice, all but whispering. Then he shook his head—a man struggling to reconcile the truth with his own disbelief—and turned away. Avery watched him climb heavily back into the truck, shift and lurch into reverse, and nod his sober good-bye. Avery stood there, holding the crate of sweating bottles, staring at the space where the fog had swallowed the white truck.

DefCon Two.

To anyone living near an SAC base, the Strategic Air Command's system of monitoring the nation's Defense Condition was common knowledge. It was a five-point sliding scale, shorthand for the degree of readiness required of all military personnel. Normally, the base wavered between a peaceable DefCon Five and a moderately alert DefCon Four. But DefCon Two—DefCon *Two*—was maximum alert, full readiness for all-out war! As far as Avery knew, the nation had never reached DefCon Two before. And if we hit DefCon One?

Avery felt the shudder from the back of his neck to the base of his spine. The milk bottles rattled their response. Blindly he turned toward the house.

His brain was numbed by the news. DefCon Two. Three small syllables that loomed so large he was very nearly knocked to his knees with dread. He closed the refrigerator door, leaned an elbow atop its cool surface, and pressed a thumb to his temple, fingers flat across his forehead, to think.

DefCon Two. A decision like that came down from the top. The Joint Chiefs alone? Or was the President involved?

The face of the man at the top of air force command reared in Avery's mind: steely eyes beneath dark glowering brows, heavy jowls, belligerent lips wrapped around a thick cigar. He was only a two-star general when he arrived on Tinian Island to assume command of the air war against Japan, but he'd already earned the nicknames of Iron Ass and Bombs Away LeMay.

Before his arrival in early '45, the B-29 crews flew high-altitude, daytime sorties against strategic military targets. But Curtis LeMay changed everything.

Memories of those first frantic weeks in late February '45 rose painfully like welts after a whipping. Rumors flew after late-night calls from crew chiefs rousted every mechanic on the island out of bed to work round-the-clock modifying the B-29s to LeMay's specifications. Unbelievably, the general's orders were to remove all defensive weapons and munitions except those of the tail-gunners and replace them with additional bombs. When reconfigured, LeMay's B-29s were an aerial apocalypse straining their engines under the jam-packed combination of highly explosive white phosphorus bombs (to crack open roofs), plus napalm and incendiary clusters (to set off the firestorm).

Flight crews dropping by the hangars were aghast, outraged, and near mutiny. But old Iron Ass ordered them up, not only defenseless and at low altitudes, but with the express command that "not being able to make it back is no reason to abort."

The night of March 9, Avery was aboard one of LeMay's 334 bombers that branded Tokyo with a fiery X, then dumped everything they had—seventeen hundred incendiary tons—from seven thousand feet. Block by block, Tokyo blew up in flames. In less than three hours, sixteen square miles of the city and one hundred thousand residents were incinerated.

The air reeked of burning wood, debris, and flesh. From the tail, Avery viewed the inferno through dark glasses against the glare of

Tokyo's searchlights. After leaving Tokyo, for more than 150 miles out, he could still see the leap of flames and debris several thousand feet high and dark clouds of smoke hurled upward to more than fifteen thousand feet. Even now, in the safety of his own home, he swallowed hard against that singular black taste—*ashes in our mouth*—and the hollow horror on the faces of his fellow crewmen.

When questioned about the switch from military targets to civic centers, old Iron Ass made no bones about it: "There are no civilians in Japan," he answered curtly. After Tokyo, sixty-six other Japanese cities (and towns when they ran out of cities) felt the wrath of Le-May's nighttime "fire jobs."

Now that crazy bastard was a Joint Chief? With a nuclear arsenal capable of incinerating the planet three times over. Did President Kennedy, a mere PT-boat commander, have what it would take to stand down LeMay's five-star bloodlust? He'd certainly shown no balls at the Bay of Pigs.

Avery shook his head in disbelief. The fate of the world rested on a bunch of old warlords and America's youngest-ever President. Not to mention that wacko Khrushchev.

He rubbed his temple. The pulse just beneath the skin had begun to race. He needed to *move*. He pushed himself straight, crossed the kitchen, and picked up the phone. The action caused Sarah's note (*TUES: Langford, 11:00 & 1st Baptist, 1:00, WED: Cherry Plaza, 1:00*) to flutter to the floor. He bent to pick it up and tucked it back behind the phone jack. Pointedly ignoring the fog-filled window, he dialed the station.

"Orange Town Texaco. Steve speakin'."

"Everything okay over there?"

"Nothin' I can't handle. But . . ."

"What?"

"Bad news from the depot. Couple of convoys stopped by, requisitioned all their mid-grade. Cleaned 'em out. We got only a thousand gallons of regular. Seven-fifty premium. Best they could do."

Avery blew out frustration in a half breath, half whistle.

"Been tellin' customers we're down to five gallons a car. Till things loosen up."

"All right," Avery said, remembering why he called. "Listen, I have to stop by the cottage on Princeton, post a FOR RENT sign. Might be a few minutes late."

"Gonna miss McNamara on TV? He's 'bout to update the press."

Avery's eyes shot to the kitchen clock. Nine twenty-nine. The navy's blockade of Cuba was set to start at ten.

"Oh, and Cap?"

"Yeah."

"There was a lady here—va–va–voom!—looking for you. Told her you'd be in at ten. She's havin' breakfast at the Rexall 'cross the street. Comin' back to see you then."

"Anybody I know?"

Steve paused. "Hard to say, Cap. But definitely worth the drive over."

AVERY DECIDED THE COTTAGE could wait and switched on the TV.

Secretary of Defense Robert McNamara stood checking his notes behind a DOD podium. The former president of Ford Motor Company, he had a reliable look—solid frame, square face, round glasses, hair combed straight back. But during the war, Avery knew, McNamara had served as Curtis LeMay's statistical analyst. How much sway, Avery worried, did old Iron Ass still have over his former lieutenant colonel?

McNamara's statement was painfully brief:

Overnight the US Navy had tightened its line of interdiction from eight hundred to five hundred miles off Cuba's coast. Despite the increased leeway, approximately twenty-five Soviet ships remained on course for Cuban ports. The first test of the quarantine, a possible clash between American and Soviet ships, could come within twenty-four hours.

Avery was struck by McNamara's gaze into the camera, the sly, calculating gleam as he told reporters it was a "fair assumption" that some of the Soviet ships were carrying offensive nuclear weapons. The man's smugness, his failure to mention that the nation's military had moved to DefCon Two, tightened the constriction in Avery's chest and the creeping numbness inside his head.

A sudden need to *get out* propelled him off the couch, through the door, and into his truck.

FOUR BLOCKS FROM HOME, away from the socked-in haze of his neighborhood, the sky was a steel-gray lid set atop the town.

At the stop sign on Smith, Avery stuck his head out the window and gulped fresh air, but the tightness in his throat and chest remained. From somewhere above the cloud cover, he heard the sound of thunder, rolling southwest. Another fighter squadron bound for McCoy. Where the heck are they putting them all?

Pulling into the station, he saw his usual parking spot was occupied by a sleek white Chrysler Imperial with a No. 3 Hillsborough County plate. He swerved into the open spot between Steve's Admiral and the street.

Out at the pumps, Steve caught his glance and gave a quick head jerk toward the office, followed by an appreciative eye roll. Clearly the lady, "va-va-voom," whoever she was, was waiting inside.

He saw her legs first. One long, silk-stockinged shin crossed over the other, nice calves, stylish black heels, and the discreet silver wink of a barely there ankle bracelet. The hem of a slim black skirt. But everything else, except for both sets of slender fingertips, nails painted dark red, was hidden from view by the held-high spread of an out-of-town newspaper—the Styles section of the *The New York Times*, probably purchased across the street at Hammond's Drugs.

Avery cleared his throat.

Her fingertips tightened their grip, then, in a quick graceful movement, closed, folded, and set the paper on the desk. She stood and looked at him, tall enough to meet his gaze eye-to-eye.

"Hello, Wes."

Avery's mind bucked at the impossible, the unimaginable, sight of her.

"K-Katharine."

"Oh, please." She smiled. "It's still Kitty. That much, at least, hasn't changed."

"B-but . . . ," he stammered. *Kitty? Alive?* "But Dolores . . . Dolores said you were *dead*." Mentally, he scrambled for the details of his mother-in-law's long-ago—five years ago? six?—late-night phone call: a car crash in California, both occupants killed, ashes scattered at sea. He and Sarah had been shocked but also (though he hated to admit it) more than a bit relieved.

"Oh, she told me the same thing," Kitty said with a dismissive toss of platinum-blond curls. Kitty alive, and *blond*! "'You're dead to me,' Mama said. But obviously . . ." She extended both arms sideways, palms up, and hitched a slim hip.

Avery's instinct ricocheted between the need to step back and steady himself against the desk and the urge to step forward and hug her, welcome her back among the living! Unsure what to do, not wanting to offend or presume, he extended his hand lamely—the polite, automatic response of a good deacon at church.

Inside his head, the edges were blurring. The world outside the office had in that moment ceased to exist. The past seventeen years, the future as he'd perceived it, had collapsed forward and backward onto themselves like a seaman's telescope. A handful, a hundred questions went off rapid as flak inside his brain.

Kitty turned to eye Steve's approach. He had a couple of credit cards in hand and would need to access the machine beside the register.

"Is there someplace else . . . ?"

Avery's mind flew through options: Here in the office, there'd be constant interruption. Home was impossible. Ditto a local restaurant. Kitty was too attractive not to . . . and someone seeing them together might . . . But of course . . .

"Yes," he said, pointing out the side door.

She picked up her purse, a shiny black envelope, slim as a cigarette case. Avery took her arm, tossed Steve a look that said he'd be back later, and steered her to the Imperial.

"It's just up the street. Like me to drive?"

"Why don't I follow you?" she suggested.

Better still. "All right," he told her, fishing his keys out of his pocket.

All the way up Princeton, he berated himself for his stiff response to her, his lack of focus on the most basic of issues. Kitty *alive;* driving a car with Hillsborough County plates. Was she living in Florida now, in Tampa? He'd been too—What? Floored? Flabbergasted? Dumbstruck! Yeah, struck dumb by the sight of her—to ask: After seventeen years of no contact, how did she find him? What was she doing here? Why now? And most basic, most important of all: *What did she want?*

Half a block before the cottage, he put on his turn signal and watched her do the same. When he swung into the drive, he pulled all the way up to the house to leave her plenty of room.

He intended to walk back and open her door. But she was out of the car and striding toward him before he could reach her. She accompanied him without comment up the drive; but at the base of the brick steps, she stopped and asked warily, "Anybody home?"

"It's an empty rental," he assured her. "Tenants moved out first of the week."

As he worked the lock and the dead bolt, she clicked open her purse, dropped in her keys, and snapped it shut. Sneaking a sideways peek, he noted she wore no rings, no other jewelry except for the ankle bracelet and a large single pearl necklace in the V of her red sweater. The cloud of platinum-blond curls was a shock, as were the fine lines around her carefully made-up eyes and lips. But, my God, her *face* was so stunningly familiar—same oval shape, elegant nose, pale, porcelain skin; yet somehow less soft, more composed than her younger sister's.

By the look of things—the clothes, the car—she's done well for herself, he thought, opening the door and stepping back. Kitty lifted her chin as she passed, as if she'd read his mind and was answering, *Yes, I have.*

She even smells expensive, he thought dizzily. Roses mixed with some exotic spice.

He watched her gaze sweep over the compact living room, the hallway to both bedrooms on the right, the archway into the dining room and kitchen on the left. She seemed to take in the small details he'd added over the years: the five-inch baseboards, a perfect match to the golden oak floors, the built-in bookcase surrounding the small window seat, the recessed china cabinet in the dining room.

"Charming," she said, stopping to touch the chair-high wainscoting and run an appreciative hand over the polished wood grain.

He followed her into the kitchen, acutely aware that, aside from the very short time he'd spent with her the week before his and Sarah's wedding, most of what he knew about Kitty—a lot of it not good—had come secondhand. From his mother-in-law, who'd flat-out lied about her own daughter's death. And from Sarah, who, from the get-go, bore her only sister a long and extremely complicated grudge.

At the sink, she leaned forward to peer out the window—her hair haloed by the diffuse light—and gave a small cry of delight at the playhouse in the back corner, a perfect miniature of the cottage right down to the white window boxes and green shutters.

She turned, and in her smile he saw that the slight overlap in her front teeth, which he'd thought endearing, was gone. Her teeth were perfect now, and obviously she no longer bit her nails.

She moved toward the door as if to step out onto the small back porch, but stopped short to study the markings on the molding beside the jamb—his and Sarah's measurements of Charlotte's height at various ages. He'd intended to move it to the new house but hadn't gotten around to it yet. Did she realize what it was? Kitty turned again, fingering the pearl on its delicate silver chain, resetting it in the soft hollow at the base of her throat.

"Mind if I smoke?" she asked.

He pulled out a chair for her at the small kitchen table, found an ashtray in the cupboard, opened the window over the sink, and sat down opposite. He watched her extract a cigarette and a slim, silver lighter from her purse, saw the slight tremor in her fingers as she got it lit, the deep and hungry drag followed by her long, ragged exhale.

"So this was Carly's happy home?" Her tone was light, but her eyes betrayed the effort.

He nodded, berating himself for not thinking about the effect the cottage might have on her. "We call her Charlotte."

"Of course you do." She took another greedy pull, then stared at her exhaled smoke, retrieving a memory. "Last thing Sarah said to me was she thought the name Carly 'common,' that she had something else in mind."

He'd forgotten about that.

Those gray eyes—the same color as Sarah's though a slightly different shape—frosted over. "How is Miss Priss, by the way?"

"Sarah's fine."

"Moved on to bigger and better digs, I s'pose?" Her eyes raked the room.

"Split-level on the lake, six blocks from here."

"So she got her happily ever after . . . except . . . What about the other kids? Thought y'all wanted a houseful."

"Didn't work out," Avery said quietly, then screwed up his courage to ask, "You?"

"Three ex-husbands, no kids."

Aw, jeez, Avery thought. At the base of his skull, the news set off a prickling alarm.

"Not that I ever wanted 'em." She stopped to drag again, her eyes half closed in a remembering squint. "When *I* turned sixteen, all I wanted was a car. Daddy found this old, beat-up roadster . . . a '24 Packard, with a rumble seat, for God's sake!" She paused to favor him with a wan smile. "Never been happier in my life. That car got me out from under Mama's thumb; it was my ticket to *freedom*! But *Sarah*? Know what Sarah asked for on her big birthday?" Her eyes mocked her absent sister. "All Sarah wanted was for Daddy to build her a cedar hope chest and for Mama to give her Grandma Ayres's Royal Albert china."

Images of the chest at the foot of their bed and the blue-and-gold china in their dining room breakfront came to mind.

"Funny thing is . . . Sarah was the one with real talent. People used to swoon over that voice of hers." She shot him a piercing look. "She ever do anything with her singing?"

"Solos in the church choir," Avery said, feeling a rush of loyalty.

"That's *it*?" she said, incredulous. "Poor Mama!" She threw back her head, red lips wide in a loud, braying laugh brittle as glass. "When we were little, Mama was convinced she was raising a pair of thoroughbreds. Had her sights set on a Miss Alabama or, the very least, a governor's or senator's wife. Turned out"—her bitterness sliced the air, shard-sharp—"I was the black sheep in horse harness and poor ol' Sarah the sacrificial lamb."

Black sheep, Avery understood. He'd heard the tales. But Sarah a sacrificial lamb? Kitty's zero-to-sixty mood shift—a hallmark of both Ayres girls and their mother—had taught him to be wary of asking. Better by far to steer things back to his mother-in-law. "You know Dolores passed, a year ago August?"

"Cousin Maura sent me the clippings." She studied the lit end of her cigarette for a moment as if re-reading them. Then she looked up, rancor discarded, eyes bright. "Tell me about Carly. What's she like?"

"Wonderful . . . an A student, state champion majorette, and as sweet a girl as you can imagine."

"Well, I'm sure that's *your* doing."

"Oh, now . . ." Avery felt compelled to rise to Sarah's defense, but Kitty cut him off with an abrupt wigwag of her hand.

"Save it, for her." Cigarette smoke zigzagged between them.

The questions he had for her were piling up inside his head. Where? How to begin?

"So you live near Tampa now?"

"Not near. *In*. Neighborhood called Bayshore. You know it?"

"Right on the water. Ritzy."

"One of the better ones. Great views of downtown. But unfortunately . . ." She paused. Her eyes bored into him, her tone turned careful. ". . . just north of MacDill."

MacDill.

Avery's thoughts spun. As if he was caught in a time warp. As if, instead of hours, only seconds had elapsed between Jimmy Simms's half-whispered warning, "DefCon Two," and Kitty's telltale remark, "just north of MacDill"—Tampa's SAC base.

In the silence, come down heavy as a hammer between them, he pictured the day he first met her. The big house on Greensboro had been bristling with family drama. Downstairs, Sarah and her mother, and a blur of female relatives, scurried about, getting ready for that weekend's wedding. Upstairs, Kitty lay hugely pregnant and alone, confined to her childhood bedroom, door closed, shades drawn. Poor kid hadn't been allowed outside in weeks, not once since her surprise return home from Rome.

Their mother, no-nonsense Dolores, had already arranged to place the infant in an orphanage when it came, but Avery, tentatively at first, then more insistently, had intervened. The day before the wedding, he and Sarah had their first argument. "I saw my fill of death and dying on Tinian, and over Japan," he told her. "And it left me certain that life is precious, and family is everything. This plan of your mother's—to just dump Kitty's baby on strangers, orphan your own flesh and blood—strikes me as coldhearted and uncaring. This baby's your family, for God's sake," he argued. "If nobody wants it here, we should take it with us to Florida; give it the love and protection it deserves." Sarah, her head full of worries about the wedding, resisted. "Why should I cover up another one of Kitty's catastrophes?" "Why not?" he countered. "I can see your sister's been judged and juried . . . but it's the *baby* being punished. Tell me, where's the justice in that?" "But, Wes, how can you even think about taking on another man's child?" she argued. "It's half Ayres, isn't it? How can we not?" In the end, she'd agreed, and helped him lobby Dolores with "The child is an innocent, and deserves a good home among loving kin."

Abruptly, Kitty got up, ground out her cigarette in the sink, and rinsed away its remains. Once again she peered out the window to the playhouse. Only then did she turn to face him.

"Seventeen years ago, I trusted you, Wes. I'd never have agreed if it weren't for you. Everyone else treating me like a leper, worried about the scandal, the precious family *name*. . . ." Her tone was sharp with remembered pain. "As if the whole town didn't know all about Daddy's tomcatting!" Then, visibly, she softened. "Everyone but *you*, Wes. You were the only one who even asked me about Carlo, who showed me any sympathy for his loss. You talked about losing your grandfather—Old Pa, you called him, remember?—and earlier on, losing your daddy in that awful accident. You still carry that broken screw in your pocket?"

"No," he told her, flattered that she remembered.

"You said how much you looked forward to kids of your own. You were kind to me, Wes. I've never forgotten that. In the hospital, when the time came, I didn't give Carly to Sarah, do you remember? I handed her to *you*."

The memory of that moment—Charlotte so tiny yet so perfect, an exquisite little doll pulsing with life, and the welling in his heart, the overwhelming need to protect her—was a touchstone for Avery. He returned to it often; as recently as yesterday, in fact, when she'd appeared at the station so fragile and frightened. Charlotte had come to him for comfort and for the truth.

And he'd always given it to her—except for this one thing.

On their honeymoon drive down to Florida, Sarah had drawn the line. "I'm her mother and you're her father. Let's just leave it at *that*." It had been easy to present themselves as Charlotte's parents, easier still after they heard from Dolores that Kitty was dead. But *now*?

Kitty's eyes blazed with intention. "Seventeen years ago, I quit Tuscaloosa and everyone in it. But not before Mama and Sarah made me promise, made me *swear* on the family Bible, 'No contact with the child, no deathbed confessions of motherhood, no nothing, *ever*.' I'm not here to break my word. But to tell you the truth, Wes—I mean, who really knows where all this missile-business is headed?—I just want to see her. If we're all bound for hell in a handbasket, I want to lay eyes on my only daughter, just once . . . before I go."

For the second time that day, Avery recalled the nauseating sense of jumping out of the known, falling through nothingness, and landing in a new, never-imagined hell. Kitty, whom everyone thought was dead, was not only alive, but wanted to see his daughter. Avery swallowed hard against the surge of bile at the back of his throat.

He was struggling to stay on top of a sudden swell of emotions. Think, man, think! In chess terms, this is surely only a check, not checkmate. What are your options?

If Sarah were here, she'd have ordered Kitty out by now, insisting she honor their agreement exactly as planned. Certainly, she'd expect him to do the same.

But under the circumstances—who knew what was going to happen?—how could he deny Kitty her request? She was, technically, Charlotte's mother. And all she wanted, she claimed, was to "lay eyes" on Charlotte. Where was the harm in that? But Sarah . . . Sarah was her mother, too. The only one Charlotte had ever known, with a lifetime of care and devotion to her.

Two mothers, one child. In the Bible, it had taken the wisdom of Solomon to set things straight. But he was no Solomon. More than that—his jaw hardened with resolve—although Charlotte had two mothers, he was her only father. Her real father, Kitty's Italian fiancé, was long gone, killed in The War the week before V-E Day. He'd never even known of Charlotte's existence. Or that Kitty, an army nurse in Rome, had been quietly discharged, come home unmarried, pregnant, and, in her family's proper southern mind, disgraced.

And what about Charlotte? What if *she* learned the truth of their lifelong lie to her: that Sarah was her aunt. That he was, in fact, her kindly uncle. By marriage. With no genuine blood ties between them. Would she forgive or reject him? The possibility that he might lose her over the untold truth, the deliberate lie, being exposed was too painful to consider.

Somehow, he *had* to help Kitty.

Not because he was kind. Not because it was the right thing to do.

No. He'd help Kitty because, bottom line, helping her might help him if Charlotte ever learned the truth.

"She's up for Homecoming Queen," he said quietly. "The parade's on Friday afternoon down Edgewater Drive, College Park's main drag. You come, you can see her then."

He heard her sharp intake of breath. "Homecoming?" Her eyes flared open, then shuttered so quickly, he couldn't be sure of her true reaction. "Thank you," she said hoarsely, barely above a whisper.

He walked her out, opened the front door, and stood back to let her pass, hoping she couldn't hear his heart hammering inside his chest. "So, you headed back to Tampa now?"

"No." She clicked open her purse. "I was going to leave this at the station in case you weren't around." She handed him a business card. "The number on the back is the Cherry Plaza Hotel. With all the action out at MacDill, I haven't slept for days. I'm hoping to catch up." She paused. "Y'know, Wes, Daddy liked to say Sarah was his songbird and I was his black cat. I got all the lives, he'd say, but Sarah . . ." She reached out and, with a red-tipped fingernail, traced the line of his jaw. "Sarah got all the luck." Her finger stopped at the base of his chin. "I sure hope she appreciates how lucky she is," she murmured, then leaned in.

Her kiss, petal-soft, nicotine-sweet, stunned him. As did the heady swirl of her perfume and the dizzying undertow of feelings between them: her gratitude for his remembered and renewed kindness; his relief that she'd come to him at the station, instead of surprising Sarah at home, or seeking out Charlotte on her own at school. He gripped the door handle with one hand and mindfully withdrew the other, which had somehow snaked around to press the small of her back. *Careful,* he thought (his life's motto).

Her smile was sultry, close-lipped. *Thank you,* her eyes said, with the barest gleam of triumph. She'd gotten what she'd come for.

As if in afterthought, she asked, "How will I know Carly?"

You'll know, he thought but couldn't bring himself to say. "Black T-bird, red interior, white dress," he said instead.

Standing in the open doorway, he watched her go. Even from this angle, it was easy to see the ways in which she favored Sarah. Same broad shoulders and slim hips; same elegant, straight-spined gait; same whorl in the curls at the back of her head—though white blond instead of dark chestnut.

When she reached the Chrysler, she gave a small wave good-bye. Avery, fighting off a fog of confusion, went back into the kitchen. He busied himself with emptying the ashtray, closing the open window, locking the rear door, erasing all evidence of her visit. But the scent of her perfume—spiced roses—still hung over the sink.

There'll be hundreds of people watching the parade. What's the harm in inviting one more? *Who you trying to kid?*

That kiss at the end, it was nothing. *Would Sarah think so?*

Well, if Sarah was here . . . He'd already calculated the meaning and potential measure of what he'd done. And he was not proud.

STEVE WAS TAKING A smoke break in the office. The mechanic stood in his habitual at-ease stance—one foot on the rung of the stool, forearms crisscrossed atop his jacked-up knee. He was frowning down at the desktop when Avery returned.

"Looky here," Steve said. A wave of his cigarette hand sent smoke curling over the front pages of the two newspapers, the local *Orlando Sentinel* and Kitty's discarded *New York Times,* laid out carefully side by side.

The *Sentinel* was dominated by two large images: the recently installed HAWK and Nike Hercules air defense missiles at Boca Chica Naval Air Station on Key West, their menacing tips trained south toward Havana, and a line of US tanks at the ready in Berlin. Both photos bristled with American strength, firepower, and defiance of the Soviet threat.

The *Times,* meanwhile, featured enlarged, carefully labeled surveillance photos: President Kennedy's "unmistakable evidence" of two Soviet medium-range ballistic missile (MRBM) sites near San Cristóbal, Cuba, and two intercontinental range (ICBM) sites at Guanajay and Remedios. Avery marveled at the small shapes labeled

SOVIET CONVOY, MISSILE TRANSPORTERS, ERECTOR/LAUNCHERS, and slash-marked LAUNCH PADS identified by US intelligence.

He cocked an eyebrow in Steve's direction. "Any mention of the U-2s? Where they're stationed?"

Steve took a long drag. "Not a peep."

Since Saturday, Avery had searched the *Orlando Sentinel,* which Steve insisted on calling the *Slantinel,* for an explanation, an update, or even a mention of the onslaught of military activity overhead at McCoy, and outside clogging the train tracks and traffic on the Trail. So far, the local paper had been mum. Even after the President's speech, the term *U-2*—the name of the all-important spy planes based nearby—had been notably absent from any reporting.

"Somebody's called a gag," Steve told him. "Keep the yokels in the dark; sidestep a panic that might slow down the convoys."

"Since when did the military trump freedom of the press?"

"Betcha a buck they'll never put the name of that plane in print."

"Bet you're right," Avery replied, turning back to the *Times* text. "Says here San Cristóbal is in *western* Cuba."

Steve's look said he'd made the same connection—Emilio was from western Cuba.

Avery remembered the teenager's suspicions, his tale of corner fences crushed by too-long trucks. How would confirmation of his worst fears affect the boy? "Think we ought to keep this from him?"

"It's the kid's own mama, right? Seems to me he's got a right to know."

Avery felt the color draining from his face. Had Steve made the connection between Kitty and Sarah? Had he guessed the truth about Charlotte?

After a moment of awkward silence, Steve ground out his cigarette. "Well, if you've got the pumps, guess I'll get back to it."

Avery nodded without looking at him.

Steve took a few steps, then stopped. "Who was she, by the way?"

"She who?" Avery asked, as casually as he could manage.

"C'mon . . . the blond bombshell with the legs?" He made a sound like the growl of a cat.

Had Kitty's hair and legs distracted Steve's attention from her face? Was it possible he didn't know? Avery tucked two fingers into his shirt pocket and came out with Kitty's card, offered it up for Steve's inspection.

"Bayshore Realty?"

Avery shrugged. "She's got a client interested in local rental property. Did a title search and my name came up on multiple addresses." Which was true. "Wanted to pick my brain about local rents, taxes, schools, and so forth." Which was not.

Steve looked wounded. "I own my own duplex. She coulda picked my brain. And anythin' else she had a mind to."

"Luck of the draw, I guess," Avery said carefully.

Steve sniffed the card. "Wild Rose of Sharon," he announced with a sigh and handed it back. "My first wife's favorite."

Avery moved behind the desk. As Steve went back to the service bay, he unlocked the middle desk drawer. Then he stashed Kitty's fragrant card in his zippered leather bank pouch, beside the shiny jumble of Charlotte's dog tags.

THE PHONE ON THE NIGHTSTAND woke Sarah, dazed from a dreamless sleep. She rolled onto her back then onto her other side, noting the time—nearly *eleven*—and grabbed the receiver off its cradle.

"He-hello, Avery residence."

"Sarah, it's Edith. You been to the Cherry Plaza yet?"

"You said one o'clock, remember?" She sat up, finger raking tangled hair out of her eyes.

"Glad I caught you, then. Listen, I just heard from General Betts's office—not the general himself, his attaché—who's asked that we soft-pedal any criticism of the public shelters. Bad for the public morale, he said."

Sarah, still groggy and bone-weary from weeks of Edith's unending demands, felt the hard flash of resentment. "Is he saying public morale's more important than the truth?"

"Well, at this point, it *is* whatever it *is*. And we don't want to be responsible for setting off any sort of panic."

"But . . ."

"Besides, Sarah—and I'm sure you learned this from your mother, as I did from mine—'you catch more flies with honey than with vinegar.'"

That phrase, Sarah remembered, had indeed been one of her childhood's staples. Mama used it often, until one particularly embarrassing night at the Tuscaloosa Country Club, when Daddy punched a fellow club member in the face and broke his nose. "Oh, Colton," Mama cried then, "what *were* you thinking?" "The man's an ass, Dolores. And everybody knows it." "But surely—" "Now don't start with that crap about catchin' more flies with honey. Makin' nice with a bully is a complete waste of time—'turn the other cheek' with a guy like that, you're just askin' for a second slap on the face!"

"Sarah?" Edith croaked. "You still there?"

"What flies, Edith?"

"Pardon me?"

"Exactly what flies are we trying to catch?"

"Oh, my dear, surely I've mentioned it. The general has as much as guaranteed us spots in the best shelter in town."

"Which is . . . ?"

"The storage vault at LaBelle Furs!" Edith's voice quivered with excitement. "All the best families will be there!"

So that's what all this—the committee work, the shelter show, the inspections—was about? Edith being able to ride out a disaster in fur-lined luxury? Sarah dropped the hand holding the receiver into her lap. It was pale blue, a new special-order Princess phone whose Southern Bell slogan, she remembered, was, "It's little . . . it's lovely . . . it lights."

"Sarah?" Edith's voice, coming from the seven small holes in the receiver's top, sounded annoying, insect-like. "Sarah?"

Sarah raised the receiver back to her ear just long enough to say, "Edith, I have to go," then recradled the phone.

Her first thought—*Of all the nerve!*—was quickly followed by: *Why didn't I see that coming?* She jammed bare feet into her slippers, pulled on her robe, and pointedly ignored the insistent ringing of the phone—Edith, no doubt, calling back. In the bathroom, she scrubbed her face, brushed her teeth, and avoided her sad and drawn image in the mirror.

Shading her eyes against the light in the kitchen—sunshine filtered bright white by the fog over the lake—she made her way to the coffeepot. She dumped out the cold coffee left from Wes and started a new pot, then went onto the porch, where the birds cawed loudly for food and fresh water. Afterward, she stood for a moment staring out at the fog-draped lake.

It was a day like this—damply gray and still—they'd buried Robbie on the bluff overlooking the mist-covered Black Warrior River. At the church, he'd looked so small, so peaceful in his blue velvet Easter suit, the one that had so perfectly matched the color of his eyes. During the service, she'd imagined, it was as if he'd only climbed in there to take a nap. But later, seated graveside at the family plot, with the old willow oaks weeping long yellow leaves like tears, she'd panicked at the sight of the closed casket. *He can't breathe in there— we've got to get him out!* She'd squeezed her sister's hand so hard that Kitty yelped and yanked it away. When Mama turned, her face shiny with tears, sad eyes staring them both into silence, Sarah's chest had grown so tight that she herself could hardly breathe. *Horrible, horrible!* she was thinking when, just as the casket disappeared from view, she heard the whisper. In hindsight, Mama said, it was just the rustling of dead leaves beneath the funeral director's feet. But Sarah insisted she'd heard the whispered words clearly: *"I am too tender for this world."* She didn't know then (and couldn't say for sure now) where that voice came from. Was it little Robbie's last good-bye to her? Or her own eight-year-old's heart, crushed by death's awful randomness and a great load of grief she'd been too young to comprehend?

"Well, I don't know," Sarah said lamely to no one. She strode back into the kitchen, swiping off sudden tears with the cuff of her robe. No time for *that*! She stood, tapping long fingers on the counter, until the coffee was ready. Cup in hand, she moved through the living room, switched on the stereo to radio function, and tuned in WDBO too soon for the noon news.

In the dining room, she fingered Charlotte's white dress, unsure where to begin. Should she focus on the machine-sewn alterations, then hand-stitch the hem afterward? And why in the world had she finished up the red dress first, which was for Saturday night's dance, when Charlotte needed the white one for Friday's parade? She stared into her coffee cup, willing it to wake her up, wishing she could make it through a single day—just one—without feeling like a poor imitation of a previous self, someone she used to be. Though who that was, and whether *that* Sarah was worth imitating, was beyond her, lost in a fog that day by day took longer and longer to lift.

She chose, finally, to forgo the sewing machine until after the caffeine kicked in. Instead, she unhung the dress and moved to the other end of the table, where the light was better for hand sewing. She opened her sewing box, selected a needle, some white thread, her grandmother's small stork-shaped scissors, and her mother's silver thimble. Donning her reading glasses, she squinted, licked the end of thread, and poked it through the eye of the needle. She pulled it long, snipped it, paired the two ends between her fingertips, and rolled them into a knot. Whenever Mama did that, she'd quote President Roosevelt: "When you get to the end of your rope, tie a knot and hold on!"

"Oh, Mama, I'm trying," Sarah said aloud, pushing the needle point in and out, up and down like a small boat through the white sea of satin, pulling the thread behind it in a thin wake.

But knots—she sighed deeply, hurting as she thought of it—like families, like dreams, like life, for that matter, can be slippery things, unwilling or unable to be held.

7.

"*O*NLY *five*, WES? YOU CAN'T BE SERIOUS!"

"But I'm flat-out empty with a *twenty*-gallon tank."

"What's *next*—ration coupons? War bonds?"

Avery played the role of beleaguered businessman. We're under-supplied, he told them, with no assurances from the depot of any more gas anytime soon. Need to stretch what we have as far as we can.

Just after noon, hoping to cut down on complaints, he unearthed a pair of A-frame signs from the back room. Normally the signs hawked a seasonal promotion—AUTHENTIC TOY FIRE TRUCK! ONLY $3.99 WITH FILL-UP OF TEXACO FIRE-CHIEF GASOLINE—but today, Avery covered them with plain white paper and painted in large green letters:

LIMIT TODAY:

5 GAL.

PER CUSTOMER

He left room at the bottom for a line he suspected he'd have to add soon, OUT OF ETHYL—the name most customers called his mid-grade Fire Chief gas with, the red pump proudly proclaimed, "natural, no-knock additives."

All the while, working on the signs, he mulled over the gap between good old reliable Wes, Rotarian, deacon, roadside Samaritan, and the man who'd just taken Kitty to the cottage, ostensibly betrayed his wife, and perpetuated a seventeen-year-old lie to his daughter.

Yesterday, he would have described himself in the plainest of terms: solid citizen, honest businessman, devoted husband and father. He might have even said that, despite the occasional bump in the road, he was living his version of the American dream.

But today? Even though nothing had happened, really, with Kitty, he felt guilty; his perfect record—in seventeen years, he'd never seriously considered another woman—sullied. Not that there hadn't been more than a few opportunities over the years. Marion Halden came to mind, the young and needy war widow who'd been their neighbor on Princeton for a while. And Vivian Whitley, his tenant on Harvard Street, who was periodically short on rent money and long on suggestions. More recently, there was redheaded Annie Flynn, a local divorcée who'd flat-out offered to trade him "regular service under the hood, yours for mine." But in all this time, he'd never strayed, not once. Why was that?

First and foremost, fidelity.

After posting the completed signs at each entrance, Avery stared out at the traffic, and pictured the words—*First and foremost, fidelity*—written in Sarah's careful hand. Back then, he was still on Tinian Island and courting her in letters. Working up the nerve to pop the question, he'd asked her instead, "What qualities are you looking for in a husband?"

"First and foremost, fidelity," she'd written in reply. It was several years later, after her father's very long, very emotional funeral—the eulogies went on forever, with more than a few female mourners weeping loudly and uncontrollably—that Sarah explained why she and her mother had sat stiffly through the whole thing in stone-faced silence. "Oh, Wes," she told him. They were standing outside the church, scanning the departing crowd for Kitty, who never showed. "Daddy had affairs with half the women here. You can't imagine the hell he put Mama through for *years!*"

First and foremost, fidelity. Her need for fidelity had paired well with his careful nature (from age ten, he'd thought of himself as the careful son of a careless father), which made what happened today at the cottage all the more confounding. Certainly Sarah would see his helping Kitty—never mind his kissing her!—as a betrayal. He'd surprised himself by how simply, how easily, he'd done it.

Now, cleaning the windshield of Lee Vomac's pickup, he caught a whiff of spiced roses and bent his head in a quick, guilty sniff. The scent of her was trapped in the crease of his right inner elbow. He studied the skin there, so much paler than his suntanned forearm, and thought, This Kitty thing has to be contained! But how?

Moments later, clicking off the gas nozzle at exactly five gallons, something else clicked, though not audibly, inside his head. It was a signal, a mental alarm sounded by that back part of his brain tasked with sorting and filing, tasked with noting a curious link or worrisome connection, and returning it, with a silent click, to conscious thought.

Two mental images, from different times and places, surfaced simultaneously: Kitty handing him her card at the cottage, saying, "The number on the back is the Cherry Plaza Hotel"; and, earlier this morning, Sarah's note, retrieved from the kitchen floor and replaced beside the phone jack, reading, *WED: Cherry Plaza, 1:00.*

The coincidence, and its potential consequences, set off a small tremor in his chest.

Within the hour, Sarah would be arriving at Orlando's Cherry Plaza, the very same luxury hotel on downtown Lake Eola where Kitty was staying! What were the chances of Kitty emerging from lunch in the lobby's lakefront restaurant just as Sarah arrived to check their public shelter supplies? Would the two sisters recognize each other? Of course. Would Kitty—who seemed as prickly about Sarah as Sarah could be about her—say why she was there, and what happened at the cottage this morning? Nightmare!

He checked his watch: twelve fifty-two. And felt a small ball of fear forming in his stomach. No doubt Sarah was already en route. It was too late to stop her. Should he try to reach Kitty instead?

He holstered the nozzle, collected $1.55 for Vomac's gas, then turned quickly toward the office. But Steve was already at the desk breaking for lunch. No way could Avery fish out Kitty's card and make that call in front of him. And—Oh, for crying out loud!—here came Sonny Geiger strolling in off Princeton.

Geiger was a fellow mechanic who maintained the fleet of trucks and tractors for Dr. Phillips's Granada Groves, the giant citrus packinghouse that abutted the train tracks behind the station.

"How's it goin', boys?" Geiger boomed, filling the office doorway in his usual plaid shirt, denim overalls, and green mesh John Deere cap. He had the habit of punctuating his sentences with an audible suck, like a small kissing sound, on his toothpick.

Steve turned half-lowered eyelids on Avery, barely veiling his contempt. Avery's return glance counseled patience. Geiger had a knack for showing up at exactly the wrong time. Like now, when Steve was eager to eat and play a bit of chess, when Avery needed to make a call to head off marital disaster.

But during the height of the citrus season, when his shop got backed up with work, Geiger sent them his overflow: usually heavy-lifting jobs like transmission replacement or an engine overhaul. Good money in the slow months after Christmas. And Granada's checks never bounced.

"Just breaking for lunch," Avery answered. "You eaten yet?"

Geiger held up a freckled ham of a hand. "Just did. Y'all go right ahead." Then, leaning his bulk against the jamb, he asked, "Seen any familiar trucks roll by?"

"Army, you mean? More'n I care to count."

"No," Geiger said, sucking his toothpick. "I mean . . . any of *our* trucks."

"Granada trucks? Not really. But it's hardly the season."

"Good thing, too." Geiger suck-kissed his pick again. "'Cause we'd be up crap creek without a Sears catalog."

"What's the story, Sonny?" Steve growled.

"Well"—Geiger crossed meaty forearms over his ample gut—"you know Howard, our plant manager? Late Sunday night . . . we're talking one o'clock in the morning here . . . night before the President's speech, remember? Ol' Howard got a call . . . at *home* . . . on his *unlisted* number. Man said he was from Ryder Truck Lines . . . said he was calling—on behalf of the *US* gov'ment—to instruct ol' Howard that he needed to make our semi-trucks and flatbed trailers available, with drivers ready, to be gone for an *indefinite* length of time." He paused to let the news sink in. "Man said the trailers had to have steel floors and had to be a certain height from the ground . . . said Heidrich Citrus up the Trail was already in for three . . . said they expected Howard to be in for *five*! Well . . ." He tongued his toothpick to the other side. "Who the hell knows how *they* knew what kind of trucks we have . . . and exactly how many . . . but Monday morning, our five and Heidrich's three took off for *parts unknown*. By the looks of things, I figure they'll be rolling back by any day now. Appreciate your keeping an eye out."

Steve looked askance at Avery.

"True story, Sonny?" Avery asked.

Geiger removed his pick, stabbed it in the air for emphasis. "Yessiree Bob! And you heard about DefCon Two?"

"*Two?*" Steve was aghast.

"One phone call short of war," Geiger insisted. "And I guaran-damn-tee ya the marines'll take Castro down in no time a-tall," he added with a smug suck-kiss.

"Who told you?"

"Officer out at McCoy called Howard break-a-day this morning . . . said they were at DefCon Two, which means all aircrews are camped out on the tarmac . . . eating and sleeping under their planes, ready to take off at a moment's notice . . . asked if the base sent over a pickup, could we fill it with oranges for the boys stuck out under the wings? We had to roust a picking crew to grab some early tangerines . . . guy from the base just left with 'em 'fore I came over."

"DefCon Two," Steve said quietly, and turned to stare out the window.

Avery thought about all the fighters he'd seen parked wingtip-to-wingtip out at McCoy. He tried to imagine their crews—two to five men apiece—camped out on the tarmac. All were waiting for a war that, once started, would mean the end of everything. He wrapped up his untouched sandwich and dropped it back in his lunch pail.

JUST AS GEIGER LEFT, there was a rush of business at the pump and in the service bays. Sally Michaels, waitress at the Cassandra Hotel, a popular honky-tonk up the Trail, drove in on a flat tire with a now bent rim. Normally a Chatty Kathy, she stood outside the service bay, chain-smoking one Pall Mall after another, staring bleakly at the convoys rolling by.

Dragster Jimmy Cope rumbled in with his younger brother Jerry in tow behind him. Jerry had apparently bungled the installation of a new Hurst shifter in his '57 Chevy Bel Air. Jimmy smirked disgust. "I told him he was a fool to try and install it himself." Jerry shrugged sheepishly. "Kinda hopin' to race it Friday night." To which Jimmy added darkly, "If there *is* a Friday night."

Avery and Steve went through the motions, attempting to service their customers as if everything were normal. But the signs were everywhere that normal was on vacation: Car radios were tuned to tense-talking newsmen providing the latest non-update on the Soviet ships headed toward the US Navy's quarantine line; a sobering convoy of military ambulances and medical trucks slowed traffic on the Trail; and some kind of air maneuvers were being flown above the cloud cover.

Just after two, with no word from Sarah or Kitty, Avery began to wonder: Had *that* particular disaster been avoided? Or, if the two sisters *had* run into each other, what would happen next? It wouldn't be Sarah's style, he decided, to come to the station and confront him in front of Steve or anyone else. Like her mother, she abhorred a public scene. Most likely, she'd retreat to the house and wait till he got home. What Kitty's style was, he hadn't a clue.

He was desperately trying to decide what he would say to Sarah—

what *could* he say to her?—when he heard, behind the station, the startling clatter of an *empty* northbound train. Within minutes, a second train, also empty, followed.

Empty trains could mean only one thing: northbound shipping of Florida's commerce in cane sugar, citrus, vegetables, cattle, lumber, and phosphate had been suspended. The military now monopolized the rails.

Was a whole season's worth of work for south Florida's muck farmers—fighting weather, weeds, and whitefly to bring in a late crop of strawberries, tomatoes, snap beans, whatever—rotting on their loading docks for lack of transport? The trains were unavailable. Had the government commandeered their big trucks, too?

By three-fifteen, Steve had managed to unbend Sally's wheel rim and put on a new tire. And Avery had diagnosed the drag racer's problem, pulled a product code out of the Hurst catalog, and called the guy with the bad news.

"You did a great job putting in the wrong shifter. Hurst makes a special C-shaped version for the '57s—*C* for 'Chevy,' right?—so second and fourth gear don't get stuck under the bench seat. I can order the right one, but who's going to put it in? Me or you?"

"How 'bout the guy knows what he's doin'?" Jerry said.

Most days yes, Avery thought glumly, but not today.

After writing up the work ticket, he called Holler Chevy's parts desk and requested a runner first thing in the morning. Gas business remained brisk. Both he and Steve were out at the pumps when Father Thomas drove up with Emilio.

The priest had barely stopped the car when the teenager jumped out shouting, "The ships! The Soviet ships! They're turning around!"

"Just now on the news. Praise be to God!" the priest crowed.

The pair's excitement swept over Avery and Steve to the customers under the station canopy. "Wahoo!" The Johnson kid hung out of his family Dodge Dart's window and cheered. Plumber Bob Myers, pulling out onto the Trail, honked his horn in jubilation. Other cars at the intersection were doing the same.

Emilio's grin eclipsed his face as he shot out his hand to shake

Avery's, then Steve's, then, caught up in the excitement, Avery and Steve shook hands, while the priest's head bobbed in smiling benediction.

"Thank God," Avery murmured, flooded with relief.

"And the United States Navy," Steve added with a wink.

There was a ballooning sense of celebration as the foursome drifted into the office. "The Soviets turned tail and ran!" "Can you believe it?" "A miracle!"

"RC Colas for everyone!" Avery declared. As Steve went to grab them, Avery saw the priest's merry eyes narrow with concern. He turned to see why.

"San Cristóbal," Emilio whispered, holding *The New York Times* in trembling hands. *"Mi madre, mi abuelos en San Cristóbal."*

"But I thought she was in Pinar—what's its name—Pines by the River?"

"Pinar del Rio is both a town and a province," Thomas was explaining, the *Times* now in his hands. "Like New York, New York."

"We lived in town," Emilio said. "But after they put Papa in prison, Mama and I moved to my *abuelos'* . . . my grandparents' coffee farm in San Cristóbal."

"Your father . . . ?"

"In prison?"

"Who?" Steve demanded, thrusting a cola into Emilio's hand. "Who put your father in prison?"

"Fidel . . . ," Emilio said bleakly. "After Tereza was murdered."

"What?" Avery exclaimed.

His father in prison? Tereza—wasn't that his sister's name?—*murdered?* How was that possible? And how, Avery wondered, had the kid carried around such terrible things and never mentioned them?

Then again, he recalled, most of Emilio's stories had been about his childhood *before Fidel.* He'd mentioned his sister just the other day, hadn't he? When he asked Charlotte to the dance—hadn't he said he'd been her practice partner?

"Please tell us, son," the priest said gently, "what happened."

"Tereza . . ." Emilio's face was taut with pain. "There were only fourteen months between us, but she was the older one . . . and beautiful. Everyone said so. Her dream was to join the Ballet Nacional de Cuba. And she might have. . . ." His gaze dropped to the bottle in his hand. He rubbed his thumb over the small crown at the base of its logo.

"Last May . . . she was one month from graduating high school, and Fidel ordered all seniors into the country . . . to teach the *quajiros,* the poor farmers, how to read and write. National literacy, he said, was our *top* priority. Tereza was excited; she *wanted* to go. But Mama, and especially Papa, feared for her safety. 'You're naïve,' he argued, 'a complete innocent with no real-life experience.' They talked back and forth for many days. 'Twelve years in a Catholic school, all girls,' Papa said, 'and you've never known anything but *cariño,* your family's loving-kindness. Never been anywhere without a chaperone.' But Tereza insisted, 'All my friends are going! And besides, educating the poor is the *key* to Cuba's future.'

"Our parents were dead set against it. But when she asked me, I told her that if she wanted to go that badly, she *should* go. I told her, 'Those poor farmers would be *lucky* to have you as a teacher. . . .'"

"It's all right, son."

"Papa . . . Papa was a respected judge. He thought he had influence, so he filed an official protest on our behalf. But by then, Fidel had imposed Patria Potestad, the law that took away parents' right to decide things for their children and gave it to the state. So . . . when the official letter arrived telling her where to go, Tereza went.

"Because she had blue eyes, like me, the locals called her *la zafir,* the sapphire. On her third night away from home . . . someone came to her cabin and dragged her into the fields. She was . . ." His fingers tightened around the bottle neck in a two-handed fist. "Raped . . . beaten . . . and left to die in the dirt.

"The next day, two children playing in the canes found her body where it had been dumped in a ditch."

"My God!" Thomas exclaimed.

Steve leaned in to give Emilio's shoulder a slow, comforting squeeze.

"I am so sorry," Avery managed, sickened. It was a father's worst nightmare.

Emilio straightened. "I was at school. Not my old school—Fidel had closed the Catholic schools by then—I was at the state school when the *policia* came to tell my parents. They claimed later that Papa went berserk, that he threatened to kill Fidel. But it wasn't true. Mama said he told them *only* that Tereza's blood was on Fidel's hands. They branded him a counterrevolutionary and hauled him off to El Principe prison in Havana. Mama . . . she tried everything, called everyone we knew. But no one, not even his fellow judges, could help.

"It was three *months* before she was allowed to visit him. And the prison guards . . . They forced her to take off all her clothes, then searched her with their filthy hands for a concealed weapon. When she finally got in to see him, Papa was shrunken but alive, she said. He told her we should leave our house and go to her parents' plantation in San Cristóbal. She couldn't . . . she didn't have the heart to tell him we'd already been kicked out of our home so three other families could move in.

"It was my grandfather who insisted we talk to their priest about the Pedro Pans. He was a Jesuit from Spain. 'I know all about the Communists,' he told us.

"Six weeks later, I had my passport, my visa, and a seat on PanAm Four Forty-Two to Miami. I know Mama is still in San Cristóbal. But Papa, God willing . . ."

"God!" Avery was surprised by the brusqueness of his own voice. The words came out without thinking, without stopping. "God had *nothing* to do with this!"

Emilio's eyes flashed from Avery to the priest, whose white brows were drawn down in thought.

After a long moment, Thomas sighed. "Mr. Avery is right. God doesn't control evildoing. He can only provide comfort to those who find themselves caught in its path."

Avery's mind was a jumble of questions and concerns for Emilio's father in Castro's prison. And the boy's mother! He tried to picture her, kicked out of her home, returned to her parents' farm, grieving the murder of her only daughter and the imprisonment of her husband. Where on earth had she found the strength to put her only son on that plane?

His mind shifted to her present-day problems, what Sarah teasingly called his "Mr. Fix-It Mode." How big was San Cristóbal? Were their streets clogged with *Russian* convoys? Would she figure that, if we attacked, the Russian missile sites would be the first thing hit? Could she pack up her parents and go? But where? The whole island was maybe three-quarters the size of Florida. *The caves!* Emilio said once that the mountains were riddled with pirate caves. Would she . . .

The insistent ring of the gas bell announced the Dodge pickup pulling into the pumps. Avery, closest to the door, made a move to go.

"Please," Emilio said, setting his soda aside. "Let me." *Work,* his look said, *would be a relief.*

Avery watched him go. *And I thought I had problems.*

"Should I stay?" Thomas asked.

"No need, Padre," Steve said quietly.

"We'll look after him," Avery added.

It was a promise, he decided, not only to the priest but also to Emilio's parents, both of them trapped in the crosshairs of a confrontation that had the whole world holding its breath.

DISTRACTED BY A RUSH of customers, Avery got home after six. He had less than thirty minutes to shower, dress, eat, and get to the church for Wednesday-night Prayer Meeting, with choir practice and deacons' meeting after.

He'd been reluctant to leave Emilio alone (and just as reluctant to go home and face whatever awaited him there), but Steve had agreed to "drop by the station later with a couple of burgers" and hang out till closing.

In his neighborhood, the morning fog was long gone. But the sky remained milky, dulling Lake Silver to a gray slate.

Charlotte greeted him at the door with a grin, dressed oddly in pedal-pushers and high heels.

"Nice look," he told her.

"Shoe practice." She made a face. "Unfortunately, these things don't walk as good as they look!" she exclaimed, wobbling off.

Avery chuckled. Usually graceful in ballet flats, penny loafers, or majorette boots, his daughter in heels reminded him of a newborn foal trying to right itself on long legs and tender hooves.

"You'll get the hang of it," he called to her, then remembered, with a guilty chill, Kitty's high-heeled glide down the drive.

"Where's Mom?" he asked.

Charlotte turned, index finger over shhh-ing lips. "Resting," she said, then pressed the same finger to the place between her eyebrows where Sarah tended to get her headaches.

Avery gingerly opened the door to their bedroom, but Sarah wasn't there. He backtracked to the hall and slowly cracked the heavy door into the pitch-dark shelter. In the light from the hallway, he saw her outline on the nearest bed. One long forearm was laid protectively across her eyes. Her pale bent elbow was to the side, a single still wing. The shelter's normally musty smell was masked by a floral air freshener.

"Sarah," he said softly.

"Y-yes," she answered.

"Did I wake you? I'm sorry."

"No."

She said it without inflection, but he instantly feared the worst— Kitty's betrayal of his betrayal that morning. He moved through the darkness, along the edges of the slim wedge of light from the hall, to stand beside her. He heard her pained sigh.

"Bad, huh?"

"Terrible."

His natural inclination—to retreat and leave her be—was overrun by his worry all afternoon, his need to know what, if anything, had happened with Kitty, and what was next. He felt his heartbeat in his chest—so loud he feared she might hear it.

"When did it hit you?"

"'Round noon, I guess." Her voice was a weary whisper.

Did he dare hope . . . ? "You have to cancel the Cherry Plaza?"

"Yes, of course."

His anxiety all afternoon had been for nothing? He was off the hook? He bent his head, closed his eyes in relief. "Want me to call Doc Mike, ask him to come by?"

"Not tonight, thanks." At times like this, he knew, she craved darkness and quiet. As he moved toward the door, she called, "Wes?"

"Yes, darlin'?"

"Tell Malcolm I'm sorry."

"Sure thing. You rest now," he said gently, and let himself out.

In the shower, he lifted his inner elbow to his nose, sniffed the now faint scent of roses one last time, then soaped himself clean.

AT CHURCH, HE LET CHOIR director Malcolm Sears know that Sarah wouldn't be making choir practice.

"She's not the only one," Sears said, surveying the rather sparse crowd. "If it wasn't for the choir, I'd be home glued to my TV set like everyone else."

"Me, too," Avery told him.

Aware that the networks had promised coverage of the next wave of Soviet ships approaching the blockade, the pastor kept things short. Avery knew the Twenty-third Psalm by heart, but tonight its verses struck him differently than at any time before.

"Yea, though I walk through the valley of the shadow of death, I will fear no evil . . ."

How is it possible *not* to fear evil? With a monster like Castro jailing innocent people, and the world's superpowers poised on the brink of mutually assured destruction? When this very minute, less than ten miles away, flight crews were camped under fully loaded planes ready to start World War III at a moment's notice? When a brave young man's mother and grandparents could be among the first to die?

"*. . . for Thou art with me. Thy rod and Thy staff, they comfort me.*"

Seen a whole lot of rods and staffs passing by the station this week—no comfort to me at all. Was he a bad Christian for thinking these things?

"*Thou anointest my head with oil, my cup runneth over.*"

Right over the top, I'd say. The scalding guilt he'd resolved to set aside—at least for the night—flooded back.

"*Surely goodness and mercy shall follow me all the days of my life.*"

Or hours. Does God know how much time we have left?

"*And I shall dwell in the house of the Lord forever.*"

Hope to get there later rather than sooner.

As usual, the minister's remarks were followed by prayer requests from the congregation. Avery was struck by the ordinariness of the requests: for this person's mother who'd fallen and broken her hip, that one's husband who was in the hospital, that one's neighbor diagnosed with lung cancer. Finally, one woman asked a prayer for her nephew "on a ship at sea."

Avery considered standing and suggesting that "we all say a prayer for the President, our nation, and the world." But quite possibly, he decided, the Catholics had that one covered. Instead he said, "I have a young friend whose family is trapped in Castro's Cuba."

Pastor Billy Wigginthal pursed his lips, then raised a palm and intoned, "Let us pray. . . ."

Avery bowed his head, closed his eyes, and hoped that God was listening to the world's prayers for peace. Would He also hear one man's plea to *deliver me from megaton bombs and platinum-blond bombshells?*

8.

AVERY SAT ALONE AT THE KITCHEN DINETTE TRYING TO READ between the lines of the *Sentinel*'s upbeat coverage of yesterday's events: ARMS SHIPS APPARENTLY TURNED BACK. KHRUSHCHEV SEEKS SUMMIT TALK. A map showed the "Cuban Missile Sites" at San Cristóbal, Guanajay, Sagua la Grande, and Remedios. Inside, there were a few of the photos that had appeared in yesterday's *New York Times*. But as usual, there was no mention of the locally based U-2s, or of the US military's maximum DefCon Two readiness for all-out war. He scowled out the window at the fog creeping snail-like off the lake—not as thick as yesterday's but still an annoyance—when a sudden movement caught his eye.

It was a man—some kind of workman in blue jeans, shirt, cap, plus a wide leather tool belt—trundling a load of wooden stakes into Avery's backyard. What the Sam Hill? The guy walked right past the window like he owned the darn place!

Avery set down his coffee mug and strode to the back door. Mindful that Sarah was still in bed, he resisted the urge to yell from the steps. Instead, he walked out after the guy until he was close enough to ask, "Can I help you?"

"Nah," the guy called over his shoulder, "I got it." And continued on his way.

"Got *what*, I'd like to know."

At that, the guy stopped and turned. And Avery saw, for the first time, the logo on his shirt pocket for Bob's Pools & Igloos.

"Oh, hi," the guy said. "I'm here to stake out your igloo. Called your wife yesterday. She said to walk right in."

"*My* wife? Not possible."

"Well, sure, got the paperwork right here," the guy said. He turned back to the wheelbarrow, removed a file folder, walked up to where Avery was standing, and handed it over.

Avery glanced over the contract for "One airtight, watertight, radiation-tight Igloo Fallout Shelter" . . . color: pool blue . . . price: an astounding $1,474.83! . . . signed by: his neighbor Roger Stout.

"You got the wrong place. Roger Stout lives"—he pointed toward their shared hibiscus hedge—"thataway."

"Oh." The guy's face fell. "Next door, huh?"

"Yup," Avery said, returning the paperwork. What in the world was Roger thinking?

The guy seemed to scan the gentle green slope of Avery's backyard with regret. "Sorry about that," he said.

Watching the fellow collect his load and roll back the way he'd come, Avery wondered, And what if I wasn't here to stop him? He shook his head. Fifteen hundred bucks for a gol-durn igloo? Roger's nuts!

Back inside the kitchen, he packed his lunch and checked the clock. He'd planned to stop by the cottage—*alone* today—to check the whole house, put up the FOR RENT sign, and, he'd noticed yesterday, run the mower over the front and back lawns. Rather than disturb Sarah with his good-bye, he left her a note: *Good morning. Please call me when you're up. Love, W.*

At the cottage, he checked all the rooms to make sure that Marjorie had left things shipshape. She had. On his way out back, he stopped beside the kitchen table. Here, right here, was where they'd stood, and right there by the door was where she'd . . . You're nuts, too, he scolded himself. This missile business seems to have knocked the whole world off its rocker.

Outside, he pulled out the mower, checked the tank, and gave the back lawn a quick once-over.

Beneath the window of the master bedroom, he stopped to inhale the heady scent of the gardenia bushes in bloom and to smile at the memory of what young Charlotte had always called her "favorite story."

How many times had he or Sarah had to tell it to her? How, after bailing out of his B-29, he'd written a thank-you note to Inspector 833 for the rubber raft that saved his life. How she'd replied, "You're most welcome," and shyly, or slyly, provided her home address. How Avery had responded with an eager letter of his own. How they'd fallen in love, not at first sight, but with no sight at all until Avery arrived at the Tuscaloosa train station in his airman's uniform to see Sarah in her dark coat and single gardenia corsage. How exactly one year—to the *very* day!—after they married, Charlotte had arrived as planned.

Avery frowned at the only part of the story that wasn't true. Their marriage was, in fact, the exact same age as Charlotte. Poor Kitty had gone into labor in the middle of the night before the wedding. Charlotte was born at the moment Avery and Sarah stood at the altar exchanging their vows. The next day, they'd taken her on their Florida honeymoon. They'd never really been without her.

Inhaling the rich perfume of the gardenias, Avery pictured newlywed Sarah pulling him to the window to point out the bushes she'd planted outside their bedroom. "Seven of them, see?" she'd said. A baker's half dozen—which, including Charlotte, was the number of children they'd planned. God, we were young, Avery thought, remembering his gawky, ham-handed farmer's passion for his elegant young wife. How he couldn't believe his incredible luck that *she* was actually *his*.

In public, Sarah was as smoothly polished as one of those glossy green buds. But privately—in those days, a look, a nod would do it— Sarah unfurled: buttons, hairpins, limbs flung wide across the bed; skin as petal-soft and pale white as those blooms.

"The scent of gardenias," Avery confessed to her once, "sets off a craving in me I can hardly stand. I want to know every inch of you, like a bee knows a blossom."

"More like a horny toad knows a sow bug." She'd laughed, hooking long legs around his hips. She had a low, throaty laugh back then, indulgent and inviting. When was the last time he'd heard her laugh like that?

For some reason, they'd never gotten around to transplanting the gardenias to the new house. Their larger yard at the lake had every-thing else—azaleas, camellias, hibiscus, poinsettias, bougainvilleas, flame vine to burn—but not a gardenia anywhere.

What would she think, he wondered, if he transplanted these bushes for her? Would she take it kindly, as a remembrance of their earlier, happier days? Or would she view it—like her abdominal scar—as a too painful reminder that the biggest of their plans had gone awry?

Avery shoved the mower around to the front. What did it mean, for instance, that after all their years of lovemaking, she'd suddenly refused him with, "Oh, Wes, what's the point?" The *point*?

Now mowing the strip of lawn beside the driveway, Avery passed the place where, this time yesterday, Kitty had parked her Imperial. It was an easy bet, he decided, that Kitty had roses—row after row of them—outside *her* bedroom window. But unlike gardenias, he real-ized, roses have thorns, don't they? Like cats have claws. And weren't three ex-husbands proof of that?

"How's it going?"

Steve, as usual, updated Avery in as few words as possible.

"Shifter's here. Lube job there. Figure we're outta ethyl by noon. Oh"—his eyelids flickered annoyance—"preacher came by, whinin' for a fill-up. Told him he'd have to talk to you."

Avery helped himself to a cup of station coffee.

"Nothin' in the *Slantinel*, as usual. Don't mind—" Steve peered across the street, felt for his Camels. "—like to check the Rexall, see if the *Times* is in."

"Fine by me," Avery said, wincing at his first sip. Steve's coffee was navy-style. Strong enough to jump into your cup, thick and black enough to grease a ship shaft.

As Steve walked off to cross the Trail, Avery scanned the fuel chart. Each morning, whoever opened the station stuck the tanks with the fuel gauge and recorded the results. Even with the five-gallon limit, business was up 74 percent. At the current clip, he figured, without more gas from the depot, we're out of business sometime tomorrow. Or Saturday at the latest.

Avery dialed the depot in Tampa.

"Join the crowd, Wes," the dispatcher told him. "Every Texaco on the Trail is hollering for fuel. We got a ship from Port Arthur past due since Monday, but the navy's jamming the lanes on both ends. Don't know what to tell you."

Avery hung up, frustrated, just as Pastor Billy Wigginthal wheeled his frost-white, three-year-old Rambler wagon (a gift from the congregation) into the pumps.

"Morning, Brother Wes," Wigginthal called cordially.

"Reverend," Avery replied warily, noting the three suits in plastic Parisian Dry Cleaners bags hanging in the rear window. At last night's deacons' meeting, Wigginthal had announced his need to visit his ailing mother in Atlanta this weekend.

"In a bit of a fix here," Wigginthal said.

Avery was silent. Wigginthal was the kind of guy who was always "in a bit of fix." Enthusiastic, Sears-catalog-handsome, charismatic with the young people and old ladies, Wigginthal had been a welcome change from his fire-and-brimstone predecessor. Early on, however, the young preacher's constant requests—for a new sound system, new aisle carpeting, new choir robes to match the new aisle color—had revealed a lack of financial prudence.

In fact, Wigginthal was the reason the church fathers had pressed Avery into service as a deacon. "We need a man with a head for figures, Wes. Someone who can manage the church budget, reel young Billy in." Avery had reeled; but over the past six-plus years, Wigginthal had shown himself to be a slippery fish—with a voracious appetite in a variety of areas. Newlywed when they arrived, his wife was now expecting their fifth child.

"My poor mother," Wigginthal continued. "I talked to her on the phone last night and she sounded so bad, I decided to fly instead of drive. Called Herndon first thing this morning and they told me the military's controlling air traffic. Most flights in and out of Orlando are either way late or outright canceled."

"You don't say." Could that be true?

"So I gotta drive. But the tank's half-empty. I really need a fill-up."

Avery crossed his arms in front of his chest. The drive to Atlanta was 438 miles straight north. He did the math out loud. "You got a twenty-gallon tank half-full. That's ten gallons. Another five'll give you fifteen. At 33 miles per gallon open road, that's 495 miles. Get you there with a couple of gallons to spare."

Wigginthal screwed up his face in protest. "But Nashville's nearly seven hun . . ."

Avery stood, statue-still, while the preacher caught himself in his own lie. Nashville, the freshly pressed suits, the sick-mother excuse all added up to one thing: Pastor Billy had the seven-year-itch for a larger congregation and this weekend was, undoubtedly, a new church tryout in Tennessee.

"Well." Wigginthal dropped his eyes and his chin, cleared his throat. "When you put it that way, I guess five gallons'll do just fine."

"Anything more," Avery remarked pleasantly, "I'm sure you can trust the Good Lord to provide." Privately, he had no quarrel with an ambitious preacher, but a lying one was on his own.

WHEN STEVE RETURNED, CIGARETTE in one hand, New York paper in the other, Avery had phoned Cliff Davis, a fellow Rotarian and travel agent, to confirm Wigginthal's claim.

"Not just Orlando, Wes. The FAA's either canceled or delayed all civilian flights south of the twenty-ninth parallel—bottom two-thirds of the state. Cruise ship departures, too," Davis said. "Till this thing blows over, I'm outta business."

"Come tomorrow, I'm right behind you," Avery told him, hanging up. With the navy blocking the Gulf shipping lanes, the army commandeering the railways and overtaking the highways, and now the air force shutting down the sky, state commerce was in free fall with no chute. Like it or not, we're in the middle of an armed camp, he decided. It was starting to feel like Tinian Island, which he preferred not to think about. He'd seen more than a few airmen go nuts on that island from all the worry, the uncertainty, the . . .

Steve was glaring at him with belligerent eyes.

"What?" Avery asked.

"Saw the preacher come and go."

"Yup."

"Get what he wanted?"

"Nope."

"Good" was all Steve said, heading out to his service bay.

Avery turned to stare out the window, chewing his lip. In some ways, you couldn't pick two people more un-alike than his best friend and his wife. Yet they were identical in confusing what was to him the difference between a simple kindness and a softhearted, or soft-headed, gullibility. To Avery, the difference between helping out a person in genuine need, like Marjorie Cook, for instance, and playing the patsy for a lying Billy Wigginthal was night and day.

And where does giving Kitty what she asked for fit in? the goad inside his head wanted to know. Avery shook off the question. The world was hardly black and white. And this week especially, every-thing seemed a different shade of gray.

BY TWELVE-THIRTY, STEVE had finished his lube job and stood, half watching the pumps, half reading the *Times,* while Avery worked under the lift, wrestling the Chevy's new shifter rods and side arms into place.

"Fella named Lippmann says here, only three ways to get those missiles outta Cuba," Steve was saying. "Invade and take 'em out. Blockade and starve 'em out. Or, according to him, sit down with the Soviets and trade 'em out—their missiles outta Cuba for our missiles outta Turkey. What d'ya think?"

"We've got missiles in Turkey?" Avery asked.

"Says here we do."

"Good old-fashioned horse trade, tit for tat? Works for me. Think Khrushchev would go for it?"

"Think he'd rather have a war?"

Under the Chevy's carriage, Avery flashed on the two faces of the Soviet premier, Nikita Khrushchev. On one hand, there was the Krazy Komrade, the short, fat cartoon Communist who pounded his shoe on the table and taunted Americans, "We will *bury* you!" On the other, there was the grinning Nikita, the former peasant farmer who'd toured Iowa a few years back, shucking ears of American seed corn. Was Khrushchev, whose farmer's roots lay deep in Ukrainian soil, capable of pushing the button that would destroy the earth?

Of course, you were a farmer, too, back in '45, he chided himself, and more than willing to help firebomb over two hundred thousand Japanese to smithereens.

Beneath the Chevy, Avery shuddered. If Khrushchev is anywhere near as obsessed with winning as we were, we'll all wind up burned to a crisp.

By twelve forty-five, their supply of Fire Chief gas was gone. Steve offered to finish up the shifter's boot while Avery got out the brush and red paint to add OUT OF ETHYL to the A-frame signs at both entrances. While he was at it, he created two more sets of signs. One for tomorrow afternoon:

CLOSED

3–6 PM

FOR HOMECOMING

PARADE

And a second set for Saturday night:

CLOSED

AFTER 6 PM

FOR HOMECOMING.

GO EAGLES!!!

As he spread the signs over the tire racks to dry, his thoughts meandered from how to steer clear of Kitty at Friday's parade to Charlotte and Emilio's weekend plans.

"How'd it go with Emilio last night?" he asked Steve.

"Pretty down at the mouth till your little girl showed up. Perked him right up, I'll tell ya."

"Charlotte?"

"Brought Leo an album she found at the record shop."

"Elvis?"

"Nah. You didn't hear the story?"

Avery shook his head. Charlotte had been deep in her homework when he'd returned from church and in a rush, as always, this morning.

"I guess most of the guys out at the camp are pretty homesick. Younger ones especially miss their mamas. So at lights-out, they play a record over the loudspeaker, some quartet—like the Cuban Andrews Sisters—that reminds them of their mamas and their aunties back home, helps 'em go to sleep. But last week, some harebrain broke the record."

"And Charlotte found a replacement?"

"She did. Leo was thrilled."

"I bet he was." Avery felt pride swell his chest. He wished Old Pa had lived to know Charlotte, to see the kindness that was so like his in her.

With suddenly watery eyes, he checked the time. One o'clock already and no word yet from Sarah? Was it possible she was still in bed? He considered calling her but resisted, not wanting to disturb her.

By two, however, with still no word from her, he told Steve he needed to run home for a few minutes, "make sure she's okay."

The kitchen was exactly as Avery had left it, coffee mug in the sink, note on the counter. No sign that Sarah had been up.

Gently, he opened the door to the shelter and, in the shadows, saw that she was in the same position as the night before: toes up, one pale forearm folded wing-like across her face. He padded closer, holding his breath in an effort to hear hers.

Nothing.

He was just about to reach out and touch her when she murmured, "I'm okay."

"Glad to hear it," he said softly, exhaling relief.

"Just tired is all."

"Catching up on your sleep?"

"Too tired to sleep."

"Want me to call Doc Mike, have him drop by on his way home?"

"No," she whispered, stiffening with resistance.

"Wouldn't want you to miss the parade tomorrow. Anything *I* can do?"

"While ago, I got up for the bathroom. Charlotte called. She forgot her baton for practice, needs it dropped off at the band room."

"Before school's out?" Avery eyed the bedside clock. He'd have to hurry.

"Yes."

What would she have done if I hadn't come home? he wondered. It wasn't like Sarah to miss a commitment.

"I better get going then," he told her. "Baton in her room?"

"Prob'ly."

"Back at six. Seven at the latest."

Wearily, her lips formed the words *Thank you*, without a sound.

WHEELING INTO THE SCHOOL's side driveway, Avery pulled up to the curb nearest the band room. Through the open windows, he heard them tuning up the Eagles fight song for tonight's homecoming bonfire by the lake. (Aptly named, the Edgewater campus was wedged between waterfront homes on Lake Silver's northeast shore.)

He parked, grabbed Charlotte's baton, and strode toward the band room at the back of the school auditorium.

Despite the band music, the rest of the campus appeared quiet and calm. *Normal* was the word in Avery's head when a sudden loud crash—the heavy thud of metal smashing metal, shattering glass—sent him running. A second crash was accompanied by loud cries and yelling. By the time he rounded the corner of the Admin Building, he was holding Charlotte's twirling baton like a club.

Myriad explanations—a car wreck, a riot, some sort of uprising or vandalism—came to mind. But none of these came close to the scene that he confronted.

A behemoth red-jerseyed lineman, surrounded by several brawny teammates, swiveled his hips, hauled a long-handled sledgehammer high over his head, then slammed it down, clobbering the front fender of an old clunker—a '47 Ford coupe spray-painted orange and black, the colors of Winter Park High, homecoming's opposing team. Off to one side, two cheerleaders whooped beside a Key Club sign inviting students to SMASH THE WILDCATS!!! 10 CENTS A WHACK, 3 FOR A QUARTER.

Avery came to a standstill, his heart hammering. Thanks to the lineman's hit, the coupe's curved grille, which had always reminded him of a friendly face, was now pinched into a permanent grimace.

He turned and wiped one sweaty palm then the other on his pant leg and retraced his path to the open band room door.

Band director Charles Beauchamp stood up front on the podium while his students packed up their sheet music, instruments, and schoolbooks in anticipation of the final bell.

"Ah, Mr. Avery," Beauchamp hailed, and looked behind him as if expecting someone else. "But where is Mrs. Avery?"

"Home resting," Avery replied.

The bell rang. "Beware the thundering herd," Beauchamp warned, nudging Avery inside his office as a crush of students rushed past, flailing a band's worth of cumbersome black instrument cases.

Beauchamp stood at the door reminding the kids: "See you tonight. Concert positions. Six forty-five *sharp*."

Watching Beauchamp, Avery thought the man's longish flop of hair, fine animated features, and dramatic gestures were all a bit over the top. *But of course,* he heard Sarah's voice inside his head, *he's a musical genius!*

"Hey, Mr. A, is that Charlotte's baton?" Charlotte's friend Brenda called. "I'll take it. We're meeting on the field."

"Thanks," Avery said, handing it over.

"See ya tonight, Mr. Bo!"

After they were gone in a swirl of skirts and ponytails, Beauchamp turned to Avery, beaming. "It's a banner year for the band, Mr. Avery. A *banner* year!"

Avery had heard that Beauchamp was busting his director's buttons over the fact that this year's Homecoming Court, normally dominated by cheerleaders, included two of the band's majorettes—Charlotte, of course, and squad captain Barbara Everly.

"Majorettes triumphant!" Beauchamp was saying. "This could be our best homecoming *ever*. Assuming"—his eyes flickered concern—"there *is* one."

"Well . . . ," Avery replied, eager to be on his way.

"Before you go . . ." Beauchamp riffled through the mess on his desk. "Last week, Mrs. Avery and I were discussing contraltos. Turns out the great Sigrid Onégin is a mutual favorite." He located a record album and held it reverently against his chest. "Do you know her?"

Avery eyed the red operatic album cover—*Prima Voce?*—then shook his head. Although Sarah often played classical recordings at home, and there were some he enjoyed, his tastes ran more to Hank Williams, Patsy Cline, and the Grand Ole Opry.

"Too bad," Beauchamp said, handing it over. "Dame Onégin's version of Bach's 'Erbarme dich'? Sublime! The woman had a *three-octave* range," he enthused, "and her *trills*? Phenomenal!"

"I'll be sure to tell Sarah," Avery said awkwardly.

"No need, I put in a note," Beauchamp said, smiling.

Without the din of the kids, Beauchamp's office had grown uncomfortably quiet. Avery palmed the album and got the heck out of there.

Driving back to the station, he felt again the widening gap between himself and others. Here, in the heart of town, things seemed calm, eerily so. People waved, smiled, and called out a friendly "Afternoon, Wes!," as they might on any ordinary day.

Insulated from the convoys on the Trail, the massive shipments rolling by on the rails, and local news sanitized by the *Sentinel,* were they unaware, untroubled by the events unfolding before his very eyes? Or were they hiding their fears same as he was?

The past week's day-by-day revelations, the constant hydraulic shifts from shock and disbelief to dread and outright dismay—plus his nagging guilt over the whole Kitty thing—were becoming corrosive. Trepidation bubbled up in his gut like ground crude.

Am I overreacting?

But hadn't he learned, at the tender age of ten, that life could turn on a dime? Or, in his father's case, the failure of a six-cent extension screw?

Throughout the war, he'd carried the two pieces of the broken screw in a leather pouch in his pocket: a reminder that a single moment's carelessness could alter everything. He'd forgotten that he'd shown it to Kitty all those years ago; but had been pleased that she remembered. And he wished he'd talked to her more about the larger picture.

As an army nurse, had she seen, as he had in the air force, that the actions of their own forces could be as dangerous as any enemy's? That within every massive military operation, there was the inevitable FUBAR—somebody's screwup that sent things Fucked Up Beyond All Recovery. It was so prevalent in the navy, Steve said once, that they had their own term: BOHICO, for Bend Over, Here It Comes. Whatever its name, Avery couldn't escape the feeling that disaster was out there, waiting to happen. Kitty must have felt it, too. Or why else would she be here?

The sun, missing for two days, had finally managed to burn a hole through the steel-gray cloud cover. The sky—what he could see of it anyway—was chicken-wired by dozens of feathering contrails from the constant maneuvers out of McCoy.

Wasn't that crisscrossed patch of blue *proof* that he wasn't overreacting? He hadn't *imagined* those jet trails, or the U-2s, or the convoys, or the barely camouflaged flatcars, or DefCon *Two!* Others might be ignorant or oblivious, but Avery could *see* with certainty that the US military was in full readiness to make the ultimate

FUBAR—war with the Soviets—a reality. Surely, somebody some-where was considering alternatives?

Hungry for news, he dialed on the truck radio. A report in prog-ress said something about US ambassador Adlai Stevenson and a special session of the United Nations Security Council in New York. Feeling the catch of some distant gear urging him on, Avery gunned the truck toward the station.

STEVE HAD MOVED THE TELEVISION out of the office and onto the workbench in his service bay. He stood watching, one leg up on a rung of the work stool, bent elbow atop bent knee. His eyes flickered from the screen to Avery. He made a face, ripe with disgust.

"What'd I miss?" Avery asked.

"Buncha Russian horseshit."

On television, America's Adlai Stevenson abruptly set down his earphones, swept off his glasses, and shot the Soviet representative an angry glare. His voice, when he spoke, rang out with simmering in-dignation.

"I want to say to you, Mr. Zorin, that I don't have your talent for ob-fuscation, for distortion, for confusing language, and for doubletalk. And I must confess to you that I'm glad I don't."

Steve's look queried Avery. "He just call that suckbag a liar?"

"Yup."

Stevenson continued. *"But if I understood what you said, you said that my position had changed, that today I was defensive because we didn't have the evidence to prove our assertions that your Government had in-stalled long-range missiles in Cuba. Well, let me say something to you, Mr. Ambassador—we do have the evidence. We have it, and it's clear and in-controvertible. And let me say something else—those weapons must be taken out of Cuba."*

"Damn straight," Steve agreed.

At the double *ding* of the gas bell, both men turned to check the pumps. It was Father Thomas, driving through to deliver Emilio. He waved from behind the wheel as Emilio sprinted in.

Steve stood up, offered Emilio the stool.

Emilio hesitated, torn between the desire to watch and the need to change into his uniform.

"Sit," Avery said. "This is important."

Stevenson had quickened his pace. "*. . . while we're asking questions, let me ask you*"—he jabbed a finger in Zorin's direction—"*why your Government—your Foreign Minister—deliberately, cynically deceived us about the nuclear build-up in Cuba.*

"*The other day, Mr. Zorin, I remind you that you didn't* deny *the existence of these weapons. Instead, we heard that they had suddenly become* defensive *weapons. But today—again, if I heard you correctly—you now say they don't* exist, *or that we haven't* proved *they exist?*

"*All right, sir. Let me ask you one simple question: Do you, Ambassador Zorin, deny that the USSR has placed and is placing medium- and intermediate-range missiles and sites in Cuba? Yes or no?*"

Avery heard Emilio's quick intake of breath. He felt his own anger rise at Zorin's infuriating grin, his dramatic fumbling for his earphones.

Stevenson bore in like an auger. "*Don't wait for the translation.* Yes or no?"

The council chambers erupted in nervous laughter. Zorin grasped his microphone, yammering in Russian. A translator spoke over him: "*I am not in an American courtroom, sir, and therefore I do not wish to answer a question that is put to me in the fashion in which a prosecutor does. In due course, sir, you will have your reply. Do not worry.*"

Avery felt Stevenson's fury. "*You are in the court of world opinion right* now *and you can answer yes or no. You have denied that they exist. I want to know if you—if this—if I've understood you correctly.*"

Zorin grumbled in Russian, his tone chiding. Tense seconds later, the translator explained, "*Sir, will you please continue your statement. You will have your answer in due course.*"

The Security Council chairman intervened, "*Mr. Stevenson, would you continue your statement, please? You will receive the answer in due course.*"

Avery held his breath. Don't let this SOB off the hook!

Stevenson reared back. *"I am prepared to wait for my answer until hell freezes over, if that's your decision! And I'm also prepared to present the evidence in this room!"*

"Yes!" Steve hissed, punching his fist into his open palm.

Emilio frowned, looked to Avery. "Hell freezes over? What does that mean?"

"As long as it takes," Avery translated.

On screen, Stevenson signaled an aide, who produced two large easels and a stack of poster-boarded photographs.

". . . in view of his statements and the statements of the Soviet Government," Stevenson was saying, *". . . denying the existence or any intention of installing such weapons in Cuba, I am going to make a portion of the evidence available right now."*

The gas bell, the arrival of a gray Renault, made Emilio jump.

"Stay," Steve ordered. "I'll get 'em," he added, striding out.

"The first of these exhibits," Stevenson continued, *"shows an area north of the village of Candelaria, near San Cristóbal . . ."*

"San Cristóbal!" Emilio shot to his feet.

". . . The first photograph shows the area in late August 1962. It was then, if you can see from where you are sitting, only a peaceful countryside."

"My grandfather's farm!" Emilio exclaimed, pointing to the top left of the picture. But just then, the camera zoomed in and shifted right. The teenager turned to Avery, wild-eyed, then snapped back to Stevenson's explanation.

"The second photograph shows the same area one day last week. A few tents and vehicles had come into the area, new spur roads had appeared, the main road had been improved. The third photograph, taken only twenty-four hours later, shows facilities for a medium-range missile battalion installed. There are tents for four or five hundred men. At the end of the new spur road, there are seven 1,000-mile missile trailers. There are four launcher-erector mechanisms for placing these missiles in erect firing position. This missile is a mobile weapon, which can be moved rapidly from one

place to another. It is identical with the 1,000-mile missiles which have been displayed in Moscow parades. All of this, I remind you, took place in twenty-four hours.

"*The second exhibit shows three successive photographic enlargements of another missile base of the same type in the area of San Cristóbal. These enlarged photographs clearly show six of these missiles on trailers and three erectors.*"

Abruptly, Emilio slumped back down onto the stool.

Avery searched for something to say—some word of comfort, an expression of hope or confidence—but his mind was blank. He reached out and laid a steadying hand on the youth's shoulder. Together they watched in silence as Stevenson moved through the rest of his exhibits. There were an unlucky thirteen Soviet sites in Cuba. So far.

"*We now know the* facts, *and so do you, sir, and we are ready to talk about them. Our job here is not to score debating points. Our job, Mr. Zorin, is to save the peace. And if you are ready to try, we are.*"

Emilio, Avery noticed, had sweated through the white shirt of his school uniform. The boy rose unsteadily to his feet, his face ashen. "I'll change now," he said, his voice ragged with emotion.

At the bench, Steve was packing up to go. He turned to Avery, moved his mouth around his thoughts, but said nothing. Avery understood. Neither one of them had believed that Stevenson had it in him. But the old man had acquitted himself superbly.

Hope, like a spidery filament, hung in the air between them, too fragile for words.

THROUGHOUT THE AFTERNOON, business was brisk.

"More work means less time to think," Emilio said stoically. Still, the worry rimming his eyes and the weighted slope of his slim shoulders belied his words.

Out front, Avery queried longtime customer Clyde Williams, "You hear Stevenson at the UN?"

"Pretty good job, considerin' Adlai's an appeaser from way back,"

Williams pronounced. "Castro ain't nothin' but a Minnie the Moocher, and an ungrateful one at that! And Khrushchev needs to learn you don't play possum with the US of A. All this pussyfootin' around. If we know where they've got those missiles, I say, Bombs away! Let's go get 'em! Then send in the marines to mop up. It'd be all-over-but-the-shoutin' by middle of next week."

"But . . ." Avery was dumbstruck. He felt himself flush red. "What about the local Cubans? The ones who are still there, stuck with Castro's boot on their neck? And what if our bombers miss one of the sites and one of their missiles gets through? What then?"

Williams narrowed his eyes. "FUBAR," he said softly. His look was that of a man who'd calculated the risks and judged them acceptable. Avery resisted the sudden, savage urge to put a fist upside Williams's fat, idiotic head.

He was still mulling over the exchange, wondering how many others in high and low places felt the same way Williams did, when the phone next to the register rang.

"Orange Town Texaco. Wes speaking."

"Dad?"

"Hey, kiddo. What's up? Why are you whispering?"

"You think Mom's all right?"

Avery bowed his head and softened his tone. "She still in bed?"

"Yeah. Says she's too tired to get up. How can she be tired when she's been in bed all day?"

"I don't know, Kitten. I was thinking, if she wasn't better by tonight, I'd give Doc Mike a call."

"I don't think you should wait, Dad."

BY THE TIME MIKE MARTELL arrived at the front door, the homecoming bonfire had been lit across the lake. Its flames, mirrored at the water's edge, seemed to pulse in time with the urgent thrum of the Eagles' fight song. Avery had asked Sarah if she'd like to join him on the back porch to watch. But, wearily, she'd declined. *Prefer the dark,* she'd mouthed.

"Evening, Doc," Avery said, stepping aside, inviting Martell in. Like Charlotte earlier, he found himself whispering, conscious of not wanting to disturb Sarah. "Really appreciate your coming."

"No problem." Martell waved off his thanks with a finely trimmed hand; his deep-set eyes scanned the living room for his patient. "Still in bed then?"

"Yes."

"Since . . ."

"Yesterday noon."

"With no sleep?"

"That's what she says."

"Don't mind, like to talk to her alone first."

"Of course." Avery led him into the hall. At the middle room's entrance, he knocked softly.

"Sarah?" He saw her wince at the shaft of light falling across the bed. "Mike's here."

Inside, Martell turned on the overhead light, and Sarah moaned.

"I'm sorry," he said, "but I can't examine you in the dark."

Martell moved a folding metal chair to the side of the bed, sat down, put his leather bag on the floor, and took her wrist. As Avery retreated, he heard Martell ask, "So tell me, Sarah, what's going on?"

Eager for an explanation, Avery lingered in the hallway.

"My headache," he heard her say. "It seems a bit better but . . . somehow I feel worse. And I haven't slept in . . . I don't know how long."

"Can you sit up?" There were the sounds of Martell opening his bag, removing small instruments, and instructing her to "Look here," "Now your ears," and "Say ahhh."

After a moment, Martell said, "Check your glands?" and "Is the pain any different? A different place?"

"Not so much pain anymore as a kind of heavy . . . sadness. Sorrow, really."

Avery heard him pick up something else—a stethoscope, he guessed—and ask her to cough. "Again, please . . . and once more."

"I've been lying here thinking . . . wondering . . ."

"About?"

"Well, I need to ask you something . . ." Her voice quavered. Avery strained to hear. ". . . about the hysterectomy?"

"What about it?"

"I never understood. . . . Nobody ever explained to me why . . . why, when the ectopic pregnancy was on one side, in one tube, right?"

"Yes," Martell said.

"Why not . . . well, why not just take out that one tube and leave the other? Why take out both plus everything else?"

"Well . . ." The metal chair creaked as the doctor sat back.

"It doesn't make any sense to me."

"Well." Martell cleared his throat. "As I recall, you'd been through all those—was it four?—miscarriages."

"Five."

"Okay, five, plus the ectopic. You were hemorrhaging badly and in so much pain—and you did have a healthy child at home—it just seemed like the right thing. . . ."

"But what if . . ." Sarah was pressing him, her tone increasingly urgent. "You *knew* I wanted another child. Wes wanted a son. So why not . . . ?"

"Well . . . uhmm." Martell began to quibble but abruptly stopped. Avery could only imagine Sarah's look—the one that said she was not about to be put off. "We did consider saving the other side, but with your history . . ."

"Did you . . . did you discuss it with Wes?"

"Not as I recall," Martell said. "The surgeon and I talked and, well, it was sort of an executive operating room decision."

"For *you* . . . ," she said suddenly, hotly. "For you, it was an *executive* decision? For me . . ." Avery stiffened at her muffled sob. "For me . . . ," she said in a pained whisper, "it was the death of hope."

"Oh, Sarah . . ."

"And I ask you," she pressed. "How am I to go on? How am I to live . . . without hope?"

Avery heard a movement. Was the doctor taking her hand? "Are you sure . . . ," Martell asked, "this isn't about Charlotte, her getting ready to go off to college? It's a common malady these days. 'Empty nest syndrome,' they call it."

For a long moment, Avery heard nothing. Then his wife sighed, and said, "I am too"—something—"for this world."

"Oh, now, that's no way to talk," Martell replied quickly. "Obviously, you're overtired, and in need of some serious sleep. I have something for that."

As the doctor rummaged through his bag, Avery stepped away, into the living room, then out onto the back porch. Across the lake, the high school's bonfire was raging at the water's edge. He could just make out the band in neat concert positions off to one side; the cheerleaders whirling in formation on the other; with the football team, in red-and-white jerseys, assembled in between.

Somewhere over there, Charlotte was in her Sunday best, a red knit dress with large white buttons, waiting with the other girls in the Homecoming Court. At some point, after they were introduced, she'd said, each girl would toss a ceremonial log onto the fire.

"Sounds like fun," he'd told her.

"Sounds like Lamesville to me," she'd retorted. "But it's part of the deal, apparently."

But as the bonfire flames leaped higher and higher, their reflection like fiery tongues licking the lake's surface, as the cries of the crowd for an Eagles victory rose to a roar, Avery couldn't help but wonder: How could two people share the same experience yet see it so differently?

For him, the night of Sarah's hysterectomy began with the inexplicable sound of suffering, an anguished animal-like cry that, in the first few moments, he thought was a doe or a fawn caught in a hunter's steel trap. Rolling out of bed, he followed it to the bathroom, where he was shocked to find her doubled over on the floor in a spreading puddle of blood. Her face was deathly white, her eyes glazed with fear and pain. Stunned, he'd run to call the doctor, then rushed back to wrap her in blankets and gently, quickly, carry her to the car.

He'd been barely aware of Charlotte slipping like a shadow into the backseat. In fact, after the frantic drive to the hospital emergency room, one hand on the wheel, the other on Sarah's bent-over back urging her to hold on, he was surprised to hear Charlotte exclaim, "There's Doc Mike, Dad, beside the gurney!" Odd word, *gurney;* he'd wondered how she knew it.

They waited for hours, unable or unwilling to put the worst of their fears into words, until finally Doc Mike appeared, exhausted but upbeat. "She was hemorrhaging badly. It was touch and go for a while, but she's fine now. She's going to be just fine." Avery had hugged the man and thanked him for saving Sarah's life. In his mind, that's what the hysterectomy was—a lifesaver.

But for her, it was "the death of hope"?

No *hope?* He'd been stunned to hear her say it. Yet hard on the heels of his surprise came the aching memory of the one and only time they'd talked about it.

"Are you . . . aren't you sad about this?" she'd asked him, in the hospital while she was still recovering.

"Well, of course I am, darlin'," he'd told her. He would have loved a son. "But isn't the important thing that you're okay and we still have Charlotte?" His attempt at optimism had triggered a bout of bitter weeping. *Children of our own* was a dream they'd both shared since the beginning. He'd done his best to comfort her, but to no avail. He remembered wondering, How do you grieve a dream?

And for how long? he asked himself now.

"Ahem." Martell stood at the kitchen door.

"Doc." Avery turned awkwardly. "Get you something to drink? Water? A soda?"

"No, thanks."

Something in the doctor's manner had the whiff of bad news. Avery braced himself for it. "What do you think?" he asked quietly.

Martell took off his glasses and tucked them into his shirt pocket. Without them, his face looked oddly undressed. He pinched the bridge of his nose between his eyes then said, "Neurasthenia."

"Nure-azz-what?"

"Nervous exhaustion. Sarah's extremely overwrought. Hanging on by a thread, I'd say . . . on the verge, if we're not careful"—his naked look admonished Avery—"of some sort of breakdown."

"Breakdown?" The word was incomprehensible. "How? Why?"

Martell spread out both palms. "You tell me. . . ."

"Well . . ." Avery was grasping for an explanation. "It's been a crazy week, that's for sure—the Civil Defense show, all this business over Cuba, plus homecoming. . . ."

"*Week?* I'd say this goes back a lot further than that. She was asking about the hysterectomy, and that was two years ago, Wes. I tried to divert her attention to something more concrete, more in the present—like the fact that Charlotte will be leaving home soon, that a lot of women dread their kids going off to college—but I'm afraid it's much more complicated than that."

Disconcerted, appalled, Avery longed to say, *Is this my fault somehow, Doc? Something I said or did?* But instead he asked, "What do we do now?"

"Well, I'm no headshrinker. But if it was up to me, she'd be in Florida San—R and R, four to six weeks."

"The sanitarium?"

"Yup."

"What'd she say about that?"

"I didn't bring it up, but it's definitely something we should explore . . . I've given her something to sleep."

"Will she . . . I mean, she's in there because it's the darkest room in the house. Should I move her back to our room? To keep an eye on her?"

"No need," Martell said confidently. "Most likely, she's already out. I'll stop by in the morning, give her something to help get her up and out of bed. And I'll call Florida San to check their availability. My best advice for now is to avoid upsetting her. Keep things as calm and quiet around here as possible."

"But what about the parade tomorrow? And the game Saturday

night, the halftime ceremony? Sarah would be horrified if she missed homecoming. If not now, definitely whenever she comes out of this . . . this what?"

Martell, frowning, held up an open hand to stop him. "Let's cross each bridge when we come to it, shall we?"

9.

"SAILOR, TURN TO!" WAS THAT A WOMAN'S VOICE—"SKIPPER ON deck!"—out of Steve's service bay? Avery did a double take.

She was a stout redhead, with rosy windburned cheeks and blue-gray eyes with a clearly flirtatious twinkle. She handed Steve a socket wrench, then sashayed across the service bay to greet Avery in the office doorway. She had an ample bosom, amply displayed, and her forthright handshake was as firm as a man's.

"Lillian," she said with a cocky grin. "Lilly for short. Sometimes Lil, but not for long. And you're Wes, of course." She surveyed him up and down, like a little admiral on inspection. "Steve said you were tall, but he never said *anything* about handsome. Why, you're a dead ringer for that actor—oh, what's his name, Steve-O?—I loved him in *Witness for the Prosecution.* The guy everybody underestimated, till he turned out to be the killer in the end?"

Steve's face appeared from under the hood of John Dunham's Eldorado. "Tyrone Power."

"Bingo!" Lilly agreed. "Steve-O says you wouldn't say 'shit' if you had a mouthful, but I always say it's the quiet ones you gotta watch."

"Steve-*OH*?" Avery echoed, with a deliberate hike of brows in Steve's direction.

"Ohhh." She had a gravelly chuckle. "That's my little pet name for a certain midshipman knows his way around a lady's lower deck."

There was a loud metallic clang in the corner. Accidentally or not, Steve had dropped the socket wrench on the service bay floor. "All right, Lilly," he said, his tone half pleading, half warning.

"Oh, I'm an old Tartar!" she trilled to Avery with another wicked wink. "Everybody says so. But a woman has *needs* same as any man. Requires *regular* maintenance, same as any car or ship. And your master mechanic over there . . ."

"Lilly!" Steve groaned, emphatically dropping the Cadillac's hood. "Watch yourself, Cap. She's a walkin', talkin' instruction manual."

Avery hoped his smile covered his embarrassment, and his curiosity. And the rapid replacement of his mental image of Steve's lady friend—Miss Lillian, the demure New Smyrna Beach nurse whom Steve visited on weekends—with *this* Lilly, the living, breathing lust bucket before him. He shot Steve an appreciative glance. *Lucky guy*, it said.

"And it ain't like *his* tongue wasn't hanging over his toes a few minutes ago!" she added cheerfully. "When *your* lady friend stopped by."

"My . . . ?"

Steve walked over, wiping his hands on a service rag. "Wild Rose of Sharon, remember? From the other day?"

Kitty? "Here?"

"Looking forward to the parade, she said. Wanted to drop off a good-luck gift for Charlotte." Steve chucked his chin toward a small flat package on the desk.

"Gift?" Avery felt the uptick in his blood. Hadn't they agreed that all she'd do was *look*? Not touch, not talk, definitely not *gift*!

"They're gloves," Lilly explained. "Long ones up to here." She pointed to the soft pink flesh above her elbow. "*Very* elegant."

And they were. Long white gloves, neatly folded inside a clear plastic bag. "For luck, she said. There's a card, see?"

Visible through the plastic was a small white card with what had to be Kitty's looping handwriting: *For C., This is your moment. Savor it! Good luck, A friend.*

C., it said. For Carly instead of Charlotte?

"Thought we oughta put 'em in The Admiral, so we don't forget," Steve said. "But she said to make sure you saw 'em first."

With some effort, Avery masked his response, stilling the muscles in his face. Inwardly he reeled with revulsion and self-recrimination. A bead of sweat crept out of his armpit and trickled down his ribs. Kitty *here,* waltzing in with a *gift* for Charlotte, wishing her luck from "a *friend*"? Where did she get the nerve? What if Charlotte had been here? Worse yet, what if *Sarah* had been here? Sarah, who was under doctor's orders to *avoid* any upset. Wouldn't seeing Kitty, on *this* of all days, be enough to push Sarah right over the edge? No doubt. So *no way* he could allow the gift, right?

But if he didn't, was it possible that Kitty would seek them out on the parade route and demand an explanation? Or worse yet, show up at the house? Good Lord, what a *disaster* that would be. And if Kitty decided to bring up the cottage?

Avery closed his eyes, shook his head at either option. When he opened them, he was confronted by the amused gleam in Lilly's blue-eyed stare.

"Got a problem?" she asked softly.

Avery blanched. The layered lilt in her tone, the smile playing across her face, implied she'd leaped to the conclusion that Kitty *was* his girlfriend, that the day was ripe with potential intrigue.

"Not at all," he managed. "I'm sure Charlotte *and* her mother will be delighted." Even to his ears, it came out lame, an obvious lie.

"Well, then, I'll just set them in the backseat for this afternoon." She was clearly unconvinced.

Steve waited till Lilly was outside to say, "Sorry, Cap. She just showed up late last night cryin'. Said that all week, people at the hospital been sayin', 'See ya tomorrow, if there *is* a tomorrow,' and that yesterday it just got to her. Said that, if this is *it,* she wanted to be with me. Besides, she knew I was lendin' The Admiral to Leo and could use a ride." His look was apologetic, his face more hound-dog than usual. "Oh, and by the way"—he handed Avery the clipboard with the fuel chart—"we're outta Supreme. Called Tampa again. Maybe somethin' Monday, maybe not."

"Somehow," Lilly announced, returning, "I thought things would be calmer away from the coast. Patrick AFB's been crazy all week, but McCoy must be a zoo! Well"—she sighed, shaking her car keys out of her pocket—"guess I'll go forage for some food. Which way's the Winn-Dixie? If this is our Last Supper, I definitely want a steak!"

"There's a Publix two blocks east of the duplex, on Edgewater Drive," Steve told her. "Need directions?"

"I'll find it. Be back at three," she said to Steve. "Should be an interesting afternoon," she added, with another disconcerting wink at Avery.

THE TWO MEN WATCHED Lilly wheel off in her '61 Pontiac Firebird.

"A Fireball Roberts reject," Steve said, "from Smokey Yunick's shop in Daytona. More car than most people could handle. But now that you've met her . . ."

Fire-engine red, Avery observed. Figures.

Reflexively, he patted the left chest pocket of his uniform. "Need to drop off a couple prescriptions for Sarah across the street. Pick up some *real* news while I'm there?"

"That'd be good," Steve agreed. The *Sentinel*'s lead stories were predictably upbeat: The naval quarantine would continue during peace talks at the UN; a Soviet oil tanker was halted but later allowed to pass into port. "Wish they'd do the same with our tanker into Tampa," he griped.

Avery, waiting for a break in the traffic to cross the street, had his mind on other things.

As the number of southbound convoys had lessened, the number of northbound cars and station wagons had swollen to a near-continuous stream. Whole families from Florida's big south counties—license plates from Broward, Palm Beach, and Miami-Dade—were heading north out of harm's way.

Watching them, Avery worried: Maybe I should have packed up Sarah and Charlotte at the first sign of trouble and gotten the heck out of Dodge. Like Marjorie did. Would that have made any difference? Would Sarah be fine if I had, instead of . . . whatever she is now?

Pharmacist Bo Hammond hailed him from behind the counter.

Avery handed over the three prescription slips that Martell had dropped off this morning. Hammond spread them out like playing cards on the counter, smiling.

"In my business, we used to call this combination 'happy-go-lucky.' Miltown, the tranquilizer," he said, stabbing an index finger at the middle slip, "a lot of people call 'em their happy pills. And the Dexedrine you probably remember from The War."

Avery nodded. Dexedrine was standard air force issue to crews facing long night flights to Japan and back. Pilots called them "go pills," or often, because of their color, "greenies." "Greenie up, boys," the pilot would call over the com system, meaning "Take your Dexedrine and stay alert."

"But poor Seconal," Hammond was saying, cradling the third slip in cupped palms.

"Sleeping pill, right?"

"Yes." He said it sadly, as if mourning the loss of an old friend. "Ever since Marilyn, it's hard to call Seconal lucky anymore." He scooped up the slips. "Be right back," he said and turned to his shelves.

Watching Hammond go about his business, Avery struggled against the sudden tilt, a sensation of spin that had his hands grasping the counter in front of him. In the briefest span of days—one week!—a dizzying gap had opened between what he considered his normal life and now:

Sarah so unnerved it would take three different pills to steady her—one of them the same powerful barbiturate that killed Marilyn Monroe? Why hadn't he seen this coming? What *should* he have done? What could he do *now* to help her?

And what about Charlotte, who, this morning, seemed lost and remote, floating out the door with a look—eyes wide and wary—that tore his heart, left him flailing with frustration at how best to protect her. What he wanted, desperately, was for all of this never to have happened; for everything to be just as it was before. Before the planes, the President's speech, the trains and convoys; before Kitty showed up. And the nure-azz-whatever-it-was that had Sarah *hanging by a thread.*

He turned away and headed toward the newspaper racks, not wanting Hammond to see his eyes tearing up at the sense of his own drowning helplessness. A man takes a wife and makes a life. He plans ahead, builds his business, puts away savings for rainy days and retirement. He cultivates a sense of competence and control. He strives to be a good husband, father, and friend. He anticipates and corrects the occasional ping, the odd blowout. But he expects the welds to hold. He does *not* expect things to fall apart in a matter of *days.*

AVERY STOOD AT THE CROSSWALK, waiting for the light, when the passing convoy slowed to a parade-like crawl. Inexplicably, several of the drivers began honking their horns and waving wild halloos out the windows. The flatbeds' cabs were uniformly taped with cardboard signs stenciled US ARMY in big black letters; but there was another uniformity beneath them that took him a moment to recognize.

"Wes! Hey, Wes, it's *me*—Bobby Odom!" the driver called through the window to Avery at the curb.

And it *was* gap-toothed Bobby Odom, longtime driver for Dr. Phillips's Granada Groves, waving from behind the wheel.

"Call my wife! Tell her I'm okay!"

Avery raised a hand, called back, "Sure thing!" and counted one, two, four barely disguised Granada trucks bearing their canvas-covered military loads to some point south.

How many trucks had the toothpick-sucking Geiger said the government requisitioned?

"Five from us, three from Heidrich," Geiger informed him over the phone.

"Well, I only laid eyes on four of yours—and Bobby Odom, for sure. You'll call his wife?"

"'Less she calls me first. All the wives been pesterin' me for days. It'll be a relief to give 'em some real news."

Real news? "Any updates from out at McCoy?"

"Not lately. Though"—Avery heard the suck-kiss—"my milkman says they got bombs stacked up along the tarmac, high as a man's head and far as the eye can see. You imagine that?"

No imagination required, Avery thought grimly. Bombs lining the tarmac like that were SOP, standard operating procedure, for Curtis LeMay's trademark fire jobs.

Peace talks? Avery's jaw hardened against yesterday's hope.

AT ONE O'CLOCK, their traditional lunchtime, Avery told Steve that he needed to run home and give Sarah her prescriptions.

Steve, carrying his own lunch pail to the desk, nodded impassively. He'd noticed the white Rexall paper bag bulging with pill bottles, the fact that Avery's real-life problems were taking precedence over their daily lunch-and-chess routine; but, uncharacteristically, he refrained from comment. And Avery was profoundly grateful.

In the truck, he set the bag of pills on top of Beauchamp's record album, still on the passenger's seat from . . . Was it only yesterday he'd been to the school to drop off Charlotte's baton?

Time—usually divided into predetermined blocks, the set and regular rhythms of waking, working, eating, and sleeping—had somehow turned fluid. Without the usual markers, it meandered like a stream across new and old territories. He was finding it too easy to lose track.

Driving toward the cottage on Princeton, he had to remind himself that he and Sarah and Charlotte no longer lived there. Though surely somehow, their younger selves still inhabited it, still breathed in Avery's mind. Charlotte learned to ride her bike just there on the walk, where the FOR RENT sign now swayed in the wind. And when he and Sarah planted that tabebuia tree in the corner, it had been a single stick with a few leaves, not quite waist-high. Now its branches arched high overhead, sheltering both his and the neighbor's yard with an umbrella of yellow trumpets each spring.

Avery felt his heart groping backward, grasping like a greedy tod-
dler toward those innocent days—days he couldn't begin to reconcile
with the two-days-ago memory of his and Kitty's secret meeting in
the kitchen. What a fiasco that was! And still might be if he wasn't
very, very careful.

Closer to the lake, the lot sizes and house volumes increased; the
youthful striving of their old neighborhood gave way to the perceived
serenity, the outwardly calm façade, of lakeside success. His new
neighbors weren't going anywhere. They'd already arrived.

And several of them were out on the sidewalk, staring in the direction of the obnoxious intrusion: the loud, machine-gun-like *rat-
tat-tat-tat* of a jackhammer emanating from an unseen space beyond
his carport.

Avery downshifted, gave the neighbors a flat-handed wave, and
turned the pickup into his driveway. Through the opening in the
hedge between his property and the Stouts', he spotted the aqua-
blue, three-quarter-ton truck from Bob's Pools & Igloos, and deduced
they were installing the gol-durn shelter in their hard clay side yard
instead of the back.

He got out quickly, slammed his door hard, aiming to confront the
guy over the noise—*My wife is under doctor's orders not to be disturbed!*
he intended to say—when the side door to his own home opened.
And there was Sarah, bleary-eyed, one hand clutching her navy-blue
bathrobe, the other clinging to the doorjamb. Her right cheek was
creased and red, her hair a tangled mess. "Oh, darlin'," he said impulsively, taking her arm.

"How about a little lunch?" he asked her gently. "Bowl of soup
maybe? Some buttered toast?"

She nodded distractedly. "Hot in here. How 'bout the back porch?"

"Of course." Mercifully, it appeared the jackhammer guy had
reached a stopping place.

"Hey, fellas," Avery said, "look who's here." The parakeets fluttered, chattering to be fed. "You'll get yours in a minute. Ladies first."

Back in the kitchen, he opened a can of Campbell's soup, added water to the pot, set it on the stove to warm, and got out the bread to toast. Tomato soup and buttered toast was what Sarah always fed them whenever he or Charlotte was sick. It was what her mother fed her, she'd explained. And Kitty, too, Avery presumed, though Sarah never mentioned her.

He served her on a tray and, while she stared at the bowl as if summoning the strength to eat, he replenished the birds' food and water, and retrieved her prescriptions and Beauchamp's album from the truck.

He left the record on the kitchen counter, filled a glass of water, and returned to Sarah. He noticed she'd forgone the spoon, instead dipping a strip of the toast into the soup and making an effort to nibble at it. He set down the water, then carefully checked the labels on each pill bottle and gave her three of the white Miltowns plus four of the small, green Dexedrines.

"This should help," he said.

"Hope so." She sighed, taking them. "Tell me the plan again."

"I'm picking up Charlotte at two-thirty, then Emilio right after. I'll drop Charlotte off here to change, and take Emilio to the station to change and pick up The Admiral. He'll follow me back here and take off with Charlotte to muster for the parade. You and I will head to the bank, where they've set up reserved seats for parents of the Homecoming Court."

"What time do we have to leave?"

"Three-fifteen at the latest. I'll be here around three if you need help."

"I'll be okay. It's Charlotte's big day." She set her tray aside. "I have to be."

Avery watched her eyes flutter shut, her head fall back tiredly against the chaise. Heading back to work, he heard the echo of Martell's advice: *One bridge at a time.*

"How's Mom?" Charlotte asked, climbing into the truck.

"Doc Mike prescribed some pills. She just took them."

"So she's up?"

"She was. Had lunch and now she's getting ready for the big parade."

Charlotte blew a relieved exhale. Avery handed her the folded sheet he'd pulled from the linen closet at home.

"What's this for?" she asked him.

"You'll be sitting on top of the backseat. Thought you'd need something to put your feet on, protect The Admiral's tuck-and-roll."

"Thanks." She flushed, fingering the pleats of her madras plaid skirt.

"Piece of cake, kiddo. All you have to do is smile and wave to the nice people."

"Yeah, and pretend everything's just fine."

"Everything *is* fine, Kitten. Or will be soon, I hope."

Emilio hailed them from the curb, stepping out of a crowd of kids in Bishop Moore's blue-and-white uniforms waiting in front of the school. The boy scrambled in next to Charlotte, his mood buoyant, expectant. She handed him the sheet and explained its purpose.

"Good idea," he said. At the same time, he studied her. "You okay?" he asked.

Avery kept his eyes straight ahead and concentrated on his driving.

"I'll just be glad when this part's over," he heard her answer.

"Rather be marching with the band, worrying about dropping your baton?" Emilio asked.

"Yes, actually."

"But then I'd be stuck pumping gas at the station. Wouldn't I, Mr. A?"

"'Fraid so."

"Instead of driving The Admiral and the best-looking girl in the parade."

Out of the corner of his eye, Avery caught Charlotte's blush, the glimmer of her smile.

"So this is all about you, huh?" she teased him.

"Me? No way. I figure it's The Admiral on parade. All we have to do," he said, leaning back expansively, "is sit back and enjoy the ride."

Avery was impressed by his effect on Charlotte's mood; he shot Emilio an *atta boy* wink. At the house, Charlotte stepped lightly to the curb, calling, "See you at three!" then bounded up the drive, pony-tail and pleats tick-tocking behind her.

At the station, Steve had The Admiral's top down and was buffing its already glossy hood to a near-blinding shine.

Emilio placed the sheet in the backseat, beside Kitty's gloves, re-trieved his hanging bag from the storage room, and went to the men's room to change. Minutes later, he emerged transformed, head high with the acquired confidence of his handsome new suit.

Avery was checking the time—*two forty-five, right on schedule*—when the station phone rang. "Orange Town Texaco, Wes spea—"

"Dad! You need to get back here. Hurry!"

RETRACING THE ROUTE HOME, Princeton to Northumberland to Bryn Mawr, Avery kept an eye on the rearview mirror to make sure Emilio and The Admiral were behind him. Meanwhile, his mind re-played Charlotte's phone call, the rising panic in her voice as she told him, "Please hurry, Dad. Mom's gone off her rocker!"

Both hands firmly on the wheel, he was willing himself calm. "Steady as she goes," a different voice—his grandfather's resonant bass—urged him.

When Old Pa arrived at their farm in central Georgia, he was surprised to learn that the only son of his only daughter had never even been on a boat.

For the next year, after chores and homework, they worked nights building a small sailboat, a Biloxi dinghy, together in the barn. His grandfather was a skilled carpenter and a retired chief engineer. He was exacting in his work, and spare in his compliments. One night, however, having carefully mortised the battens and fastened the planks with inch-and-a-quarter copper nails clinched two inches apart, his grandfather pronounced, "You got your good looks, your head for figures from your daddy, boy; but the talent in these hams"—he grasped Avery's oversized hands with his own—"is from me."

The day they finally set sail for the first time, having hauled the boat fifty-five miles northeast to Lake Sinclair, his grandfather insisted that Avery man the stern for their maiden voyage. "Feed the sail and starve the tiller, son." "Firm hand, steady as she goes!" It had become Avery's motto for life.

Now, looking at his hands on the wheel, hands that grew more and more like his grandfather's with each passing year, Avery prayed he was up to whatever lay ahead.

CHARLOTTE, STANDING IN THE open front doorway, took his breath away.

With her dark hair piled high on top of her head and her long dress, a white sheath shimmering with silver threads, she was *transformed*—no longer the ponytailed teenager he'd dropped off less than an hour ago. Like in that movie *Sabrina,* Avery thought, when Audrey Hepburn went off to Paris a gawky schoolgirl and came back a stunner. In a gesture that reminded him of Kitty at the cottage, she touched the pearls in the hollow of her throat.

"She's in the dining room," she whispered, eyes wide.

"You go on ahead," he told her. "We'll be all right."

Charlotte gnawed her lip. "I don't know, Dad. . . ."

"Go," he assured her, and flicked a hand at Emilio, parking in the drive, to come and get her. "Take care," he called after them. "Wave to us in front of the bank."

Inside, the dining room appeared empty. Had Sarah moved to the kitchen?

She was on her hands and knees under the table. He spotted the bottoms of her stockinged feet first, then the glow of her red skirt, a flash of white blouse.

"Sarah?"

She didn't respond, so he called again. "Sarah? Sarah!"

She was intent on *something* under the table. And what was she saying to herself so urgently, over and over?

He placed one hand on the tabletop, the other on the floor, and squatted down to listen. Beyond the mounds of her hip and shoulder, he saw her long fluttering fingers picking rapidly through the carpet, loop by loop. And heard the rise and fall, the repetitive rhythm of some kind of rhyme. The third time through, it came to him. His mother used to say the same thing: "Drop a pin, let it lie, rue the day you passed it by."

She was looking for lost pins?

"Sarah, can I help you?" he asked, gently touching the heel of her nearest foot.

Her yelp—a short, high animal cry of alarm—surprised him; as did the sudden, ruthless kick of her foot, and the blazing look she shot him over her shoulder. Her eyes, normally slate gray, had pupils so enlarged they were gleaming black; their expression hooded and hostile. "No!" she insisted, then resumed her picking and muttering.

Avery stood. Beside her sewing machine, he saw the empty pin box, the picked-clean strawberry pincushion, the neat rows of shiny pins separated—it appeared—into groups of ten. He ran back through the kitchen and outside, around her car and his truck to the small workshop that buttressed the carport on its far side. He grabbed the red horseshoe-shaped magnet he kept on a hook by the door, returned to the dining room, and knelt down in front of her, all the while wondering which of the pills she'd taken—the white Miltowns or the green Dexedrines—might be fueling her apparent agitation.

"Try this?"

She seemed startled by his reappearance and leery of the magnet.

"I use it for dropped nails and screws. Should work for pins, too," he promised her.

She shrank back warily to watch him.

Slowly, he drew the magnet over the carpet just in front of her. "Well, looky here," he said, smiling, showing her the pin attached to the magnet.

Sarah snatched the pin and studied it. After a moment, she rocked back on her heels, her head barely missing the table rim, and put it on the tabletop.

"See a pin, pick it up, all the day you'll have good luck, right?" he told her. "How many are we missing?"

"Five—"

"Minus that one, four." He moved the magnet in a wider arc around the chair, where earlier in the week she'd been sewing, and came up with three more. Once again, she took them and placed them on the table.

"We have a parade to go to," he reminded her.

Sarah shook her head fiercely. "Bad luck to leave without it."

He made another wider but unproductive pass of the magnet over the carpet, worrying, Do I dare take her out like this?

When he came up empty-handed, he saw the alarm flare in her eerily all-black eyes.

"It's okay, darlin'. We'll find it. Here it is!" he exclaimed. "The last one, lost and found."

She dropped her face into her hands. Her shoulders shuddered in dry, gulping sobs. He set the magnet and pin aside, and helped her up and into his arms.

"There now," he crooned, stroking her snarled hair away from her face. "Everything's fine now, isn't it? Still feel like seeing a parade?"

Her hand flew up to cover her open mouth. "What time is it?" she gasped.

He checked his watch: three twenty-five. Even if they walked out the door this minute, it was too late to cross Edgewater Drive to their reserved seats in front of the bank, which, he decided, was probably a blessing.

Sarah turned frantically and ran toward the hall. "I need my shoes . . . my jacket . . . my . . ."

He followed her into their room, where she disappeared into the closet in search of the dark red jacket and pumps that matched her skirt. "I'll be right there," she called, out of breath.

He went out, grabbed two folding lawn chairs off the back wall of his workshop, and at the last minute reached into the Buick for her dark glasses.

She came out of the house pinning her hair into a French twist. With red lipstick and a bit of makeup, she looked more like herself— except for her eyes. They scanned the yard, the truck, and *him* as if seeing it all for the first time.

"You look great," he lied, and gently helped her into the truck. "Pretty glary out here," he added, handing her the dark glasses.

The parade had mustered south of downtown at Dartmouth Street, and would be heading north on Edgewater Drive to wind up at the high school. Avery drove three blocks east to the relatively quiet corner where Bryn Mawr crossed Edgewater. The wooden saw- horses were already up, and about twenty-five people crowded the street behind them. Avery was relieved to see that most of them were what he called their "nodding neighbors," people who knew them on sight but not much else. He made a two-point turn and backed up behind them. He set the lawn chairs in the truck bed, and helped Sarah up and into one, then sat down beside her.

"Balcony seats," she said, seeming relieved by the privacy of the elevated truck.

A whirl of flashing lights, the wail of a siren, and blare of a horn drew their attention to the street. The big red engine, pride of the College Park volunteer fire force, announced that the parade was on its way.

The girls in the convertibles were interspersed between floats that were frothy concoctions of chicken wire and crepe paper, each created by a different grade level, all variations on the theme of the mighty Edgewater Eagles bashing, smashing, trashing, and lambasting the wimpy Winter Park Wildcats.

The first two girls to pass by in convertibles, both blond, were cheerleaders who smiled and waved like pros to the people rimming the parade route.

Charlotte was third. Dressed in shimmering white, ensconced above The Admiral's red leather backseat, its gleaming black trunk and fins, she'd never looked lovelier, a spectacular pearl in a radiant black-and-red box.

Avery put two fingers to his lips and blew out his loudest whistle, a holdover from his farm days calling home the cows. Charlotte recognized it and turned. Avery stood and windmilled his arms to get her attention. He was rewarded with her eager wave, her shy and tremulous smile. Emilio, sharply handsome at the wheel, turned and waved.

To his right, Avery heard Sarah's sharp intake of breath. "Kitty," she croaked.

"What?" Avery felt the wildfire spread of alarm. He scanned the crowd across the street. "Where?"

Of all the blocks and intersections along the parade route, how on earth could Kitty be *here*?

Avery grabbed the chair back to steady himself. He'd been a fool to invite her. And an even bigger fool to let Sarah out of the house in this condition. She couldn't possibly handle seeing her long-lost sister here and now. And when the truth came out—how Kitty had come to be here—he was doomed. Everything, every single thing he cared about, was lost in a disaster of his own making.

"Her *gloves*, Wes," Sarah insisted. "Kitty wore gloves just like that when she was crowned Homecoming Queen. Where in the world did they come from?"

It wasn't Kitty she'd seen. It was her gloves. Her gol-durn *gloves*. Avery felt the damp cling of his shirt to his back, and the high hammering of his pulse. He dropped back down into his chair, kept his eyes straight ahead.

"Oh, Wes," his wife whispered. "Isn't she beautiful?"

"BUT WE HAVEN'T SEEN the *band*," Sarah exclaimed, protesting Avery's suggestion that they go. "Or the other two girls!"

So they stayed to watch the other floats; the fourth girl, another blond cheerleader, rail-thin, all teeth; and the fifth and last girl, gorgeous Barbara Everly in Charlie Novak's cherry-red Corvette.

Though *girl* was hardly the word for Barbara, Avery decided. Where Charlotte in white had reminded him of a pearl, a polished princess, Barbara in the same color was a sparkling diamond. On looks alone, she was the smoldering queen of the girlish court.

Finally, the twirls were in sight, and behind them the Fighting Eagles marching band. Avery spotted director Charles Beauchamp striding beside the band, admonishing the lines to stay straight and in step.

Suddenly Sarah leaped up from her chair. "Charles," she shrilled, waving. "Oh, *Charles!*"

"Sarah, hi! See Charlotte? A vision, an absolute *vision!*" Beauchamp called back, gathering his fingertips to his lips then letting them fly in her direction.

It seemed, to Avery, a ridiculous, overly dramatic gesture. Beside him, Sarah flushed pink with delight.

"Brava, Madame Sarah. Bra-*vah!*" Beauchamp yelled. His elaborate salute and knee-deep bow set Sarah off in a trill of schoolgirl giggling.

Sarah *giggling?*

Avery stared dumbly at his twin reflection in Sarah's dark glasses. A barrage of questions went off flak-fast in his head: Was Sarah somehow involved with Beauchamp? Was it possible? Was this the moment, was it *him*—not the band or Barbara Everly—she'd lingered to see? Had something real just happened between them? Or was his own guilt over Kitty making something out of nothing? Sarah and *Beauchamp?* He found the very idea of such a thing repugnant and, as he thought about it, insulting. Sarah, who was always so publicly poised and proper, and Beauchamp, the flamboyant genius? Did he dare confront her? Not with the doctor saying to "keep things calm and as quiet as possible." But good Lord, *Beauchamp?*

"Don't wanna cook," she was saying—he noted the slight slurring of her words—on the short drive home. "How 'bout a night out on the town?" she asked, removing her glasses, her eyes still over-bright. She was brimming with nervous energy—as if her inner engine had shifted from rough idle into overdrive. Was this the result of seeing Beauchamp? Or was it just the "happy pills" kicking in?

The words *I'm closing* froze on Avery's lips. Both Steve and Emilio had the night off, and Avery was scheduled to man the station from six till nine. But what kind of trouble might Sarah get into if he left her alone? Craving activity, what if she took a notion to pick up the phone and invite someone over? He shied away from picturing who. Would she visit the neighbors? Or, God forbid, get behind the wheel of her car and go somewhere on her own? How could he let *that* happen?

I can't, he decided.

But Steve had worked a full day and had Lilly in town. And Emilio was headed off with Charlotte to an after-the-parade party with the twirls. For the first time in seventeen years, he realized, Orange Town Texaco would have to be closed with no advance notice to his customers. He had no other choice.

"Okay," he told her. "But I'll need to shower, and stop by the station on our way over."

CLEAN-SHAVEN AND IN FRESH CIVIES, Avery was warming up to the idea of a night out. "Fried chicken and cathead biscuits at Chastain's?" he asked hopefully.

Sarah, inexplicably, had changed into a bright-blue flowered dress he hadn't seen in years, a souvenir from a family trip to Key West. She'd untwisted her hair and brushed it out into a soft drape, one side tucked behind her ear. She fluttered around the living room, fluffing pillows, adjusting lamp shades, straightening magazines, like an actress on stage playing the good wife—a far cry from the woman who, just hours ago, had panicked over a lost pin.

"Chastain's?" She shook her head, her mouth in a coquette's pout. "How about . . . Gary's Duck Inn! That would be fun!"

The one and only time they'd been to Gary's Duck Inn, with its flaming tiki torches, lava rock waterfall, and tropical drinks with tiny paper parasols, she'd pronounced it "too tacky for my taste."

Now it would be *fun?*

Seeing her float toward the kitchen to "take my pills," Avery asked, "Do you really think you need some more?"

"Oh, yes," she trilled. "It's definitely time."

When she returned to the living room, she was holding Beauchamp's record album. "Whuz this?"

Avery eyed her carefully. "A loan from the musical genius," he said amiably. "He gave it to me when I dropped off Charlotte's baton."

"Charles?" she repeated, with a husky laugh. "How sweet of him!" She set the album atop the stereo, then turned. Her smile, her whole face, seemed secondary to her darkly gleaming gaze. "Shall we go?"

Forgoing the truck, he helped her into the Buick, his mind churning with questions he couldn't, or wouldn't, ask. At the station, he swung into his usual parking spot. "Back in a few," he told her.

He replaced the day's signs (CLOSED 3–6 PM FOR HOMECOMING PARADE) with those intended for tomorrow (CLOSED AFTER 6 PM FOR HOMECOMING) and transferred the contents of the till to the floor safe. He was composing a quick note for Steve—*Closed early. I'll explain tomorrow.*—when the phone on the desk startled him.

"Orange Town Texa—"

"Wes, it's Kitty."

"Hel-lo." He eyed Sarah, who was eyeing herself in the Buick's flip-down vanity mirror.

"I see she liked the gloves."

"Apparently."

"Oh, Wes, she's lovely!"

"Thank you. We think so."

"I . . . well, I've decided to stay over another day. I couldn't stand heading back to Tampa without seeing whether or not she won."

Avery felt the sharp clench of his gut, its rapid pull on his breath.

"Don't worry. I'll wear a hat and hang out on the other school's side until halftime. Nobody will even know I'm there."

I'll know, Avery thought. His jaw jutted at the thought of repeating today's nightmare of nerves at tomorrow's game.

"You've no idea what it felt like, seeing her," Kitty prattled on. "I used to wonder, but I never imagined she'd be so ... And she has ..." Avery heard the catch in her throat. "... Carlo's smile. *Exactly.* I wasn't prepared for that."

"You ..." Avery hesitated, pained that she'd misread his silence as permission. For days now, the entire week, he'd felt the constant push of things, people, predicaments spinning out of his control. He wanted—and needed—to push back.

But how?

Everything he cared about—his daughter, his wife (who was now looking his way, long fingers drumming the dashboard), his business, his entire life felt like a house of cards in the advancing path of gale-force winds. How could he explain that to Kitty?

"It's impossible. If Sarah sees you, there'll be all hell to pay."

"Sarah's had her for seventeen *years,* Wes," Kitty snapped. "Surely, she—or *you*—can't begrudge me a few *minutes.*"

Avery heard the hunger, the hardening resolve in her voice. Careful, he warned himself. Don't let this get ugly.

"Does she *know,* Wes?"

"Know what?" he asked, too quickly.

"About me? Me and Carlo. That you and Sarah—"

"No," he interrupted flatly. "She knows nothing."

He felt the long, slow intake of her breath, like a rasp drawn sorely across his heart.

"Doesn't seem exactly fair, does it?"

For the second time that afternoon, Avery felt the high, flailing hammer of his pulse. Only this time, it wasn't Sarah's state of mind at stake; it was his daughter's entire world.

"I want to meet her, Wes," Kitty was saying.

Avery felt lost, falling headlong through the dark into a new hell. With nobody, not one single person around to save him. Worse yet, outside the window, Sarah was opening the Buick door.

"W-wait a minute, j-j-just *one minute,*" he stammered. His fist dropped on the desk so hard it made the phone shudder, its inner bell ding.

"You *can't* . . . *I* can't talk about this right now, but we have to . . . we *will* talk about this tomorrow! Okay?"

"Why, sure, Wes. I'm not going anywhere. How about one o'clock—no, one-thirty—at the cottage where we met before?"

No way. His mind balked. Not the cottage, not again. No way, Hozay. Tell her no. Say it, you fool! Say no, *say NO now!*

"All right," he heard himself say, "one-thirty tomorrow," and banged down the receiver.

High afternoon winds had chopped the cloud cover into long rippling rows, like roof tiles, or fish scales, glazed gold to pink to peach by the setting sun. A mackerel sky, Old Pa would have called it. "Mare's tails and mackerel scales make lofty ships take in their sails," he would have said—a warning to batten down the hatches, rough seas ahead. Like things could get worse than they are already?

THEIR WAITER WAS A smiling Filipino who handed them the ornate, leather-bound menus and asked, "Something to drink, boss?"

Avery gave their standard order: "Two sweet teas, please."

"Oh, no! What's that?" Sarah asked, pointing toward a nearby table. "With the gardenia in it?"

"That's a scorpion, miss."

"Yes, please." She nodded happily. "And he'll have a rum and Coke."

We're drinking now? Avery wondered.

When the drinks arrived, Sarah removed the fragrant gardenia floating in her drink and stuck it in her hair above one ear. "Remember gardenias?" she asked, a deliberate flirt.

Her pupils had once again eclipsed her irises.

She's already high as a kite, Avery realized. His heart sank. So what happens when you add alcohol to the mix? Wish I'd had the good sense to ask, he was thinking, when he was suddenly confounded by a silk-stockinged foot snaking its way under his pant cuff, above his sock, to the bare skin on his shin.

He stared at the woman who resembled his wife but who was acting like somebody else entirely. "Gardenias? How could I forget?" he
told her.

He ordered the fried shrimp platter while she, on the waiter's suggestion, went for something called Flounder en Papillote, which
turned out to be a fillet baked inside a paper bag. She ordered another
drink.

"Another sting of the scorpion's tail, miss?" the waiter joshed her.

"Absolutely!"

Where had *this* Sarah come from? And where did the real one go?
Had this wilder side of her always been lurking about, waiting to be
set free by seven little pills and a couple of scorpions?

On the drive home, she leaned into him, nuzzling his neck, nib-
bling his ear, crooning softly a song from their early days, "Gonna
take a senti-men-tal jour-ney . . ."

The scent of gardenia filled the front seat. Avery found himself
hoping Charlotte wasn't home.

"Never thought my heart could be so yearn-y," Sarah continued,
her voice velvety, her breath warm and rummy against his neck.

Sarah half staggered, half stumbled backward into the house,
hands tugging at his belt, fingers fumbling for his buckle and then his
fly. Avery tottered after her awkwardly, one eye on the open curtains
to the street, the other on their path through the darkened living
room and down the hall.

At their bedroom, she flung open the door and lurched sideways,
reeling him in. Avery one-armed the door closed and with the other
kept her from falling backward onto the hard corner of the cedar
chest at the foot of their bed.

She fell on the floor instead, grasping and tugging him down on
top of her, teasing his chin, neck, and ear with her tongue as his hands
sought the soft snaps connecting stockings to girdle covering panties
and the musky hollow below.

"C'mon, c'mon," she was saying. She seemed fierce and feral and
not at all Sarah-like as she undid the last snap herself, and somehow

freed the patch within the tangle of their clothes, guiding him, "here," urging him, "in, in," urgently "now!"

The question swooped through his mind—Is it wrong to take advantage of her in this state?—but only briefly. What could be wrong with a man making love to his wife?

10.

THE STORM, HERALDED BY LAST NIGHT'S MACKEREL SKY, COM-
menced with a steady downpour before dawn. When Avery woke, the
windows were rain-darkened, their bedroom deep in the blue gloom
of very early morning. He turned to check the clock and was surprised by the time. Nearly eight o'clock. He hadn't slept so well in . . .
who knew how long?

Thank God it was Steve's turn to open.

He lay back, replaying the evening's events.

They'd been hard at it like honeymooners when Charlotte knocked
on the door to say she was home.

"Thanks, kiddo," Avery had called. "Good night."

"Mom okay?" she'd asked tentatively.

"A-okay," Sarah had trilled beneath him. "Never better!"

What had Charlotte made of that? He'd wanted to wait for the
sound of her door closing down the hall. The interruption had softened him. But Sarah, knees locked tightly around his hips, had rolled
them over and, with a skill he didn't know she had, rocked him back
into hardness.

Afterward, though, she'd simply rolled off him, stood, and stag-
gered into the bathroom, where he heard her retching her dinner, plus
the two scorpion drinks, into the toilet. He'd scrambled up to help
her—hearing in his mind the waiter's mocking "Another sting of the

scorpion's tail, miss?"—but she'd waved him off. He'd wet a wash-cloth then, at her pained request, found and opened the prescription bottle for her sleeping pills.

Avery glanced over at her now, sound asleep; a soft, rasping snore muffled by the curtain of her hair. Had the combination of the drugs and the drinks prompted last night's wild ride? Or was this the way a woman "hanging by a thread" acted, seesawing from one extreme to another? He wished he knew.

He checked the clock again. Yesterday, she'd slept half the day away. Would she do the same today? And which Sarah would she be when she woke up?

SHOWERED, SHAVED, AND DRESSED for work, he stood on the pro-tected stoop under the carport, contemplating the amount of rain between him and his plastic-bagged newspaper out on the drive. On the stoop, half a dozen foil-capped milk bottles glistened with water droplets in their aluminum wire crate. Simms must have come while he was in the shower. Avery was sorry to have missed him and what-ever air base update he might have offered.

Lousy day to be a milkman, he thought, retrieving the crate, de-ciding he'd pick up his paper on the drive out.

By nine-forty, Charlotte still wasn't up. Avery was reluctant to wake her. Still, he needed to know what her plans were today. More specifically, he needed her to keep an eye on Sarah while he was at work. He frowned over the notepad. It was their family custom to leave messages for each other on the kitchen counter. If he slipped it under her door, Charlotte might miss it. But what if, for some reason, Sarah got up first? Avery thought about that, then wrote:

Good morning, Sleeping Beauties. Please call me soon as you're up. Love, Dad/W.

Backing out in the rain, he maneuvered the truck to the right of the plastic-wrapped newspaper, opened his door, scooped it up, and tossed it onto the seat beside him. When he arrived at the station, he removed the *Sentinel* from its wrapper and unfolded it on the desk beside *The New York Times* Steve had purchased on his way in. Avery read the matching headlines and felt the news like the point of a spear pressed against his chest.

RUSSIANS SPEED BUILDING OF MISSILE SITES IN CUBA, the *Sentinel* blared.

US FINDS CUBA SPEEDING BUILD-UP OF BASES, WARNS OF FURTHER ACTION, the *Times* read. Construction of the Soviet bases *"was proceeding at a rapid rate with the apparent intention of achieving a full operational capacity as soon as possible. High officials said that such work could not be allowed to continue indefinitely,"* the lead paragraph informed him.

"Do these guys *want* a war?" he asked aloud, dumbfounded.

"Looks like it, don't it?" Steve's hound-dog face looked grimmer than he'd ever seen it.

What were the Soviets thinking? And how would the brass hats respond?

Avery's eyes scanned the rest of the story, past the White House demands and the UN concerns, looking for the Pentagon's reaction. It was there, in the *Times'* final paragraphs:

Two Thors, the 1,500-mile intermediate-range ballistic missile, were used in scientific booster missions, one in the launching of a nuclear device over Johnston Island in the Pacific last midnight, and the other in the launching of an unidentified satellite from Vandenberg Air Force Base in California.

Also at Vandenberg, an Atlas intercontinental ballistic missile (ICBM), with a credited range of 6,000 miles, was launched in a "routine training" test. Titan II ICBM was launched 5,000 miles in a development test at Patrick Air Force Base, Florida, the Pentagon said.

Avery heard the quickening drumbeat inside each sentence, the rattling of the Joint Chiefs' sabers over who controlled the fate of the world. His mind flashed on the combined memory of bombs stacked head-high as far as the eye could see and General Curtis LeMay's glowering, cigar-chomping swagger. Somewhere, he imagined the bonfire of Bombs Away LeMay's war lust leaping into full flame. Will the other Chiefs follow? Will our too young, untested President let them?

Wasn't this exactly what Ike warned us about in his farewell speech? The old soldier understood the momentum of war, how swiftly the reporting of enemy outrages, the public outcry for action, the Joint Chiefs' assurances of a fast and easy victory could sweep us all into the ultimate debacle.

Avery attempted a deep breath to steady himself, but the fear of clear and imminent disaster seemed to have sucked all the air out of the room.

CHARLOTTE CALLED IN AT ten twenty-seven.

"Hey, kiddo, how was the party after the parade?"

"It was fabulous, Dad. A bunch of us made plans to take Emilio water skiing on Lake Fairview today. But with all this rain, I guess that's off."

On any other day, Avery might have noted the addition of a new event, outside homecoming, to his daughter's and Emilio's schedule—and the expansion of mutual interest it represented—but not today.

"Mom up yet?"

"No."

Although Steve was out of earshot and Sarah was apparently still asleep, he and Charlotte slipped into a kind of conspiratorial code talk. She agreed on the need to "keep an eye out," and he insisted she call him "if anything seems sideways." Neither of them was willing or able, Avery realized, to address Sarah's erratic behavior yesterday directly. It was obvious that their shared but unspoken hope was that she'd wake up today and be herself again; though the chances of that happening, Avery feared, were slim.

Out front, the stream of evacuee traffic had swollen with the rain into a rushing river of headlights streaming north.

Working opposite sides of the pumps, Avery and Steve tended the ones who peeled off briefly for a quick infusion of five gallons of gas. The cars were crowded, but the people inside were eerily silent. Grim-lipped men sat behind the wheel, their round-eyed wives beside them and blank-faced kids clutching the family dog or cat or the occasional grandparent in the back. Eager to rejoin the pack, most of them waved off his offer to check their oil, handed over their cash, and were gone, leaving the smell of their fear ripe in his nostrils.

At half past eleven, Avery checked the fuel chart, tallied the receipts, and could no longer ignore the obvious. He went to the storeroom, got out the paint, a brush, and a pair of blank posters, and prepared the signs:

OUT OF GAS—
SERVICE BAYS OPEN
TILL 6 PM

In a break in the action out at the pumps, Steve stood beside him and mentioned, a bit too casually, his eyes on the paintbrush: "Didn't see you outside the bank yesterday."

Avery attempted nonchalance. "Sarah was running a little late. We wound up watching at the corner of Edgewater and Bryn Mawr."

"Charlotte looked great."

"Yes," Avery agreed, relieved to have the conversation veer off Sarah. "She did, didn't she?"

"Lilly thought so, too. Had a kinda crazy idea"—Steve paused, rubbed his chin thoughtfully—"that something about Charlotte—she couldn't put her finger on it—sort of favored Wild Rose of Sharon."

Kitty? Avery stilled his brush.

"*Kinda* crazy?"

"I know," Steve said, scratching an eyebrow. "But all dressed up—like a movie star almost—I could kinda see . . ." The question—*Who is Kitty, really?*—hung unasked between them.

Avery resumed painting while he considered his options. Without Lilly, he might have told Steve the truth. The stalwart bantam rooster of a man was, after all, his best friend. But Lilly was a wild card who leaped to conclusions and, to his mind, talked too much.

Avery shrugged. "I never even laid eyes on Kitty Ayres around here . . . till the other day. You?"

"Nope," Steve replied. "I surely would've remembered *that* if I had!" He grinned, allowing Avery to squirm gratefully off the hook.

AT EXACTLY NOON, LILLY'S flaming red Firebird rolled into the shelter of the station's canopy. She and Steve had made plans to walk across the street for a meal at the Rexall lunch counter; but because of the rain, still coming down in sheets, they decided to drive.

Avery stood at the pumps and watched them go, watched the Firebird nose its insistent way cross-stream, saw the river of northbound traffic close up behind them.

Watching the continuous flow of cars and humanity passing him by, Avery felt oddly isolated and left behind. When his father died, their farmhouse had filled up with people—county neighbors and far-flung relatives—who, after the funeral and the big potluck, left him and his mother standing on the porch, watching their waving processional slide away like a giant snake into the distance.

His mother's hands, with long, pale fingers grasping the porch railing, were beside his. He remembered reaching out to touch the white knob of her wrist protruding beneath her dyed-black cuff. His gesture startled her and she jerked away, red-rimmed eyes suddenly round with surprise that he was still standing there. Where else would I be? he'd wondered.

"Now what?" his ten-year-old self asked her.

"I have no idea," she'd answered hollowly and looked away, leaving him to feel the hard yoke of her loneliness descend on him as well.

Wearily, Avery turned toward the office. He'd resolved to check in with Sarah's doctor, but this was the first spare moment he'd had all morning. He retrieved the phone book from the lower desk drawer and was scanning the M's for Martell when the phone at his elbow went off with a sudden, insistent ring.

"Dad, Mr. Beauchamp just called. He says the field's a soggy mess so they've canceled the game."

"Too bad. What about the dance?"

"It's still on, in the gym."

"And the ceremony?"

"Eight o'clock, in the gym."

"Oh-kay." Avery's mind leaped to Kitty. Would she insist on coming to the gym?

"The thing is, Dad, Mr. Beauchamp wanted Mom to call her list of band parents, let them know the game is off."

"And, your mother is . . ."

"In the living room. She asked not to be disturbed. She's got her head in the stereo, listening to the same song over and over."

"What song?"

"I don't know, Dad. Something foreign. German maybe?"

"Like opera?"

"Yeah, something like that. And, Dad—" Charlotte took a deep breath. Avery heard it and braced himself. "—she's crying her eyes out. Can you come?"

"Steve's out to lunch. I'll leave as soon he gets back."

"Okay. Please hurry, Dad."

"Good afternoon. Cherry Plaza Hotel."

"Yes." Avery cleared his throat. "I'm calling one of your guests. Miss Ayres, Kitty Ayres?"

"One moment, please . . . I'm sorry, sir. Miss Ayres doesn't answer. May I take a message?"

"No message. Thank you."

He strode to the office doorway, peered across the street for the return of the red Firebird. He considered calling Bo Hammond to summon Steve and Lilly back to the station; but he had enough on his plate without setting off another round of Lilly's suspicions. Besides, they were due back at one and it was already twelve forty-seven.

Thirteen minutes, he thought, plus the four-minute drive home. Surely Sarah and Charlotte would be okay till then.

Intent on the traffic, he was surprised to find his view suddenly blocked by the side panel of a large white truck, and to hear, magnified beneath the rain-enclosed canopy, the keening squeal of the Divco brakes.

Milkman Jimmy Simms sat slumped in his seat. His face, normally ruddy, was drained of color. His eyes stared blindly ahead; both hands gripped the wheel tightly. On the dash beside him, the microphone of his two-way radio squawked static.

Was he having a heart attack? "Jimmy, you okay?"

Simms's eyes floated in Avery's direction but failed to focus.

Avery put a hand on Simms's shoulder. "Jimmy? You all right?"

"They lost one," Simms said, his tone disbelieving.

"One what, Jimmy?"

"One of them turkey buzzard planes you were so hot to see. Took off early. Didn't come back. Sonuvabitch Castro shot it down, just like Powers over Russia!"

"A U-2?"

Simms nodded. "Not one of them black ones, though. Buddy at the barn says they're all there. Musta been a silver."

With the lone air force star. Avery flinched in alarm. Shooting down an air force plane was a clear-cut act of war. And no doubt the very thing LeMay and the other Chiefs had been hungering for.

This was the trumpet's call to the final horror—a war of missiles that, once started, would be over before most people even knew it had begun.

RACING HOME, HIS SPIRITS in a sickening spiral, Avery tried to recall what he'd told Steve about needing to go, about not coming back for the rest of the day. He failed.

In fact, turning onto his own street, he realized he remembered nothing of the mile-and-a-half drive except his quick stop at the empty cottage to scribble a note to Kitty: *Game canceled on account of rain. Sarah not well. Had to go. Sorry, Wes.*

The air inside the cab was too close and, with the defroster blasting, too warm. Avery felt chased by the downpour of rain, trapped behind the slap of the wipers on the windshield and the rain-muffled roar and whine of jet engines overhead. He swung into his own driveway a bit too quickly and felt the truck's rear end give way in the curve. He braked into his usual space under the carport, took the truck out of gear, and nearly opened his door into Charlotte, who'd come rushing out of the house.

"She's gone *bonkers,* Dad!"

"What do you mean?"

"All I did was offer to make her a sandwich and she looked at me like she'd seen a ghost—"

"A ghost? What did she say?"

"Nothing, Dad. She just ran out the door, onto the back porch, and started yelling at the poor parakeets!"

"Still there?"

"No. After that, she ran outside. She's out there now . . . standing in the rain! I tried . . . I really tried to get her to come in, but . . . she wouldn't come." Charlotte was weeping.

He reached out and gave her shoulder a comforting squeeze. "Okay, Kitten. I'll go out and talk to her. Meanwhile, you drive up to Doc Mike's. Tell him we need him right away."

She wilted with relief. "I called Mr. Beauchamp back. Told him Mom was sick and somebody else needed to make her calls."

"Good thinking, kiddo."

"I tried calling Emilio, too. To let him know about the game," she said in a rush, climbing into the truck, "but nobody's answering out at the camp."

Were they evacuating the Pedro Pans? Where to? "How 'bout after Mike's, you run by the Catholic church. Look up the priest—Thomas is his name."

"Father Tom? Of course. Well, maybe . . ." She touched the side of her head and nibbled her lip, torn between the desire to go and the need to return. "If you think . . ."

He held up a palm, waved her away. *Go,* it said. "We'll be fine," he promised, and hoped he wasn't lying.

He was halfway across the covered back porch when he finally saw her through the rain-streaked screen. The unlikeliness of the scene stopped him short.

Sarah, who routinely took baths instead of showers because she disliked "water splashing on my face," stood, face raised to the downpour, hair and rain streaming down her back. Sarah, who never emerged from their bedroom without robe and slippers, stood barefoot on the grass, her sleeveless, rain-soaked nightgown cupping her buttocks and clinging to her legs. Her long, bare arms were outstretched toward the lake, flapping wildly like wings, and she was calling urgently, inexplicably, "Shoo! Go on! You're free!"

None of this made any sense to Avery. Until he saw, beside her on the grass, the three birdcages, doors ajar, pegs empty.

For reasons known only to her, Sarah had set all three of her parakeets free in the middle of a downpour.

Avery grabbed the cotton lap robe from the chaise. Sarah startled at the sound of the door and stepped farther down the lawn, her arms flapping more wildly. "Shoo!"

A spooked horse can't be forced, he'd learned in his childhood. You have to show it your respect, and gentle it back into the barn.

"Come in now, Sarah," he said softly, draping the robe gently over her shoulders. "You'll catch your death out here."

Rivulets of water striped her face. Rain or tears? It was impossible to tell. He reached out, tucked a strand of wet hair behind her ear. "Come back into the house, darlin'."

She swung around to face him. Her eyes were coal black again and red-veined with misery. He wanted to fold her in his arms, carry her inside the way you would a terrified child. But the determined jut of her chin warned him away from trying.

"Catch my death? I'm half-dead already!" She stood her ground—

though she was trembling all over, her teeth chattering—and let the robe fall to the grass.

Rain streamed down her body, over the two small mounds of her breasts, parting around each dark nipple, visible through the thin, wet nightgown.

"Please, darlin'," he urged softly, stretching out one hand, placing the other lightly at her back. He could feel her heartbeat racing between her ribs. "Come in with me."

"I let them go, Wes."

"I see that."

"I wanted *song*birds. Canaries! But I let the guy at the shop talk me into parakeets. I *settled*, Wes. And I never heard a single note out of any one of them. Nothing but Ack! Ack! Ack! and ARK! ARK! ARK! I just couldn't *stand* it anymore! I'm *done*, Wesss." She'd stiffened with warning, and pronounced his name with an unnerving hiss. "I'm done *settling*. . . ."

"Nice rain we're having, don't you think?"

Avery turned. Mike Martell stood beside them, doctor's bag in one hand and a large orange-and-blue golf umbrella in the other.

"Oh, yes, isn't it!" Sarah warbled, a now smiling coquette.

Martell handed Avery his bag and umbrella and said, "Perhaps you could open the door and . . ." He took Sarah's hand and slipped it under his arm, escort-style. "A blanket sounds nice, doesn't it?" He patted her hand. "Maybe some hot coffee?"

Sarah made a flirt's pouty face. "Not coffee. Chocolate. *Hot* chocolate. With marshmallows on top!"

Avery held the umbrella high over their heads while Martell slowly, ceremoniously walked her toward the door and out of the rain.

Stepping in behind them, he set down the doctor's things, rushed off to grab a blanket, towels, and Sarah's robe and slippers. He thrust the bulk of it to Martell, save the robe, which he draped around her shoulders, then headed to the kitchen to put on coffee plus a small pan of milk for hot chocolate. Once he had those started, he dashed into their bedroom to exchange his own drenched clothes for dry ones.

Back in the kitchen, he stood watching the milk for bubbles and struggling to get a handle on his fears. All of them—Sarah nearly *naked* in the rain letting the birds go, Simms dumbstruck over the downed U-2, not to mention his standing up to Kitty at the cottage— swirled around him. Each was a potential disaster. But combined? His mind was a fog of imminent doom.

The metal shudder of the pan on the burner—the milk had begun to boil—brought him back to the task at hand. He grabbed mugs, spooned cocoa, poured hot milk into Sarah's mug, coffee into Martell's.

Martell had pulled up a chair beside the chaise, where Sarah sat facing him, bundled in her robe and the blanket; wet hair turbaned in a towel. They were talking urgently.

Avery, feeling odd man out, cleared his throat. Sarah glanced up, accepted her cup with a bright smile that immediately dimmed. "No marshmallows?"

"Sorry," he faltered and, after handing off Martell's coffee, turned back toward the kitchen.

"I'll just be a minute," he heard Martell say, heard his footsteps click cross the porch's dark terrazzo. Inside the kitchen, the doctor scowled. "You know that bridge we talked about crossing the other day?"

"Yes."

"It's here."

Avery was silent.

"She needs to go to Florida San, Wes. And soon. Mind if I make a call?"

While Martell dialed the number, Avery watched himself, as if from a distance, fish the plastic bag of miniature marshmallows off the pantry shelf, walk across the kitchen, step out onto the porch, and fill the top of Sarah's cup.

"Thank you," she said quietly. She sipped on her mug, not looking at him.

He was glad, because he was trying—oh, how *hard* he was trying— not to look guilty over what they—he—was about to do to her.

Avery the observer watched himself squirm through a knot of questions: Did Martell bring his car? Will we drive her to the sanitarium together? In the doctor's car or Sarah's Buick? Has she forgotten about homecoming? What will we do if she refuses to go?

Martell appeared in the doorway, lips pursed in obvious aggravation. He curled a single finger in Avery's direction. *Come,* it said.

Avery looked at Sarah. She was licking a combination of chocolate and marshmallow foam off her lips and staring out at the rain. She seemed, impossibly, content.

"Everything okay, Sarah? Would you like another?"

"Another what?" she asked flatly.

In the brief hardening of her eyes, the sharpening of her features, Avery felt again the shadowy brush of a furtive, feral wildness. Instinctively, he folded one arm over the other, hoping to disguise the rise of gooseflesh on both his forearms.

"Another hot chocolate, darlin'."

Her look softened instantly. "Yes, please. And a grilled cheese?"

"Of course. Be right back."

Martell, who'd been watching their exchange from the doorway, backed silently into the kitchen.

Avery crossed the distance slowly, sensing the other shoe and dreading its inevitable drop.

"They're telling me the ward is full; that we'll have to wait for an empty bed. The chief surgeon and I were in med school together at Gainesville. I'll pull some strings, but it might take awhile. Tomorrow at the latest."

"What'll we do till then?" The guilt he'd felt earlier, Avery realized, had been lined with relief that Sarah would be safely away from Kitty and in someone else's professional care. Now what?

"For starters, we'll take her off the Dexedrine; it's obviously overstimulating her. And let's up the Miltown, which should calm things down a bit. The Seconal's been working at night, right?"

"Yes," Avery answered, eyeing the doorway. What if Sarah walked in and found him huddled in conversation instead of fixing her cocoa?

She was so erratic. . . . "Could you write it down?" Avery pointed to the counter notepad and pen. He got out more milk, bread, cheese, and butter, set them down beside the stove, pulled out a frying pan, and refired the burners.

"Tonight of all nights," he was thinking. And was surprised to hear he'd said it out loud.

Martell looked up, blinked confusion, then apparent understanding. "Oh, yes. The dance. Nancy and I are chaperoning." He had a daughter, too, Avery remembered, a pretty cheerleader who'd be a senior next year. "This is Charlotte's big night, isn't it?"

Avery nodded, resigned to missing it. Sarah wasn't going anywhere this evening.

Martell tapped the tip of his pen on the paper. "Look here, Wes. We're supposed to be there at seven-fifteen. I could come here instead. Then you could go on with Nancy, watch the ceremony, and come back."

"I couldn't ask you to do that—"

"Oh, yes, you could. Y'see"—Martell shot Avery a conspiratorial wink—"the Gators are in Baton Rouge and they're televising the game at seven. I come here, I could probably catch the first quarter, maybe even the first half."

"And Sarah?"

"This'll knock her out for the rest of the day," he replied, ripping his note off the pad. "When I come back, I'll give her a shot that'll take her through to tomorrow morning."

Before Martell left, he explained her new dosage to Sarah.

"An afternoon nap?" she asked.

"Absolutely!"

Avery, bringing out lunch on a tray, heard Martell's follow-up lie: "You need your beauty sleep for homecoming tonight, right?"

"Y-yes, I guess so."

After lunch, at the doctor's suggestion, Avery drew a hot bath. The new dosage, four round white Miltowns plus two Seconals, appeared to take the edge off her, but he was hesitant to leave her alone in the tub. He left the bathroom door slightly open and, keeping her in view, moved to sit down on the unmade bed. But the sight of it jarred him.

Sarah was a stickler about making the bed. From their earliest days, she'd always had the same unfailing morning routine—get up, put on robe and slippers, make the bed, brush teeth then hair, in that order.

Would seeing the bed a mess stop her the way it had just stopped him? Put her off from taking her prescribed nap? Not wanting to risk it, he quietly tucked and smoothed their bedding into place for her.

In the tub, Sarah began to hum a low, mournful tune. Then slowly, softly, she began to sing a song he hadn't heard in years.

"I am a po-or wayfaring stranger, a-travelin thro-ugh this world of woe." Avery sat down on the bed, listening.

"Yet there's no sick-ness, toil or dan-ger in that bright world to which I go. I'm going the-re to see my father. . . ."

They'd sprinkled the aisle of the revival tent with sawdust. Just like at the circus. The smell of it had clogged his nostrils, reminding him then, as it did even now, of his father. Strong arms swinging the honed ax blade high above his head, then down in a perfect arc onto a stump, splitting logs for his mother's cookstove. It was the smell of sawdust, and the bright promise of relief from his crushing grief, that had propelled him out of his seat.

"I'm only go-ing over Jordan, I'm only go-ing over home," Sarah was singing in her deep, rich contralto, while Avery, in his mind, was walking the sawdust aisle. *"I know dark clouds will ga-ther 'round me. I know my way is rough and steep. Yet, beauteous fields lie just be-fore me, where God's re-deemed their vigils keep."*

Up at the front of the tent, he'd declared to the preacher his desire, his eleven-year-old's overwhelming need, to "see my father," to know that his strong arms, mangled and flayed to the bone by the tractor's axle, his life's blood pooled in the dirt of the barn floor, had been made whole again in heaven.

"Yes," the man had promised. "Yes," his mother, overjoyed, had nodded to him from afar. And the choir, as if on cue, had sung:

"I'm going the-re to see my mother. She said she'd me-et me when I come. I'm only go-ing over Jordan, I'm only go-ing over home."

He'd believed it then and, in a post-revival fervor, he'd been baptized and pronounced born again. It was afterward, however, when the promised vision of his father returned-to-wholeness never appeared, when his mother's demands for more and more attendance at church events reached shrill levels, that he'd given up on blind faith and fervent religion, and adopted instead his grandfather's more quiet, more practical spiritual creed. "Life, like the sea, comes at us hard," he could hear Old Pa saying. "It's kindness—simple, human kindness—that buffers the blows."

"Why, Wes!" Sarah, in her robe, was surprised to see him there.

"I was enjoying the singing."

"Of cours-se you were."

Avery noticed the smiling slur in Sarah's speech, the slight unsteadiness in her step. The pills appeared to be working.

"You know I've always loved your voice." He stood up to take her arm and help her to the velvet stool in front of her vanity. Did she know—had he ever told her?—how, after his father died, that song came to signal the official end of his childhood?

"You s-should've heard me in high school." She picked up the tortoiseshell comb she used to untangle her wet hair. "I was the sophomore s-star of the s-senior follies!"

"Really?"

"Oh, yes-s. I even auditioned wi' the great Frank La Forge— touring the S-south in search of the nex' big star! You have any idea who Frank La Forrge was, Wes?" she asked, yawning widely.

"Can't say that I do, darlin'." Avery took the comb from her and gently ran it through her hair. It was something he used to love doing when they were newly married. Then Charlotte got big enough to try and took over. Then, at some point, he didn't remember when, Sarah did it herself.

"Frank La Forge trained Mar-yan Anderson. Turned her from a gospel singer 'nto an innernation'l *star.*"

"Is that so? And you auditioned with him?"

"Yes-s. Said I reminded 'im of a young Sigrid Onégin."

The singer on Beauchamp's record, Avery recalled.

"He invited me to study with 'im in New York."

"But . . ." He caught Sarah's eyes in the mirror. ". . . you chose not to go, right?"

"Cho-se?" Her voice rose and cracked bitterly on the word. "Who told you that?"

His mind raced back, to her early letters, his brief stay in Tuscaloosa. "I . . . well, actually, I don't know. I just thought . . ."

"Y'thought wrong, Wes. There was no choice involved."

"Why not? Dolores wouldn't let you go?"

Sarah's pale face froze with recalled pain. "Kitty got pregnant, Wes."

"What?" Avery saw his own astonishment reflected in her mirror. He'd dropped the comb on the carpet. As he bent to pick it up, he did the math in his head. He couldn't square the dates.

"After th' dance, night she was Homecoming Queen. Somebody slipped her a mickey. Spanish fly. Whatever. Afterw'rds she couldn't remember who, or what, or even how many."

"My God!" This happened in high school? When Kitty was what? Seventeen? Same as Charlotte is now. Which made Sarah what? Fifteen?

Her eyes had become ashy coals, burning heat in his direction. "All Mama wanted was for it to go 'way. She made Daddy sell Kitty's car f'r the money, but day it was s'posed to happen . . . Kitty woke up bleedin'. She lost it. Lost them. Twins."

She took the comb from him and studied it, fingering the tangle of loose hairs from its teeth into a small nest in her palm. "First time I ever heard th' word *miscarriage.* Or that women in our fam-ly were prone to 'em." She dropped the nest into the small wastebasket at her feet.

"Oh, darlin'." Avery drew her up and into his arms. "How horrible for you both."

For a moment, she leaned heavily against him, head bent, face buried in his shoulder. Then she drew back to tell him the rest of it.

"'Twas bad for me, but worse for her. You can't 'magine the things got scrawled in the halls: 'Whore-Coming Queen,' 'Kitty, Queen of Alley Cats.' 'Kitty lost her litter.' Stuff like that."

Avery stepped her to the bed, helped her sit on it, then sat down beside her, steadying arms around her waist.

"She had to get outta Tuscaloosa . . . go to a private school upstate. 'Course . . . they couldn't afford that *and* sendin' me to New York."

The words *New York* seemed to sap whatever strength she had left. She collapsed onto the bed and lay facedown, shoulders shuddering, chest heaving with dry, despairing sobs. Avery knelt beside her, stroking her hair. "There, there," he told her, feeling incapable of soothing her. So that's what Kitty meant, calling Sarah the "sacrificial lamb"?

"I know . . ." She was speaking so softly he had to lean in to hear her. "You got t' Tuscaloosa, you thought us monsters. But . . . you got no idea . . . *no idea* how much we scrimped 'nd scraped to keep 'er at that fancy school . . . only to have 'er run off 'nd join the WAACs . . . wind up back home . . . same fix all over again."

"But . . ." Questions, explanations were clogging his brain.

"You'd think . . ." She turned on her side to face him, reached out and grabbed his forearm, her grip surprisingly strong. "You'd think what happen'd to her would've tamed 'er . . . certainly did *me* . . . but only made her wilder. She got kicked out of th' army, Wes. Not 'cause she was pregnant . . . Mama checked . . . She was dishonor'bly discharged. *Morals* charges! 'Hellcat in heat,' one guy tol' Mama. 'Little more than a *whore*,' 'nother guy said. Nobody b'lieved that cockamamie story 'bout Carlo . . . nobody but *you*."

"But . . ." Was Kitty lying back then? And as recently as the other day? Was she even in real estate, as she claimed? If not, where did the money for the Chrysler and the cashmere come from?

"'Twas too late to abort," Sarah rushed on, "all we could hope was she'd lose it . . . You will never know . . . ," she said quietly, painfully confessing, ". . . how long, how hard I prayed she'd miscarry again 'nd be gone 'fore you came."

"Oh, Sarah." He felt a rush of pain for her.

Her shoulders sagged. "I know . . ." She looked lost. Avery knew that look, and the loneliness behind it tore at his heart.

"When I was little, Kitty's wildness . . . terr'fied me. When I see signs of it in Charlotte, I'm scared all over again. But . . . I don' know . . . mebbe a *little* wildness isn't so bad. Because . . . well . . . a too tame life . . ." Her eyes returned to him, squinting as one might at a stranger at a distance, then wandered past him, and through him, to the dark pleated curtains tightly closed against the light; the small chest of drawers where she kept her "unmentionables"; the pale slipper chair and matching footstool where every morning she put on her stockings and every evening she sat to remove them. ". . . can feel . . . ," she whispered, her gaze floating to the ceiling, ". . . like a kind of livin' death."

Her chest heaved with misery, and a wave of raw pity consumed him. He felt numb and mute and enormously sad. He reached out to stroke her surprisingly dry cheek, remembering Charlotte saying that Sarah was "crying her eyes out." Was it possible to run out of tears?

He sat with her, adjusting her pillows, the covers, the light beside the bed until, finally, exhausted, she fell asleep.

He unplugged the phone on the nightstand, and closed the bedroom door quietly behind him. How was it, in seventeen years, he'd never heard the whole story . . . until now? And even if he had heard it, what could he have said or done to help her feel differently? What could he say or do *now*? He felt overwhelmed by Sarah's truth, her guilt and suffering over wishing Charlotte had never been born, and, worst of all, her crushing disappointment. "A too tame life," she'd said, "a kind of living death." The words—and the judgment in them—stabbed deep.

Wandering back into the living room, Avery heard the sound, saw the flash of green from his own truck pulling into the carport. He went to the side door to greet Charlotte, intending to tell her that her mother was calm and resting. But the look on her face stopped him.

"What is it, kiddo?"

"Turn on the TV, Dad. The Pentagon's about to make an important announcement."

11.

"WHERE'S MOM?" CHARLOTTE ASKED, WARILY SCANNING THE living room.

"Took a hot bath and went to bed. Doc Mike changed her pills and"—Avery lowered his voice, glanced toward the hallway leading to their bedroom—"he's making arrangements for Florida San, probably tomorrow."

Charlotte took a shaky breath and let it out softly. Her face reflected a painful, shifting mix of emotions: worry over her mother's welfare, doubt over the doctor's arrangement, then, finally, a glum nodding assent. *This won't be easy,* her eyes seemed to say, *but we have no other choice, do we?*

Avery shook his head. *No, we don't.*

She crossed the room to stand beside him. She offered and he accepted a comforting hug. Then, releasing him, she turned and snapped on the TV.

All three networks—Channels 2, 6, and 9—were tuned to the briefing room of the Pentagon, where a spokesman stood at the podium on the flag-draped dais. His statement was delivered bluntly:

"A US military reconnaissance aircraft conducting surveillance over Cuba is missing and presumed lost. A large air and sea search for the plane and its US Air Force pilot, Major Rudolph Anderson Jr. of Greenville,

South Carolina, is currently under way, and will continue throughout this afternoon and evening."

Jimmy Simms was right.

"At the request of the secretary of defense, the air force has called up 24 troop carrier squadrons and their supporting units, approximately 14,000 air force reservists, to immediate active duty. . . ."

When the reporters in front of the podium erupted with questions, the spokesman held up a hand—*No answers,* it said—and stepped aside.

In the shouts that followed him off the dais, before the round, eyeball-shaped logo of the CBS network silenced them, Avery heard the reporters giving voice to his own fears: *". . . escalation?" ". . . retaliation?"* And most sobering of all, *". . . World War Three?"*

Aware of his instinct to shield Charlotte from his own concerns, not to mention CBS anchor Charles Collingwood's comments—how could his analysis be anything but dire?—Avery snapped off the television.

"They're going to invade Cuba, aren't they?" Charlotte's arms were crossed in front of her chest. Her face was very pale.

"I hope not."

"Dad, *twenty-four* troop carrier squadrons? Where else would they be going?"

"Look, kiddo . . ." He stopped, at a loss how to comfort her.

"I'm not a kid anymore, Dad." She said it sharply. "Emilio says one of the guys got a call through to his parents in Havana. They've been expecting the marines for months. . . ."

Months? Not days or weeks, but *months?* So . . . who started this mess anyway? Did Khrushchev put the missiles in Cuba so *he* could intimidate us? Or did all our military exercises this past spring and summer convince him that *we* were about to attack them?

". . . Castro's ordered everyone on high alert, ready to fight," Charlotte was saying. "'Fatherland or death,' he's telling them."

Avery had a painful mental picture: Somewhere in Washington, a fiery, black-browed Curtis LeMay was insisting, "There are no civilians in Cuba, either!" If LeMay had his way . . .

Charlotte was staring at him and, without warning, burst into tears.

He stepped forward to comfort her, and she crumpled against his chest, wrapping her arms around his waist and sobbing into his shirt. "There, there, Kitten," he whispered, holding her as he had when she was little, gently patting her back. "All right now, you're all right."

After a long while, she withdrew from him, blotting her eyes with the sleeve of her sweatshirt. "The thing is, Da-addy . . . ," she said quietly.

Her quivering break on the word *Daddy* (she hadn't called him that in years) tore his heart.

"I don't understand why all this is hap-pening. . . ." She waved her hand at the television, the room, the whole wide world. "And why *now*? I-I don't want to die. Not now . . . just when I'm starting to live!"

Nobody's dying, he wanted to say but didn't. They were both beyond his usual Happy Pappy sugarcoating. Instead, he tried to remember what they'd been talking about before, to pick up the thread before she'd lost it.

"So you found Emilio? At the church?" he asked her, lamely. "What was he doing there?"

Charlotte's eyes hung on him a second too long before she answered, "All the guys from the camp are there, handing out coffee and doughnuts to the crowd."

"There's a crowd? In the middle of the afternoon?"

"It's a *madhouse*, Dad." Avery winced internally at the word. "The pews are packed with people praying, and there are long lines waiting for the priests to hear their confessions. While I was there, one woman with a brand-new baby was on her knees, hysterical, insisting somebody christen it immediately, so the poor thing wouldn't wind up in limbo. What the heck is limbo anyway?"

"I have no idea."

"They're handing out flyers, too. *Eight Simple Air Raid Rules*. I left ours in the truck. And"—she fished a crumpled piece of paper out of her pocket, and handed it to him—"Father Tom asked you to please call him at this number between four and four-fifteen. And . . . oh, jeez." She glanced at her watch. "I've got to jump in the shower. Emilio's picking me up at five-thirty."

"Five-thirty? I thought the dance starts at seven-thirty."

"He's taking me to dinner first." She flashed the first smile he'd seen from her all day. "We have reservations at The Villa Rosa."

In that instant, the screen of mental horrors that had been rolling like newsreel through the back of Avery's mind went blank. He stared at Charlotte and saw, in her smiling eyes, in the wispy, rainy-day curls framing her lovely face, the little girl who'd always loved The Villa Rosa, who requested it for special holidays and birthdays, and insisted that the restaurant's red-and-white checked tablecloths, its dripping candles in straw-covered Chianti bottles, its tinny Italian accordion music reminded her *exactly* of her favorite scene in the movie when Lady and the Tramp shared their first bowl of spaghetti together.

In the midst of all the craziness surrounding them, Charlotte was about to have the date she'd dreamed of for years.

And why not? he thought. With all these two have been through the past few days, why not?

"Gotta go," she said, turning on her heel, bounding gracefully out of the room, leaving Avery despairing: Where did the years, and that little girl, go?

"Saint Charles Church, this is Debbie."

"Thomas O'Meara, please."

"Father Tom? One moment."

"Hello?"

"Thomas? It's Wes Avery."

"Wes . . . I was, uh . . . pleased to meet your daughter today . . . Lovely girl."

"Thank you. She said you asked me to call?"

"Uh, yes . . . Well, look, it's an unusual request, but these are unusual times . . . perhaps you'll understand?"

Avery waited. He couldn't imagine what the priest wanted. But he hoped it wasn't gas. Not even the pope himself could get a fill-up today.

"The monsignor has decided . . . with everything going on, or about to go on . . . best not leave our boys, our Cuban boys, out at the camp tonight. They're all deeply concerned . . . as you can imagine . . . about their families in Cuba. Monsignor thinks they're better . . . safer . . . in a family setting. We have parishioners but . . . Well, I wondered . . . with Emilio's plans tonight, if he might stay with you? Only for the night, mind you . . . we'll need him back for nine a.m. Mass . . . Until or unless . . . well . . ."

The man was frazzled. But if I'd spent hours in a two-person box—with endless lines of people coming in to confess their darkest secrets and deepest fears—I guess I'd be frazzled, too.

"Or, if it's inconvenient . . . Perhaps Mr. Steve? You two have been . . ."

"Of course, send him over."

It made sense, didn't it? That, after the dance, Emilio should stay here. By the look of things, Charlotte wouldn't mind. And Sarah . . . well, according to Martell, Sarah was out for the night, right? And by the time she woke up tomorrow, Emilio would be long gone to church. Assuming—there was no denying the possibility—there *was* a tomorrow.

Within seconds after he'd hung up, the phone rang, startling him. Was it the priest calling back? He picked it up after the first ring.

"Hello?"

"So I guess I'll see you in the gym."

Kitty. "You got my message?"

"About the game? Yes. But I drove by the school just now. Sign out front says the dance is still on."

Avery felt the jab of her suspicion that he'd deliberately tried to derail her. "Yeah, well, I wasn't sure myself when—"

"Right," she said, obviously not buying it. "I'll see you there." She hung up.

Avery stood in the empty kitchen, staring at the now dead receiver in his hand as if seeing it for the first time. Bakelite, he remembered, fingering the molded black plastic. Same stuff the Brits used to make hand grenades during The War. Number 69 Bakelite Grenade, he thought, recalling the young paratrooper who'd showed him one, its surprisingly light heft. "Only problem . . ." the young man had warned him, returning the grenade to its hook, ". . . if you're the least bit careless, you'll blow your own head off."

EMILIO ARRIVED PROMPTLY AT five with his suit bag, a small duffel, and the white sheet from The Admiral's backseat in hand.

"Mr. A, thank you so much. It's just been . . ." The boy's face betrayed his shaky hold on his emotions.

"No problem." Avery waved off the need for further explanation. He tossed the sheet onto the bench beside the door, and ushered Emilio into the guest room that was also the family "shelter." Emilio's eyes widened at the spartan metal bunks, the floor-to-ceiling racks of food and supplies, and (to Avery's mind) the tomb-like gloom of the place.

"You can change in here," Avery told him, "but I think you'll sleep more comfortably on the sofa in the living room."

Twenty minutes later, the youth emerged much more composed—shaved, combed, polished, and sharply handsome in his dark suit, white shirt, and skinny black tie.

Charlotte swept into the living room at five-thirty and stunned both of them into silence. Not because her garnet-red gown set off her pale skin and pearls, her dark eyes and curls to perfection—though the overall effect *was* stunning. It was, for Avery, because at that moment her shy-but-head-held-high elegance, eyes bright with anticipation, cheeks pink with excitement, reminded him—*exactly*—of Sarah on the platform of the Tuscaloosa train station awaiting his arrival. Charlotte was, at this moment, every inch Sarah's daughter. His heart ached at the realization that Sarah wasn't beside him to see it.

The only jarring note, to him, was the one long white glove she wore, its twin held loosely in her hand.

Charlotte creased her brow. "Mom's asleep and I can't decide. Gloves?" she asked, showing him and Emilio one side, the side with the glove on. "Or not?" she said, pivoting to show the other long slim arm, delicate wrist, and pale, perfectly polished fingers.

Emilio, who'd shot to his feet when she entered, grinned. "Either way works for me."

"I think *not*," Avery decreed firmly. "You're perfect without them."

"Thanks, Dad." She removed the glove, setting both aside on the bench beside the door, gliding over to kiss him on the cheek. "Are we ready?" she asked Emilio, who immediately, proudly, offered up his arm.

"I'll see you in the gym," Avery told them, and saw her eyes cloud with concern for her mother. "No, no. Doc Mike's coming by to keep an eye out," he assured her in their code.

"Good." She favored him with a dazzling, relieved smile that set his father's heart swelling to button-popping proportions. "See you there."

The rain had stopped. Avery watched Emilio escort her to the passenger's side of The Admiral, open the door, and tuck her in as though she were made of spun glass.

"Take care," he called, and Emilio waved. Of course, he would take care. But it comforted Avery to say the words.

PEERING INTO THE FRIGIDAIRE's open freezer compartment, he recalled Lilly's comment at the station—"If this is our Last Supper, I definitely want a steak!" He quirked a corner of his mouth in a rueful grin and pulled out the brown-and-red TV dinner box labeled SALIS- BURY STEAK.

Ain't the House of Beef's porterhouse (which would have been his preference), but it'll have to do.

He checked the instructions, set the oven, removed the foil-covered aluminum tray from its box, slid it into the heat, and set the timer for twenty-five minutes.

One eye on the clock—he was counting down to the six o'clock news—he washed and put away the dishes from lunch, set up a TV tray with knife, fork, and napkin, and poured himself a glass of sweet tea.

At five fifty-nine, he sat down with his steaming tray on his lap, expecting the Saturday stand-in for his weekday favorites, Chet Huntley and David Brinkley. The opening chords—*bomp-bomp, bomp-bomp, bomp-bomp, BOMP-bomp*—of "a special Weekend Edition of *The Huntley-Brinkley report*" were a surprise, as was the appearance of Huntley, circles puddling darker than ever under his eyes, in New York and Brinkley, wary as always, in Washington.

Clearly, the news was bad and getting worse.

"President Kennedy has revealed that Premier Khrushchev offered an acceptable solution for the Cuban crisis and then pulled away from it."

Why would he do that?

"In a letter to the Soviet leader tonight," Brinkley continued, *"President Kennedy called on him to stand by an offer made in a private communication last night to remove Soviet missiles from Cuba under United Nations supervision.*

"At the same time, the President brushed aside a subsequent proposal from Premier Khrushchev this morning offering to eliminate Soviet missile bases in Cuba if the United States would remove its missile bases in Turkey."

So Khushchev's trying the old bait-and-switch? Now the bastard wants the trade, their missiles for ours?

"In an effort to persuade Mr. Khrushchev to revert to his previous offer, the President said that if he would agree to remove the weapons from Cuba under inspection, the United States would halt the blockade and give assurances against an invasion of Cuba."

And they're stuck with Castro forever?

Huntley, always the heavy, weighed in. *"But even as the White House was trying to retrieve a situation that earlier began to look promising, of-*

ficials said the crisis was escalating. Several events seemed to bear out their fears:

"In Cuba, a United States U-2 reconnaissance aircraft was reported missing while attempting to observe what was happening at the Soviet missile bases there. And another United States plane was fired upon, apparently by Cubans and not by the Russians.

"Also, the Castro Government appeared to be taking a much more belligerent attitude than the Soviet Government, possibly in fear that it was being sold out by Moscow. It announced that its forces intended to oppose the United States reconnaissance planes.

"At the Pentagon, the Defense Department threatened retaliation if United States planes were fired on."

Avery set his tray aside, his appetite vanished. He leaned forward, forearms on his knees, hands clasped between them, ear cocked to his own thoughts. It was his chess player's pose, struck when evaluating next moves.

The broadcast ended with their ritual exchange of good night.

"Good luck," Avery muttered, switching them off, returning to his doleful thoughts.

What was it Steve read in the New York paper? Only three ways to get those missiles out of Cuba: Invade and take 'em out. Blockade and starve 'em out. Or sit down with the Soviets and trade 'em out?

Obviously, Khrushchev wanted the trade.

Obviously, he and Castro knew the Pentagon was gearing up to invade. And both of them seemed itching for the fight, ready to start things on their own if need be.

But where was JFK on all this? Stalling for time, it appeared; hoping to make the best move possible—that was obvious.

Avery found himself wondering if Khrushchev and Kennedy were chess players. And, if so, which parts of the game were their strengths? Every player had a strong and a weak spot. Steve's strength, for instance, was his opening gambit, and middle transition; Avery's was his endgame.

And Khrushchev's? Kennedy's? Contemplating the global game played out over the past week, Avery had the dizzying realization that they'd reached every chess player's worst nightmare: *zugzwang*.

Zugzwang, the endgame perfected by Persian chess masters over a thousand years ago, occurred when every move left is "bad" and whichever player has the next move will, as a result of his move, lose.

In the thermonuclear-charged game between Khrushchev and Kennedy, having reached zugzwang, the only question left to answer was: *Whose turn is it?* Was it Kennedy's, due to Khrushchev's downing of the U-2? Or was it Khrushchev's because of some secret move on Kennedy's part?

Avery stood up, to counter the burn of bile in his gut, and went into the kitchen to dispose of his dinner. The gravy had coagulated into gray gunk, and the green-beans-and-carrots medley had the look of melted wax. If this was indeed his Last Supper, he'd just as soon go hungry.

Besides, Martell would be here soon and he needed to get ready.

In their bedroom, Avery left off the light so as not to wake Sarah and padded softly through the darkened room. He gathered his suit and shoes from the closet. He stripped and stepped into the shower, and adjusted the stream to as hot as he could stand it. With palms on either side of the showerhead, he leaned in, bowed his head beneath the flow, and let the heat massage the tightness in his neck and shoulders and cascade warmth down his back, buttocks, calves, and heels. Eyes closed, he could feel the centrifugal force of things spiraling out of control—the world, like Sarah, hanging by a thread—so he opened them, anchoring himself within the shower's careful grid of gray and green tiles.

With a dripping forefinger, he traced the grout around one square tile. *Careful.* If ever a word summed up a man, a life, *careful* was his. It had been his priority and his watchword: "Take care," he'd told his customers, his wife, and his daughter every day for as long as he could remember. But in the past handful of days, he'd discovered the joke: All the care in a man's world can't protect him, or his family, or anyone from the greater perils outside his control. At this point—perhaps at any point?—careful didn't count, and control was the punch line in the big joke. It all boiled down to—what? Luck of the draw? Your spot on the giant chessboard? Despite the hot water, Avery shivered. He wrenched off the flow and toweled himself off, shoulders high and tight.

What are the chances, he asked the grim eyes in the mirror, that Kennedy, the young sailor, or Khrushchev, the crafty old farmer, isn't making his final move now, at this moment, and we are all about to lose everything?

Perversely, the voice inside his head jeered: Is there a Russian word for global FUBAR? And by the way, what in the world are you going to tell Kitty to head off her own personal endgame against Charlotte?

HALF AN HOUR LATER, Avery found himself helping his doctor's sturdy wife into his truck.

"Take your time," Martell told them, one eye already on the television, intent on turning on the game.

"They really should have canceled this thing, don't you think?" Nancy Martell complained, shifting Charlotte's forgotten flyer from the church, *Eight Simple Air Raid Rules,* into the space on the seat between them.

"Tough call," Avery replied, thinking how disappointed Charlotte and Emilio would be if they had.

In the crepe-paper-draped gym, he scanned the early arrivals for Kitty, and for Charlotte and Emilio—no dice—and allowed himself to be pressed into service transporting ice and opening juice cans for the red-and-white-draped punch bowls.

Just after seven-thirty, Avery saw Charlotte and Emilio come through the door; saw the chaperone direct Charlotte to the girls' locker room to join the others backstage preparing for their grand entrance; saw Emilio step away and hesitantly seek a place to wait for her. The place was starting to fill with students dressed for dancing. The band, five guys sporting identical ducktails, tight pants, and dark sunglasses who called themselves the Shades, was tuning up with the theme from the TV show *Bonanza.*

Avery was weaving through the onlookers milling around the edges, his eyes on the door, when a woman stepped deliberately in his path. A flowered silk scarf covered her hair and wrapped around her neck in the style that Grace Kelly made famous. A black raincoat concealed her clothing, and her face was dominated by a pair of large, black, rather thick cat-eye glasses. But there was no mistaking the scent of spiced roses, or the single pearl in the hollow of her throat.

"Hello, Kitty," he said quietly.

"Nice to see you, Wes. Sarah still under the weather?" Her tone dripped sarcasm.

Before he could find the right words, another voice, vaguely familiar, called out to both of them: "Well, hail, hail, the gang's all here!"

Avery turned to acknowledge it and felt the spread of alarm at the sight of Lilly's florid face and, behind her, Steve's squint asking the obvious question, *What's* she *doin' here?*

"Curiosity killed the cat, they say," Kitty said, sizing up the situation instantly and slipping into Realtor mode. "But I don't buy that, do you? When I met Wes the other day, I was so taken by his affection for his daughter, I couldn't help but wonder whether or not she won. These little traditions are what make a community great, don't you think? And America, too, for that matter. And of course, a great school like this is nothing but *good* for property values."

Lilly listened to Kitty's entire spiel open-mouthed, then, self-consciously, closed her trap. Steve, who'd stood nodding in pleasant enough agreement, turned questioning eyes back to Avery.

Avery was still struggling to recover. "Surprised to see you two here," he said, tossing the ball into Steve's court.

Steve took a hasty look around, then stepped closer and said softy, "Lilly's been called back to work tomorrow. All the hospitals on the coast are on red alert, ready to receive the wounded after the invasion." He shot Avery a long, level look. "We came to tell Leo I need to pick up The Admiral out at the camp, first thing tomorrow mornin'."

Avery absorbed this news—somehow worse than any other he'd

heard today—and felt trapped inside a still, airless space, its edges a blur of clueless, carefree teenagers.

"The camp . . . ," he said, swallowing hard, ". . . is closed. The priests have farmed out the boys to local families. Emilio's with us tonight. You can come by the house instead."

"There you are!" And suddenly, there Emilio was—where had he been?—grinning relief. "And Mr. Steve! Hello!"

"Leo, this is Miss Lilly," Steve told him, disconcerted.

"Hello, Emilio." Kitty offered him an elegant hand. "I'm Kitty, friend of the family."

"Ladies and gentlemen," the principal announced from in front of the band, "please join me in welcoming Edgewater High's Class of 1963 Homecoming Court!"

On cue, the lights in the gym dimmed. The Shades attempted some sort of ceremonial march. The theater teacher turned spotlights on the boys and girls entering two by two as the principal announced their names.

To Avery, the whole scene felt increasingly surreal. There was his Charlotte, a radiant jewel, the three pretty blondes, and lovely Barbara Everly parading into the gym on the arms of their handsome escorts.

Meanwhile, somewhere not far south, tens of thousands of paratroopers, fighter pilots, seamen, marines, and infantrymen stood ready, waiting at this very moment for the command to go to war.

Greg Lund, captain of the football team, emerged—he and his teammates had the privilege of the final vote—with two cheerleaders. One carried five bouquets, four small and one large spray of red roses for the winner. The other held the two crowns for the night's king and queen.

Somewhere in Washington, someone was calculating the expected casualties and wounded. And, armed with those numbers, someone else was issuing alerts to who-knew-how-many hospitals to have beds and bandages and operating rooms ready for them.

Even though the commander in chief was actively pursuing peace, the giant machine of war was out there, idling, ready at an instant's notice to roll. Once started, it would be near impossible to stop. Not until it had reached the awful end, which with today's powerful weapons would be the annihilation of everything.

The couples stood in a spotlit semicircle. Kitty had moved to Avery's outer elbow, away from the others. As the Shades' drummer whipped up the crowd with a suspenseful drumroll, and Lund took the first small bouquet of white roses and walked dramatically toward one of the blondes, then zigzagged to another, Kitty leaned in. She whispered, "What do you know about him?"

Avery turned toward her, astonished to discover she'd taken his arm.

"Him," she repeated insistently, and darted her eyes toward Emilio.

The crowd was applauding the first blonde, whose pretty face was frozen in a cheerful loser's smile.

Avery leaned in to Kitty's ear. "Good boy, fine family; works for me."

Another drumroll. This time Lund was headed toward Barbara Everly, but at the last minute—relishing the tension he was creating—he zigzagged toward another blonde, the thin one with big teeth.

In the applause that followed, Avery was aware that Kitty was eyeing him, clearly wondering, *How much do you know?*

The thought occurred to him: *Is it possible she's here to* protect *Charlotte? To make sure what happened to her doesn't . . .*

It was the third drumroll, and Lund was headed straight for Charlotte. Without zigzagging this time, he pivoted abruptly toward the third blonde. Only Charlotte and Barbara, the two brunettes standing side by side, remained without flowers.

At the final drumroll, Kitty's fingers squeezed his elbow in anticipation. Greg Lund carried two bouquets, one small white, one large red. He walked slowly to stand midway between Barbara on his right and Charlotte on his left. The crowd murmured: Was it significant that the white bouquet was in his right hand and the large red one on his left? Had Barbara lost? Was Charlotte the winner?

Avery watched his daughter's smile wobble. Win or lose, he decided, she's still the prettiest girl in the room.

Milking the drama to its final drops, Lund raised both bouquets. He handed Charlotte the white one and Barbara the winner's red roses. The crowd roared. Lund's cheerleader helpers moved in to place the crowns upon the new queen and king.

Charlotte grinned, her face flushing.

Beside him, Kitty huffed disappointment.

"It's okay," Avery told her. "She didn't want to win."

Kitty cocked a lip corner in disbelief.

"No, really. Look at her." There was nothing fake about Charlotte's dazzlingly happy smile.

The Shades switched tunes. Now they were playing that song from *West Side Story*—*"There's a place for us, somewhere a place for us"*—with an outer-space Telstar spin. The principal announced the Royal Dance and invited the king and queen and the rest of the court to begin the ceremonial first waltz. After a brief few bars, the principal invited the rest of the crowd to join them.

Greg Lund cut in on Barbara's partner, and Emilio, apparently as instructed, did the same with Charlotte's.

Kitty nudged his arm. "You should cut in," she urged him.

"I should?"

"You wouldn't be the first." She pointed out one of the cheerleaders' dads, already waltzing with his daughter. "And when you're done, you can bring her over here and introduce me."

Avery turned to face her, keeping his back to Steve and Lilly so they couldn't hear. "No, I can't." He said it quietly.

Anger flared in her eyes like an artillery shell. "Why the hell not?"

"This is Charlotte's night. Not yours, not mine or Sarah's. The thing is . . ." He paused, needing to get it right. "The most important thing about parenting is . . . you put the kid's needs ahead of your own. Do you . . . Can you understand that? Charlotte doesn't *need* to have old history rehashed tonight. She *needs* to have the time of her life because, quite frankly, who knows if she'll get another chance?"

He watched her take it in, absorbing not just his words but his resolve. He saw her cast a hungry glance toward Charlotte, saw her calculate her chances of getting past him, saw her decide, long before she said the words, "All right, Wes," and held up her hands in temporary surrender. "For now, all right. So *go*," she insisted, giving him a not-so-subtle push. "Dance with your daughter while you still can."

Avery felt the flush of triumph, and relished his first taste of empowerment all this awful week. He tapped Emilio on the shoulder. "Borrow my girl for a minute?" he asked.

"Of course." Emilio stepped back.

And Charlotte smiled; her heart in her eyes.

"You look beautiful, Ki—" He stopped himself. The evidence before him was incontrovertible. She was no kitten anymore.

"Thanks, Dad."

"Sorry you didn't win."

"I never cared about winning. I'm just happy to be here."

The band was done with "Somewhere" and jumped immediately into "C'mon, baby, let's do the twist!"

Avery laughed—"That's it for me!"—and escorted her back to Emilio.

"We won't be late, Dad."

"Enjoy yourselves," he called, waving them off.

Steve stood where he'd left him, hands in the pockets of the navy-blue serge he called his funeral suit.

Avery looked around. "Where'd Kitty go?"

"She took off, said to tell you she'd be in touch. Lilly's gone to find the ladies' room."

They watched the gyrating dancers for a moment. Then Steve turned to face him.

"Look here, Cap," he said earnestly. "My plan is to follow Lilly over to the coast, stick with her whatever comes. I . . . Well, look . . . I wanta thank you." He thrust out his hand. "You been nothin' but first-rate."

Avery's throat clamped with a sudden sense of loss. *He's my best friend. And he's telling me good-bye.* His own hand shot out to grasp Steve's, which was considerably smaller and heavily callused. But as always, the other man's grip was a steel vise.

"Taught me everything I know, partner," Avery said quietly. Then, swept up with emotion, he threw his arm around Steve's shoulder, pulled him into a hard hug, and whispered, his throat closing on the words: "Good luck."

NANCY MARTELL WAS AT the punch bowl when Avery told her he was leaving, and that: "Mike should be here soon."

"If he can tear himself away from the game, y'mean," the doctor's wife snorted.

He made his way back to the truck and home. He parked in the carport, picked the forgotten flyer off the seat, and carried it into the house, vaguely curious which *Eight Simple Rules* might mitigate a nuclear disaster.

Martell stood up, disgusted.

"Damn Tigers. The Gators haven't stopped 'em once all night. Hell of a thing—just as we're heading into Amen Corner!"

"Amen Corner?" Was that doctor-talk for World War III?

"Don't you know, Wes? The part of the season where we play Auburn and Georgia back-to-back?"

"No, I didn't know that." Avery glanced toward the hall. "Heard anything out of Sarah?"

"Not a thing. I doubt she even felt the shot I gave her. Looked in about three punts ago—realized I was yelling at Coach Graves to get something going and might have disturbed her—but apparently she's dead to the world till tomorrow."

"Nice way of putting it, Doc."

"Sorry." Martell shrugged. "You know what I mean. Chlorpromazine works like a charm."

"Any word on Florida San?"

"Not yet. My guess is my buddy's either at the game or watching it. Don't worry, though. We'll get her in tomorrow. First thing, I hope."

"Will we have to drive her over there?"

"With any luck, he'll send an ambulance—without the siren, of course. I'll meet 'em here. It'll be easier on everyone that way."

Avery couldn't imagine how sending Sarah off to the sanitarium would be easy on anyone.

"Well, I suppose Nancy's looking for me. I promised her one dance," Martell said, turning toward the door. "Oh," he added, turning back, "did Charlotte win?"

"No. But she didn't expect to. Said she was happy just to be there."

"Too bad," Martell pronounced, with a final grimace at the game. "See you tomorrow," he said and was out the door.

"Thanks, Doc," Avery called from the stoop.

Martell acknowledged him with a brusque backward wave of his hand.

Football. Avery felt the twinge of envy. The world's on the brink and all he's got on his mind is football.

Avery closed the door, switched off the television, checked on Sarah—who was indeed sleeping soundly—and returned to his chair with the flyer from the church in hand.

EIGHT SIMPLE AIR RAID RULES, the heading read above two columns of type. Each of the four rules in the left column began with the word ALWAYS in capital letters.

ALWAYS shut windows and doors. *If the warning comes in time, shut all doors and windows and pull down the shades or blinds. Turn off all pilot lights, and close all stove and furnace doors.*

And if it doesn't come in time? Avery recalled the moonscape of Hiroshima.

ALWAYS seek shelter. *If there's time, go below ground, into a subway, into the basement of a large building or in the cellar of your home.*

Obviously, whoever wrote this thing knew nothing about Florida's high water table.

If you haven't time to get to the shelter, at least duck under a bed or table. If you're caught out of doors, flatten out against the base of a wall or dive into a ditch or a doorway.

Only two rules down and he was already irritated.
Number three was

ALWAYS drop flat on your stomach. *Even if you only have a few seconds' warning, wherever you are, drop flat on your stomach and put your face in your folded arms. Even if you've seen the flash, do the same thing right away.*

Sure. It's probably better than standing out on the street, watching the whole thing, but . . .

ALWAYS follow instructions. *Instructions will come to you after a raid by radio, sound truck, or some other way.*

How's that? Telepathy?

Follow them exactly.

Roger that.
The remaining four rules in the right column each began with the word NEVER.

NEVER look up. *To avoid temporary blinding by the flash, never look up to see what's coming. When you drop to the floor or the ground, keep your face in your folded arms for at least 20 seconds after the explosion in order to keep flying glass out of your eyes.*

Yup, Avery thought. Never mind the massive five-mile-wide fire-ball of pulverizing heat and radiation.

NEVER rush outside after a bombing. *A second bomb may follow the first. Besides, the longer you wait, the more chance there will be for lingering radioactivity to die down.*

Who in the world came up with this crap? He checked the line at the bottom of the sheet. Richard Gerstell, PhD, Consultant, Civil Defense Office, National Security Resources Board. Unbelievable.

NEVER take chances with food or water. *Whenever there is any reason to suspect that lingering radioactivity is around, don't take chances on open food or water. Stick to canned and bottled things that have not yet been opened, things in a closed refrigerator, and the water in covered pails or bottles or jars which you have filled before the attack.*

Covered with what?
The eighth and shortest rule was

NEVER start rumors. *A single wild rumor could start a panic that might cost you your life.*

Avery, now outraged, crumpled the flyer into a ball, crushed it tightly inside his fist. Isn't the worst rumor the false hope that you could actually survive one of these things? Or that, honestly, you'd *want* to?

Launching himself out of his chair, he dropped the ball of crap into the trash, tugged at his tie, and wrenched open his collar. Craving fresh air, he strode onto the porch. He was bound toward the bench on the dock but a small movement, a puzzling spot of bright color, stopped him.

He froze, wishing he'd thought to bring a flashlight, when the thing, whatever it was, hopped like a giant grasshopper in his direction. Another hop brought it into the rectangle of light falling out of the window and across the grass. It was . . . one of Sarah's parakeets?

"Well, hey, fella, hey," Avery called gently. It was the blue one. He'd never gotten their names straight but knew them by color: yellow, blue, and green. "Here, boy, Blue Boy." Avery dropped to one knee, offered the bird his index finger as a friendly perch.

The bird cocked a cautious eye at him but hopped closer. The light from the kitchen lit up his white speckled head, his mottled gray wings, and the bright blue puff of his chest.

"Had enough of the wild life, guy?"

The bird chortled a still-wary response.

"Want your old one back? Me, too."

The bird chortled again and hopped, then stepped one careful foot, and then the other, onto Avery's finger. Something about its small tentative movements, its fragile little feet, its shiny black trusting eye tore the too tight lid off Avery's pent-up emotions. He looked at the small bird now settled on his own big ham and something inside him shattered.

With raw, coughing sobs, Avery wept. He slumped down on the wet grass, heedless of his suit, cradling the blue bird in both hands, and cried—for the simple, sweet life he'd believed he had, little more than a week ago; for Sarah's misery, her rejection of their life as "a living death"; for Charlotte's growing up so fast, right before his eyes; for his best friend's quiet good-bye; for the airmen roaring by high overhead; for his country, his beleaguered President, his dangling-by-a-thread world. And for his own inability to do anything, *any thing*, about any of it.

Stripped of all sense of safety or security, he felt lost, helpless, and utterly overwhelmed by a crushing sense of failure. His only hope was that when the end came, it would be fast. Better by far to be pulverized, reduced to radioactive dust by the fiery blast following the blinding flash of light, than to lose a limb and bleed out in the dirt (as his father had) or to endure the lingering, flesh-eating horror of radiation poisoning like the cancer that took its terrible time with his mother.

Chilled by his conviction—hopeless, hopeless—Avery shuddered and the bird shrieked and rustled its wings in protest. Tiny feet grasped a toehold on callused flesh.

Avery saw the bird, the rectangle of light on the grass, the lit kitchen window through a mist of tears that gave the scene—his entire life?—a mirage-like shimmer. He felt spent, light-headed, muscles too weak, bones too soft to move. He might die right here. It would be appropriate, wouldn't it? Now, as always, outside looking in.

No, you won't, the voice that was inside him, yet somehow watching him from elsewhere, insisted. At its imperious urging, he managed to haul himself up—careful of the bird, of Blue Boy—carry the bird, retrieve its empty cage, still upended on the grass, and make his way into the kitchen. Once there, he set both bird and cage onto the counter and stared at them.

Resolutely, he wiped the wires and each of the wooden rungs clean and dry. He found and folded a newspaper lining and settled it into place. Then he filled and repositioned the plastic cups with food and water.

Each action set off a flurry of grateful fluttering and chortling.

"There you go," Avery said, lifting Blue Boy back into his cage. "Feel better now?"

He watched the bird peck greedily at its seed, crack the kernel from the shell in its beak, head-shake the empty hull to the floor of the cage, swallow, then start the whole process all over again.

He remembered his own dinner, congealing in the trash. The thought of food repulsed him. Despair, like a pair of dirty hands, gripped him by the throat.

He went into the living room and sat in his chair to wait—for Charlotte and Emilio's return, and for whatever came after that.

JUST BEFORE MIDNIGHT, AVERY saw the headlights then heard The Admiral rumble up the drive.

As Emilio killed the engine and the lights, Avery scooped up the *National Geographic* beside his chair and pretended fascination in the cover story, "Seattle Fair Looks to the 21st Century." Forty years from now? Fat chance.

He heard Emilio walk around the car to open the door for Charlotte, heard the two of them stroll up the drive. He looked up when they entered—Charlotte with her runner-up's roses in one hand, Emilio's arm in the other, both their faces lit with youth. Feeling like a counterfeit Ward Cleaver, he asked, "Have a good time, kids?"

Past them, through the picture window, he caught the slow glide of a long white car, a Chrysler Imperial, and the face of its driver briefly illuminated by the streetlight on Bryn Mawr.

Had Kitty followed them here? Was she just making sure Charlotte got home safely? Or did she expect him to let her in?

"Oh, Dad, it was *great*!" Charlotte enthused. "We danced the whole night."

"And I've got the blisters to prove it," Emilio added with a rueful grin.

Avery stood, stepped to the front window, and pulled the drapes firmly closed. No way was Kitty getting in. Not here. Not now.

"Emilio and the twirls got a conga line going. Most of the crowd joined in except for Todd Jenkins and his crew." Charlotte made a face. "They kept calling Emilio 'Jose Jimenez,' saying stupid things like 'Better dead than red.'"

Avery turned. "But . . ."

"Doc Mike told 'em to knock it off. He was about to give 'em the boot when Emilio invited them to hook on at the back of the line."

"And they did?" Avery asked.

Charlotte gave a proud nod.

Emilio shrugged. "They were just jealous because all the best-looking girls were dancing with me."

Avery would have liked to hear more, but Charlotte's pointed glance was clearly beseeching him to leave.

"Well, since we're all in . . ." He made a show of locking the front door, then added lamely, ". . . guess I'll close up shop."

He took his time covering Blue Boy's cage, picking up the random seed hulls on the counter, dawdling over the trash.

At last, he heard Emilio's deliberate call, "Good night, Mr. A," and more softly, "Good night, Charlotte."

He heard her high-heeled footfall across the dining room, turned to see her push through the swinging door into the kitchen.

"Thought I'd put these in water." She grabbed a vase from under the sink, filling it first with water then with the roses. "There," she said. When she was done, she gave him a heartfelt hug. "Good night, Dad," she said. "Thanks for everything." Even all dressed up, the little girl she'd been was still there, sparkling, in her smile.

"You're welcome, sweetheart. See you in the morning." A father's promise of tomorrow. The lie of it sickened him.

After she'd gone to bed, he helped Emilio, now in pajamas, make up the sofa with linens from the closet and wished him good night. Then, one by one, as if for the last time, he turned off the lights and, remembering the Chrysler, the fact that Kitty was still out there somewhere, checked and locked all the windows, closed all the curtains, and dead-bolted the doors—something he'd never before felt compelled to do in this neighborhood.

He undressed in the dark, hangering his grass-stained suit, racking his tie, placing his dress shoes in their usual spot, and putting his shirt, socks, and boxer shorts in the laundry basket. As he accomplished each task, he found himself thinking, There, that's done. And that. And that, too, with the sense that if this was the last time, he wanted it done right.

Finally, he slid into bed. Sarah, beside him, was snoring softly. "Dead to the world," Martell had said. Avery envied her. He thought briefly of finding her bottle of Seconals and taking some himself. But that seemed the coward's way out.

Instead, he lay on his back in the dark, listening to the rise and fall of her breath.

He pictured their location on a map, from a plane's, or God's, view. Florida, the pistol-shaped state cocked straight at Cuba, the great green crocodile of the Caribbean. Deadly missiles lining its spine like scales, Havana due south of Key West. Somewhere he'd read that the crocodile has the strongest jaws, the most powerful bite of any animal on earth—ironically true, if Cuba proved the planet's undoing.

Every sound outside the house startled him, made him wonder if it signaled the beginning of the end. A car passing by, a formation of jets swooping overhead, a boat engine roaring to life across the lake. Surely, they'd use the Civil Defense sirens if they could. But what if there wasn't enough time? What would be the final sound—the last one he would hear?

The roaring of the giant fireball, he decided. The airmen who'd delivered The Bomb to Hiroshima reported it was unlike anything they'd ever heard or seen. "Louder than all hell," one said.

His mind darted between dark and darker scenarios, feeding the most primal of his fears. Engulfed by fire, they said, it wasn't the flames that killed you, it was the lack of oxygen. If you were lucky, you died before you felt the pain.

And then what?

Pearly Gates, streets of gold, a fitting for a new white robe?

Avery knew he was long past believing the revivalist's version of heaven. On the other hand, he couldn't conceive an alternative. His mind was a blank, afterlife a complete unknown. Unknowable till you got there. Like the way the world would be after the bombs fell. All life reduced to dust, blown about by a poisoned wind.

What was the use of wondering? Let go, let it go. You'll have the answers soon enough.

His eyes and ears searched the dark, not for rescue but for acceptance.

12.

*A*VERY WOKE WITH A START AND WAS STUNNED TO FIND HE was still alive.

His first thought was, My God, we're still here! He rolled over to embrace Sarah but stopped himself. Not wanting to wake her, he resisted the urge to run his palm down the smooth curve of her shape, shoulder to waist, or over the soft hill of her hip. It was early enough to slip out, he decided, while everyone else was still asleep, and watch the dawn he hadn't expected to see come up on the lake.

He pulled on jeans and a T-shirt and padded barefoot through the house. He was tempted to check the TV or turn on the radio for news, but he didn't want to wake Emilio, who was tossing fitfully on the sofa.

Blue Boy heard him coming and chattered to be uncovered. "Morning, fella. Take a look," Avery whispered as he lifted the cover from the cage. "We made it to another day."

He unlocked the back door, crossed the screened porch, and let himself out, reveling in the feel of the grass beneath his feet, the scented breeze rippling the lake's surface, and the squawk of the night heron scolding the tardiness of his daytime replacement.

He sat down on the bench and breathed in the muck-sweet air hanging over the water in delicate wisps. He watched the soft advance of the dawn ripening the clouds and lake from pale to pure peach, lavender to plum. Then he stood to watch the sunrise coming up over his own rooftop. Suddenly it struck him. How oddly quiet the morning was. No jet engines rumbled overhead. No new contrails scarred the sky.

But was this just the calm before the coming firestorm? Was the war machine still out there, revving its engines? Or was it possible they'd brokered a peace? That prospect filled him with an enormous, a momentous, sense of hope and gratitude—to God in His heaven, to President Kennedy, even to crazy old Comrade Khrushchev, if that was the case.

He rose, exulting in the idea that maybe, just maybe, all was not lost.

And then he heard the scream from the house.

He broke into a run—off the dock, up the dew-slippery slope of the lawn, banging open the screen door onto the porch, through the kitchen's swinging door into the dining room, and barged into the living room.

Sarah was in the entrance to the hall, hand at her throat, vibrating with anger and upset.

Beside the sofa, Emilio stood in his pale-blue pajamas, with the wide-eyed look of a prisoner facing a firing squad. Beside him, Charlotte, dark hair tousled about her face, red robe revealing a bit of white nightgown underneath, glowered with outrage.

"It is not, it is *not* what you think!" his daughter screamed.

"What *I* think? What I *think* is"—Sarah was yelling at fever pitch—"this is *all* your *father's* fault! You—" She jabbed an angry finger in Avery's direction. "*You* allowed this to happen. While I was sleeping, *you* let this happen in our home, our *home!*"

"*Mom!*" Charlotte was pleading. "We didn't . . . Dad didn't . . ."

"Oh, no! *No!* Of *course* not! Dad never does anything wrong in *your* eyes, does he?"

"C'mon, now, darlin'." Avery stepped toward her to lay a calming hand on Sarah's shoulder.

She shook him off violently. "*You* c'mon, Wes Avery! For seventeen *years*, I've tried—oh, how I've *tried*—to fight this girl's nature with good nurturing, to build some sort of moral bulwark against her inborn inclinations. You know what I mean. You know *exactly* what I mean." She was spitting with a fury he'd never seen before. "And the minute, the *second* I'm unavailable, the very first chance you get, you put this little romance together—and you not only suggested it, you *encouraged* it by inviting this . . . this slick young spic—"

"Sarah!" Avery thundered, cutting her off.

She was hysterical, her face drained of color, her eyes bloodshot. She was sweating and trembling, and staggering forward, arms out-flung.

In the movies, Avery thought, the man slaps a hysterical woman, first one cheek and then the other, until she "comes to." But he'd never in his life struck a woman. He wasn't about to begin now.

"Sarah," he insisted levelly, "you need to calm down."

"You want me *calm*? Call the doctor! Have him come over and fill me up with *happy* pills! Maybe send me to the *loony* bin! That would simplify everything, wouldn't it? For you and for this little . . ." She shot Charlotte a scorching look.

What had she seen? What in the world did she think they'd done?

The fierce and feral thing that he'd only glimpsed yesterday seemed to have taken her over completely today. In the far reaches of his mind, he heard the doorbell ring.

Steve flashed through his mind, come early to pick up The Admiral. But Steve would never bang like that.

"Oh, here he is *now*, I'll bet!" Sarah pushed past Avery and stag-gered toward the front door. "Good old Doc Mike come to carry off crazy old Sarah. I won't go, Wes. I *won't*. And I'll tell you something else." Her fingers were clawing at the lock, attempting to lock the doctor out, not realizing she was instead unlocking and releasing the door. She turned back to glare at him, eyes crazed, chest heaving, gasping for breath. "I am *done*! I can*not* . . . I *will not* raise another *whore's* child!"

At that moment, the door swung open and standing there, eyes wide with horror . . . Kitty.

Sarah froze. In a long, slow pivot from Kitty to Avery, her blazing eyes branded him her traitor. Then the sound, an injured animal's shrill heart-wrenching howl, filled the room. Without warning, her body pitched headlong. She began to convulse in movements that were as unnerving as they were unnatural.

Kitty stepped in briskly, saw the folded sheet on the entry bench, and seized it. Dropping down beside Sarah, she secured, in a few deft twists, Sarah's wildly flailing arms and stopped her hands from clawing at her eyes.

Avery, Charlotte, and Emilio stood rapt, trapped in place until Kitty looked up and ordered, "Call the doctor! Tell him we need an ambulance!"

"Go get Doc Mike," Avery barked. *"Run!"* he added as together they flew out the open door.

Sarah continued to buck and groan on the floor, eyes rolled back to the whites, tongue like a separate thing trying to escape her mouth.

Avery dropped down opposite Kitty, unsure whether or where to touch Sarah to soothe her. "H-how did you know what to do?" he asked Kitty.

"Army nurse, remember? She's like a soldier in shell shock. Most important thing is to keep her from hurting herself. Stroke her hair. It might calm her."

Avery did what he was told. "There, there, darlin'," he crooned, and it did seem to help settle her, some.

"Wes, when you said she wasn't well . . ." Kitty's face was flushed with remorse. "I'm so sorry."

"It's not your fault; this has been . . ." He didn't have the words.

"I never would have . . ." Kitty's eyes darted toward the door. "Look, you need to stay right here. If she starts to get agitated again, keep her from rolling into the table." She was rising to her feet, fishing her keys out of her pocket.

"Where are you going?"

"My car's blocking the drive. I-I'm going to move it . . . for the ambulance."

"But I . . ." Avery looked from Sarah, who was keening and rocking side to side, to Kitty, who was halfway out the door.

"Stay with her, Wes. I'm sure the doctor's on his way."

Through the open doorway, Avery heard her run to the car, open and slam the door, start the engine, slide it into reverse. Moments later he heard footsteps running up the drive. Charlotte, Emilio, and Martell burst into the room.

"How is she?" Charlotte demanded, breathless, eyes on her mother.

"A little better, I think."

"Ambulance should be here shortly." Martell was feeling for Sarah's pulse at the juncture of her neck and jaw.

"Where did Kitty go?" Emilio asked.

"Putting her car on the street," Avery answered.

"No, she's not," Steve announced from the doorway.

"She took off when we pulled up," Lilly added. She reached out, touched Martell lightly on the shoulder. "I'm a nurse. How can I help?"

Sometime during the confusion that accompanied the arrival of the ambulance and Sarah's transfer by the paramedics to the gurney in the back, Charlotte, intent on going to the hospital, disappeared. She returned in jeans and a red Fighting Eagles sweatshirt. Emilio emerged from the powder room dressed for church.

It was Steve's idea that Lilly drive Avery and Charlotte to Florida San. "Ain't an ambulance driver alive who can lose or outrun her," he said. Meanwhile, he volunteered to get Emilio to the church and to remain available for whatever was needed afterward.

The ride to the sanitarium in Lilly's Firebird passed in a blur. Avery kept his eyes glued on the shadowy movements of the paramedics barely visible through the ambulance's back window. At the emergency entrance, they unloaded Sarah swiftly and wheeled her through the double doors, directing Avery, Charlotte, and Lilly to the lobby.

The intake counter was buzzing with the news: "Y'all hear about Cuba? It's all over the radio."

"Khrushchev backed down! He's pulling the missiles outta there!"

"Everybody's thrilled except Castro," an orderly said. "Seems like he's the only one really *wanted* a war."

"Oh, I'm certain there were others," a nurse said grimly, "who'll live to fight another day."

The world was saved—but somehow Sarah was lost, Avery thought. Would they ever get her back?

The next several hours were a haze of worry. After Lilly called her own hospital, and learned she was no longer needed at the coast, she took charge of Avery and Charlotte.

"You two sit here and hold on," she told them gently. "I'm going to chat up the nurses, see if they'll check with the doctors, find out exactly what's going on back there."

Although hard information was sparse, and delays overlong, she was a fountain of reassurance to their mounting concerns. "Sarah will be fine. You'll see. But unfortunately, this nerve business takes time. She's the patient, but you're the ones whose patience will be tested."

When, at last, Martell emerged to introduce his friend, Dr. Jake Walton, head of the ward, they were told Sarah was sedated and resting comfortably. Martell urged them to go home.

But Avery resisted. "I have to see her. I need to be here, to explain, when she wakes up."

"Oh, she won't be waking up anytime soon." Dr. Walton shook his head. "And when she does, tomorrow maybe or the next day, we'll want her to remain calm."

Lilly ushered them out the door and insisted on driving them through the Steak 'n Shake—"You may not feel like eating now, but you'll thank me later"—then drove them home.

Avery and Charlotte invited her in, but Lilly refused. "It's been a rough day; you two need some rest."

Once inside the house, Avery discovered he "might be a bit hungry after all."

Charlotte told him to sit down in his usual place at the dinette, while she unpacked the take-out burgers and fries and set out the chocolate shakes.

Unexpectedly ravenous, they blessed Lilly for her foresight and wolfed down their burgers. Afterward, Charlotte cleared the table then sat back down, hands clasped, eyes focused and unblinking.

"He was crying, Dad," she said simply.

"Who?"

"Emilio. I heard him early this morning. He was sobbing. Worried sick over his family in Cuba."

"You can't blame him for that."

"I didn't. I just went out to make sure he was okay."

Avery nodded. It made sense. If only Sarah had let her explain . . .

"He was telling me about his sister and crying, and I was holding him and crying, too. Then, next thing we knew, there's Mom screaming her head off."

"I'm sorry, kiddo. If I'd been there, I could have . . ."

"What did she mean, Dad . . . when she said that . . . what she said . . . about me?"

Truth be told. There was no sidestepping it, was there? Cat—and Kitty—finally out of the bag. Avery took a ragged breath. "Your mother had a sister. Older, for sure. Prettier, she thought, but I'd beg to differ."

"Kitty." Charlotte nodded. Her eyes stayed on his face.

"How'd you know that?"

"The summer I was thirteen, Grandma Do took me to downtown Tuscaloosa. A lady at the hat store said something about me being the spitting image of Kitty. Grandma told me Kitty was my aunt who died, and not to bring her up to you or Mom. Later on, I heard her and Mom whispering in the kitchen. 'That little laugh of hers?' Grandma said. 'The way she bats her eyes at Wes, has him wrapped around her little finger?' 'I know . . .' Mom said. 'It's Kitty all over again.'"

Her mimicry of both Dolores and Sarah was spot-on. "I never heard that."

"I never told you. The only time Mom ever mentioned Kitty was the other night, when she told me Kitty was Homecoming Queen and something bad happened afterward. I figured that was why she was so dead set against Emilio. So . . . ?"

Avery, who'd been content to let her talk, realized she'd circled back to her original question: What did Sarah's outraged and outrageous statement—*I will not raise another whore's child!*—mean? He swallowed hard.

"It was back during The War. Kitty left college to join the WAACs—the Women's Auxiliary Army Corps—and became a nurse. She was stationed in Rome and fell in love, I guess, with an Italian soldier named Carlo. They got engaged. But before she could tell him she was pregnant, he was killed. Charlotte." He leaned over and gently took her hand. "It was you Kitty was pregnant with."

She sat there, liquid eyes absorbing the news; her only reaction a single, slow blink. But Avery saw the sea change in her: One moment she was his only daughter asking him for information. The next, she was the stunned offspring of somebody else entirely, her mother's sister and a foreign father called Carlo.

"*Kitty* is my mother?"

Avery nodded.

"And my father never knew . . . about me?"

"No, honey, he didn't."

She withdrew her hand from his.

"So she came home to Tuscaloosa and . . ." He could see her piecing it together, rearranging everything she thought she knew about her life into something else entirely. ". . . had me . . ."

"On our wedding day. Her plan was to give you up, to an adoption agency. But your Mom and I . . . we took one look at you and everything changed. You were ours. Kitty agreed. And the three of us—you, your mom, and me—left for Florida the next day."

Somehow, he'd expected anger. *I'd be mad if it was me.* But a single tear rolled down her cheek and hung—a small shivering bead—off her jaw. He reached out, intending to collect it and to comfort her; but she leaned away from him, not wanting to be touched.

"Grandma Do must have had a cow."

"A whole herd, I'd say."

"And . . . how'd you talk her into it?"

"Who?"

"Mom . . . ," she said brokenly, then added, "I mean Sarah."

Her correction grieved him. Who else would "Mom" be? And if Sarah wasn't clearly Mom, then he . . .

"I never had to," he lied on Sarah's behalf. "All it took was one look. . . . You were just the tiniest, most perfect thing in the world, no bigger than this," he told her, indicating the space between his fingertips and the inside of his elbow.

Her eyes drifted from his hands to his face with an expression he found unreadable, which was—for him—unbearable.

"Your mom was out of her head today. You have to know that, Ki . . . Charlotte."

She stared out the window. It was twilight, and an evening breeze was raising small phosphorous whitecaps on the lake. On the opposite shore, other families in other homes were turning on their lakefront lights; sitting down to supper, he imagined, or settling in on sofas in front of televisions for an ordinary evening.

She closed her eyes against the view.

"But why did Grandma Do say she was dead? And Mom, too? And what was she doing here?"

"I can't begin to guess why your grandmother lied about that—to both of us—which is why it was such a shock to have her suddenly show up."

"But how did Kitty know . . . ?" She asked it in a small, flat voice. "Why was she at the dance last night?"

"You saw her?"

"No. But Emilio said you introduced them."

"She just showed up at the station on . . . Wednesday, I think it was . . . said she wanted to see you. With everything going on, she was afraid she might not get another chance."

"That's it? She just came to *look* at me?"

"Well, yes. But then, after she saw you in the parade, she wanted to meet you, too. But I . . . well, I wouldn't let her. Not last night. I didn't want to spoil—"

"That why she came here this morning?" she interrupted.

"I don't know. But then your mother . . . Sarah . . ." God, now *he* was correcting himself.

Charlotte bit her lip. "Think Kitty's coming back?"

"I have no idea. But . . ." A wave of nausea churned inside his stomach. "She lives in Tampa. I have her number if you'd—"

"I don't know what hurts worse," she cut in quietly, "the truth or the lie." Her eyes were clouded with anguish.

"I am so sorry. . . ."

"It's okay," she said automatically. "Well, not really, but it *will* be, I guess . . . eventually. I'd be lying if I said it doesn't change things; it can't help but change things. But . . . for now, Dad . . . let's just leave it at that."

Avery nodded his acceptance and his gratitude, though the words *for now*—implying, as they did, some sort of future reckoning and the peril of potential loss—were devastating.

How stupid he'd been to think that all his proper "taking care" would protect her, or Sarah, from pain and disappointment— including their separate disappointments in *him*.

And yet . . . *yet* . . . she'd called him "Dad," hadn't she? He clung to that small gift—an unconscious kindness on her part—like a drowning man thrown a life ring.

13.

QUESTION OF THE WEEK: HOW DO YOU GRIEVE A DREAM?

Sarah's headshrinker was big on "the question of the week." Avery had noticed the guy used it every time to signal the end of their session—"Well, that's the question of the week, isn't it?"—as a more polite version of "Time's up; see you next week." And whatever the question was, the guy always wrote it down in your ever-fattening file and expected you to think about it and come back prepared to discuss your answer.

And the next time you showed up, he opened the file that you never got to see, peered into it through the wire-rimmed reading glasses that were always there (either on his nose or pushed up onto his forehead like a second set of silver eyebrows). He used his stubby index finger to scan the last page of his notes, muttering, "Now, let's see . . . the question of the week was . . . ?"

After six weeks—no, seven; this week made it seven—Sarah's headshrinker was technically Avery's headshrinker also, but she'd had him so much longer—almost a year now—Avery was resistant to laying claim.

But today, Dr. Flanagan was in for a surprise. This week, Avery had given serious thought to the question and written down his answers front and back on a piece of ORANGE TOWN TEXACO stationery that he intended to hand over, so he could be certain what was on at least one of those pages in the file marked: AVERY, WESLEY L.

Fact was . . . he'd sat up most of the past six nights thinking it out, and he'd organized his thoughts carefully under the heading, **HOW TO GRIEVE A DREAM: EIGHT SIMPLE RULES.** Then he'd drawn a line down the middle of the sheet, front and back. Each of the four rules in the left column began with the word ALWAYS in capital letters.

Rule number one was

ALWAYS shut windows and doors. *Especially after the 247th well-meaning person tells you, "This was God's will," and you find yourself standing in the middle of your kitchen at 3 A.M. in the morning screaming your head off that "GOD HAD NOTHING TO DO WITH THIS!!!," frightening one poor parakeet half to death.*

Number two was

ALWAYS respect a true friend. *If you're lucky enough to have a best friend who's been through some tough stuff himself and has the guts to tell you straight-out that you could use some help, have the good sense not to bite his head off. Realize that, in some ways, he knows you better than you know yourself and he can see when you're about to go 'round the bend in the bitterness department.*

Then,

ALWAYS put something in your stomach. *Even when you don't feel like it, when the thought of food makes you want to retch, find something—some one thing—to eat. Otherwise, you might waste away into such a bony old scarecrow that you won't even recognize the guy in the morning mirror whose black, sinkhole eyes want to*

*know, "Who the hell are you?" You can live on TV dinners if you
have to, especially when your wife's away and your only daughter's
gone off to college—where, no matter how much she's "worried
about you," she <u>belongs</u>—257 miles away. Or, at the very least,
you can haul yourself out of the house to the drive-in for a chocolate
shake. It goes down easier than a Swanson's Salisbury Steak, and
you won't have to talk to anyone but the girl on skates, and she's
not about to ask you questions that you have no earthly idea how
to answer.*

ALWAYS get out of bed. *Sometimes it's the only thing you <u>can</u> do.
Sit up, put one foot in front of the other, and feed the damn bird.
That little parakeet may starve otherwise. And it's not his fault
that you feel like Humpty Dumpty fallen off the wall, and there
are no king's horses or king's men to put you together again—as if
they could, or you'd want them to—because the person that you
thought you were, the life you thought you had no longer exists.*

The remaining four rules in the right column each began with the
word NEVER.

NEVER give up, until you have no other choice. *Take every
book off your shelf and look for answers, search your bank accounts,
sort through your wife's hope chest, read through your long-ago
letters to her from your younger self. Try to figure out where you
came up with the idea that you could dream, plan, buy, or will into
existence a life without suffering. Go ahead. You'll suffer anyway.
And at some point—perhaps at 3 A.M. some other night—you'll
realize the truth about your own false self, the one that's been
hiding out for years inside the carefully constructed shell of a
supposedly successful life.*

NEVER take any unnecessary chances. *If that was your
philosophy, it may also be your problem: Stick to the slow lane.
Better yet, live your entire life by the side of the road. Preach safety*

and practice careful control. Work harder than your employees. Be kind to, yet appallingly judgmental of, your friends, neighbors, and customers. Prize and protect your daughter's innocence. And, while you're at it, ignore your wife's obvious suffering. In the end, it won't protect a damn thing. You and your wife and your daughter will suffer anyway.

NEVER see the forest for the trees. *Not until you find yourself so desperately deep in the woods that you sit down in darkness, certain you'll never see the light again. And it somehow makes sense to unearth your wife's left-behind sleeping pills and you think: Wouldn't it be easier to say sayonara to the whole thing? And it probably would. But then you ask yourself: What about the damn bird? And it hits you like a crowbar over the head: It's not about you. It's about the bird. You can make the choice at any time, to feed the worms—Sayonara, suckers!—or to feed the bird. So you follow the sound of its hungry chattering back into the kitchen, you fill up the little cups, and you see this fragile little thing chirp gratefully, flutter fearlessly, and eat like there's no tomorrow. And on some soul-deep level that defies your ability to explain it, that bird feeds you.*

The eighth and shortest rule was

NEVER say, "Never again." *Take another lesson from your best friend, a two-time loser who just invited you to be his best man again. With a new wife and a practically adopted Cuban son attending the local JC, he's got the family he always claimed he never wanted. And you're the one living like an old bachelor. The old saying "Be careful what you wish for" ought to be revised; it ought to say instead: "Be very careful what you take for granted."*

Bottom line: How do you grieve a dream? In any way you must. For as long as it takes. Until you're able, or ready, to think about some thing or some one other than yourself.

. . . . .

WES AVERY WHEELED PAST the Florida San guard shack and waved at Ray, the Sunday guard, who smiled and raised the red-and-white gate without the usual visitor rigmarole.

As he drove past the crowded front parking lot toward the lesser-known lot in the back, an ambulance arrived at the side entrance followed by a pale Chevy Impala full of family members, eyes panicked, faces ashen with fear and concern.

He felt a flood of sympathy for the patient and the family and for all that lay ahead of them: the painful early weeks of lockdown with no contact allowed; the initial family visits weighed down by so much expectation and emotion that they were bound to be a disappointment for everyone; the various treatments (medicines, therapies, and, most frightening of all, electroshocks) tried and failed and tried again; the eventual transfers to lesser and lesser security floors; and, in Sarah's case, to one of the independent living cottages on the back grounds.

It would be easier, Avery decided, if they gave you a guide early on so you knew what to expect. Then again, as the doctors told Charlotte and him often: Treatment, like life, is not an exact science. You learn to take things as they come—or go (which, apparently, was the case with Kitty, who'd disappeared without a word, a peep, since last October).

Tentatively, he and Charlotte had learned their way around, like the fact that they kept the comas and the catatonics on the top floor, above the ward for schizophrenics. "Be thankful she doesn't hear voices," one nurse told them early on, "or see things that aren't really there." But the hard-core psychotics got transferred to Whitfield, over near Jackson.

He parked the truck near the outbuilding that housed Dr. Flanagan's office and made his way into the small, sparse waiting room—more of a vestibule, really, with two chairs and one small table—which was empty, as usual. He removed the station envelope with his answers to the question of the week from his shirt pocket and slipped it under the headshrinker's inner office door.

He returned to the truck, opened the tailgate, pulled out the wheelbarrow, a few tools, a bag of soil, two flats of bright flowers, and wheeled them all onto the sidewalk, around the outbuildings, to the back grounds and the small cottage, third on the left.

She sat on the bench on the cottage's narrow front porch—eyes closed, face tipped to the sun, relaxed in the khaki slacks and denim shirt that identified her as an "independent" resident. He called to her and she roused slowly, a soft smile spreading across her face, short chestnut hair grown back curly since the treatments, with a pale off-center streak of gray.

She stepped off the porch to see what he'd brought her and ran her fingers lightly over the petals of her favorites: pink dianthus, purple snapdragons, some yellow chrysanthemums, and the bright purple-and-yellow faces of cool-weather Johnny-jump-ups. She watched him spread and turn the soil beside the steps. Then he watched her set out the plants the way she wanted them. Wearing the gloves he'd brought from home, they worked side by side; she placing the plants in the holes he'd dug, patting the soil around tender roots. When they were done, she sat back on her heels, eyes lit with delight.

"Beautiful," she decreed. "Thank you."

"You're most welcome," he told her.

He filled the watering can from a groundskeeper's spigot and stood on the sidewalk, dribbling rain onto each plant in the small garden they'd made. She returned to the bench up on the porch of the cottage he'd yet to set foot in. (She'll let you know when she's ready for that, the shrink had promised.)

He looked up at her, smiling. "Anything else, Sarah?" he asked gently.

She patted the empty space beside her on the bench.

He set down the watering can, took off his gloves, and, heart thudding, hope billowing like a sail before him, Avery stepped up. Together they sat in the warm slant of afternoon sunlight, watching the rain-heads pile up in preparation for a dazzling sunset.

"Red sky at night?" she asked him.

"Sailors' delight," he said. It was one of Old Pa's maxims. His letters to her from Tinian had been full of them.

"Never quite understood that."

"It's a warning and a promise, y'see," he told her. "Storm tonight; clear skies and steady winds tomorrow."

Years ago, he'd written her: "We'll go sailing, Sarah. Florida has more lakes than you can imagine and I can't wait to sail them with you." But an unexpected newborn and a fledgling business, and everything else since then, had gotten in the way. Sailing was one of his lost dreams. Just as music, he'd realized, was one of hers.

"I was thinking . . . if you'd like, Sarah . . . maybe next time I could bring you a record player and some of your records? We could listen to some music?"

She cocked her head.

He wondered if she'd understood him. Anything beyond the here and now is a still an abstract, the shrink had explained.

"Music?"

"Yes. Any kind you'd like."

For a long moment, she searched his face. "Yes," she said finally, smiling. "Music would be nice."

Avery felt the flush, the warm spread of her agreement and of his profound gratitude—to her, to the doctors, to Whomever—for the fragile bloom of trust lighting up her eyes.

14.

Subject: Your Class of '63 Questionnaire
Date: 11/3/2013 4:48:21 P.M. Eastern Daylight Time
From: CAvery833@aol.com

To: Susan@SusanCarolMcCarthy.com
Sent from the Internet (Details)

Dear Ms. McCarthy:

Emilio Alvarado, Class of '63 Bishop Moore High School, has forwarded your questionnaire and strongly encouraged me to participate. (Apparently your project—a Cuban Missile Crisis story set in College Park—was quite the talk of last week's 50th BMHS reunion.) To be clear, I'm also Class of '63 but from Edgewater High, the public high school up the street from Bishop Moore. But, as Emilio was quick to point out, your questions don't appear to be school-specific and, further, he insists, I'll get around to answering long before he will.

Full disclosure: The week of the Cuban Missile Crisis was also Homecoming Week at Edgewater High and Emilio was my date for the big dance. We went through a lot that week, some of it wonderful, some of it incredibly painful. I'm guessing he wants me to decide what should be told or withheld. And therein lies the difference between his life as a high-profile defense attorney and mine as a clinical psychologist.

You ask if, as a resident of the Orlando area, I had any inkling of the Crisis in advance of President Kennedy's televised speech on Monday night, October 22, 1962. Yes. My dad was ex-air-force (a WWII tail-gunner) whose business (the local

Texaco station) was in the flight path of Orlando's SAC base. On Friday, he'd noticed a lot of unusual plane activity so, that Sunday, he and I drove over to McCoy to check things out. The runways were jam-packed with more bombers, fighters, and troop carriers than we could count. Plus, off to one side, there was an entire squadron of the super-secret U-2 spy planes that, it became obvious later, were providing the President with photographic proof of the missiles in Cuba. I remember my dad saying, "Something's up, Kitten—something *big*." And, although he tried to hide it, I could tell he was shaken by what we'd seen.

You ask for any specific memories surrounding the President's speech. I remember that my mom took me out of school early that day to shop for homecoming dresses. We were on the escalator in the new Jordan Marsh store and suddenly everyone was talking about the President and some big announcement at seven o'clock. We rushed home to watch it with Dad.

I'd never seen the President's face so serious. And his first sentence was a stunner: "unmistakable evidence," he said, of "missiles in Cuba" with "nuclear strike capability against the Western Hemisphere." He talked about the Soviets' "weapons of *sudden* mass destruction" "capable of striking Washington, DC, the Panama Canal, *Cape Canaveral,* Mexico City, and . . ." Whatever came after that, I couldn't say. My mind froze on the idea that, after the Capitol and the canal, the cape (*our* cape) was Target Number Three on the list, Number Two in the continental US! To a central Florida kid like me—who'd grown up marching out onto the playground at "T-minus-two-minutes and counting" to stand and scan for the silver rockets rising in the east; to cheer the trails of sun gold thrust, the fireworks flare of booster separation, and the arc of light, Tinker Bell bright, as our heroes soared off into space—the President's singling out of *our* cape, less than sixty miles away, felt like a bull's-eye on my very soul. I remember trying to joke with my parents afterward—"There goes homecoming!"—but they were both too horrified to laugh.

You wonder what changes, if any, we noticed the next day. Overnight, Highway 441, the state's main north-south artery (which ran in front of my father's station), was clogged with gray-green convoys. The railway (behind the station) rumbled with incredibly long trains of canvas-covered missiles, tanks, and armaments. The skies seemed alive with planes of every imaginable type. And both the Atlantic and the Gulf, we heard, were rimmed with warships. Honestly, it was terrifying.

For the rest of his life, my dad read every book and collected every statistic he could find on the Crisis. I was shocked to learn: Two-thirds of the rolling stock of railroads in the southeastern US were requisitioned by the President for the transportation of troops, vehicles, and ordnance to south Florida. The army alone moved more than 100,000 troops and 100,000 tons of equipment in less than 150 hours. The marines' strength was at 40,000; the navy, 30,000. The air force reserve added another 14,000 to those already jam-packed onto every available air base, causing one brass hat to comment, "Florida looked like the deck of an aircraft carrier. . . . Every bit of cement in the state had an aircraft on it."

Within that week, Dad found, there were more military personnel, more boots on the ground among us, than Truman sent into Korea. Florida, the pistol-shaped state, was cocked and ready to unload on Cuba an invasion force one and a half times that of the combined Allied forces at Normandy on D-Day. To put it mildly, we were civilians directly in the path of the largest, fastest mobilization of military might ever made on American soil. "To put it accurately," Dad liked to say, "we were modern-day Jonahs in the belly of a fully breaching whale."

What was the rest of that week like? Certainly, we all held our breath on Wednesday when the Soviets' ships were approaching the US Navy's "line of interdiction" at sea. One of my teachers called it "the most dangerous game of chicken ever played." And, boy, were we relieved when the Soviet ships swerved and turned around! Many people thought the Crisis was over then. But of course the missiles were still in Cuba, and in Florida every arm of the American military remained at full DefCon 2 readiness for World War Three, the war we all knew would be the end of everything. On a personal note, however, it was still Homecoming Week—with dresses to be fitted, boutonnieres to order, the big bonfire, the parade, and, although the game was rained out, there was still the big dance and my first date with Emilio. Despite everything, maybe even because of everything, I was falling in love that week. I bounced like a pinball between sheer terror and pure bliss.

You ask when or how did I hear the news that the Crisis was over and how did it affect me? Tough question. That Sunday morning, after a week on top of several years of incredible stress, my mother had a "nervous breakdown." That was the term back then, though today we'd call it a "psychic break" due to the post-traumatic stress of an unnecessary hysterectomy, not to mention some severe over-medication. My mother had been rushed in an ambulance to Florida

Sanitarium and I was standing in the hospital lobby with Dad when we heard the news that Khrushchev was pulling the missiles out of Cuba. I can only remember thinking, "The world is saved. But my family is lost."

Of course, if my dad was answering your survey, he'd be quick to point out that the Crisis was far from over on October 28. For Floridians, especially those of us living anywhere near the state's five Strategic Air Command bases, the military stand-down and "return to normal" took much longer. Those three tense weeks, October 23 through November 15, 1962, were the one and only time in US history that the nation's SAC bases stood at DefCon 2—round-the-clock defensive readiness for all-out nuclear war.

You ask if I had any personal opinions at the time about the way the Crisis was resolved. I didn't, but my father sure did. After the announcement that it was "over," Dad insisted there was no way in hell that Khrushchev, that belligerent, shoe-thumping bully, had simply backed off. "Kennedy cut a deal," he said. It would be twenty-seven years before Dad was proven right. I'll never forget his phone call in 1989 telling me that Ted Sorensen, Kennedy's special counsel and speechwriter, had finally copped to the secret deal Robert Kennedy cut with Soviet ambassador Anatoly Dobrynin—America's Jupiter missiles out of Turkey in exchange for the Soviets' missiles out of Cuba—in the eleventh hour of the twelfth night of those Thirteen Days.

What do I perceive were the short- or long-term effects of the Crisis? Short-term, my mother's "breakdown" was devastating, for her and for us. But we weren't alone. I remember the staff telling us they were overwhelmed for months with psychiatric patients. I researched it later, in college, and found that the state's psychiatric hospitals and clinics experienced a 22% surge in patients needing help between late October '62 and January '63. By the way, another interesting surge occurred nine months after the Crisis. In late July and August, the state's live birth rate spiked a whopping 34%!

Over the years, my father, Emilio, and I had many discussions about the long-term effects of the Crisis, especially the myths that evolved to cover the hidden lie over the secret deal. As President Kennedy said, "The great enemy of the truth is very often not the lie—deliberate, contrived and dishonest—but the myth—persistent, persuasive and unrealistic."

And perhaps the biggest, most persistent, most damaging myth was that the Crisis resolved itself—because Kennedy and America hung tough, stood tall, went eyeball-to-eyeball with the enemy until the other fellow, mesmerized by America's resolve and mind-boggling military might, simply blinked and backed off.

This may be way more information than you want, but Dad was a big fan of historian Ned Lebow, who wrote that the mythical version of the Crisis promoted by the Kennedy brothers and many others—that Khrushchev blinked and backed off—had plenty of disastrous effects: the Vietnam War and the nuclear arms race, accelerated by Soviet determination never again to be so humiliated by the United States. On the positive side, perhaps, was the global perception that Khrushchev had failed. The Chinese were particularly sensitive to Khrushchev's "loss of face" and Chinese-Soviet relations cooled. Dad agreed with Thomas Schelling, one of the nation's leading nuclear thinkers, who wrote that the Cuban Missile Crisis helped us avoid further direct confrontation with the Soviets, and it resolved the Berlin issue.

Also good, I suppose, was, after peering into the nuclear abyss, John Kennedy and Nikita Khrushchev resolved to be more careful in the future. Almost immediately, they established the telephone hotline so both leaders could speak directly in a crisis. And in 1963, they initiated the first Nuclear Test Ban Treaty.

Of course, Emilio views it all a bit differently. You may be interested to know that he was a Pedro Pan, one of the 14,000+ Cuban children whose Catholic parents sent them to the US to escape Castro's Godless Communism. Like most Cuban Americans, Emilio sees President Kennedy's pledge to Khrushchev not to invade Cuba as a complete betrayal. It not only cemented Fidel's 50-year stranglehold on the island, it turned south Florida's powerful Cuban American voting bloc passionately anti-Kennedy, anti-Democrat, and pro-Republican.

You ask what, if any, personal changes came about as a result of the Crisis? Another tough question. That week changed everything for me. For starters, my mother's "breakdown" taught me things about myself I'd never known. I struggled, and got a lot of help from Emilio, over who I really was. We became high school and later college sweethearts. Eventually, the distance between med school in Gainesville and law school in Miami, and the differences in our opinions over the Vietnam War, proved too great. Although we each married others, we remain like family to each other. That week also changed both my parents; they struggled, too, for quite a while. Before that week, I was intent on a career in aeronautical engineering. Watching my mother's treatment and recovery, however, spurred my interest and eventual career in psychology with specialties in infertility and adoption issues. I'm also involved in a study exploring the link between early electroshock therapy and the later onset of Alzheimer's. We lost Dad in 2008. Thanks to Alzheimer's, my mother never knew of Dad's death and she no longer knows me, but she does entertain fellow residents at her facility with a once-a-week performance of operatic arias. Go figure.

I find your final question—have I experienced any echoes of the Crisis or of history repeating itself?—intriguing. Here's what I know . . .

Not long after September 11, 2001, I began to have Armageddon-like nightmares in which I was a teenager again at Edgewater High. It took me awhile to figure out that my subconscious had somehow melded the Cuban Missile Crisis of my youth with the attack on the Twin Towers. Nearly four decades apart, my response to 9/11—shock and outrage, anxiety and fear—sent me back to a place I knew well. But obviously, I wasn't the only one.

In 2002, forty years after the Cuban Missile Crisis, like most Americans I watched in horror as, once again, a grim-faced American President appeared on national television to announce the discovery of "weapons of mass destruction" in Iraq. (President Bush omitted President Kennedy's additional adjective— sudden.) Once again, a US diplomat—Secretary of State Colin Powell—went before the United Nations with extensive charts and photographs to have his "Adlai Stevenson moment."

More chilling for me, however, was the memory of John Kennedy, having stood down the Joint Chiefs' clamor to invade Cuba and secretly negotiated the peace, explaining, "The essence of ultimate decision remains impenetrable to the observer—often, indeed, to the decider himself." Forty years later, President George W. Bush said simply, "I'm the decider," and commenced the ten-year "regime-change" war in Iraq. For those of us old enough to remember the 1962 original, it was eerily similar rhetoric masking an unmistakably different intent and outcome.

Best of luck with your project, Ms. McCarthy. Again, I apologize if this is too much information, but your questions really got me thinking. I look forward to reading your finished book!

Sincerely,
Charlotte Avery, PhD, ABPP
Ponte Vedra, FL

ACKNOWLEDGMENTS

*T*HIS BOOK BEGAN AS A WAY OF SETTING DOWN MY OWN VIVID childhood memories of the Cuban Missile Crisis, but it would never have been finished without the generosity of so many others, whose insights helped me grasp the larger, communal story.

Thank you, Maggie Aguiar of Miami and former Florida senator Mel Martinez, for sharing your poignant Pedro Pan stories, and to Isabel Roach of Verona, New Jersey, for your mother's Cuban exile story as well as that of your family's tragic 9/11 loss of your beloved Stephen. Thank you, TSgt. Glenn R. "Chap" Chapman, whose memoir, *Me and U-2: My Affair with Dragon Lady,* confirmed that the strange, dragonfly-shaped planes my father took me to see on the runway of Orlando's McCoy AFB were indeed the mysterious U-2 spy planes that supplied President Kennedy with photographic evidence of the missiles in Cuba. Chap was a U-2 mechanic at McCoy that fall ("We were armpit to armpit with other crews at that place!"). He put me in touch with Air Force Captain and U-2 pilot Tony Bevacqua, whose stories brought the mission as well as his good friends and fellow U-2 pilots Gary Powers and Rudy Anderson to life. Thanks also to A3D pilot Bob Provencer for taking me to school on the role of the navy's aviators who flew defensive cover for the unarmed Air Force and CIA U-2s and later, during the peak of the Crisis, provided dangerous low-level surveillance of missile site activities. Also helpful were Bill Saavedra of the Air Force History Support Office at Bolling AFB in Washington, D.C.; Barbara Angel at Patrick AFB; Herb McConnell at Andrews AFT; Fraser Jones of FAA Public Affairs; and Molly Townsend of Martin-Marietta Public Affairs.

Tana Porter of the Orange County Regional History Center dug up long-buried information on Orlando's Cold War Civil Defense Plan, its seven woefully undersupplied shelter sites, plus the delightful detail that many of the city's first families thought the storage vault of LaBelle Furs the safest place in town. Nena Runyon Stevens, Bishop Moore High School Class of '63, gathered friends and fellow classmates Gale Hergenroether Deming, Karin Economon, and Maureen Carpenter Odom for an evening of shared laughs and senior year memories. In addition, Nena contacted classmate Patty Heidrich, who forwarded her father's emailed memory of the late-night middle-of-the-Crisis phone call "requesting" the immediate loan of Heidrich Citrus flatbed trucks and drivers for "an unspecified length of time."

Jean Caldwell Presley, school secretary, provided access to Edgewater High's 1963 yearbook as well as back issues of the school's newspaper, *The Eagle Eye*. Jean also treated me to her stories of growing up across the street from Apopka baseball and racing phenom Edward Glenn "Fireball" Roberts. More than a few former Edgewater High teachers and students kindly contributed their memories of the fall of 1962, including art teacher Glen Bischof, band director Delbert Kieffner, and graduates David Hughes, Carl Weisinger, Karen Scofied Marshall, Pat Raymond Hodge, and Wayne Rich. Thanks, everyone. And to Edgewater High's actual Homecoming Queen Beverly Arnold Wheeler; longtime College Park residents Reta Rivers Jackson and her daughter Teressa Jackson Carver; Donna Whelchel; Clifford Davis; and Bob Patterson, owner of Bob's Texaco (now Sunoco) on Edgewater Drive—special thanks for helping me fill in so many blanks. To Brenda Bray, sister friend since kindergarten, thanks for letting me hang out at your lovely home on Lake Silver and absorb the peaceful ambiance of lakeside College Park living, a world away from the tiny rented cottage on busy Princeton Street I inhabited just after college. Billie Nunan, thank you, too, for sharing your 1962 panicked, hormonal mother-of-a-newborn story, begging your parish priest to baptize the baby immediately to avoid limbo. "It's too soon" was the priest's epic reply. "But if it looks like the end is near, I'll give you a call."

As a writer, I received some incredibly helpful responses from my intrepid group of readers; some have been with me since the first tentative draft of *Trumpet,* others newer to the process yet expert at spotting unintended holes beneath the polished surface of a final draft. Thanks so much to Monika and Kevin Stout; Julie Clark and her dad, Joe Bear; Sarah Browne; Chuck Gordon; and, of course, my brilliant book club ladies and friends: Anne Spindel, Barbara Goetz, Carol Parker, Diane Mandle, Gwenn Adams, Jan Brownell, Joan Thatcher, Karen Evans, Tricia Rowe, and dear Val Gilbert. It was their wonderful suggestion that the final chapter originally written as an author afterword, be recast from an adult Charlotte's point of view. Giant heartfelt thanks to Debra Douglass and Joanne Martinez, my two most dedicated readers, who made time to read, discuss, and often debate almost every version of this years-in-the-writing story.

Whenever I lost heart, my agent, Jill Marr, jumped in with excellent advice, sound opinions, and fine humor. Thanks, Jill, and Andrea Cavallaro, Elise Capron, Thao Le, the inimitable Sandy Dijkstra herself, and everyone at the "Best in the West" Sandra Dijkstra Literary Agency.

My editor, Kate Miciak, has been terrific through three books now. Many, many thanks, Kate, for always challenging me to do better, and better still, and for never failing to cheer me on while I spent months "just five or six pages" away from being done. Big buckets of gratitude also to Julia Maguire for excellent editorial assistance; Kelly Chian and Angela McNally in production; and our esteemed Senior Vice President, Editor in Chief, and Associate Publisher Jennifer Hershey.

Paul, thank you for the inspiration of your long-ago after-school job at Charlie's Chevron in San Rafael, and for the ties that bind us together, no matter what. Connor, your gifts with language, especially for the spot-on metaphor, delight me to no end. Thanks for understanding that on all your adventures all over the world, my heart is a reluctant stowaway soothed only by a well-timed POL. Joanne, we've been best friends for thirty-five years, and always will be. Ultimately, this book belongs to Travis. The shattering loss of that bright spirit, dark humor, and booming belly laugh taught us all how thin, how fragile the line between normal and nightmare, and the painful, humbling lessons of How to Grieve a Dream. Firstborn darling of my heart, not a day goes by . . .

ABOUT THE AUTHOR

SUSAN CAROL MCCARTHY is the award-winning author of two novels, *Lay That Trumpet in Our Hands* and *True Fires,* and the nonfiction *Boomers 101: The Definitive Collection.* Her debut novel has been widely adopted by U.S. schools and selected by libraries and universities for their One Book–One Community and Freshman Year Read programs. A native Floridian, she now lives in Carlsbad, California.

Susan Carol McCarthy is available for select readings and lectures. To inquire about a possible appearance, please contact the Penguin Random House Speakers Bureau at speakers@penguinrandomhouse.com or (212) 572-2013.

www.SusanCarolMcCarthy.com

This book was set in Caslon, a typeface first designed in 1722 by William Caslon (1692–1766). Its widespread use by most English printers in the early eighteenth century soon supplanted the Dutch typefaces that had formerly prevailed. The roman is considered a "workhorse" typeface due to its pleasant, open appearance, while the italic is exceedingly decorative.